GH(

"VERDICT: A paranormal thriller that offers thrills and chills in addition to a touching exploration of grief, love, and moving on."
—*Library Journal*

"Ghosts and the hunt for a possibly malevolent spirit sweep through the pages of Meredith Lyons' *Ghost Tamer*. In this fast-paced debut, a young woman discovers why she was the lucky one to survive a train crash while also facing, and conquering, shadows from her past that won't let her go." —**Georgina Cross, bestselling author of** *The Stepdaughter*, **as well as** *Nanny Needed, One Night*, **and** *The Niece*

"Meredith Lyons' sizzling debut has a lot of heart and the perfect amount of snark. *Ghost Tamer* is a paranormal joyride!"
—**James L'Etoile, award-winning author of** *Black Label, Dead Drop*, **and the Detective Penley series**

"Meredith Lyons' *Ghost Tamer* is a superbly-written and wholly original debut. A witty, fast-paced, and frightening supernatural thrill ride!" —**Bruce Robert Coffin, award-winning author of the Detective Byron mysteries**

"Debut author, Meredith Lyons has created an entertaining tale that upends tropes and brings readers something rare—a unique ghost story. A page-turning must-read novel for fans of mystery, fantasy, and the supernatural." —**Jeffrey James Higgins, award-winning author of** *Furious and Unseen*

"Meredith R. Lyons writes with an intensity of emotion and an abundance of sass. Her debut novel *Ghost Tamer* has just the right mix of spunky and spooky. The pages turn all by themselves. It's uncanny." —**John DeDakis, Writing Coach, Novelist, and former Senior Copy Editor for CNN's** *The Situation Room with Wolf Blitzer*

GHOST
TAMER

GHOST
TAMER

MEREDITH R. LYONS

CamCat
Books

CamCat Publishing, LLC
Fort Collins, Colorado 80524
camcatpublishing.com

Hardcover ISBN 9780744302790
Paperback ISBN 9780744302813
Large-Print Paperback ISBN 9780744302820
eBook ISBN 9780744302837
Audiobook ISBN 9780744302851

Library of Congress Control Number: 2023932282

Book and cover design by Maryann Appel

5   3   1   2   4

For my Momza,
who knew this day would come.

For Erin, for Jason, for Jake.
Each of you is remembered within these pages.

For all who have lost someone indelibly
lodged in their soul.

1

"IT'S COMING. LET'S RUN."

Joe and I sprinted through the thick snowflakes toward the El platform, pounding up the salt-strewn stairs two at a time. Scanned our passes lickety-split and leapt onto the very first car just as the warning bell chimed and the doors glided shut.

"Winners." Joe held his gloved hand up without turning around and I smacked my mittened palm against his for a muffled high five. He pointed to the front of the car. "Hey, Raely, your favorite seats. Must be your lucky day, girl."

"Excellent!" I clamped onto my friend's shoulder and wove after him through the passengers as the elevated train bobbed and swayed.

It was a few hours after the rush, and the train was not uncomfortably packed. Joe and I lucked into those first two seats at the front behind the driver. I loved being able to see out to the tracks in front. Made it almost like a carnival ride. As soon as I was settled in my seat, leaning back against the side window, Joe launched into an impassioned critique of my stand-up set. We were both out of breath from our sprint. Still buzzing from the adrenaline of recent stage time.

"I mean, you have to feel good about that bit with the birthday cup," he said. "That one is solid . . ." We had just finished five-minute solo sets at an early evening open mic. I liked the earlier ones, fewer people. Although Joe was trying to get me to commit to a 'real' one—8 p.m. or later, true show time—sometime before spring.

Other passengers surrounding us in our little section of the train stood either reading or plugged into music or podcasts. Everyone created their own space. Joe's ardent critique of my set didn't register to the average commuter, although a few smiled to themselves, glancing over at him, perhaps catching some of his clever turns of phrase. Since he was in flow, he was still standing, gesticulating, while I gazed up at him.

I flung my legs across the seat he had not yet taken and studied him. He was one of those guys who would always be okay. He could easily transition from his office job to any bohemian shenanigans that he may get the urge to dabble in with a simple change of clothes and an alteration of mousse pattern. His set had been perfect. He'd nailed every bit. And for some reason, he always wanted me to do just as well.

"Okay, now you do mine," he demanded, one gloved hand gripping the upright post as he swayed with the train, the fluorescent overhead lights gilding his dirty-blond hair, bleaching him into overexposure. "What did you think? Where do I need to tighten it up? I thought the part about the reunion email was a little *meh* . . ."

"Joe, none of it was '*meh.*'" I'd spent much of his set resisting the urge to tell the people next to me, *That's my best friend up there.* "I think you should just go for the whole ten minutes next time. It was spot-on. The audience was with you the entire time. I think they were disappointed when you were done, honestly."

"I still think if we got into Second City, it would take our skills to the next level." He scooted a little closer as the train made another stop, but only a few people pushed through the doors before they slid shut again. "Improv is an essential skill."

"Oh, for sure," I said. "I just don't know that I'm—"

"Stop saying you don't think you're ready, you never think you're ready for anything. You just need to *do*." He leaned toward me, grinning and pointing. The train jostled, but he swayed with it. I couldn't help but smile back. City lights flashed by in the windows behind him as we sped through the Chicago Loop, leaving the near south side. The tiny squares of high-rise windows carved bright, symmetrical specks into the dark winter sky.

It had finally stopped snowing. I peeked out the front window. The train gobbled up the line of track before us ever more quickly as it picked up speed.

"So," I nudged his leg with my boot. "We're done with our sets, no more secrets. What's the big, exciting thing you're doing this weekend that trumps game night? I was ready to clean up at Telestrations."

Joe's smile broadened. He smacked my boots, pushing them to the floor, and took the seat, leaning toward me. "I'm proposing to Mia."

I straightened away from the window. "Shut. UP!"

He grinned and grasped a finger of his glove, wiggling his hand free and reaching for an inside coat pocket. "Wanna see it?"

"Yes, I wanna see it! Oh my God! Joe!" I scooted closer, a silly grin spilling over my face, and extended my palm. I loved Mia. And I loved who Joe was *with* Mia. Joe grinned back at me and unfastened the first two buttons of his coat to access the pocket.

The full moon gilded the metal of the tracks ahead of us as the train whipped toward the river, to the turn just ahead. The hairs on the back of my neck stood up.

"Joe," I said, catching his eye. "The train is going too fast."

We turned away from each other, gazes locked on the front window. The curve was looming. Shiny, bright metal, arcing gracefully to the left. And the train wasn't slowing down. My heart expanded, uncomfortably filling my chest. Electricity shot through my limbs. Our car sped forward relentlessly.

My eyes found Joe's. The metallic taste of fear coated the back of my tongue. I meant to say that we should grab on to something, even as my body compelled both hands to grasp the railing of the seat beside me. Joe opened his mouth to say something and then . . .

There was a wrench. A screaming of metal fighting metal. The train tore off the rails. For one second, we were all suspended together. As if existing inside a gasp. Not a human sound. Conversation ceased. Silence was our collective scream.

Then chaos. Everyone yelled, cried, cursed. The lights strobed, then cut out. Every body and bag on the train hurtled toward the front of the car, tagging every metal guardrail along the way. Gravity found us again with a sickening crunch.

Pain sliced into my side, but I couldn't move. Couldn't make space. Pressure increased. I couldn't breathe. Panic clawed at my ribcage. I wanted to fight but there was nothing to defeat. No air to breathe. I couldn't move. Nowhere to go.

Blackness.

When consciousness found me again, I was disoriented.

My head hurt. My lungs heaved as if I had been underwater. I wheezed like a drowning victim. Someone pulled at me. Under my arms. Hauling. My feet were caught. Yanked free.

A yelp died escaping my throat. I struggled to open my eyes, my eyelids impossibly heavy.

"Joe?" Raspy. Rusty voice.

"I'm getting you outside. They'll find you more easily outside. You need to stay very still."

I wrenched my eyes open. I watched my legs being pulled through the shattered window of the train as if they belonged to someone else. My booted feet thudding to the ground. Dragging trenches through the fresh powder. I had never given thought to how big the trains were when I rode them every day, but now, seeing one crashed in the snow, it was like a blue whale.

"Joe . . ." I croaked.

"You need to think about surviving. You're hurt. You need to stay relaxed and then you need to do what the medical people say. Look up. Look up and stay calm."

He laid me down in the fresh snow and I looked up. I could see the moon. Full. I could even see a few stars. *Never see stars in Chicago. Not downtown.*

I heard sirens. Helicopters. Someone was in trouble. I knew I should help. But I was so tired. Lying in the snow and looking up seemed the right thing to do.

The edges of my vision blurred. Whoever had been pulling me was no longer nearby. I heard voices. Turned my head to the side. It seemed to take a long time. The world went in and out of focus. I saw people. Lights. Lots of lights, painting the glittering snow with pulses of pink. I wondered why I didn't feel cold. I didn't feel anything. A crimson semi-circle blossomed through the snow at my left side. The bloom slowly grew. It was beautiful. Red against the white.

People. Running closer. Boots spraying the fresh snow. Shouting, lights flashing, the whirring of the helicopters throbbed against my eardrums. I pulled my gaze back to the train to search for Joe. I tried to call for him, but my mouth wouldn't move.

2

DAYS IN THE HOSPITAL PASSED BY IN A BLUR. I'd had surgery and was going to have a ginormous scar on my left side, sure to be very attractive come bikini season and fun to explain the next time I managed to sustain a relationship to "that stage."

I was the only one in the first car to survive.

My mom drove up from the suburbs immediately and had the sense to contact the personal injury lawyers I used to work for part-time.

No one would tell me anything about Joe. Not that I was conscious much at first. They waited until I was "out of the woods" to break the news that he hadn't made it. Apparently, that kind of shock can affect the healing process.

Mom was neatly Tetris-ing flowers and get-well cards into a box she had coaxed from hospital staff, which had "lubricating jelly" stamped on the side. Mia had just left. Her visit had been awkward and painful with neither of us knowing how to talk to each other. Now I slumped in my wheelchair, exhausted and hollowed out from that halting attempt at conversation, cocooned in my invisible blanket of grief and pain, a stuffed Pooh Bear wedged next to me.

When Mom had placed it in my lap, I'd rolled my eyes and reminded her that I was twenty-six but tucked him under my arm when she turned her back.

Another nurse finished a chatty farewell with Mom—who, of course, had befriended the entire staff by now. She reminded me to take it easy and swept out of the room with my recently autographed discharge papers.

"Where's that tall dude with the shaggy hair? Is he coming to say goodbye, too?" I sounded crabby. But crabby was one of my more pleasant moods lately.

"Who?" Mom didn't look up from her packing.

"That guy. He came here like . . . three or four times? Usually during the night? I figured he was a night shift person. He never stayed long or did anything useful, but he sure did come by a lot. What?"

She had stopped packing and was staring at me, brow furrowed. She looked much too concerned to be merely trying to come up with someone's name.

"What?" I repeated.

"The first few nights after surgery you talked to yourself sometimes. We assumed you were . . . sleep-talking, like you used to do when you were little. You would ask about Joe or—"

"So, you never saw that guy?"

"I think you must have been imagining it. You've had a lot of morphine."

She nodded to the stack of get-well cards in her hand and resumed collecting bouquets.

Exhaustion pulled at me. The ever-present ache in my chest flared, reminding me that Joe was dead. In the end, I didn't care who had visited, and so I let it go.

THREE WEEKS LATER, I limped up the well-salted sidewalk to my lawyer's River North office, buzzed the receptionist from the street-level intercom, and announced myself. After yanking the door open, I debated taking the stairs up to the second story, decided to heed the throbbing ache in my leg, and opted for the elevator. I was on track for a full recovery, they said, but it sure was taking a hell of a long time.

Minutes later I was in the small, familiar conference room with a bottle of water in my hand and a notepad on the shiny wooden table in front of me. I'd worked part time for Dubin and Cantor for almost three years and still came in to help occasionally if they were shorthanded. They'd apparently managed to grab the cases of a few more of the survivors in adjacent cars. And some of the . . . not survivors. Anyway, it was nice to have lawyers you trusted.

James Cantor, my former boss, came striding in. He was short, athletic, and energetic, with an accordion file under one arm and a coffee in hand. I managed to wrestle a weak smile from somewhere to meet his blast of energy. Normally, I blasted right along in tandem.

"Raely! You look tons better. How do you feel? You feel like crap, right? Yeah, well, just keep putting one foot in front of the other. I promise you. Night and day. You may not feel it yet, but you're healing."

"Thanks," I said, the corner of my mouth creeping up the left side of my face. I hauled my latest batch of medical records out of my messenger bag. "My ortho has started emailing me these directly, so I printed them off at the comedy club."

"Excellent!" He dived for the records. "So you don't need copies? Great. I'll have Helen enter them. Hey, you want a coffee? You look like you could use a coffee. Fake plant milk, right? Helen!"

Helen shuffled in briskly, a warm grin already in place. Her iron gray hair and sensible sweater-and-skirt ensemble contrasted with James's artfully faded jeans and black button up—rolled to the elbows, of course. He gave her my coffee order, which I knew was coming out of a Keurig, so I didn't feel too guilty about it, and passed her the records.

"Yeah, I guess the doc likes me. Is it true love? Or am I merely a fascinating case? We may never know," I said. Helen chuckled and trotted off.

James teased a folder out from the large accordion file with 'Raely Videc' printed on the side in large block letters. So strange to see one with my name on it.

"Got your police report back and even have photos of the scene."

"Really? Wow, that was fast."

"Yeah, so, we gotta work on your statement. I know you were in shock and it's completely understandable that your memory may be hazy or incomplete." He carefully spread the papers and photographs across the shiny table, placing each 8 x 10 as if it belonged in a specific spot. I accepted my coffee from Helen with a nod of thanks and scooted closer to the table.

"I don't think my memories were too hazy." I took a gulp of coffee, summoning patience. We'd had several versions of this conversation before.

"You said you were pulled from the car."

"I was pulled from the car."

"You said someone pulled you out through the window of the car and dragged you away from the rest of the train."

"Yeah. 'Cause that's what happened."

He pushed a photograph toward me. I spun it around and slid it closer. It was an aerial view of the wreck, obviously taken from a helicopter. Maybe stills from a video. I could see the smashed front car, the second car dangling, and the third car teetering. I could see myself. A lone, tiny figure, limbs splayed like a snow angel, a crimson blotch at my side. I forced my emotions into a little box. Stuffed them into my mental basement. I would deal with them later. Or never. Never was fine.

"Yes, look." I jammed my finger at the photo, pushing it to the space between us, suppressed emotion thickening my Chitown accent. "You can see drag marks from my legs. I was sitting on the opposite side of the train. How could I have been thrown from the window on *this* side? There woulda been glass all over me. I woulda hit my head or something."

"Look here." As James circled his finger over the snow surrounding my body, his accent broadened in response to mine.

I glared at the section he indicated, then clung to a polite tone with effort. "I don't see anything."

"Precisely."

What was he talking about?

"What *don't* you see?"

My brow furrowed. I looked at the photo, then shook my head.

James leaned forward, palms on the table. "Footprints."

My breath caught. I snatched the photograph off the table. Held it close to my nose and scanned. He was right. Other than the trenches my feet had dug into the powder and the craters pocked by fallen debris, the snow was perfect.

"The paramedics came immediately after this was taken. You can see them off to the side. They saw no one nearby. If someone had pulled you from the train, there would be footprints somewhere."

3

MY FIRST NIGHT SHIFT BACK AT THE CLUB WAS A TUESDAY. As soon as my physical therapist cleared me for long-term standing, I'd called up George Rosen, the owner. He put me on the floor that week. I did the weekday shifts while my leg was still sore. Less running around. Even at a comedy club, working behind the bar can get intense during breaks between sets.

On my first Friday night shift, I was working with Luck, my favorite fellow drink-slinger. He had been there a while but never gave you the impression that he was "too senior" to do side work or help a coworker in the weeds.

He was a comic himself, as were most of us in some iteration, and his set wasn't half bad. It didn't hurt that he was easy on the eyes. He had perennially bronze skin, light gray eyes, and short, dark curls. And a killer understated callback joke for every conversation that would have you chuckling when it popped into your head two days later. If I had an option, and Luck was either on the schedule or doing a set, that's the night I'd choose. Luck was always down to hang out afterward, too. A not-so-small bonus.

During the first two hours of the shift, my heart felt lighter than it had since the accident. The easy banter with patrons and Luck—who seemed just as happy to have me back on Fridays as I was to be there—the feeling of doing something normal, and the *almost* complete absence of pain . . . it was a balm. There were even stretches of time where I didn't consciously mourn Joe.

I spotted the shaggy-haired hospital guy at the end of the bar. I gave him a small smile and a wave to let him know I'd be down there when it was his turn. His hair looked more anime than shaggy in this light. Perhaps he'd applied product for a night out.

"Hey!" I raised my voice over the din of the crowd once I'd taken care of customers ahead of him. "From the hospital, right? Nice to see you in the real world."

He stared back at me like I had grown three heads.

My professional dazzling smile dropped a watt or two. "Well, what can I get you?"

"Are you talking to me?" said the guy behind him. I started to tell him to wait his turn, but as he squished his way up to the bar, giving his order, he *walked right through* the anime-haired guy.

My blood turned to ice and a dull roaring filled my ears as Anime shook his head and backed away. Through at least one other person. It took tremendous effort to wrench my focus back to the man in front of me and ask him to repeat his order.

Maybe it was a blessing that my thirty-second chat with Anime had put me one inch away from the weeds. I was forced to concentrate on taking orders and slinging drinks until the next set started. Luck was working furiously, too.

I waited until the next act was going strong—an experienced standup, thank God, because he had the crowd fully contained within seconds—and told Luck that I needed some air. I got his blessing, pulled a bottle of warm water from one of the cases in the storage closet as I passed, and pushed open the stage door to the alley, being careful to leave the worn, wooden doorstop in its jam to avoid being locked out. I plunked down on the steps with a raspy exhale, sipped my tepid water, and tried to think through what I had just seen. Some kind of PTSD effect, maybe?

I put my water bottle on the step beside me, closed my eyes and pressed the heels of my hands into them. I was wearing contacts, so I had to be careful, but sometimes I still enjoyed seeing the little stars I could create. When I lifted my face, he was there.

I closed my eyes. Assessed the position of my contact lenses and found them to be fine. I blinked several times upon reopening. He was still there. There had to be a logical explanation for this. He looked totally normal; I must have imagined him misting through people.

I stared him right in the eye, grabbed my water bottle, and took a pull. Sad that it was not whiskey. "Who are you, and what do you want?"

He glanced around, settled his gaze back on me, then took a step forward.

I dropped the bottle and jerked to a standing position. Neither of us watched it clunk down the remaining two steps, splashing its contents over the concrete, and rolling to a stop at his feet.

"You can see me?" he asked, tilting his head as if *I* were the one behaving oddly.

"No fucking shit, Sherlock, now why are you stalking me?" I edged up a step closer to the door, never taking my eyes off him.

He blinked. Stuck his hands in his pockets. It was then that I noticed he was wearing dark jeans and a light jacket in the middle of winter. No scarf. No gloves. Not even a hipster hat.

"I'm not stalking you." He looked just as confused as I felt. Applause erupted from the theatre at my back. The set was done. "You need to go back to work." He stepped backward and *vanished into the building across the alley.* I started hyperventilating.

Luck threw open the door, thankfully a full two inches shy of knocking me off the steps. "Hey, Raely, I need you. Full house." He flashed me a smile and darted back inside. I shook myself, grabbed the door before it slammed shut and followed. I forced myself to focus on work until I was done. Then I had a few drinks with Luck and the comics to try to numb myself.

⁓ ∽ ∽ ∽ ⁓

I TREATED MYSELF to a Lyft once I was comfortably anesthetized.

Some voice in the back of my head told me that it wasn't safe to be hobbling around on public transportation in the snow with a bum leg, regardless of whether less-than-corporeal, anime-looking men were in fact stalking me. I felt under my coat for the little canister of pepper spray that my mom had tucked into my stocking every year since I moved into the city. *They expire, you know.*

Fat lot of good it would do in my jeans pocket under all my layers.

I moved it to the pocket of my coat and kept my hand wrapped around it, telling myself I was going to start carrying it everywhere, at the ready. Maybe go over those palm-strike maneuvers that I'd learned in that self-defense class until I had this figured out.

Had what figured out, exactly?

I tried to settle my whiskey-flavored thoughts into a coherent line as my Lyft driver fiddled with the radio. I'd stared out the window after the barest of polite greetings to avoid her feeling like she had to make small talk with me to get that top-star rating. I idly wondered if she carried pepper spray.

I definitely saw this guy at the hospital. My brain had moved this issue to Priority One. It made sense from a self-preservation standpoint, but mainly it gave me a break from my previous Priority One—survivor's guilt and crushing sadness. *It was definitely the same guy at the club tonight.* And he had definitely vanished through solid people, and at least one wall. All of which had appeared to go unnoticed by anyone else. He'd spoken to me, though. And he *looked* solid enough. That is, until he collided with someone or something else.

I was avoiding it. Avoiding labeling him a ghost. But . . . I had no better word. So, why would a ghost haunt me at the hospital and comedy club? Was he someone who had been on the train with me? Someone who hadn't made it?

I only half paid attention as I thanked the driver and clomped up the walk to my apartment. I gave her the full star rating and a generous tip for being out so late. When I looked up from my phone, I saw a girl in shorts and a T-shirt peering into the windows on the lower level.

"Oh, hey, are you locked out?" I fished my keys out of my coat pocket. She had to be freezing.

She whipped around. The shock on her face made me pause.

"Sorry, I didn't mean to scare you. I get off work late." I gestured toward the building, making sure to show my keys. Maybe I was slurring. Maybe I sounded like some drunk asshole, and she thought I was making fun of her. "I live here too. Are you locked out?"

She shook her head, one side of her mouth quirking up as if she were trying not to smile. She staggered back onto the snowy lawn and ran around the side of the building.

"The fuck . . ." I breathed. She hadn't even been wearing shoes! To run off through the snow barefoot . . . I looked at the ground where she had run from the window. No footprints.

I didn't remember unlocking the front door or hurtling up the stairs. I didn't remember throwing the deadbolt, locking the doorknob, and putting the chain on my door. In the morning, I would have trouble opening the door before I remembered. I would also laugh at myself for thinking a deadbolt was going to keep out ghosts.

I threw on every light in the place as I stumbled through the motions of preparing for bed, simultaneously terrified to end up there. Defenseless. In the dark. *Maybe I'm seeing things. Maybe I should call the doctor. Make that appointment.* In the end, I pulled Blitz, my disgruntled black-and-white cat, into bed with me. I even bribed him with cheese so he'd stay. He had no interest in cuddling, but I wanted him in the room. Cats could sense ghosts, right?

I tried to tell myself that I was tired. Drunk. That I had imagined the girl outside. Hadn't looked closely enough for the footprints. That I just needed to sleep. Sleep would fix my brain. I just needed to take better care of myself, that's all. Some sleep. Less booze. Some good, healthy food tomorrow. I found a book that I'd read a million times and lost myself in the familiar story. Blitz eventually deigned to curl up between my feet. At some point, I fell asleep, the book dropping from my fingers.

I woke up before dawn and he was there. Standing in the corner of my room. Watching me while Blitz washed his paws without a hint of concern.

I squeezed my eyes shut as adrenaline surged through me. *Nonononono NO! This isn't real.* I opened my eyes, and he hadn't moved. My chest caved. The adrenaline dissipated as quickly as it had come and left me enervated.

A strange guy in my bedroom, stalking me, and I didn't feel an overwhelming sense of terror or an instinctive desire to scream; instead, I felt a bottomless well of despair.

Funny.

I pushed myself into a sitting position, careful not to disrupt Blitz out of long-ingrained habit. A heavy, dark sadness pressed on my heart. Some distant part of my brain clocked that as abnormal. I dismissed it. No time for that.

"Why are you here?" My voice sounded dull and tired, even to myself. I thought of the pepper spray, resting in a dish on the nightstand, but didn't so much as look at it. What was the point? "What do you want from me?"

He stiffened and blinked. "I don't understand."

A bark of laughter leapt from my throat, startling Blitz and Anime. "You're in my *bedroom*. You've been following me around, and I wake up and you're staring at me like a . . . a . . . I don't know, but it's creepy as fuck and I'm tired and I hurt everywhere and I just want to know what the hell you *want*."

My voice broke on the last word. I thought I might cry as the weight on my heart continued to press down, but my eyes were dry. Blitz resumed bathing himself as if there were no strange intruder, badly in need of a comb, hanging out in a shadowy corner of my bedroom.

"I don't understand how you can see me. How you can hear me. You never did before."

The weight gradually lifted, replaced by a slowly spreading numbness. I looked him in the eye. Dark, like his hair, but I couldn't tell the color. "What?" The word crept out of me, barely audible.

"I thought in the hospital that it was temporary, because you came so close to death. Or the drugs . . . but something permanent must have shifted." His eyebrows drew together. Two dark slashes above his eyes, a small crinkle deepening between them. "I've been with you for . . . years. You never saw me before."

I squeezed my eyes shut. Drunk. I'm still drunk. Please let me still be drunk. Asleep. Yes. I'm having a nightmare.

I felt Blitz kneading the covers next to my legs and flinched. I opened my eyes, focusing on the cat. Calmly purring. I could still see him, the . . . ghost, peripherally. My arms began to shake, and my eyes started to burn. *No. Do not show fear.*

My snarky subconscious piped up: *He's a ghost, not an angry dog.*

So helpful. Still, I forced a few deep breaths into my lungs and dragged my eyes back up to his. I made myself take a real look at him. I was pretty good at reading people, surely ghosts were at least . . . person-lite.

His eyes were wide—I still couldn't discern their color in the darkness of the corner he had pressed himself into—but they were fixed on me. He hunched against the wall like a lanky crescent moon. Hands in the pockets of his jacket. It looked just like a jacket a friend of mine once had in high school. I'd always envied it—cargo chic, he had called it, utilitarian, but fitted. Robbie had to alter his thrift store finds in the costume shop during lunch. Anime's jeans reminded me of photographs of my dad in the '70s. Worn blue converse peaked out from underneath them. He didn't seem threatening.

"What's your name?" I asked.

He flinched, I snorted.

"What?"

"Your name? Do you . . . do gh—. You know what? Let's start with what you are."

The left corner of his mouth twitched up, and he ducked his head. Christ. A shy ghost? I squinted, but in the pre-dawn light, I couldn't tell if he was blushing. Smart-ass internal voice quipped about having conversations with spirits in the dark. I reached over and smacked my bedside lamp. Warm orange light spilled into the room.

He blinked. "I like that thing."

Surprise bubbled against my sternum. I glanced back at the lamp. It was in the shape of a bare silver tree, little fairy lights at the ends of each branch. I found it charming also. "Thank y— Hang on. I refuse to have polite conversation with a strange entity in my bedroom that declines to give me a straight goddamn answer."

"Entity?" His eyebrows floated up to disappear behind his messy fringe.

"Cut the crap, Casper. Tell me what you are and what your name is, and then get the hell out of my life forever."

He curled up into himself and slid down the wall to the ground as if I had hurt his feelings. I shook my head and grabbed the glass of water from my nightstand. I took a big gulp, still keeping an eye on him in my periphery. My arms were still trembling, but the fear had been blunted by a myriad of other unpleasant emotions. I wanted to yell at him. Tell him that I was tired, that this was *my bedroom*, and for him to be acting like I was the one being mean was completely inappropriate. I was also done with being the only one talking. Determined to wait him out, I sipped my water and gripped the edge of my comforter as if it were woven from threads of my patience.

After an eternity, broken only by the sleepy purrs of Blitz, who was now curled in my lap, the sulky spirit lifted his forehead from his arms and looked up at me, as if checking to see if I was going to throw something at him. In fairness, I had considered throwing the rest of my water on him to see if perhaps he might melt, but I merely raised my eyebrows.

He uncurled enough to sit cross-legged on the floor. He looked about my age, but then, I'd never been great at guessing ages. He muttered something.

"What's that?" My voice sounded loud even to me in the dead silence of what was probably near sunrise.

"I said I don't know my name, and I'm not entirely sure what I am. All I know is I've been with you as long as I can remember." He spoke to his fingers as he clasped and unclasped them.

"Well, things have changed," I said, exhaustion peeling away any tactful filters that might normally have been in place. "I can see you now, and we seem to be conversing. I need something to call you and we have to establish some ground rules while we figure out this . . . situation."

A beat. He stopped fidgeting.

"Okay," he said. "You called me Casper. Is that a name I can use?"

Deep inside, a more awake version of myself probably smiled. "Casper is absurdly perfect. If you're a friendly ghost. For the purposes of this discussion, let's assume you are."

He nodded. He even smiled a little. Sat up straighter. "I think I am some kind of ghost," he said, as if pleased to be diagnosed. Almost as if he were saying, "I think I am lactose intolerant."

"Wouldn't you know?" I asked. "I feel like that's a thing you know about yourself."

He shrugged. "Most ghosts do know that they're ghosts. And know what they want and where they came from. I probably am a ghost; I just don't remember where I came from."

"Since you've apparently interacted with *other* ghosts, let's just say you're definitely a ghost. Cool?"

He nodded. He seemed happy with this.

I shook my head. "Alright, Casper, rule number one: You can't be hanging around me all the time. Especially not in my bedroom watching me sleep."

He shot onto his knees with lightning speed, thrusting upturned palms toward me. "How else am I supposed to keep you *safe*? Sorry."

I'd flung the water glass spasmodically in his direction and leapt to my feet in a tangle of sheets and cat. My heart was still thudding loudly as I removed an offended Blitz's claws from my oversized T-shirt and set him gently back upon the bed, my eyes narrowed on Casper. "No sudden movements. Please."

I bent to retrieve the glass. It had rolled to a stop against the bed frame after splashing its remaining contents over the wall and window. I set it back on the nightstand and leaned against the wall opposite him, still standing.

"Let's back up to the keeping me safe thing. What exactly are you keeping me safe from?"

He shrugged, now fiddling with his shoelaces. "Just . . . anything. Most of the time it's not hard. I can just remind you to look if you're about to bump into something or tell you that going down the alley is a bad idea and you should go the other way—"

"How would you tell me to not go down an alley, for example?"

He looked up, deadpan. "Hey, don't go down that alley."

I rolled my eyes. "Okay, so you would talk to me, and I wouldn't hear you but . . ."

"But most of the time, you would do what I said, yeah. Sometimes you ignored me and did stupid stuff anyway."

"What sage advice of yours have I ignored to my great misfortune?"

"Hey, this isn't a good part of the woods to poop in."

"Oh, so you know what poison ivy looks like?"

"Better than you, apparently."

"Wait, you watched me—"

"No! Gross, once it was obvious you were ignoring me, I took off for a while."

"Okay, you can come on long trail runs." My heart sank. "Once I'm able to run again."

The corners of his mouth twitched upward.

I pushed my injuries out of mind. "Does everyone have little ghost protectors following them around? Yelling warnings at them when they're about to do stupid things?"

His smile vanished, and his eyes dropped to the floor again. "No. Hardly anyone. Some people have spirits—ghosts, whatever you want to call it—following them, but usually they're just watching. They don't try to help them. Most of the time, warning you is enough. But when your train crashed I . . . had to get more involved."

My spine locked. The air left the room. My hand drifted up to press against my mouth. He remained seated, peered up at me through his messy hair. I dropped to my knees. With effort, I pulled my hand down, pressing it flat to the floor. "*You* pulled me out," I whispered.

He nodded.

"I heard you talking to me. And no one believed me because there were no footprints."

He scrubbed his hands through his hair, making it messier against all odds. "Maybe something happened when I touched you. I've never done that before."

"How could you drag me out of a wrecked train and not leave any footprints?"

"It's not something I could always have done. It takes a lot of effort to physically affect anything. I was not concentrating on making footprints. I was concentrating on moving you."

I slumped against the wall. The sky outside the window was beginning to lighten. Thank God I had the day off.

"How long have you been playing guardian angel for me?"

"As long as I can remember. As long as you've been alive."

Gooseflesh spread over my skin. I shook my head. This was too much to take in. "So that girl downstairs in the shorts, who left no footprints, she was a ghost too?"

He went still, eyes wide. My breath hitched.

"You're seeing other ones?" Fear shadowed his eyes. Dark blue eyes.

My stomach tightened. "I think so . . ."

"That's not good."

4

"I DON'T THINK YOU'RE SUPPOSED TO GO OUT in the cold with your hair still wet."

"Is this the kind of life-saving advice you dispense regularly?" I asked, trudging through the snow, adjusting the straps of my laden backpack. "The kind of thing you constantly yammer in my ear, and it's only annoying because I can hear you now?"

"Geez, you are cranky."

I spun around to face him. He was standing in a snow drift to my left, leaving no prints of course. "Casper, I did not get a lot of sleep last night, in case you didn't notice. I had more whiskey than is generally advisable, the sun's not fully up, I'm cold, and you've been dumping indigestible facts on me for the last hour or so. I apologize if I'm snappy, but—"

A girl wearing a Starbucks cap shuffled quickly by, doing her best to pretend she had not seen or heard the crazy woman talking to the air. I sighed and watched her round the corner. *I'll give it a second so*

she can get a block closer to the train without thinking I'm following her.
I pulled my attention back to Casper.

"You still look like you're in a dimly lit room. Is that a ghost thing?"

He shook his head. "What do you mean?"

"I mean . . . you're standing in the fabulous dawn sunbeams and I still . . . I feel like my contacts are fuzzy when I look at you or something." I saw another couple beginning to make their way up the sidewalk toward us. I turned on my heel, muttering under my breath, "Let's just go. I need coffee, then I'll be a better person."

The coffee shop didn't open for another two minutes, so we waited outside. I dug around in my backpack for my thermos and moved my wallet to my coat pocket to expedite my transaction time, then peered at the bakery shelf through the window and tried to make an advanced decision on some carbs.

"I like this place," Casper said, sliding up next to me. "I like the different art that they hang. There's something new to look at every month. Everyone's always relaxed in here."

I nodded, keeping my eyes on the muffins.

"Early on a weekend though, so not too many people hanging out, right?"

"Mmmhmm." Normal people were cuddled in their warm beds.

A familiar barista trotted over to unlock the door, tossing me a bright wave. I stretched my mouth into my friendliest pre-coffee grimace. As the door clanged open, Casper continued to prattle away about the old movie playing on the shop's tiny TV, the bagel options, and on and on, as if he couldn't bear to leave one portion of the room untouched by his comments. I hung on to my patience, telling myself it was probably natural to be excited if no one had ever been able to hear your opinions before.

I handed over my coffee thermos with a request for a dark roast and weighed my muffin choices. There were also some nice, fat croissants . . .

Casper was suddenly speaking in my ear. "Hey, what flavor are you gonna get?"

"Wait. Until. We sit down. Please!" I hissed.

"What was that?" The barista snapped his head toward me, eyes wide.

I straightened, pasting on my sanest smile. "Can't wait. To get. That cinnamon! Muffin! Please!"

Fortunately, he noticed nothing amiss, his face brightening into an "aw shucks" grin as he trotted over to the pastry case like a happy puppy. "Little tired this morning?" he chirped.

"You have no idea." I paid, grabbed my muffin, tossed sweetener into my coffee, and headed into the seating area—a larger room separate from the tiny coffee counter—my pet ghost trailing sulkily in my wake. Although the cafe was empty, I chose a small two-seater table all the way in the back corner near an outlet, and unpacked my laptop, headphones, and a notepad. Casper perched himself on the stool opposite me.

"Why do you need all that stuff? How long are we staying?"

"I need to look like I'm doing something—having a Zoom meeting, or muttering to myself about work—so nobody notices I'm talking to the air like a crazy person." I plugged my headphones into the laptop and popped one of them into my ear.

He folded his arms and glared, the dark slashes of his eyebrows nearly meeting over his nose.

"I'm not turning any music on, calm down." I took a life-saving gulp of coffee and sighed. This was the right choice. I took another healthy swig and leaned back against the wall, letting my eyes fall shut. Yes, I could make coffee at home, but this was so much better.

"Is it really that good?"

I raised my head and opened my eyes.

"It's magical." I took another, more moderate sip, set the thermos down, and carefully unwrapped my muffin, making sure as little of it as possible stuck to the wrapper. "Do you not remember eating or drinking things? I mean, you can't always have been a ghost, right?"

His brow furrowed. "Can't I have?"

I blinked. Tore off a piece of muffin and shrugged. "I kind of thought you were going to be the expert on this one."

"If I was ever something else, I don't remember it. My earliest memories are with you."

My mouth went dry, the muffin sticking to the top. I took another gulp of coffee. "That statement causes feelings that I don't care to process right now. Can we discuss the assertion you made last night regarding me seeing ghosts as a negative thing?"

"Oh, so you're ready to talk about that now?" he said, with a touch of attitude.

I narrowed my eyes. When he had initially dropped this bomb, I had stormed off into the shower, biting out a mature, *I didn't ask for this!* and had barely spoken to him until I was ready to head out the door. "Yes, please. I am appropriately fortified." I demonstrated with another sip of blessed caffeine.

He shifted in his seat, fidgeting with the hem of his jacket. Other than looking a bit like he was in a dim room rather than a cheery coffee shop, he appeared completely solid and human to me. I wondered why I wasn't scared of him. If what he said was true, and he'd always been there, maybe on some level I knew I didn't need to be afraid. I munched on my muffin—*so good!*—and waited for him to speak.

"There are lots of other types of . . . ghosts," he said finally, "and there are others . . . like you."

"Other people who can see ghosts?" I opened my web browser and began clicking around.

He nodded. "I haven't seen very many of them. But there are some ghosts who aren't good. They're not good for other ghosts—they'll attack if they're bored, try to siphon energy—and they're not good for people. But they're very, *very* bad for people who can see them."

The muffin was sticking again. I swallowed hard. "How do I know you're not 'bad for people,'" I finger-quoted. "You could be a bad ghost for all I know."

His eyebrows dropped and he narrowed his eyes. "Not once have I tried to hurt you."

"You've been painfully annoying."

He folded his arms and glared.

"Fine. Then what's the difference between you and a real bad ghost. What do they do?" I found an interesting site and scribbled a few notes while he explained.

"It depends on what they want. Some of them just want energy. They can make you sick or depressed. Some of them have been around for a long time and they just . . . they want to cause harm for fun. Or make you feel certain emotions that they enjoy. I've seen only a few types that want to interact. They want to make themselves known to people, and they want to tell them things—"

"Just getting information doesn't sound so bad. Didn't you say you told me stuff all the time?" I put my pen down and clicked over to a different page.

"It's not the same. I was just telling you not to walk into traffic and stuff," he said. "I followed an Oracle around for a day or two because he knew so much. Time isn't linear for Oracles. They can go forward or backward. Wherever they want. This particular Oracle liked telling living people things. Just one thing to one person at first. Sometimes good things, sometimes things they shouldn't have known. Things they didn't want to know. Then he became really interested in one person who could see him. He whispered things to the guy all the time, wouldn't leave him alone."

My stomach dipped as if I were in a car that caught a little air off a speed bump. I glanced up from my screen. "True things?"

"They were true. But most hadn't happened yet. A lot were horrible. He was wrecking the living guy's life. I stayed away from him after that. He wasn't that interested in me, anyway. He had a lot of other ghosts following him around."

"Can't I just like, ignore them? Refuse to listen? I don't know."

He smirked. "It would be better if you could, but the kinds of ghosts that will be interested in you won't let you ignore them once they know you can see them."

"Ignoring shit I don't want to deal with is one of my special skills," I said, pointedly going back to my screen.

Casper stared right at me. Then he reached out and slammed my laptop shut, *nearly* amputating my fingers. I flinched, but before I could protest, he kicked over my backpack and began pulling stuff out.

"Hey, hey, *hey!*" I set my coffee down, yanked my earbud out and flung myself on the ground next to my bag, batting uselessly at his arms. My hands just swept right through them. He stopped, however, having made his point.

"I thought you said that was really difficult," I murmured, glancing around, reassuring myself that the room was still empty. No one else had heard my outburst or witnessed my possessions ostensibly flinging themselves out of my backpack.

"I said it took a lot of concentration and effort for *me.*" He settled back onto his stool, folding his arms across his chest, watching as I rearranged items back into my bag. "I haven't been a . . . ghost, or whatever, for as long as a lot of the bad ones."

Still kneeling on the ground, I unfolded a crumpled piece of paper that had been dislodged and examined it to see if it was something I still needed to keep. "How many—"

"Shhh!" he hissed, standing abruptly over me, too close. "Pretend you can't see me."

"What?" I looked up at him.

His eyes were wide, staring through the windows and into the street. "Look away! It's 'special skills' time."

His fear was almost tangible.

I fixed my eyes on the paper in my hand without seeing it. The temperature in the room seemed to drop. The hairs on the back of my neck rose.

"This one's mine," Casper snarled, kicking my bag again, and earning an unfeigned yelp from me.

A horrible, rattling exhale filled the room. "*Yours . . .*" The word stretched out into a skin-crawling hiss. I tried to act like my veins hadn't just turned to ice. I reached for my bag but stopped when my coffee thermos shot across the room, slamming against the wall in front of me, its contents splashing across the floor.

I gasped and scuttled backwards, away from the thermos and froze, crouching against the wall.

"Mine!" Casper said firmly.

A nerve-grating, rusty cackle clawed my eardrums followed by the scrape of a table. I couldn't help it, I looked up.

A black-coated figure lifted the table I had occupied. My things slid off onto the floor, and I watched in horror as he hurled it at me. A cry punched from my throat as the edge of the tabletop slammed into my ribs. The barista and another customer pelted into the seating area.

"*Yours . . . for now.*" With a final rattling breath, the figure floated back through the wall and vanished.

5

THE BARISTA AND THE FEW OTHER PATRONS in the coffee shop that morning were so concerned with my well-being that they didn't spend too much time trying to piece together what had happened. After all, how and why would I throw a table on top of myself? After helping me collect my belongings—my laptop had fallen on top of my bag and escaped damage—I was gifted a free refill to take on my way. The poor barista seemed thrilled that I only wanted to get out of there and did not appear inclined to pursue legal action against the furniture.

I said very little as I scraped myself together and limped out the door, other than assuring everyone that I was fine and just wanted to go home—partially because I was shaken up and partially because it was difficult to process the questions from the living humans while Casper fretted over me simultaneously.

I stumbled down the street as quickly as my bum leg would allow. My ribs were sore, and my stomach was still in knots. I had mostly accepted the refill because it was less work than refusing.

"Are you okay? I'm so sorry I kicked—"

"I know why you did it. It's fine. And of course I'm not fucking okay. This is so far from okay—"

"Where are we going?" Casper stopped walking.

I didn't break stride. "*I'm* going to the grocery store; I don't know what anybody else is doing."

"Don't you want to get home after that? I thought you said—"

"I am not going home until I've bought stuff to create wards and protect my space." I pulled a coffee-stained piece of paper out of my pocket. "If you decide to come with me, don't be offended if I pretend you don't exist."

"Probably for the best," Casper muttered.

He trailed me silently through a Farmer's Market, a grocery store, and a hardware store. Although he would comment occasionally, he made no objection to me either answering in grunts or not at all. I didn't look directly at him or speak to him until we were back in my apartment.

I fed Blitz a large helping of kibble in hopes of keeping him out of my way while I assembled my smudges on the scuffed card table that I used as a desk/dinner table in the cramped but brightly lit kitchen. I stuck the scribbled sheet of instructions I had labeled "*How to Make* ~~Shit~~ *Wards to Keep* ~~All~~ *Bad Ghosts Out*" under a saltshaker and sifted through my ingredients.

Casper plopped onto the counter, feet dangling several inches off the floor, looking just like a normal human guy hanging out at his friend's house, watching her do some kooky thing and letting it play out.

Joe had perched in that very spot countless times.

My fingers trembled. I lost my grip on the twine I was endeavoring to wrap around my messy bundle of sage and lavender. Several sprigs jerked free, scuttling across the table and onto the floor. I dropped everything, pressing my palms flat to the scuffed surface, trying to steady them. Trying to breathe.

"Is that part of your internet instructions?" Casper deadpanned, leaning over to peer at my scribbled notes.

A laugh bubbled up but lodged in my throat, changing into something more painful. The constricted sensation spread downward across my chest, squeezing my heart. I clamped my eyes shut. *Inhale deep, exhale slow, inhale deep, exhale slow . . .*

"Raely?" It was the first time he'd said my name. Or the first time I was able to hear him say it. A sob pushed its way out of my mouth, and I clamped my hand over it to prevent others from following.

My eyes were still shut tight, but I felt Casper slide off the counter to stand next to me. When he gently set his chilled arm across my shoulders, my body relaxed, and that scared me too. I took a breath. "I thought you couldn't do that."

"I hadn't done it *before*," he said softly. "This is easier than dragging you out of a train. And you looked . . . like you needed a hug or something."

I pried my eyes open and pressed my hand back down to the table. I made myself look at him. He was clearer than he had seemed this morning. His dark blue irises contracted when the light hit them, just like anyone else's would.

"What if I'm going insane?" I whispered. He gazed steadily at me, the weight of his arm across my back unchanged. "Joe's dead, and I'm . . . here. It's not fair. It doesn't make sense. I know it's not my fault, but I feel guilty. I keep thinking things like, I'm the one who said we should run and catch that train. And now I don't have a best friend anymore. And what if . . ."

The words got stuck. I snatched a handful of takeout napkins from the corner of the table and swiped them roughly across my nose before pushing the rest of the words out.

"What if I've just manufactured a new best friend to follow me around and hang out with me, because I'm so lonely and consumed by guilt?"

He patted my shoulder awkwardly. The chill of his touch made me thankful for the forced heat of the radiator near the kitchen table. "You're not going insane, Raely. I've been here the whole time. I knew Joe too. And all your friends. Your mom. Blitz even likes me."

I couldn't deny that. Blitz had never once freaked out in his presence. But that didn't necessarily mean he wasn't a figment of my imagination. Might even be proof that he was. I chewed on my lower lip.

He blew out a breath that moved no air and stepped back to the counter, folding his arms. "Okay, manufacturing me out of survivor's guilt is one thing, but you didn't manufacture the violent coffee shop ghost. How could you have thrown a table on yourself? Not even your guilt is powerful enough for that."

"Oh, do not underestimate the strength of my guilt and despair," I said. "But you do have a point."

"Maybe you should talk about it in your therapy session." Casper glanced at me sideways.

My shoulders tensed. I narrowed my eyes. I hadn't made, nor did I intend to make, the PTSD therapy appointment that the doctors—and my *lawyer*—had recommended. I had no interest in picking apart the accident or Joe's death. There was nothing I could do to change it. I just needed to move forward.

"This has been a lovely chat," I said tightly.

"It *has* been really nice talking to you." Casper's voice was soft.

He was pulling the zip up and down his open jacket, staring at his feet.

"I thought you always talked to me," I said.

"I guess I just mean that it's nice having you answer me. Even if you're kind of mean sometimes." The corner of his mouth twitched up, and his eyes flicked up to mine briefly before dropping to his shoes. His smile fell away.

"I'm sorry I couldn't save Joe, too."

My heart froze mid-beat.

Casper was still. Leaning against the counter, face drawn, eyes bleak.

"I did try." His voice had dropped to a whisper. "I just didn't have any energy left, and he was . . . It was too late. I'm so sorry, Raely. I'm going to miss him too."

It took a few tries, but I managed to force the question out. "He's not a ghost then?"

Casper shook his head. "I don't think so."

I nodded, staring at a crack in the floor's ancient linoleum, welcoming the numbness that swept through my limbs. Any vague hopes I'd been secretly harboring about running into a ghostly Joe dissolved. Probably for the best. For Joe. My gaze traveled back to Casper. What a lonely existence he must've had. Following me around, chattering away in my ear and hoping my subconscious would heed him. My heart cracked.

"Why would you hang around someone for your entire life that couldn't see or hear you?" I asked quietly.

"I knew you heard me. Sometimes when you were asleep you would answer me."

"And we're back to creepy."

Casper snorted. "Sorry."

I took a deep breath, then blew it out. A few sprigs of lavender tumbled across the table. "So, I'm not insane. And I'm not imagining you."

"You're not."

"Well, shit."

⁓⁓⁓⁓

AFTER THOROUGHLY SMUDGING the apartment, carefully following the most legitimate online instructions, I switched to a different tab, continuing my interrupted research from earlier.

"Don't you want to take a nap or something?" Casper asked.

I snorted. "Yeah, after being attacked by a spooky-ass . . . what the hell kind of ghost was that, anyway? One of those Oracles you were talking about?"

"If it's what I think it is, it's called a Jimani. I've only ever seen one other one. They're . . . really bad." Casper shuddered. Awesome. A spirit that made another ghost shiver was potentially interested in me. "We really don't want it following you around."

"Why not?" I asked, eyes glued to the screen.

Casper sighed. "They're powerful. And violent. I mean, you saw how easily they can move stuff and how little they care if they hurt anyone. They enjoy causing pain and creating problems for the living."

"What kinds of problems? Besides being terrifying and tossing furniture around."

Casper shifted from foot to foot. "Disclaimer: I don't know a lot about this—"

"Whatever you know can only enhance the utter lack of knowledge I currently possess."

Casper took a breath. "If they decide to kill you, they can take over your soul before you get to move on."

My stomach turned to ice. "Great." I grabbed my thermos and spun the laptop around to face him. "This is our next stop."

Casper's eyes roved over the screen. The corners of his mouth pulled down further the more he read. "Ghost hunters? That's a terrible webpage."

I snapped the laptop shut, drained my coffee, and banged the thermos back down. "I didn't realize afterlife web design was a thing." I grabbed my coat.

"You're just going to go down there?"

"They don't have a phone number listed. And the email I sent before we were attacked hasn't been answered. Got any better ideas?"

He only glowered, his mouth twisting to one side in clear disapproval.

"Cool. Let's go."

6

WE CAUGHT A BUS TO A WEST SIDE NEIGHBORHOOD that housing ads would call "up and coming." I sat much farther back than usual, because I didn't enjoy watching people sit on or walk through Casper, although he assured me that it happened all the time and was likely more uncomfortable for the living person than it was for him.

I noticed that those who did pass through him often appeared to have a sudden upset stomach or a chill afterward. But everyone was cold in February.

The ride was long, and the day was a frosty steel gray. Buses were almost always warmer than trains, which I appreciated. I kept an eye on the street names and occasionally scanned the directions I had typed into my phone. Casper and I were the only ones to disembark at our stop. I had already developed a bad habit of holding doors open for him unnecessarily.

The sidewalks were largely unshoveled, so I took my time, not wanting a slip to reverse any of the dubious progress physical therapy had made on my injured leg. I looked up at intervals to check house numbers but mainly concentrated on where I was putting my feet.

Casper, however, was taking in the sights.

"This is a crappy neighborhood."

"Oh, I'm sorry, where was your mansion again?"

"Just keep your eyes open. Don't get mugged or something."

"You know, that's something we should discuss. Are you just a useless backseat driver in my life, dispensing opinions like an annoying cartoon angel on my shoulder? Or would you be of any use should hypothetical muggers leap out of the snow drifts and attempt to rob me of my train pass and the two dollars of liquid capital on my person?"

I glanced at Casper as he exhaled in exasperation. His breath didn't cloud the air as mine did, which should have stopped surprising me by now. He kept his eyes forward, his dark eyebrows pulling closer together. "I wouldn't be that useful, no. I haven't had a lot of practice at physically affecting things. Or people."

"Well, don't worry about it," I said, pausing in front of a rotting wooden fence to squint at the ice-blurred house number. "People don't normally mug that many people when it's below freezing. This is us."

I started to pick my way through the gap in the fence, where presumably a gate was once attached, when Casper stepped in front of me.

"Raely, this is a shithole."

"You're incredibly judgy today."

"You're not going into this dump. Mission aborted." He folded his arms across his chest. As if he had authority over me. A weird burning sensation effervesced against my sternum. I wanted both to laugh and to punch him.

"Okay, all of those with corporeal forms are entitled to vote on whether the mission proceeds." I walked through him. "Look at that, the mission is proceeding."

I heard something like a growl behind me, but I ignored it and banged on the door. There was a faded, handwritten scrap of lined notebook paper stuck behind the glass above the mail slot that read, "Barrett, Roberts & Marsh/Ghosthunters, Inc." From somewhere within the house, a male voice hailed. Another answered with a guffaw. There were some thumps, a few more inarticulate shouts back and forth, then footsteps. Casper appeared at my elbow, glaring at the peeling paint on the door, his eyebrows lower than ever.

A chain rattled, and I heard the deadbolt slide back. The door swung open to reveal a taller-than-average man with short, black hair and hazel eyes. He couldn't have been much older than I was. He was wearing jeans and a faded Johnny Cash T-shirt over a long-sleeved thermal.

He gave me a quick once-over, blinked, then leaned against the doorframe and flashed a smile full of even, white teeth. It was the kind of smile I occasionally got at the club, approximately five minutes before the predictable 'What time do you get off work?'

"Well hello, doll, and to what do I owe the pleasure?"

Casper snorted. I ignored him.

"Hi, sorry, I didn't see any way to make an appointment. I got the address on your website, and I was hoping I could talk to someone about . . . ghost . . . problems?"

"Hey, you've come to the right place!" He straightened and stuck out his hand. I extended my mittened paw in return and shook. "Dylan Barrett, come on in. My partners and I were just going through some footage we got at our last job."

I stepped into what was probably intended to be a living room but looked more like a low-rent version of a hacker control center in a B movie. Computers and equipment on card tables lined the perimeter of the space, interspersed with beat-up couches and milk crates containing jumbles of electronics.

A couple of mismatched thrift store coffee tables, placed with no real care for the room's feng shui, held empty pizza boxes and stacks of files and papers.

"Thanks." I stepped over a pile of unopened mail and into the warmth, pulling off my mittens and pushing them into my coat pockets. "I'm Raely—"

"Holy shit, Dylan! This meter is going nuts!" A shorter, scruffier man with dirty blond hair shuffled over to us, expertly dodging piles of detritus, clutching what looked like a cross between a walkie-talkie and a battery tester. "Hi. Chris Roberts," he said, barely glancing at me. He was dressed in an oversized flannel, like a shrunken lumberjack.

Dylan crossed to his side and gazed at the meter, which had some kind of green-on-black line jumping up and down on its Game Boy–esque screen. He waved at the last of the college frat rejects, beckoning him over. "Greg, are you catching this on the big one?"

I flinched when what I had first taken to be a pile of laundry in the corner rose from an overstuffed chair. Greg stumbled over with a larger "meter" connected to a handheld antenna, tripping over a milk carton en route. The most generic of the three, in a blue polo and rumpled khakis, he waved the antenna around, as if he were blowing soap bubbles with it, his eyes darting between the faces of both meters.

"Yeah, the big one is going nuts too. This is wild! It started right when she came in."

As one, they all looked up from the meters, eyes widening on me as if Christmas and their birthdays had rolled in the door all at once.

"You have some serious energy around you," Greg said. "You must have been around a lot of spiritual activity lately."

I heard Casper mutter something that sounded like "Jesus Christ" under his breath.

"Well, yeah," I said. "That's kind of why—"

"Where do you live?" Chris interrupted me again. "Is it super haunted? God, I'd love to do a stakeout and see what's causing this."

"I live in a very ordinary apartment, but I have a ghost standing right next to me, so that's probably why your . . ." I waved my hand at the contraptions they clutched. "Those meter things are . . . doing whatever."

In a moment of stillness they all stared at me, mouths like guppies, the metallic clinking of the radiator the only sound.

Greg thrust his antenna to one side of me. "A ghost right there?"

"Other side."

He swatted the antenna in Casper's direction, almost taking off my nose. His meter jumped. This fully adult man pranced in place, whooping like he was at a sports game. Casper glared down his nose at the antenna bouncing up and down inches from his face.

"I don't like this," he said.

"You're kinda annoying him," I told Greg, fighting a losing battle with the smirk spreading across my face. "He didn't really want to come here in the first place."

Like comedic marionettes, they turned as one to stare at me again. Had there been any insects flying around, they'd have certainly been eating them for breakfast. I clenched my own jaw as if it would signal them to shut their mouths. My cheeks flushed. This was becoming uncomfortable. I cleared my throat. "So, like, my budget isn't huge, but let's get down to business, if that's alright. What kind of services—"

"Wait, you can *talk* to the ghost you want to get rid of?" Dylan cut me off. I was bored with being interrupted.

"No! Well, yes, I can talk to him, but Casper's not the ghost I want to get rid of, he's kind of a protector gho—"

Chris's meter slipped a few inches, almost sliding from his grip. "Your friendly ghost is named *Casper*?" He howled with laughter and the other two joined him.

"Oh, that's the best," Greg crowed. "That's the best thing I've heard all year."

"I'm changing my fucking name," Casper gritted out.

"Okay, can everyone in the room, living or otherwise, please get a grip? This is unprofessional, and I'm tired of everyone talking over me and interrupting me." I fished my mittens out of my pockets, stuffing my hands back into them. "You should say on your website how to make appointments or, I dunno, list a business number or something. This is obviously a bad time. C'mon, Casper."

"Thank God." Casper turned and stalked through the solid wall as if he couldn't stand to remain in the house for another second. The bleeping meters instantly went silent.

I was nearly to the door when Dylan's hand wrapped around my upper arm and spun me around with surprising force. I instinctively froze.

"Hey, Raely, c'mon. Give us a break. We've never had a girl walk in with an actual benevolent spirit attached. You can't blame us for getting a little excited. It's not a big deal that you stopped by, but you could have emailed—"

"I did email," I said, my eyes dropped down to his hand, still gripping my arm tightly. He followed the line of my gaze and let go.

"Okay, well, we don't always comb through the inbox at the crack of dawn." He laughed. "No worries, I get it, you were freaked out about something and wanted someone to help you right away. How about this? I'll get some things together, and you and I can meet to strategize later. I may even throw in a discount for the awkward timing." Greg frowned at the back of Dylan's head.

I hesitated. A little warning bell pinging. He must have seen it on my face.

"Right, you're careful." He smiled. "Smart. We'll meet in public, coffee or something. Say, around 4 p.m.?"

Casper poked his head back through the door to see what the hell was keeping me. I took a step toward him. "I can meet you to strategize," I said, "but don't be offended if I don't order anything. I don't like having caffeine after the a.m. hours."

"Ah, sensitive to caffeine. That's alright, doll." He clapped his hands together. "Even better. I'll get lunch. Or dinner. Whatever you eat at that time. My treat for pissing off your ghost. Hang on a second." He grabbed my arm again when I turned to the door—a bit more gently—then unearthed a bag from beneath a rumpled coat on one of the couches and dug around in it until he produced a battered business card. "Here's my cell number. Just text me with yours whenever you get somewhere that's not freezing, and we'll go from there."

I took the card, thanked them all, and stepped out into the wintry gloom, trudging back toward the bus stop. Snow was drifting down from the endless clouds above.

"Tear that up and throw it away," Casper said.

"Excuse me?"

"Those guys were idiots. You can't seriously be considering going to meet him?"

My face heated. I caught myself as my boot skidded on an icy patch. "In case you haven't noticed, we don't have a ton of options. And their equipment *did* pick you up, so obviously they're doing something right."

"Dylan is just hitting on you."

"Oh my God."

"Buy you dinner." He snorted. My spine went rigid. "Did he offer you a discount too? Did he even ask which ghosts you *do* want to be rid of?"

Snowflakes had to be combusting in the air inches from my flaming hot skin. I had my own reservations about Dylan, but I hadn't found any other ghostbusting services online. We ducked under the bus shelter. I pulled my knit hat off and smacked it against my thigh, dislodging a small shower of snowflakes. No bus in sight, of course.

"And why do you have to meet him somewhere else? Why couldn't he just give you a ballpark price now? Throw it away." Casper pointed bossily into the mouth of a nearby trash can. His entire person was completely free of the snow, now swirling down in huge, fat flakes. He raised his eyebrows as if to ask what I was waiting for.

I opened my mouth to inquire as to who died and made him king, then snapped it shut. He had probably been bossing me around like this my entire life. Would past-Raely have listened to him? Like a remote-controlled toy, blindly obeying what she'd taken for a gut feeling? Something hardened in my chest. If I was honest with myself, Dylan's mannerisms had raised some of my own red flags. Not the least of which was the fact that, despite his grabbiness, I still wanted to meet with him. Which, given my history, meant I probably shouldn't.

But had those implanted red flags come from me or from Casper? How much subconscious "guidance" had he given me over the years? My fingers curled into fists inside my mittens, and my lips tightened into a hard, thin line. Present-Raely had a goddamn mind of her own.

I glared at him, jammed my hat back on, yanked off my right mitten, and pulled my phone and the business card from my pocket. I swiped it open and punched in numbers as the skin on my hand slowly chilled. Casper's eyes widened as I hit send, slid both phone and card back into my pocket, and wiggled my fingers back inside my mitten. I turned my back to him and stared up the street, willing a bus to appear. The vapor of my own breath floated around my face. I was huffing as if I had just sprinted up the block.

I felt Casper standing behind me. Neither of us spoke as we watched the headlights of an oncoming bus gradually grow larger. Neither of us was happy.

7

"WHY ARE YOU PUTTING ON MAKEUP?" Casper was leaning against the doorframe of my tiny bathroom, peering in through narrowed eyes. I stood at the sink two feet away, my back to the door—and Casper—and pawed through tubes of the finest drugstore makeup brands I'd spread out on the counter. I plucked a mascara from the pile—waterproof, in case of snow. The bathroom was the only room in the apartment I had warded so thoroughly that even Casper couldn't enter. Because he had no business in the bathroom, and I needed a place for privacy.

Which I was not getting.

"Because I'm going to a restaurant for a business meeting," I said to his reflection—apparently, I could see ghostly reflections—in the mirror while I layered mascara onto my eyelashes.

"You keep telling yourself that."

I twirled around and shut the door in his face.

Spinning back to the mirror, I tested two different lipstick options against the back of my hand as I checked my phone. *4:30 p.m.* Dylan and I had changed our meeting to 5 p.m. because the restaurant he had chosen didn't start seating until then. At least it was walking distance from my place. I had not been looking forward to another jaunt to the unshoveled West Side on my bum leg.

After being rather pushy about meeting for dinner instead of coffee, Dylan had offered to pick me up in his car, but I had been firm on that point. I didn't need Casper's overprotective vibe to remind me not to take rides from men I didn't know on the first . . . meeting.

Not a date.

Still, it didn't hurt to look nice. I did want the guy to help me, after all. Although, had I looked deep in my heart of hearts, I could have said there was no reason to be putting forth this amount of effort. I was familiar with Dylan's type, and, unfortunately for me, that type had always drawn me in. Once I'd learned this, I'd assiduously avoided the Dylans of the world. Until today.

I told myself I hadn't been out since the accident. It was natural to want to dress up. I told myself that I was on an ever-shrinking budget. Maybe he would charge me less if he thought I was cute. I nodded at my reflection. *Solid plan.* I chose the darker shade of red, applied the lipstick, then flipped my flat iron to high heat and turned my attention to my hair.

"JESUS H. CHRIST," Casper said fifteen minutes later as I strode from the bathroom, a cloud of perfume wafting behind me.

"Fuck off." I didn't look at him as I stalked to my closet for an appropriate sweater to layer over my slinky, spaghetti-strapped top.

"Hypothermia much? It's *February.* There's a *snowstorm.*"

"Is that how you died? Hypothermia? Is that why you know so much about it?" I yanked two sweaters off their hangers, considering which would strike the right balance between foxy and "oh this old thing."

"They're called layers, and the place is two blocks away." The clingy black one. I tossed it on and sat on the bed to zip my tall boots over my jeans. Adequately shod, I stood, threw on my coat, grabbed my keys, a notebook, and a pen, and headed for the door.

"What's the notebook for?" Casper's tone was decidedly derisive.

"Notebooks are for notes. Business meeting, remember?" I yanked the door open.

"Tell that to the come-fuck-me boots."

I slammed the door and stomped down the stairs with as much speed as my leg would allow, almost walking through Casper on the landing. "These boots have excellent traction," I snapped, skirting around him. He followed me.

"Does the lipstick have excellent traction too?"

"*Why on earth* are you still near me?" I hissed, finally looking at him.

"Business meeting, remember?" He smirked. His obnoxious face was less hazy than it had been this morning, and his eyes sparkled malevolently. "I'm part of the business. Seems it would only be weird for me to come along if it was a date. But since it's not—"

"It's not. It's just that I hate you so much right now, I thought you might buzz off and go float around a cemetery or something." I shoved open the front door of the building with more force than necessary, jarring my right wrist. I bit back a yelp but didn't break stride, thrusting my hands into my pockets.

"No mittens?" Casper's voice was shellacked in sarcasm. "But it's dropped a couple degrees since the sun went down."

I clenched my jaw and said nothing. He was doing a great job of keeping me from feeling the cold. I was positive my fury was thawing all snow-covered objects in my wake.

"Okay, Raely, I'll stop. But please calm down. If you stay this worked up, you might attract mean ghosts." He'd dropped the sarcasm, but his tone lilted with laughter. We were half a block from the main thoroughfare. I glanced around. No one on the street. I stopped and spun to face him.

"Apologize."

His jaw dropped open. "For *what*? Telling the truth?"

"For being a dick about my outfit."

"For the record, you're a dick pretty much all the time about just about everything."

I stared at him and folded my arms.

He sighed and rolled his eyes heavenward.

I stared.

"Okay, I'm sorry if something I said really upset you. I just . . . do not have a good feeling about this operation."

I nodded stiffly once, turned, and clomped through the slush to meet my ghostbuster.

BAD DOG WAS a casual restaurant, but the food was expensive enough that you could find people clad in anything from T-shirts and ratty jeans to cocktail dresses. It was a classic winter-city pub, with a long hallway on the other side of the main entrance to keep the cold from following you too far in. The walls were lined with pictures of dogs. Some of them were wearing jaunty hats and happy doggy grins. I almost made a comment about it to Casper when I realized that: One, I would look like I was talking to myself, and two, he had probably visited this place with me before and already knew what I was going to say. This resulted in me turning to speak, changing my mind halfway, and tripping over the carpet runner.

"Nervous about your date?"

"You said you'd stop," I muttered, keeping my eyes trained ahead.

The empty host's stand greeted me. I took a moment to remember what day it was. Saturday.

It was still Saturday. Surely the longest Saturday of my life. Fatigue settled heavily onto my shoulders. I shrugged out of my coat and looped it over an arm, trying to shake the feeling. No wonder the host wasn't here; they were probably seating people.

"He's in the back by the fireplace," Casper said, with all the enthusiasm of Eeyore.

"Oh! Thanks for checking." I hadn't even noticed him leave and return. I fumbled with my coat, locating the pocket with my notebook and pen and fishing them out.

Business meeting.

He shrugged. "You should start walking back there," he said on a long-suffering exhale. "People are starting to look at you because of the boots."

He was right, there were a few guys at the bar looking over.

"They're looking at me because I'm talking to myself," I snapped, but strode toward the back of the restaurant. "At least he got a good spot," I muttered. I loved the fireplace tables in the winter. And they were incredibly difficult to get. If a fireplace table was available on a Saturday night in the winter—time to play the lottery.

Dylan was seated facing the entrance. He spotted me immediately and waved me over with a smile. He had apparently showered, applied hair product, and changed into a black button-down. He'd grabbed a two-top right in front of the fireplace.

And he had wine.

"Date," Casper whispered in my ear.

I swatted the air as if a fly was buzzing nearby.

"Hi, Dylan." I tossed my coat over the back of my chair and slid into the seat across from him. The warmth from the fireplace was delicious.

I opened my notebook to a clean page and placed it and my pen deliberately in front of me.

Not a date.

"Raely, you look nice. Your hair looks better that way. Less frizzy." He grabbed the wine and poured me a glass. "I took a chance you might like red."

I considered refusing. He hadn't even asked. And the backhanded compliment about my hair ticked another "warning" box. Two internal Raelys fought a vicious battle in my head. Business meeting! Delicious wine! Not a date! Really bad, no good, very long day! The battle was short-lived.

"I have a difficult time turning down self-medication after a day like today." I pushed out a small smile.

"Just don't get trashed," Casper sighed, and strolled over to lean against the fireplace.

"Please fuck off. Sorry. Not you."

Dylan had paused in the midst of pouring my wine, a flash of anger behind his eyes, but it quickly vanished when I rolled my eyes in Casper's direction. So quickly I decided I'd imagined it.

"Sorry, Casper has opinions about me drinking."

"First rule of dealing with ghosts: Don't let them run things." He gave me a wink and filled my glass almost to the brim. I chuckled awkwardly at the over-pour but pulled the glass toward me, taking a sip without lifting it to ensure I wouldn't spill.

"So, is he constantly talking to you?" Observing my notebook, Dylan pulled out one of his own, clicked his pen against the table, and poised to take notes.

I relaxed a fraction.

"Feels like it." I took another sip of wine then pushed the glass to the side, grabbing my own pen. "But no, he just told me not to get trashed. He's staring moodily at the fire right now."

Casper flipped me off without breaking his emo fireplace reverie.

"So how long has he been attached to you?" Dylan was interrupted when a waiter dropped off a plate of fried calamari. "Oh, I went ahead and ordered. The calamari here is great. You'll love it."

"Oh. Yeah, I come here pretty regularly." Casper gave me a pointed glare over his shoulder, but said nothing. I took another sip of wine. Yes, there were red flags—pink flags really, so what if he had ordered a few things?—but this was *not a date*. I wasn't getting romantically involved. All the same, I opted to leave my sweater on. The strappy top could make an appearance some other night out.

After trying at first to restrain myself, I couldn't help enthusiastically digging into the calamari. I'd forgotten lunch completely—a bad habit I'd developed since the accident—and was starving. The calamari were the perfect temperature. The sauce had just the right amount of spice.

"He says he's always been with me, but I've only just recently begun to see him. Honestly, as annoying as he is sometimes, he's not the problem. It's the other ghosts I want to keep away from me." I pulled out my best charming smile, honed to perfection by slinging booze for tips. "I'm hoping you have some kind of magic formula or like, I dunno, an amulet or something so I can get some sleep tonight."

He laughed and tossed back his wine, finishing the glass. "If I had that, we'd be at a much better restaurant right now." He winked.

I kept my smile plastered on my face, but my heart deflated. I took a solid swig of wine and soldiered on. Yes, it was fine to dress up and drink decent wine for a change, but I had come here for answers.

"Okay, well, what *can* you do? What do you guys do with your . . . meters and stuff?"

"Alright! Down to business, I like it." His lips split into a toothy grin.

Irritation grated against my sternum, but I'd become highly proficient at faking smiles. I snatched the last two calamari rings so that my face wouldn't have to hold the position too long, doggedly ignoring the nudge at the back of my mind telling me Casper may have been right.

"Generally, we're hired out to haunted locations. We use the EMF meters and digital thermometers, different types of cameras—you know, infrared, night vision, the works—to check for paranormal activity. But investigating an actual haunted *person* is new, and one reason I was able to get the team on board."

"So they weren't interested?" I found their names in the back of my brain. "Greg and . . . Chris?"

"Well, Chris is down for anything, Greg just doesn't like change. But let's talk about you for a minute. These other ghosts, the ones you want to get rid of—what do they do? Follow you around? Move your stuff—?"

"This morning I had a ghost throw a table on top of me at a coffee shop. Casper said he's a kind of ghost called a Jimani." I nervously sipped my wine—keeping my voice at a level that I hoped would prevent other patrons from overhearing—and watched for Dylan's reaction to the name, but he just kept writing. My heart sank further. "Anyway, apparently he's a ghost that's been around for a really long time and gets off on causing strife in the living."

Casper remained near the fireplace, but his back was to the fire. He was watching Dylan now.

"Okay, wow." Dylan finished scribbling in his notebook, then looked up at me. "Don't worry, doll." He reached across the table and grabbed my hand with a smile. "I'm sorry that happened. We'll figure it out."

With effort, I lifted the corners of my mouth upward. "Thanks. So have you heard of that type of ghost?" I pulled my hand from his and pretended to wipe something off my jeans with my napkin.

"I haven't heard that name, no, but Casper obviously knows different terminology than I do, which is very exciting. We've dealt with malevolent spirits before, though. Don't worry."

The waiter stopped by to see if he could get us anything else and topped off our wine. I didn't protest. My eyes were dry with exhaustion, and the realization that I wouldn't get any solutions tonight was slowly draping itself over me like a weighted blanket. Only the thought that this was my only lead—and my stubborn resistance to the idea that Casper had likely been right—kept me in the chair.

For the rest of the meeting—still not a date—Dylan peppered me with questions about ghosts. How and why they would find me. What they were attracted to. Eventually, I waved Casper over for clarification.

"So, they know you can see ghosts, and they like that?"

I angled my head toward Casper without looking away from the table, which had become my signal that I wanted his input. He had taken up a new position to my right, leaning on the back of my chair.

"Strong emotions will attract them; grief, anger, terror. They like directing the emotions of vulnerable people. Some of them like the . . . taste of certain emotions. They'll latch on to normal people also, but it's easier to manipulate someone who can see them. Especially an older or more powerful spirit that likes to cause fear."

I translated this for Dylan, who at least looked serious about taking notes. My notebook lay open and unused, aside from some random doodles I had drawn in the spaces of silence. The bottle of wine was empty. I had finished my glass and both my water and Dylan's. I excused myself to go to the restroom and when I came back, a fresh glass of wine was waiting for me. I was about to protest that I didn't need any more alcohol, but Casper, who had waited for me outside the bathroom, saw it and said, "No. I said do *not* get trashed."

"You're *not* the boss of me," I hissed. My irritation and exhaustion combined thrust me into full-on anger. I plopped into my seat and defiantly took a sip.

"This was so much fucking easier when you couldn't see me." Casper took up a new perch across the table, behind Dylan, and glared at me.

A slow burn began in my stomach and crept up into my chest, where it settled into a steady, hot flame. I could feel my cheeks heating, either an effect of the wine or Casper pushing my buttons. I tore my gaze from his and focused on Dylan.

"Thanks for the extra glass," I said sweetly. Casper shook his head and stalked over to the fire.

"No problem. You seemed like you needed it. And I still have mine to finish. Don't wanna drink alone." He flashed his salesman grin and winked at me. Was it normal for a person to wink so often?

I took another sip of wine and looked around when I realized that Casper wasn't glaring at me from the fireplace. My irritation vanished, and my stomach dropped. He was gone.

"Okay, let's see if I've got this straight." Dylan flipped back a page of his notebook.

I forced my attention back to him. Surely ghosts didn't need to use the restroom?

"They like it if you can see them, because they can fuck with you more easily. They like certain emotions, often negative ones. They like feeling as if they can influence or upset the living. If they know you can see them, they'll seek you out. Strong emotions will sometimes attract them. And your biggest concern is this 'Jimani' type becoming interested in you. Is that the gist of it?"

"I think so," I said, my eyes darting around for Casper. He wouldn't leave me, surely. I refocused on Dylan. "I don't know how it is that they *know* if I can see them or not. Unless, of course, they see me talking to Casper. Mostly I try to pretend I don't see them if I can, but it's . . ."

"It gets harder if they're throwing furniture at you?"

I looked up at him. He wasn't smiling. He wasn't making fun of me. Something eased in my chest. "Yeah."

He reached across the table and took my hand. This time I let him. "Look, I know this sucks, and I know you wanted an immediate answer, and I'm sorry that I can't give it to you, but we're going to figure this out. My team is the best."

I smiled, my first real smile of the night. "Okay."

Dylan squeezed and released my hand. "Alright, let's talk about compensation."

Oof, it was like the air being let out of that brief bubble of well-being. I cleared my throat. "Well, I'll figure something out, whatever it ends up being. I'm not fully back to work yet. Do you have payment plans . . .?"

"I'm going to stop you there, Raely," Dylan said, leaning back in his chair and folding his arms behind his head. "Remember how I said that we typically do haunted locations? Well, since this is a new experience for us, we're willing to take on your case *pro bono*. That is, if you let us document it for future research."

"Wow, really? That seems . . . what do you mean, 'document'?"

"Well, we'll want to bring you over to the house a couple of times, with Casper, and record any readings we get. Maybe record you talking about your experience. Stuff like that. Then, if any other ghosts come by, we'll record those interactions, too, and we'll work out what attracts them and what might be used to repel them more permanently. Sound good?"

I wasn't entirely comfortable with the idea of being filmed, but my lack of funds made this a difficult proposal to resist. I tried to weigh the pros and cons but . . . I shouldn't have had so much wine. "When you record things, it's just for your own records, right? For like, diagnostics? I mean, I'll be honest, I do not want this showing up on social media or anywhere public. Also, I don't think I can talk about the accident—"

"Yeah, yeah, we'll discuss all that." Dylan said, leaning forward again and waving the waiter over. He was a little too blasé about this for my taste. The server produced a card reader, and Dylan handed over his credit card. "I'll give you a release form to look over and sign when we set up the first recording."

I hesitated. "I can read the form before we film anything?"

"Sure, yeah, of course," he nodded while signing the receipt.

I could insist on looking it over before they started recording. If I was uncomfortable with the terms, I didn't have to sign it or agree to be recorded. I could just leave. "Okay."

Casper reappeared suddenly, but my relief was short-lived. "Make him walk you home," he said. "If you see any ghosts, don't say anything about it. Don't tell him. I'll wait upstairs."

"Is everything okay?" I said out loud without thinking.

"There's a lot of activity. More than usual. And the Jimani is one of them. I'm going to take off. If he sees me following you, he's more likely to recognize you from this morning, and I don't want him taking notice of you. At. All. So please, make Dylan walk you home. And don't say anything about this. Get home in ten minutes or less, or I'm going to come back and look for you." He vanished.

"What's going on?" Dylan was shrugging into his jacket. He grinned at me. "Casper being jealous?"

"He told me to get you to walk me home. He's taking off for a bit." The mention of the Jimani had flooded my system with so much adrenaline that my ears were ringing, but I obeyed Casper and didn't mention what he had seen. Normal. Be normal and unremarkable.

"I guess I should feel flattered." He offered his arm to me as if we were in an old-fashioned movie.

"One sec." I downed the last of my wine and set the glass on the table before hooking my hand around his elbow. "Never leave a soldier in the field."

He laughed, and I tried to smile back as we made our way toward the exit. *Deep breaths. Don't let them sense your panic.* By the time we reached the front door, I had asked Dylan some inane question about where he was from, he was talking about the Mitten of Michigan, and I thought I had a handle on things. He held the door open, and I stepped outside.

Ghosts everywhere.

At first, I tried to tell myself that they were just people out and about, but they weren't behaving like living people. They were . . . waiting. One or two might attach themselves to a late-night reveler or follow a couple, but they all seemed to be drawn by something. I didn't want to look too closely at any of them. Would I even recognize the Jimani? I didn't want to. I dove into the booze and focused my entire being on Dylan.

"So when can I expect to hear from your team again? I'm this way." I guided him toward my street. Passing three ghosts, one of which Dylan walked straight through. I shuddered, and Dylan removed my hand from his elbow and put his arm around my shoulders, pulling me closer. He *was* hitting on me. My stomach flipped, and I concentrated on that.

"Cold?" He rubbed a hand up and down my arm a few times, like that ever helps anyone who's cold. "What's your work schedule? We could probably figure something out tomorrow . . ."

"Oh, I have to go see my lawyer during the day, and I work at the bar tomorrow night—"

"What bar?"

For two blocks, I focused my full attention on Dylan's questions and answers. I even tried to think about what they might mean. I thought about my bed at home. My cat. Anything but Casper. Anything but the dozens of ghosts decorating the corners.

One of them detached itself from two others and trailed after us. It was him. I didn't even have to look at him. A feeling of dread settled into my stomach just as it had in the coffee shop. I forced myself to think only of Dylan, even though my brain strained to reach out to Casper for help. The way Dylan's hand had slid off my arm and hooked around my waist. The way our frosted breath mingled as we spoke. I pushed the fear and panic back back back to a distant part of my brain and heart. It was working. We were going to make it. As we neared my place, I noticed fewer and fewer ghosts. They were drawn to the energy of the main thoroughfare. Had they always been there? Had I drawn them? The feeling of dread was slowly seeping away. Perhaps the Jimani hadn't recognized me. We made it to the courtyard. Once in front of my door, I tried to pull away gently. I wanted to run upstairs as fast as my legs could carry me, but ingrained midwestern politeness wouldn't allow it. "Thank you so much for walking me home. We'll be in touch."

He had not released my waist when I turned around and instead caught my other side with his free hand. He appeared to have completely enjoyed the walk. For a ghost hunter, he was remarkably insensitive to the presence of ghosts. "Not so fast, doll."

I laughed awkwardly and pressed my hands against his arms to disengage. It had started snowing in earnest again, and his silhouette was framed by the streetlight and streaming snowflakes behind him. Instead of releasing me, he pulled me in, leaned forward, and kissed me.

The booze-muted feelings at my core began to uncurl. Before I pulled myself out of my ghost-panic enough to react, he had tightened the hug. My arms were pressed against his chest. He slid one hand beneath my hair to grasp the back of my neck. He deepened the kiss until there was no space between us. I tested pulling away, but his grip tightened.

My breath quickened. The red flags waved, but they were so familiar it was almost nice to see them again—

"Ugh! Jesus Christ, I said ten minutes! Fuck. I can't unsee this."

It was like cold water being thrown over me. I jerked out of the kiss in time to see Casper fleeing through a wall with his hands over his ears. Like that was going to help him unsee my make-out session.

"Thanks again," I said breathlessly, as I shoved out of his arms and staggered toward the door. "I'll talk to you soon; you have my number." I jammed my key into the lock but Dylan caught my arm and spun me around.

"Hang on, we were just getting started." He was too close. My back was against the door, and I had nowhere to go.

You've been here before. You know what to do. "I really appreciate you taking the time to meet with me," I said calmly, as if he hadn't just backed me against my own door. "But I'd like to keep things professional." *Diffuse. Diffuse.*

I blocked his hand as he reached up to grab my neck again. His eyes flashed. Just then the door across the courtyard banged open and three of my neighbors poured out laughing, one of them pulling out a phone to get a rideshare. Dylan backed off.

"You wanna keep things professional, maybe you shouldn't dress like a tease and inhale wine like a lush." He spun on his heel and stalked off.

I pushed aside the feelings he'd scraped with his words and pivoted to the door, turning my key with mechanical fluidity and flying up the stairs.

Casper was pacing in the front room. Blitz was waiting by his food bowl.

Without taking off my coat, I poured food for Blitz, then stomped into the kitchen, tracking snow everywhere, to grab the remainder of the smudge stick I had made earlier. My hands shook as I lit it with a long BBQ lighter. I anointed the door and each of the windows with the smoke, intoning under my breath to cast out any negative energy. My phone buzzed in my pocket. I peeked at the screen. Dylan. I ignored it.

Casper watched me in silence, leaning against the front door as if he could hold back anything—or anyone—that might try to come calling. I wondered if he could somehow train to morph into a stronger ghost.

I was heating up inside my coat as I finished the bedroom windows. I grabbed a pillow off the bed and a book off the nightstand and headed for the bathroom, where I finally shed my coat, letting it drop to the floor. Casper leaned up against the doorframe just outside the room as I unzipped my still slushy boots and tossed them into the tub where they would do less damage. I snatched up some toilet paper and mopped my tracks up off the floor and then washed my face. My hands were still trembling. After scrubbing most of the makeup off, I grabbed the glass on the side that I kept my toothbrush in, filled it at the sink and downed it. I repeated the process three times.

Normally I'd be thinking about the guy who had just kissed me downstairs two seconds before calling me a lush. I'd glanced over the texts he'd sent. Eloquent apologies. I could have predicted it. It seemed an almost-inconsequential detail now. All I could think about was how I was going to have to deal with ghosts for however-many-more days and somehow still had to conduct my life. I yanked a brush roughly through my hair, focusing on the sensation rather than the cold pit growing along the bottom of my stomach.

After brushing my teeth, I tossed my pillow against the wall by the door and sank down to the floor, leaning against it. Casper slid to a seat against the other side of the doorframe. I could feel him looking at me, but I kept my gaze on my hands as I grabbed my coat and arranged it, blanket-like, over my legs. "Have there always been that many?"

"There are usually more on the weekends when the bars and restaurants are active, but tonight seemed especially crowded."

I finally looked at him. "Is that because of me?"

"Honestly, I don't know. I just knew that if I was following you, I'd draw more attention to you. And I really don't want that Jimani seeing you again." He paused. "Dylan didn't notice them at all, did he?"

I shook my head, looking back down at my lap.

"Look, Raely—"

"If you're going to start in about how you were right that he was hitting on me, I don't need to hear it. That much was obvious." I didn't mention what had happened after he'd fled back upstairs.

"I've watched people interact with you your entire life; I know the signs."

I looked into his face again. He was even less hazy than he had been while walking over to the restaurant. He looked like someone I knew from somewhere. Maybe a movie. He sounded exhausted. "I just don't think you should put all your eggs in this guy's basket. If you wanna . . ." he made weird hand gestures and mumbled inarticulately, ". . . with him, fine—"

My chest tightened and my face heated. "Stop it! I'm not . . . *whatevering* with him," I mimicked his gestures. This was good. Sarcastic derision grounded me. "Since presumably you don't have to pay rent anywhere, you may have forgotten, but I have a limited amount of savings that I'm living on at the moment, so the fact that he's not charging me is a bonus."

I stopped and took a breath. Casper's eyebrows lifted. "He's not charging?"

"They've never had a haunted person before. They want to use the case for future research or something." I pulled my book off the bathroom countertop and plopped it on the floor next to my pillow, trying to ignore the eels in my stomach. When I said it out loud, it sounded too good to be true. But Casper seemed to have decided not to needle me further.

I dropped some frankincense oil into my diffuser and then turned it on, making sure to push the button that allowed the light within it to fade through a spectrum of soft colors as it hummed away. I turned off the main bathroom light and, grateful for my plush bathmat, lay down on the pillow, pulling my long coat up to my chest. Thankfully the bathroom had its own radiator and was warm.

Once Blitz had seen that this was where I was settling for the night, he trotted in and made a nest at my feet.

Casper slid down until he was fully reclined on his back.

"Are you going to tell me that I'm being ridiculous sleeping in the bathroom?"

"No." He lay on his back facing the ceiling. "You've obviously warded it properly, and I'd be more concerned if you weren't a little freaked out after the day you've had."

"Is that comfortable?"

He shrugged. "I don't think I feel discomfort the same way you do. This isn't worse than anywhere else."

"Are you going to stay there all night?"

He turned his head and stared at me for a beat. "Do you want me to go?"

"No."

"Good, I'd rather stay. Not that I think anything is going to get in, but there was more activity out there than I was comfortable with."

We lay on the floor listening to the radiator hissing and Blitz purring. I didn't want Casper to go. As freaked out as I had been to see him in my bedroom in the wee hours of the morning, the thought of him leaving now made me nervous. I didn't want to be alone. In the space of a day, I'd gone from wishing him away to being more comfortable with him around than I'd been with Joe. And I hadn't cursed Joe out nearly as often.

I pushed the thought away. I couldn't go down the Joe rabbit hole. The "what-ifs" and "what would Joe do" ripped me up and ultimately weren't constructive.

"Do you want to read my book with me?"

"Is it one of the ones with fairy people having sex all the time?"

"No, it's *The Princess Bride*."

"Then yes."

"They don't have sex *all the time*. It's not like erotica." I scootched my upper body over near the doorframe so Casper could see the pages and resettled my pillow.

"They have sex a lot. What would you call it?"

"Adult Fantasy with a strong romantic component."

He snorted.

"Hey wait, you've never watched me when I've—"

"OH MY GOD NO!" He put his hands over his ears again and was squeezing his eyes shut. "Why the *fuck* would I want to see that? Ugh!" He finished with an exaggerated full body shudder. Such drama.

"Good, that makes me feel better." I flipped open the book just as a horrible squelching . . . *thing* screeched along one of the windows. My blood froze, Blitz dove under my coat, Casper sat bolt upright.

A small eternity passed while we listened to more squelching, as if something heavy and slimy were dragging itself against the glass. It stopped as suddenly as it had started. I shivered and reminded myself to breathe.

"It's gone," Casper said, finally. "So, the smudging works too."

I didn't ask what it was. I didn't want to know. I'd ask in the daylight. Blitz was trembling between my calves. At that moment, I registered that he had never had a bad reaction to Casper, although apparently, he did sense ghosts. One part of my brain began wondering about all those times he'd been staring at seemingly empty corners.

"I'm not going to be able to sleep. What if they just keep coming?"

Casper lay back down on the floor. "The best thing you can do is forget about them."

"So helpful. Were you a therapist in your mortal life?"

"I don't sleep, Raely, and I'll be here all night. Open the book."

8

IN MY SLOW RISE TO CONSCIOUSNESS from deep in the ocean of sleep, I first became aware of someone saying my name, as if from a great height. I drifted toward it reluctantly. Then my body registered something cold splashing over my face.

No. Splashing *through* my face.

I blinked my eyes open, and Casper was waving his hand back and forth through my head. I jerked back and smacked my crown on the wall.

"Sorry," he said, "but you said you had to get to your lawyer's at eleven, and it's after ten."

"Oh shit." I struggled out from under my coat and staggered into the next room to feed an already clamoring Blitz. I stumbled blearily back into the bathroom, pulled my boots out of the tub and got the water running, sprinted into the bedroom and rifled through my clothes for something appropriate for both meeting my lawyer and working at the comedy club.

Post shower, I threw my hair back, twisting it into a spiky bun that I hoped looked like I was being intentionally cool and not just short on time, threw my makeup kit into my shoulder bag and headed for the door.

"Did any more try to get in last night?" I asked Casper as I walked to the train station as briskly as the snow and my stiff leg would allow.

"Maybe one. They dropped off after you fell asleep. The first one was the worst."

"What was that?"

"Lixivier," he said, "it tries to find places to stay in for a while. It feeds on whatever fear or negativity is already there and tries to grow it. Sometimes if it gets someone with a . . . specific kind of energy, it can use that energy to affect the physical environment."

"Awesome." I fished my train pass out of my coat pocket.

"Raely, this has gotten really intense really quickly." As I tapped my card on the reader, Casper walked through and waited on the other side. "If you want to work with the ghost hunters, fine, but I think we need to start looking at other options as well. And you should keep some of that smudge on you all the time."

Without answering, I shoved my pass back into my coat pocket, pulled the stump of sage smudge out of my opposite pocket, waved it at him, then replaced it. I plugged my headphones into my phone so that I could pretend to be on a call while I talked to him. "That's great, Casper, and I'm not opposed, but I don't exactly have time to be scouring the city for experts today."

A train to the Loop was approaching. I quickened my pace toward the platform. My stomach clenched and my feet began to sweat in my boots whenever I got on a train lately. But it was how I got around. I couldn't afford a car and taking rideshares everywhere was also prohibitively expensive. It was just a matter of forcing my feet to step on.

"I know, and I think you'll be okay going to your lawyer's and work on your own, so I'm going to do some research, okay?"

I stopped and spun toward him, the train screeching to a halt behind me. "How . . . how are you going to find anything?"

He shrugged, smiled, and backed toward the station doors. "It's time I looked around. You've got enough on your plate."

The doors of the train whooshed opened behind me with a gust of heated air, but I didn't move. I just gaped at him, not even checking to see if I was holding my phone at an angle that looked like I was still receiving news from someone on the line.

Casper stepped back toward me quickly. "Go. Look, if you're really in trouble, I always feel it, and I can be right there. It'll be fine, I promise. You know how to handle yourself." He smacked a chilly kiss on my forehead and vanished. I blinked and darted through the doors as they slid shut.

———

AT MY LAWYER'S office, James—thank God—gave me coffee and a bunch of documents to sign while he grabbed my file. I had agreed over the phone to alter my statement and say that I was incapacitated when the accident happened and didn't really remember what had occurred or how I was ejected from the train. Being untruthful bothered me, but, as Casper reasoned, it wasn't like they could call him as a witness, and James wanted to make sure there were no questions or hiccups so that everything got settled as quickly as possible. There was no reason to make it more complicated. James had even agreed to stop by the office to meet me on a Sunday to get it done.

He came bustling in as I finished the last of the signatures, tossed his newspaper on the table, and asked if I needed more coffee as he thumbed through my documents, checking to see that I had signed in all the right spots. I handed over the last one, telling him that I was okay for now but might take a go-cup, to which he smiled and gave me the shooty-finger before turning his attention back to the pages.

I cupped my coffee in my hands and glanced at his newspaper. My entire body went numb when I saw Joe's picture on the folded-open page. Acting of its own accord, my right hand fastened itself around the edge of the paper and dragged it toward me. My left hand set down my coffee.

It was a memorial column on those who had died in the front car of the train. *CTA Crash Eclipses Historical 1977 Incident, Remembering Lives Lost.* Each person had several inches of space and a photo. Funeral arrangements were listed for some, Joe's among them. I had the information memorized, of course, but seeing it in print hit differently.

I saw one tear fall and splotch the newsprint before I got a hold of myself and jumped back into my body's pilot seat. I cleared my throat and pushed the paper away, grabbing for my coffee, which I downed like a shot. The pain of the liquid burning all the way down my throat and into my stomach pulled me back from the brink of the yawning black hole beckoning me.

James was watching, pen poised over the documents. His stare was like a physical tap on the side of my face, but I refused to look over.

"You're gonna go, right?"

"He was my best friend. Of course I'm going." I cleared my scorched throat. Fidgeted with my now-empty coffee cup. I had nothing to do with my hands. I began folding and pleating the paper cup as if it were the most important thing I would do that day.

"Is anyone going with you?"

Pleat. Fold. Pleat. "I dunno. Maybe some people from work." Lie.

"Have you talked to his family?"

"At the hospital. You know that; it's in my statement." Fold. Pleat.

James slid the documents carefully into their folders. "I thought you might have spoken to them since then."

"I'll see them there." Fold. Pleat. Rip.

"Right." He stared at me again. Again, I refused to look.

"You know, I'm going too. I'm representing the family as well, so the wife and I will be there. If you need a ride. To or from. Lindsey would love a chance to see you." He had gathered the folders into a neat pile, holding them in his lap.

Rip. Tear. Fold. Tear. Rip.

"I guess I'll see you there, then. I think I have a ride. But thanks." Lie again.

"Okay, I'm glad." He stood quickly, tucking the folders under his arm. "These all look good. I'm just gonna grab you a new cup. Looks like that one fell apart. I'll get you a lid too. We have those." He strode briskly from the office.

Once he was gone, I tossed the tattered remains of my coffee cup into the trash can and stood, shrugging my coat back on and looping my messenger bag over my shoulder. I glanced back at the newspaper. Paused.

I reached over and pulled out the section with Joe's picture, then folded the rest back to the front page. I shoved my stolen sheet unceremoniously into my messenger bag without paying too much attention to whether it was ripped or torn. When James came back with my coffee, I had my hat and mittens on.

<hr/>

I STILL HAD two hours before work, so I took my time and walked, sipping my coffee. I had once worked at the Starbucks at Adams and Wabash. It was so busy, they had their coffee urns out in the cafe area and would just give you the cup when they rang you up. I stopped there and refilled. No one noticed.

I walked out to the Big Feet sculpture in Grant Park, empty in frigid February. I wiped the snow off a bench, sat down, and stared at the frost-covered sculptures. It was the first time in a while I'd had time just to think.

I pulled out the newspaper sheet, set my coffee on the bench beside me, and did my best to flatten the page out over my lap.

Joseph (Joe) Grabrowski, an aspiring stand-up comic and a graduate of the Chicago Art Institute, was twenty-seven years old on the evening of the accident and had recently told family and friends that he had met "the one" . . .

I let the tears run down my face, freezing in tracks as I read my friend's life condensed and cut down into two inch–wide columns. Half of the second column was taken up by the names of people who survived him. Whoever had written it had included his girlfriend Mia. And me.

I felt her before I saw her. My stomach turned to ice as a chill that had nothing to do with the weather settled onto the bench beside me. I kept my eyes on the page and took a good look through my peripheral vision.

I knew she was a ghost when I saw the bright summer dress. Fuck. My grief must have attracted her.

She leaned through me to get a look at what I was reading, and I sucked in my breath. It was highly uncomfortable in a way that Casper's touch had never been, but I hoped it meant that she didn't know I could see her. I did what I thought a normal person would do, I shivered, downed my coffee, and tossed the cup into the trash can by the bench. Then I stood, stamped my feet, shoved the paper into my coat pocket, and headed toward the bus stop.

She followed me.

"Someone you love died," she whispered. "Were you 'the one' I wonder?"

I felt an icy touch on my neck and shrugged my shoulders, turtling deeper into my scarf.

"Did he think about you before he died? Maybe you were the last thought that went through his head . . ."

Even though I knew it was what she wanted, I couldn't stop the swell of emotion that lodged in my throat. I had been the last person with Joe. I might very well have been the last person he thought about. A sob broke through the tight line of my lips, and she laughed.

I wanted to turn around and tell her to fuck off. I wanted to ask her about the last person she thought of before she died. Or if she even had anyone to think of. I wanted to be mean back. I wanted to pull up my anger and snark like a shield and wield it against her, but I knew it would make things worse if I acknowledged her. It didn't take much to let grief take over, and I was a sobbing mess as I approached the bus stop, enduring her taunts the entire way.

There were two men in their thirties already at the stop, much to my mortification. I tried to pull myself together upon seeing them. That's what a normal person who couldn't see ghosts would do. But now that she had me undone, she didn't want to stop. She had taken to hissing, "Joe's dead, Joe's dead, you'll never see Joe again . . ." over and over. I couldn't pull it together. I collapsed onto the bench, weeping loudly.

"Oh, honey." One of the men sat next to me and patted my back. "Honey, are you okay?"

In answer, I pulled the crumpled piece of newsprint out of my pocket, folded it awkwardly to Joe's picture, and handed it to him. I still couldn't speak, but the ghost stopped hissing at me. He glanced over it and handed it to his companion before pulling out a clean handkerchief and asking me if I wanted a hug. I nodded wordlessly and allowed this stranger to wrap me up in his arms while the other man said how so, so sorry he was.

The ghost, apparently not interested in watching me receive sympathy, vanished.

THE MEN, WHO introduced themselves as Andre and Steven, were on their way to a dinner date and then drinks with friends. They sat with me on the bus and even stayed on for an extra stop to walk me to the comedy club. I was in control again by the time we parted ways. They said they went to the club occasionally and would keep an eye out to see if I was working next time. I promised them a couple of drinks on me. I was able to duck into the restroom and fix my makeup before anyone at work saw me. Sunday nights were never as slammed as Fridays, but still not as dead as a Monday or Tuesday, and I threw myself into the rhythm, focused on keeping drink orders in my head and making my hands do what they needed to do with a smile on my face.

At least until Dylan showed up.

My stomach flipped when I spotted him approaching the bar. He'd apologized via text message for what had happened in the courtyard, saying he'd had too much wine and had been carried away. Blah blah. I'd been there before. It was my *MO*. Guys who were bad for me but good at apologizing for what they never intended to stop doing. It was what I was comfortable with because that's how I'd grown up. I'd worked hard to break out of it. But since the accident, I slid into my bad habits like an old, ratty-but-comfortable hoodie that didn't really keep me warm, but I couldn't resist wrapping myself in when I didn't care how I looked.

He smiled as he waited his turn, not the least bit abashed. I noticed that he had once again applied hair product and was wearing a nice shirt. Was he really pursuing me? Or just interested in my ghostly attachments?

It had been a while since a guy had shown this level of interest. It was kind of flattering, but I didn't want to mix business with personal. And the red flags could no longer be ignored. Casper would have been so grumpy if he were here.

Dylan edged up to the bar. I put my game face on. He may just have wandered in to see the show. He may have been in the neighborhood. I'd be professional.

"Hi there," I said. "Do you know someone in the show?"

"No, I know someone behind the bar." He winked. "And I owe her an apology."

Heat crept across my cheekbones. Okay, that answered that question. "Is that so? Well, okay, accepted." I looked pointedly at the customers behind him before turning my gaze back to him. Was he done?

"Thank you. Won't happen again. All right if I get a drink?"

I bit back the words, *Well, it is a bar,* and threw on a smile. "Sure."

He glanced down the length of the bar, which was two deep all the way. "I guess having my drink up here isn't an option?"

"Not tonight. The lineup is good though; you should try to snag a table. What'll it be?" I supposed it was nice that he showed up in person to apologize, but I really did need to get this operation moving.

"I guess that depends." He dropped his elbows onto the bar, winked at me, and lowered his voice so that I had to lean in to hear him. "What's on the house?"

I slid my commiserating bartender, it's-not-me-it's-the-rules smile in place. "They count the bottles. I could give you a well whiskey but—"

"Can I get that with coke?"

Why had I just not said nothing's on the house? I anchored my smile in place. "Sure." I examined my irritation as I grabbed a clean glass and shoveled some ice from the trough. I felt like I owed him, because he wasn't charging me. Even though he hadn't really done anything yet. *He did buy you calamari and wine,* I reminded myself. *That I didn't ask for,* I responded. *This is how it starts.* I also wasn't used to people visiting at work. I was caught off guard. Whenever Joe came during my shifts, he watched the show, and we caught up afterward. *As is polite,* my internal voice snapped. *He might not be familiar . . .* I argued in his favor, but why was I making excuses for him?

Regardless, he really was holding up the line, so I poured him a Jack Daniels Green Label and Pepsi, making a show of using the jigger with that little extra splash on top so he felt like he was getting more than a shot. I even garnished it with a lime.

"Thanks, Ray."

Oh, I did not like it when people called me Ray, but I usually let it pass once.

"My pleasure." I forced another practiced smile, relieved when he finally gave up his spot. I lost sight of him as I took care of the backlog of patrons. By the time Luck and I had cleared the bar, the show was in full swing, and we were somehow low on bar fruit. The shift before us hadn't restocked.

Luck and I made a contest around the side work. Whoever made the other laugh hardest was exempt from fruit prep. With all the tragedy around me to alchemize into comedy, I was sure that I would win. I'm hilarious when I'm uncomfortable. However, Luck had me gasping with laughter in under thirty seconds, Dylan totally forgotten. I nearly slumped to the floor, doubled over when one of Luck's bits just kept going, and he wrapped an arm around my waist to keep me upright, which gave me pleasant tingly feelings. He smelled nice.

Ever the gentleman, he still offered to help, but a deal was a deal. In the end, he fetched the fruit, but I insisted on slicing it so he could take his well-earned break. I liked chopping things anyway. It was a nice, easy activity that I could absorb myself in and either think about what I was doing or let my mind wander, all while wrapped in a pleasant, citrusy smell. I was slicing away, still chuckling at Luck's bits and wondering how Casper was progressing, when I was interrupted.

"Hey." Dylan bellied back up to the bar. To his credit, he was speaking low enough to avoid disturbing anyone watching the show, but talking during someone's set still felt rude.

"Hi," I said, in an even lower tone of voice, continuing my slicing. "Do you need another drink?"

"Sure." He winked. "I'll take one more."

You're going to have to talk to him now, Raely. I grimaced. I was probably right. Why had I let Luck leave? I didn't bother with the show this time. I just gave him a lot of whiskey. I topped it off with the Pepsi and a lime and slid it over. Then I moved my cutting board a foot away so I could see the stage clearly and resumed fruit-chopping.

Apparently as oblivious to my signals as he was of sensing ghosts, he slid a seat over so that he was in front of me again. I'd had patrons flirt with me during shows before, as had Luck, and we were always good at playing "bad cop" and shushing the other one when it happened. I glanced around for him now, hoping to signal him, but my heart sank when I saw that he had joined DeAndre in the light booth to watch the show. He'd even brought them both beers. I was on my own. If Dylan had been a random patron, I would have known exactly how to handle this politely and efficiently, but I was thrown. My gaze flicked over to the back room where my coat hung on the coatrack, my phone resting in its pocket. I considered texting Luck to keep an eye on us, but remembered his phone was probably in his coat pocket also. On silent. As it should be.

"So, where's Casper?" Dylan stage-whispered. It was almost funny. *Somewhere being right about you,* I thought. Then I reined myself in. *It's still possible that the ghost hunters can help,* I told myself. He'd apologized for the incident in the courtyard. I had no other leads. Desperate times. "He took off today to do his own thing. He's not always stuck to me."

Dylan raised an eyebrow and glanced around. "But what if that . . . Jimini ghost comes at you?"

I lowered my voice again. God help me if anyone heard us talking about ghosts. "Jimani. Casper felt like I could handle myself today. He knew where I was going. And he's not that strong of a ghost. If the Jimani really wanted to do something, Casper doesn't think he'd be able to stop him on his own, anyway."

Dylan blinked. I thought I saw his eyes light up, but when I looked again, I was sure I had imagined it. He took a sip of his drink, reached across the bar, and touched my arm. "Wow. Like . . . are you okay? How do you feel about all of this?"

I pulled my arm away, picked up the cutting board, and used my knife to slide the fruit into the proper compartments. "I mean, I don't know if I'll ever be okay with it. I wish the train crash had never happened. I wish my best friend had never died—"

"Wait, your best friend died in that crash?"

That was a gut punch. I'd forgotten how much I had not talked about this. "Yeah—" I ducked down into the cooler as if to place the uncut fruit there, popped one of the more potent trappist ales, downed a swig, then tucked the bottle just inside the door before I stood back up. Fully in control of my emotions. "Joe Grabrowski. We were coming back from an open mic together. He was in the car with me. The funeral is Wednesday."

"Wait . . . are you talking about that big train crash in the loop? You were in that? Holy shit. Wow, Raely, I'm so sorry. And the funeral is Wednesday?"

"It's fine." I blinked. "I don't know why I said that. It's not fine. I'm just not used to having this conversation at work. Thank you. I guess."

Behind him, the crowd laughed uproariously at the comic's punchline. I glanced up at the stage. Marcus Green. I tucked away thoughts of Joe and watched Marcus.

He was a talented comic. He'd be moving off Sundays soon. Probably to a good Wednesday or Thursday slot. I'd miss him. He'd usually have a beer with us after and was just as funny offstage. But maybe he'd move to the Friday lineup quickly, and then I could see him again. We also lived in the same neighborhood, so it was possible we'd just run into each other . . .

"Hey, Ray, where'd you go?"

I blinked again and refocused on Dylan. I couldn't let the second Ray slide. There's no coming back from a third.

"I was watching the show. Sorry, I don't like being called Ray." Some inner compulsion had me smiling to take any sting off my boundary-setting.

He snorted and stirred his drink. "Why don't you like being called Ray?"

"It was my dad's name."

"Ah, you don't get along with your dad?" He took a gulp of his free future headache.

I ducked down "to get a towel" and took another swig of my Chimay. I popped back up and energetically wiped the fruit remnants off the bar.

"He's dead. But he was kinda shitty to my mom and me, and I don't want to talk about it." *And he's probably the reason I gravitate toward abusive assholes.* I moved down the bar away from him. Wiping the entire thing.

There wasn't that much bar though, and I could only be convincing for a certain amount of time. My gaze darted to the light booth. Both Luck and DeAndre were enjoying their *second* beers, and I knew that Marcus was good for another twenty minutes. I tossed my towel into the bin just outside the door to the back and headed over to my fridge to "get another one," taking two gulps of my Chimay while deciding how to tactfully but firmly tell Dylan that this might not be the best place to get to know each other. I tossed a new towel over my shoulder and stood, full of resolution.

"Hey, I'm sorry I brought up all that stuff about your family and your friend. I just wanted to get to know you. I didn't mean to get you all emotional." He lowered his voice and leaned forward. "When do you get off work?"

I glanced up at the stage. Marcus was killing it. The crowd was in stitches. He'd been trying out new material tonight, and I hadn't even been able to listen. "He's one of my favorites," I said, ignoring Dylan's question.

Dylan once again didn't take the hint. "So, I was thinking that we could set up a sting in a couple of days."

"I'm sorry, what?"

"A sting operation. Catch some ghosts." He winked again. He was potentially the biggest winker I had ever met. I quashed the strong desire to ask if that worked for him in life, love, and business.

"I'm listening." Maybe he didn't just come to flirt and poach drinks. "Do you think you can actually . . . catch and contain them?"

"Oh no, not contain them," he chuckled. My heart dropped a little, but he continued, gazing up at the stage lights and smoothing an errant strand of hair off his forehead. "Our plan is to figure out what they want and convince them to move on from you. Maybe even move on permanently from this plane of existence."

"How do you do that?" My Chimay was calling me from the fridge.

"We've got a couple of things to try," Dylan said. His whiskey was getting low, but I wasn't going to offer him another.

"That's frustratingly vague," I said.

He laughed as if I had intentionally been funny. "We'll set it up for this week sometime. Don't worry, let us handle it. All you have to do is show up with ghosts."

"What if there aren't any ghosts with me?" This plan seemed very disorganized.

"Then we'll cut our losses and use what data we can get from any readings with you and Casper." He finished his drink. Marcus was wrapping up onstage. "So, what time did you say you get off work? I could hang around, maybe we could get some diner food?"

My stomach flipped again, but this was a *no.* Absolutely *no.* Even as emotionally discombobulated as I was, this was not the obliteration I craved. "Not tonight," I said, smiling again. *He still might help.* "I'm exhausted from running around all day, and I really need to crash as soon as I get off. But thanks for the offer. Maybe another time?" He looked as if he was marshaling a counter-offer, so I continued. "In fact, this show is wrapping up, so I really need to get ready for the next wave. I'll go ahead and say goodbye now in case I get cut off. Thanks for stopping by and keep me updated on the . . . sting operation."

With that, I purposefully stacked rocks glasses to move to the other side of the bar. This was completely unnecessary, but I wanted to look busy. A large part of me had converted to the Casper-was-right-about-Dylan congregation.

"Absolutely, we'll be in touch, Raely." He grinned, forgoing the wink this time.

I smiled back, strode to the other end of the bar with my glasses, set them down, and went into the back room to grab two six-packs of beer. We didn't necessarily need them, but if I had to, I could busy myself finding space for them until Dylan left. The gods had shown mercy, and he was already gone by the time I returned. I blew out a breath and schlepped the beer over to the fridge where I had hidden my Chimay. I plunked both six-packs inside, grabbed the bottle, sat on the floor, and finished it off while Marcus tied up his set to thunderous applause.

<hr />

WHEN CASPER CAME back to the apartment, he found me lying on the floor in the living room, staring at the slowly rotating ceiling fan with Blitz curled up by my feet. Despite what I'd told Dylan, I'd stayed after the show and had a few more drinks with Marcus, Luck, and DeAndre until I'd successfully chased away all worries about ghosts following me home, ruminations on Joe's death, and any lingering irritation from Dylan's visit.

Now, Casper stood near my head, peering down at me. "Why do you have the fan on in winter?"

"Well, mister smarty-pants." I lifted an arm and pointed at the fan, circling my finger. "If you flip that little switch up there on the base, the blades rotate the opposite way and push the hot air down."

He sat down on the floor next to my head.

"Careful of my water glass." I let my arm flop to my side, still staring at the fan.

"It's empty. I wouldn't be able to knock it over even if I wanted to, unless I concentrated. Are you drunk again?"

"So what if I am."

"That's three nights in a row. Maybe you should give it a rest."

"It's so good to know that you can count. And I've had a rough day, so you can lay off."

"Did you even eat anything today?"

I realized that I had not, in fact, eaten anything aside from a few bags of potato chips at the club. I hadn't even felt hungry. I didn't answer. Casper being right was annoying.

"I think you need to eat a sandwich or something and go to bed."

"And write down three things I'm grateful for at the end of every day," I sing-songed. "You sound like the counselor from the hospital."

"Maybe you should just make that PTSD therapy appointment."

The fact that he knew about that pissed me off. He knew fucking everything. I had no privacy. Little flames curled around my stomach. I had been so blissfully numb before he got here. "I think you need to stop bossing me around."

"I've bossed you around your entire life," he snapped. "It's only now that you don't think the thoughts are coming from you that you've started being so contrary."

Fire exploded in my stomach, burning hot into my chest, and spreading fast. I shoved myself up to face him. "So what you're saying is every decision I've ever made came from you? You've been walking around manipulating me my entire life?" The flames grew white-hot. I felt like I was combusting and had no outlet, no way to vent the conflagration. "Well, look where all that great advice has gotten me, Casper! You lost your own life, so you've just been following me around to fuck up mine?" I grabbed the thing nearest to my hand and hurled it as hard as I could.

My empty water glass shattered against the wall, and Blitz bolted from the room.

The fire instantly turned to ice. I covered my eyes with a hand. What the hell was wrong with me?

"Oh, Blitzy, I'm so sorry . . ." I stood and started after him but froze after two steps. My heart shriveled up and sank down to hide behind my stomach. "Casper, I'm sorry." He didn't say anything. I didn't look at him. I dropped to my knees and started collecting the bigger chunks of glass. "I'm being a huge asshole. I don't know why."

He knelt in front of me, and although I knew he couldn't feel it, it bothered me to see his knees on the broken glass. I kept my eyes down, unable to look at him.

"Raely," he said, as if to a spooked puppy. I squeezed my eyes shut, my face burning. I didn't deserve gentleness, I deserved to be smacked upside the head. "Please go get a dustpan. You'll cut yourself."

I didn't argue that throwing shit around in a temper meant I had earned the cuts.

That was the kind of stuff my dad used to do, and I'd always sworn I was not going to be that way. I carried my little cape of shame with me as I collected the dustpan, a plastic bag, and a damp paper towel from the kitchen and returned.

Casper had moved off the glass and was sitting to one side. "I haven't been making all of your decisions your entire life," he said. "That came out wrong, because you were being snotty."

"Snotty seems to be my default setting lately." I dumped the glass in the plastic bag and wiped the area down with the paper towel.

"No kidding."

"You bring it out in me."

"Raely," he exhaled slowly, "I'm not trying to manipulate or control you—"

"I know, I'm sorry. I don't know why that made me so mad." I tossed the paper towel in with the glass and tied the bag closed. Then I plopped down and leaned against the wall. The room tilted slightly then righted itself. *I should probably have a sandwich. Dammit.* "Just the idea that you've been floating around behind me, telling me what to do like I can't think for myself—"

"That is *not* what I do." Once again, he shifted until he was cross-legged in front of me.

This time I looked at him.

"You don't normally require this much looking after."

I snorted despite myself.

He half-smiled. "You're just in a rough spot right now."

"Tell me about it."

I COAXED BLITZ out from under the bed, gave him some apology cheese, and made some toast for myself to eat while I smudged the windows. I was going to need to buy some more smudging supplies soon. I did an extra round of smudging in the bedroom because I wanted to sleep in the bed. A little while later, I was bundled under the covers, staring at my little tree lamp and trying to decide if I would leave it on, when Casper reappeared.

"Don't you want to know how my day went?"

"Oh, wow, I am rude. Sorry, how was your day?"

"I found someone to help you."

I sat up. "For real?"

He smiled and nodded. "She said at least she'd try. We can go by tomorrow."

"She said she'd—" I blinked. "She could see you?"

Casper's grin widened. He nodded.

9

THE FOLLOWING MORNING, CASPER WOKE ME up earlier than I would have liked. I popped two Advil with my toast and tried in earnest to avoid snapping at him. He was downright chipper, and it was indecent.

Despite my hangover, I was intrigued by this mystery woman who could see him. I made an honest effort, but I was sluggish and we didn't get going until after 11 a.m.

The day was cloudless, clear, and overly bright, warm enough for me to forgo my mittens. As we marched to the train station, the sun reflected brightly off the snow, and I was thankful for my sunglasses. "Where are we headed? Maybe I can get some coffee somewhere on the way."

I had avoided my usual coffee shop since The Incident and, although I was sure he'd noticed, Casper hadn't mentioned it. "We'll head to the Loop," he said, "and then take the Green Line west—"

"I'm not taking the Green Line. What other way can we go?"

"Raely, it will take, like, an hour and a half to go any other way."

"We're punching a clock now?"

"No, but—" He paused. When he spoke again, the fucking *understanding* in his tone grated on my already-raw nerves. "Don't you think—"

"No, Casper. I don't *think*. I *feel*. I feel very strongly that I don't ever want to ride the fucking Green Line again. This is not something I want to get over. It's irrational and emotional and I don't fucking care. Give me the address, and I'll find an alternate route."

I felt his stupid ghostly eyes on me. My gaze snapped to his. The sympathy sitting nakedly on his face tapped against my heart until it started to crack. I looked away, bit down on my tongue, and held my breath until the cracks smoothed out again.

"We can double back on the Pink Line," he said finally. "And either get a bus or walk ten blocks."

"Well, it's a beautiful goddamn day for a walk."

The train wasn't crowded late in the morning. Casper and I still rode in silence. A bonus to riding public trans with a ghost: Even though people couldn't see him, they rarely tried to take the seemingly unoccupied space. In fact, most of them steered clear of us in general.

I scrolled through my phone, checking emails. There was a new one from the admin for the Improv class I'd dropped—since I was all hospitalized and stuff during the final weeks—offering to let me retake the section for free. They were very sorry about what happened and would love to have me back when I was up for it. I deleted it. There was an email from Lawyer James Esquire with electronic copies of the papers I had signed, letting me know that the offer of a ride to the funeral still stood. I filed it away under "Train Crash Stuff." An invite to a theatre benefit. Delete. An invitation to audition for a sketch comedy show. Delete.

An email from Joe's mom.

My finger froze in midair over the icon. The subject was "funeral assist."

"You should probably read that."

I swiped the screen, closing the app, and shoved the phone into my pocket. "I understand that your literature options are limited, what with your non-corporeal hands and lack of a library card, but *must* you continually read everything over my shoulder? When did you learn how to read, anyway?"

He blinked at me. "When you did."

I stared unblinkingly.

"I told you, I've been with you for your whole life. I went to school with you and did homework with you and all that crap. I even helped you on tests sometimes."

I pushed my sunglasses up onto my head. "You went to all of my classes with me?"

He grimaced. "I skipped sex ed. And sometimes I left if they were boring and did other things, but mostly, yeah."

"So, when I was like, six years old, I had a full-grown ghost person just . . . trailing me to school? That's super creepy, Casper."

"It wasn't creepy! When you were six, I was six." He folded his arms and glared toward the front of the car like he was offended.

"I'm sorry, my brain just exploded. Did you say that you were six when I was six?"

He shrugged, still staring straight ahead. "I mean, I don't know exactly how old I am, but I've always been . . . the same size as you. Growth-wise."

I stared at him for so long he finally looked back. One man who had been sitting two rows up from us moved all the way to the other end of the car.

"What?"

I popped my headphones in and turned sideways on the seat, leaning against the window and pulling my feet up onto the bench near Casper, lifting my phone so that I could conceivably be talking on it. "Do ghosts usually . . . grow after death?" I whispered.

He shrugged. "I did."

"Okay, but like . . . seriously, Casper, this seems odd. How many other ghosts do you know that—"

"I'm going to stop you there," he said. "I know you think I should be an expert on this, but it's not like there are big . . . ghostly gatherings where we all get together and talk about ourselves. I don't know if you've noticed, but a lot of ghosts are not that friendly. By and large, they're much more interested in the living than in other ghosts. Most of the interactions I've had with other ghosts are discussions of territory or occasional power-posturing. I've seen spirits team up, but usually they were connected in life somehow." He shrugged. "Some of them were nicer to me when I was younger, and I could ask more questions then, but I was mostly interested in doing whatever you were doing. Let's switch trains here."

I plopped my sunglasses back down and followed him, thinking hard. When we reached the opposite platform, we waited for the Pink Line to arrive, standing several feet away from the other commuters.

"Why did you pick me to follow around?" I asked, looking down at my phone screen. "Why didn't you pick, like, another boy or like some family with lots of kids, so you'd have more options?"

He sighed and looked down at his shoes. So like the ones I used to have. Then I realized that everything he was wearing looked like something I had once owned or once admired.

"I don't remember *picking* you. I just remember . . . always being with you. When we were really little, you could still see me and we'd play games."

My hand flew to my mouth. "My mom said I used to have an imaginary friend. She thought I was just coping with a stressful home environment."

He frowned. "Your dad was a dick." Then his eyes cleared. "But yeah, that was me. We even had a tea party once. I didn't want to do it at first, but it was kind of fun."

The train pulled up. I headed for a seat near the back of the mostly empty car. "When did I stop seeing you," I mumbled into my headphones as we passed a couple scouring a map of downtown.

"Gradually, after you started kindergarten and started hanging around with . . . real kids."

I glanced over as we slid into two seats in the back. "Just because you're not alive doesn't mean you're not . . . real."

One side of his mouth quirked up. He was looking down at his hands, examining a thumbnail. "That's just something you said when we were little. When you were differentiating between them and me. They were the real kids."

"I'm sorry."

"It's okay. I mean, I couldn't argue with you. It made sense at the time."

"Still . . ."

There were no buses in sight when we disembarked, so we began walking the ten blocks, checking over our shoulders each time we passed a bus stop to see if we could spot one coming. Despite my pessimism, my leg *was* getting better, so I opted to keep going rather than wait at a bus shelter.

"So, who is this person anyway? How did you find her?"

"You'll see. She's amazing." He grinned like he had a delicious secret.

"Are you like, dating her or something? What's with the reverence?"

"No! Jesus. She's just . . . you'll just have to see for yourself."

I shrugged. I didn't feel like dragging information out of him. After a few more blocks, I pulled out my phone and opened the email app, clicked on the email from Joe's mom and scanned it.

"Hang on a sec." I thumbed a quick response before I dropped the phone into my pocket and resumed walking.

"What did she want?" Casper asked quietly, as if he wanted me to be able to pretend I didn't hear him if I wanted to.

"Pictures of Joe for the memorial. I told her I'd send some tonight."

"Oh. That's . . . nice of you."

We walked on in silence a bit longer until my phone pinged. I pulled it out. Checked the email. Stopped dead in the middle of the sidewalk for two full seconds. Closed the app, put the phone on silent, and continued walking.

"What was that?"

"She said—" My throat closed over the words. I cleared it and tried again. "She said that anyone who wants to can speak at the service. About him."

I crunched through the slushy sidewalks. The sun was evaporating some of the snow before it could melt, making what remained icier and crispier. I paid special attention to where I placed my feet, intentionally crushing patches of glittering ice.

"Are you going to speak?"

Crunch. Crunch. Crunch.

"I don't think so."

Crunch. Crunch. Crunch. Crunch.

"Do you want to tal—"

"How much further?"

Casper sighed softly.

I ignored it. Crunching carefully.

"It's on this block, three more doors."

I knew it instantly once it came into view. My stomach clenched as Casper continued guiding us blithely toward a corner storefront with heavy black and purple curtains behind all the windows, preventing any glimpse of what lay inside. One window was garnished with an open palm and the words *Psychic Readings. Séances.*

10

"YOU'VE GOT TO BE KIDDING ME," I said. The little hairs all over my body slowly rose to attention as I stared at the place.

He had nearly reached the door and turned around when I spoke. When he realized that I had stopped five feet away, he walked back toward me.

"You're not kidding me?"

"And the ghost hunters were such a home run?" he sassed.

When I didn't come back with a pithy remark, and probably looked like I was about to bolt—because honestly, I was considering it—he spoke more gently. "Look, just keep an open mind. I promise I wouldn't have brought you all the way out here if I didn't think she could help."

I scanned the building. The dark curtains. The old-fashioned façade, painted black. There was no indication of light or movement on the other side of those walls. It felt forbidding. The whole place had an air of "Don't come in here just for shits and giggles." No sign proclaiming the hours or saying that they were open, or even "by appointment only" with a phone number. No welcome mat, although the steps were salted and swept clear of snow. I thought I detected a whiff of sandalwood. When I looked down at the first step, my palms grew clammy at the mere thought of lifting my foot and placing it there.

"I don't want to go in there, Casper."

"Why the fuck not?" He didn't sound angry. He sounded exasperated.

I looked right into his eyes. My head shook, just slightly back and forth.

His expression changed. His dark eyebrows drew closer together, and he reached out and gave my arm a tap. "What is it?"

"I don't know." I couldn't explain it, but the place had a presence. Something *other* emanating from it that I did not want to tangle with. "I'm scared, I think."

"I promise there's no reason to be. I wouldn't bring you here if I thought anything bad was going to happen."

I forced my gaze back to the door. I tried again to put my foot on the step. I shifted slightly forward, but my chest tightened, my breath caught. I shook my head. Trembling. "I can't go in there." I knew my reaction made no sense.

Yes, the place was creepy, but it was just a place. Just a hokey psychic shop, right? Why were my legs shaking?

Casper reached down and physically took my hand. I felt it, just like anyone else's hand, but as if he'd been sitting in a cold room for a while. I knew it took a lot of energy and concentration, so it surprised me further when he gently tugged me forward. "I'll be with you the whole time."

For some reason, it did help. I scaled the first step. Then the second. There were five, and I took each of them like a small child. *Step, step, pause. Step, step, pause.* Casper held my hand the entire way. I managed to push the door open with the other.

It wasn't cold inside, but it wasn't overly warm like many busi-nesses in winter. It was also dark. I pulled my sunglasses off, tucking them in my pocket, and waited for my eyes to adjust to the mood lighting. The heavy, old-fashioned door slammed shut behind me. I flinched and squeezed Casper's hand hard. "Sorry," I whispered reflex-ively. Then I looked down at our hands. His was just wrapped around mine. No fingers interlacing. We looked like two kids who had been told to hold hands before crossing the street. He swung our joined ap-pendages back and forth a little, probably trying to lighten my mood, but all it did was solidify the toddler image in my mind. It was oddly comforting.

"You're better at this than I thought you'd be. The whole physical touching thing," I whispered. It felt *very* disrespectful to make noise in this place.

"I told you, she's awesome. She helped me understand how that works a little yesterday. How my energy can affect things on your plane." He was smiling down at me, waiting for me to chill out and get excited, I guess. It wasn't happening.

I looked around. It wasn't a large area. Or perhaps it was just very cluttered. There were three Tiffany lamps providing the only light in the room. One was on a table at the center of the space, which had sev-eral baskets arranged on it with different kinds of trinkets. The baskets were adorned with labels: "for protection," "for healing," "for clarity," and "for conjuring." I shivered.

Another lamp sat on a counter straight ahead of us, which also boasted an old-fashioned cash register that looked like it was made of brass but couldn't possibly be. The third was at the end of a long table that held more baskets of trinkets, as well as necklaces and what looked like scarves of some kind. There was a curtained entryway beyond the table. An 8 x 10 piece of printer paper, affixed to the curtain with a safety pin, read, "Séance in session. Please be quiet."

Séance? I wanted to get out of here.

I started to tell Casper so, when suddenly a voice behind me with a distinctive, flat accent intoned, "Ah, brother ghost, you did bring her." I endured several seconds of cardiac arrest before turning around.

Behind us stood a short, ageless woman. Her small black eyes sparkled within the crinkles of her skin. I think she was smiling. It was difficult to tell. Her salt-and-pepper hair stood out in a wavy halo around her head. She was neither fat nor thin and, despite the chill, she wore loose, flowing garments that, although they covered her from wrist to ankle, would have been comfortable in a much warmer climate. She trundled around to stand in front of us and gazed up into my face. Her grin broadened, and a low chuckle escaped her.

The hairs on the back of my neck stood up.

I squeezed Casper's cold, cold hand. *Please let's go. Please let's go.*

He only squeezed back and jiggled our connected arms a bit. "Raely, this is the person I've been telling you about." He turned his smile on the grinning woman. "This is—"

"I know who she is," she interrupted, her eyes boring into mine. "Are you ready to face your ghosts?" She was Cajun, I realized. I'd had a Cajun roommate in college from Plaisance. She was the first in her family to move away. Her dad called her every Sunday, and the longer she was on FaceTime with him, the more steadily her accent would revert to that soft, flat, comfortable rhythm. I used to time naps on the couch to coincide with her calls home.

This woman's voice did not make me want to take a nap.

My mouth went dry, and my heart was pounding. I didn't know what to say. Face my ghosts? *My* ghost was right here, holding my freakin' hand. Wasn't she supposed to be able to see him?

She didn't wait for an answer, but reached out and took my right hand, the one Casper wasn't holding. I fought the urge to yank it back.

She spread my fingers, flattening my palm face-up. She gazed at it for some time, occasionally tracing her fingertips lightly over the surface. My legs were trembling violently now. Surely she must be able to feel it? Surely Casper must, too? Surely, I would collapse onto the floor in a matter of seconds.

"And what will you do with your gift, little seer?" she said finally, looking back up at me with those sparkly black marbles. Irises. People should all have discernable irises. It's the law of nature.

"Gift?" I croaked out. "Send it back? With thanks, of course."

She chuckled low again, and for the second time, the tiny hairs stood at attention. I tried to gently withdraw my hand, but she held it firm. She patted my palm with her other hand as she looked at Casper.

"Ooh, brother ghost, I'm not sure." She smiled that crinkly smile up at him and gave a slight shake of her head.

"You said you'd try, though," Casper said, almost pleading. It was strange, seeing him talk to someone else. Ask someone else for something he desperately wanted like he was afraid he wouldn't get it. I found myself wanting to defend him. It was fine for me to tell Casper to go to hell, but not other people. He was *my* ghost.

"I'll . . . I'll try to be ready. For . . . whatever ghosts," I heard myself saying. What the hell was wrong with me? "Just . . . tell me what to do, I guess."

She tilted her head to the side, examining my face, trying to read something there as she had with the lines of my palm. She seemed to come to a decision. Her hand stilled, and she clasped mine, encasing it within both of hers. Her skin was like stiff, warm sheets, just out of the dryer but not yet smoothed out and folded. She pressed my palm more firmly. "We will try." Her gaze intensified, boring into mine. "Brother ghost, can you hold?" She didn't look at Casper, but continued to press my palm.

"Yes," I heard him say, and he squeezed my hand again.

It occurred to me for the smallest sliver of a second that my hands were trapped between a ghost and a psychic before the floor beneath me tilted, and I was falling away.

I wasn't in the creepy shop anymore. I wasn't in my body anymore. I didn't have a body.

I didn't have a fucking *body*.

You're fine, you're okay. It was Casper, but he wasn't speaking. He was somehow in my head, or I could somehow understand him. With no auditory receptors. Or brain.

I am not fucking okay!

There it was. That alto Cajun chuckle again, just the feeling of it from somewhere. She seemed to approve. I didn't catch any . . . thoughts from her, but I felt her pleasant surprise that I was "talking" back to Casper.

You are *okay. I'm with you. We'll go back soon.*

Go back from bloody where?

Bodiless chuckle again. *We will try. Now.*

It was a wind unlike any I had ever felt. My very essence was swept up in it. It wasn't warm, it wasn't cold, there was no *air* to possess temperature. But I was moving in some current unlike a river. A river has weight, has drag and pull. This was disconnected to any earth or solid foundation. There was nothing to grab, had I even possessed hands.

I flailed wildly. The only thing keeping me from complete panic was the slim tether to Casper. I didn't want to thrash too hard; I didn't want to lose the connection to the one thing I knew. I forced myself to stop writhing and grabbed onto Casper with everything that I had.

I'm still here. You're still okay.

Not the worst, came the flat tones. *Better than expected, and yet . . .*

I had no voice or thoughts anymore. Just an internal screaming and clinging to Casper's essence with my own as *things* buffeted my . . . soul?

Ugly things. Fearful things. So much hurt, molded from pain and sadness. They flew by, clinging, hammering, crashing into me. They swept through me. I felt them take something from me with each pass. There was an absence of good, no light. No giving, only taking. There would be nothing left. There would be nothing left if we stayed here. There wasn't enough of me. Already they had to have torn half of me away.

Casper, I can't! It's too much! It's destroying me!

We tried, the flat voice sighed.

It was like being siphoned the wrong way through a whirlpool. Dizzy and disoriented, I was dumped back into the dark room, on my knees, my left hand still clutching Casper's cold one in a death grip. My right hand was pressed into the pocked hardwood floor. A gray plastic trash can with a flimsy liner was thrust into my line of view, and I clutched it, wrapping my entire right arm around it and hugging it to me as I vomited up my pitiful toast breakfast with bile. My stomach continued clenching long after it was empty, until I was completely depleted and lying in a crumpled heap on the creepy-ass floor, my left hand the only thing suspended as Casper still held tight. I was no longer holding on to him.

Cajun lady handed me some leftover fast-food napkins. I cleaned up and stumbled to my feet. When she grabbed my right hand again, this time I did try to yank it away, but she had an iron grip. Unexpected.

She looked at Casper, who was panting a bit. His shaggy hair looked extra windswept. "I'm sorry, brother ghost. She is not yet ready."

"His name is Casper," I spat, trying one more time to get my hand back.

She kept her eyes on Casper as she answered through one of those bone-chilling chuckles. "That is not his name, but you do not yet know. You will." She patted Casper's shoulder. It even resonated as if he were solid. "It will get worse. Much worse," she said to him, her hand still on his arm, nodding solemnly. He nodded back, like they had discussed this before and come to some agreement.

I was sweaty, shaky, and angry. I yanked hard on my hand and she turned back to me, but didn't let go. She looked as if she had just noticed there was a human attached to the wrist she was gripping. Her glinting, fathomless eyes bored into mine. "You cannot throw away your gift, even if you wish to. You must accept it."

She smacked something hard into my palm and curled my fingers around it. "Keep this with you always. Hold it and think good thoughts when you are able. Then when you are not, it will be able to do it for you."

"Think good thoughts?" I growled. *Unfuckingbelievable.*

The dark chuckle. "Light thoughts, then. Love. Even if it's painful. Forgiveness, even when it's hard. Happiness, even if it's the only thing you have."

She chuckled again and finally released my hand. I wasted no time in staggering for the door. I heard her tell Casper that she would see us soon.

11

MY HEART WAS STILL HAMMERING at breakneck speed as I stumbled down the steps, my bad leg twinging sharply. Cursing, I fumbled around for my sunglasses, before looking around and realizing that the sun was setting.

The fucking sun was setting.

I pulled out my phone. My palms were sweaty, but I managed to hang on to it and activate the screen. It was 4:34 p.m. Somehow, we had been in that place for over two hours. That was impossible. But I'd thought out-of-body experiences were impossible up until a few minutes—hours—ago.

I didn't wait or even check behind me for Casper as I limped across the street toward the nearest bus shelter. There was a bus coming in the direction I wanted. Casper appeared at my elbow while I scrabbled around in my pockets for my pass.

"Raely—"

"I need you to leave me alone right now."

I found the pass. The bus slowed. There were only three people waiting ahead of me.

"Raely, please calm down—"

I spun to face him. "You know what the worst thing in the world to say to a *justifiably* upset person is?" I hissed. One of the people ahead of me glanced over his shoulder and turned quickly back around. "Please leave me the fuck alone for a bit. God, I need a goddamn drink—"

"What if you try not crawling into a bottle every time things get a little rough?"

"FUCK. OFF!" I turned and jumped onto the bus just as the driver was about to close the doors. Everyone thought I was a goddamn nutjob. I didn't give two shits. I tapped my pass onto the reader and pushed my way to the back. I noticed my legs were still trembling when I plopped into the seat harder than I intended. Just before I leaned my head back against the window and closed my eyes, I saw Casper standing several feet away, keeping an eye on me. I stuck my headphones in and blasted music.

Casper stayed at a distance but followed me as I transferred to the Pink Line, watched me switch to the Brown Line, then disappeared. Presumably to wait for me back at home. Although I tried very hard not to admit it to myself, it was comforting to know that he was tailing me. It was also very nice not to talk to or be near him for a bit. For several blissful minutes, I pretended everything was normal. That I'd never seen a ghost, never left my body, and I was just a regular person riding a train.

While on the bus, I had looked at the thing the crazy psychic had pressed into my hand. It was a big chunk of amethyst crystal. I'd used some of my remaining 20 percent of phone life googling it. It was apparently mostly for protection and healing. But it had a ton of other mystical properties attached, including "spiritual awakening." Yeah, right. The angry, feeling-violated-and-blindsided Raely came very close to tossing it into the next garbage can while making sure Casper was watching. The scared, any-protection-is-good-protection Raely decided to hang on to it. It was pretty, anyway.

Two stops before mine, Casper appeared in front of me. The train was jammed with the rush-hour crowd heading home, so he had no way to sit, but he stood in front of me, saying something. I pointed to my headphones and shrugged, then turned away pointedly.

He yanked one of the earbuds out of my ear, shocking me to attention. "Stay on an extra stop, the Jimani is hanging around your station." My blood turned to ice. I managed a stiff nod. He vanished again. I replaced my earbud and glanced around me. No one seemed to have noticed anything. We pulled up to the stop before mine, the doors opened, several people got out. The aisles were thinning now. The doors slid shut and the train glided forward again.

My heart pounded in my ears as my stop approached. My feet were sweating inside my boots. *He likes fear, get rid of the fear.* I brought my phone up to my face, randomly flipping open apps to distract myself. When I opened my browser, a large picture of an amethyst filled the screen. The train slowed, I slipped my hand into my coat pocket and found the stone. I pulled it out and clutched it to my chest. I heard the doors whoosh open and felt the chill air gust in. I couldn't help it, I looked up.

The Jimani was striding up the platform, clearer than ever before. His face, unlike Casper's, was somehow less human the more distinct he became. He didn't appear to have dark hair under his charcoal fedora but black, mottled skin. Where his eyes should have been were only sunken holes with something hard glinting at the center. He slowly oscillated his desiccated face from side to side as if scenting the air. He began to turn my way. I looked down at my phone, squeezing the crystal in my other hand, and willed him not to notice me.

The doors slid shut ever so slowly. As the train inched forward, I felt a sharp stab lance through my collarbone. I squeezed the crystal harder. *Do not react, do not react.* As the train sped farther away, the pain vanished. I exhaled the breath I'd been unconsciously holding. My hand was trembling. I slowly unclenched my fingers from around the crystal and tucked it carefully into my pocket. I stood shakily when the train slowed at the next platform and almost walked through Casper when I exited the car.

I stepped around him and continued toward the station.

"Raely, we need to talk about all of this," he said, two steps behind me.

I checked that my headphones were still in, then started up my music. I picked my "Angry/Brooding/Workout" playlist and turned it up. My stomach was churning, and my limbs were vibrating with pent-up emotions. I didn't know which one to feel; they kept flipping through me as if they were all in line and fighting to be at the front. Fear. Anger. Grief. Hurt. Anger was the easiest to deal with, so I clung to it, shoving the others to the back of the queue.

Casper stepped in front of me and walked backwards until I pressed pause to hear what he had to say.

"Where the hell are you going? I know you're pissed or whatever, but aren't you going home?"

"There's a grocery store up here. I need more smudge supplies."

"Maybe while you're there you should get something to—"

I pressed play.

Once inside the store, I relented and took one earbud out and paused my music. I nabbed a basket and headed for the produce area, grabbing sage first. Casper trailed me silently without attempting to engage me in conversation.

To show my approval, I snagged a frozen pizza and plopped it into my basket. Once I had everything I needed, I swung through the wine aisle and grabbed a double bottle, looking right at Casper and daring him to say something.

He didn't speak but glowered at me like he was posing for the cover of an emo album.

Cheez-Its. That's what I fucking need. I circled back to the cracker aisle. White Cheddar Cheez-Its. Yes. I plucked two boxes from the shelf and headed to the checkout, tossing a cat toy for Blitz into the basket on the way. Add it to the ocean of debt that was currently my life.

Casper was silent until we had exited the store. My hands were now full, so I was unable to replace my one earbud and turn my music on. Well played, Casper.

"So, we need to have a talk about what happened this afternoon and—"

"No shit. I am fucking furious with you."

"You have made that *patently* obvious, Raely, but if you could climb down off your goddamn righteous plinth for a second and deign to listen to someone else who's in this situation with you, maybe you'll understand a little more about what we were trying to do and how it might be the only thing that can fucking help you."

My anger slipped, and I lost my grip on it. Hurt scrambled to the front of the line and pushed tears out of the corners of my eyes. The change happened so quickly, Casper didn't notice. I fought to control myself, but the more I tried to pull back, the worse it got. My lungs shuddered and squeezed. I couldn't breathe. Before I knew what was happening, silent sobs were wracking my body.

Casper was still stalking a few inches ahead, assuming that I was giving him the silent treatment. It wasn't until I pulled in a wheezing breath that he turned around. His expression shifted from pissed to freaked just as quickly as my own switch had flipped, and it was clear that he didn't know how to handle me coming completely unglued. He glanced up and down the street as I continued to fight to calm myself while lugging my sad groceries through the melting snow.

"Raely, please, please . . ." He looked around again. We were about two blocks from the apartment. "Shit, Raely, I . . . I really don't want to attract anyone else here. I know you know that . . . fuck. I'm sorry I shouted at you, okay?"

I nodded and tried a deep inhale, but it didn't help. I couldn't stop. I tried cursing under my breath. Tried to pull up angry thoughts, happy thoughts. It was like trying to grab on to slippery eels. No one else was in line now. Grief was insisting on his turn.

"Okay, we need to get you upstairs. Give me these." He snatched the bags from my hands and vanished.

I stopped crying. Because what the—?

I stared stupidly at my hands, hiccupping for a few seconds, then broke into a run. I yanked the one earbud out of my ear and squashed my headphones into my pocket as I clomped up the mostly snow-free sidewalk to my door. My keys were already in my hand when I reached it. Panting, I jammed the key into the lock and continued running up the stairs, letting the lobby doors slam behind me, wincing as I belatedly glanced at the "Please don't let doors slam. Sincerely, your first-floor neighbors" signs.

Casper was in the kitchen, sitting on the floor looking as if he had run a marathon, with Blitz perched on the table next to the grocery bags peering curiously down at him. I shrugged out of my coat, tossing it toward the couch as I approached.

"Okay, that was new." I grabbed a paper towel off the roll, wiped my face and blew my nose.

"I told you," Casper said faintly. "She helped me with some stuff. Yesterday."

"So you participated in ghost boot camp and can ignore the laws of physics now?"

He smiled weakly. If a ghost could be paler than normal, Casper had achieved it. I sat down on the floor across from him. My phone pinged and I pulled it out of my jeans, tossing my tangled headphones onto the table as I tapped the screen to read the message.

"It's Dylan," I said. "He wants to do a . . . sting operation at the ghost hunters' on Wednesday."

Casper just rolled his eyes.

He must be tired if that's all the derision he can muster, I thought. "That's Joe's funeral, though." I started texting that back to Dylan. "I should tell my mom. She wanted to know when the funeral was."

"You haven't told her yet?"

"No, I've been waiting until the last minute, so she won't be able to come." My phone pinged again. "Dylan says I can come after the funeral." I texted back an affirmative, put my phone on the table, and turned my attention to my exhausted pet ghost.

"Why don't you want your mom to come? Don't you want someone to be there with you?" Casper pushed himself more upright against the wall, still panting slightly.

I shrugged. "You'll be with me, right?"

He stared at me, ribs expanding airlessly in and out, until I started getting worried.

"You *will* be with me, right? Do you want a . . . glass of imaginary water or something?"

He smiled. "I'll be okay, that just took more energy than I expected. And if you really want me to come, I guess I can, it's just . . . frowned upon."

"What's frowned upon? And who's doing the frowning?"

"Unless your living family is visiting you, ghosts aren't really supposed to go to graveyards. And especially not funerals. It's just . . . I can't remember why, it's something I was informed of when I was young. It's in bad taste or something." He shrugged. "But if you want me to go, then . . . I think that counts as my living people looking for me."

"Well, as long as you don't think you'll get in trouble with the ghost police. I'd hate for you to be uninvited to all the spring coming-out parties."

He puffed a laugh, then leaned forward, putting his head on his knees. "Look, Raely, I need to go recharge. This whole afternoon took a lot more out of me than I thought. Are you in for the night?"

I nodded. "Are you okay?"

"I'm fine. I know we still need to talk, and I know you're still mad. I'll recharge and come back as soon as I can."

"Where do you go to—"

But he had already faded away.

12

I SAT ON THE FLOOR FOR A FEW SECONDS, staring at the place where Casper had vanished. But very shortly my emotions tried to reclaim my attention, and I was not having that. I pushed up off the floor, put away the groceries, fed Blitz, gave him his new toy, and did a full changeover of his litter box.

After making a couple of new smudge sticks, I gave the entire apartment a very thorough smudging, then opened a box of Cheez-Its and I texted my mom the date of Joe's funeral.

As expected, she wouldn't be able to get off work on such short notice. She wanted to know if there was a place to donate in lieu of flowers or if she should just send flowers or do both. I successfully avoided all emotion while I texted her back that donations were to go to the animal shelter in Joe's memory. The same shelter where he'd said he was going to get a dog once he and Mia moved in together. We used to walk by and window-shop on the way to an open mic we frequented. I told Mom I needed to go and that I'd call/visit soon.

I dug out the corkscrew and cracked open my BABOW. (Big Ass Bottle of Wine. A term I credited to my old Cajun roommate but had long since become part of my own lexicon.) I owned one wine glass purchased at a liquor store. They used to break open the gift boxes that hadn't sold and put whatever glasses or flasks that came inside them at the register to sell separately. This was probably not strictly legal, but it's where I had acquired some of my favorite glassware on the cheap.

I gave myself a ginormous pour, grabbed my box of Cheez-Its and, as an afterthought, the roll of paper towels, and hauled it all over to where I had set up my laptop on the battered wooden coffee table. I took a large gulp of wine while the laptop powered up, then popped a few crackers into my mouth. *Ahh, excellent pairing.* Once the laptop was up and running, I clicked over to the photos. Facial recognition software had already created folders for the people who appeared most often, so there was one for Joe just sitting there at the ready.

I needed to get comfortable before I did this. Bringing my glass with me into the bedroom, I changed into an oversized T-shirt, flannel pants, and cozy socks. I tried to convince Blitz to come sit with me, but since I wasn't eating real cheese, he wasn't interested. I toted the entire bottle into the living room and topped off my glass. No more procrastinating.

I found several good pictures right away and attached them to an email. Even some I had taken with Joe and Mia when he'd first introduced us. The pictures stretched back for years. In some, we were just out of high school and looked like fresh-faced babies. I was able to feel warm fuzzies about some of the older ones in addition to the ache in my chest. The more recent ones were difficult, too soon for warm fuzzies, but it was the videos that killed me. Why had I taken so many? Should I send them? I decided to copy them all onto a flash drive and give them to Joe's mom at the funeral. She could decide if she wanted to watch them. I clicked on a long, untitled one I didn't recognize, pressed play, burrowed deeper into the couch cushions, and dug into my half-empty box of Cheez-Its. I recognized the back porch of Joe's apartment at night from the still shot, but didn't know when it had been taken. The camera scanned the balcony as muted sounds of a party filtered in from somewhere.

"Joe! Joe! Look over here!" *Past Raely was narrating and obviously well into her cups.*

Past Joe swung around, clad in a button-down shirt and adorned with a glow stick necklace. Light-up, fake glasses were perched on the end of his nose, and one hand was wrapped around the neck of a bottle of champagne. He struck a pose.

Past Raely laughed. "No! I'm taking a video! What day is it today, Joe?"

"Fucking New Year's Eve, baby! Wait . . . no, it's New Year's Day! It's a brand-new goddamn day and a brand-new goddamn year!" *He took an exuberant swig of champagne straight from the bottle.*

"And what did you just say that you were going to do this year?"

"You want me to say all that again?" *He leaned forward in exaggerated disbelief, grinning at the camera, his light-up glasses blinking ridiculously.*

"For posteriority! Prosperity! For . . . having a record—"

"A'ight, a'ight, a'ight. Here goes." *Another swig. He pushed the glasses off his face until they were nestled in his blond, spiky hair and looked seriously into the camera while they continued to blink on and off, highlighting his hair in pink, green, blue, pink, green, blue.* "This is gonna be a great year, my friend. We've both nailed down bad-ass, cool day jobs. We're gonna do some awesome comedy. YOU. You. Are gonna do some awesome comedy. And I am. Both of us. People are gonna be blown away"—*he swept his arms wide*—"by our comedic genius. And for all you viewers just tuning in . . ." *He smiled, one-hundred watts, and pointed at the camera.* "As I just said to my best friend, Raely, I'm gonna get married. I'm gonna get fucking married! Or at least engaged. To Mia. Of course. Not just to anybody. If you're watching this later, babe, of course I'm talking about you. But wait, maybe don't show her this until after I propose, it should be kind of a surprise."

Past Raely giggled. "I won't. Maybe we can play it at your wedding."

"Yes!" He pointed again. "Because you are going to be my best man!"

"Hell yeah, I am! I've already got ideas for the bachelor party."

"Okay, now your turn, you can give a speech. For practice." Past Joe reached for the camera, and there was some fumbling and exclamations until the phone swung around and Past Raely was in focus. Past Joe thrust the champagne bottle at her. She laughed, accepted it with both hands, and took a sip.

Past Raely was wearing a sparkly blue spaghetti strap top under a leather jacket. Her hair was curled, she had a circular glow stick perched on her head like a tiara, her cheeks were flushed, and she couldn't stop smiling. "Wait, what am I supposed to say?"

"Uhhhhh, what you're gonna do this year! Be confident! Own it!"

"Okay, I'll try." Another sip. "It's gonna be a great year! I'm going to own this year!"

"You're gonna get on at Second City!"

"Let's be realistic here—"

"OWN IT!"

"I'M GONNA GET ON AT SECOND CITY! AND MAKE EVERY LAST PERSON DIE LAUGHING!" She brandished the bottle, thrusting it high in the air.

"Yeah!"

"Maybe I'll get a boyfriend."

"You'll get a GODDAMN AWESOME boyfriend! Maybe you'll meet him at my wedding."

"Can I meet him before your wedding so that I have a date?"

"Oh yeah, that works."

Past Raely laughed, then looked out over the balcony, smiling softly. She put her elbows on the railing, still holding the neck of the champagne *bottle in one hand, and turned back to look at Past Joe over her shoulder. "It's gonna be a great year, Joe." She looked back out. "Now stop filming. We have champagne to drink."*

I was completely numb. That had been *weeks* ago. Joe had been right here and whole, just weeks ago.

I had been here and whole.

I didn't recognize myself. I couldn't remember the last time I'd laughed like that. So relaxed. Smiling so easily. It came from within, rather than serving as a mask I'd pasted on at work just to fake my way through human interaction.

I couldn't even wrap my head around how it was possible to smile like that anymore. My past self was in full color, and I was a faded sepia version.

I was never going to a stupid New Year's Eve party ever again. I was never going to jinx myself or anyone else by shouting to the universe about the great year ahead. And I certainly wasn't going to be getting anywhere near Second City. I snorted at the thought.

I wouldn't be doing any comedy this year. Probably never again. How was I supposed to make other people laugh when I couldn't laugh myself?

What the hell was I even still doing in this city? What the fuck was my purpose? Why was I still here and Joe gone? My life wasn't worth any more than his. Less, even. I wasn't about to get engaged. I hadn't found the love of my life. I was barely even a contributing member of society. I was meaningless in comparison. If our roles were reversed, Joe would be doing more. Hell, he was donating to the animal shelter *postmortem*. He'd probably have organized a 5K in my memory by now.

I didn't watch any more videos. Just copied them onto the drive. I finished sending the pictures to Joe's mom, then decided to twist the knife just a little by playing them on a slideshow while I sat on the couch and drank. The box of Cheez-Its now fully consumed, I considered getting the other one but didn't want to move. I dug the amethyst out of my coat pocket and held it while I watched pictures of Joe flashing by. *Love, even when it hurts,* she had said. Well, this hurts pretty good.

⁓ ⁓ ⁓ ⁓

BY THE TIME Casper came back, I thought I was fine.

When he walked in—or faded in, whichever—I was lying sideways on the couch with half a glass of wine on the floor near my head and my computer open in front of me, still playing the pictures on a loop. There were several wadded-up paper towels strewn about the floor about five feet away, where I had lobbed at the trash can and missed. When I saw him, I grabbed my wine and pushed myself up to a seated position, scooting over to make room.

He crossed over, face tight as he spotted my wine, and sat down next to me. He glanced at the computer screen, and his expression shifted. The hard lines smoothed out, and his eyes darkened with sympathy.

"Raely . . . what are you doing?" His voice was soft. For no good reason, as I was the epitome of acceptance and composure.

"I was sending the pictures to Joe's mom. I made her a flash drive, too." I held it up. *See? I'm totally fine.* "I put the videos and extra pictures on here in case she wants them someday. I figured I'd give it to her at the funeral."

"Okay," he said, sounding as if he was expecting me to break apart.

Nope. All done with that. I took a polite sip of wine.

"Did you eat your pizza?"

I pointed to the empty box of Cheez-Its.

He chewed on his bottom lip for a moment like he was holding something back, then said, "Dinner of champions."

"I texted my mom, too. She can't come but she's going to make a donation to the animal shelter in Joe's name, which is what they requested in lieu of flowers. And send a card. Oh, shit, I should get a card." I took another sip of wine. "I can do that tomorrow."

Casper was staring at the slideshow on the computer screen.

"I can turn that off, I've seen it like, a billion times at this point." I shut the computer down, closed the laptop and tucked it back into its case.

"Okay." Casper still sounded like he was walking on eggshells. Even though I was *perfectly fine.* "Did you do your smudging stuff?"

"Yeah, I did an extra . . . dose, I guess, around the whole place. I even charged this thing." I picked up the amethyst. "Just in case. At least I think I did." I popped it back into my pajama pants pocket. "Gave it a shot anyway. What about you? You said you were gonna explain some shit to me."

"Recharging took longer than I thought, and you've had a hard night, so why don't we do that in the morning?"

"I'm *completely* fine. Let's do it now. Is it gonna be long? Should I get a refill?" I finished my glass. "I'll get a refill."

"Holy shit," Casper muttered when I pulled my big bottle off the floor.

"Whatever, you were right there when I bought it."

"I didn't know you were planning on drinking the entire fucking thing in one night."

"There's still like . . ." I held the bottle up to the light. "Three glasses left at least."

He sighed and scrubbed his face with his hands. "Look, we can talk about all the heavy stuff in the morning. We can go get you some coffee or something . . . just . . . tonight, how about you enjoy your wine and we can talk about . . . comedy or Joe or—"

"I want. To talk. About the batshit crazy place you brought me today." I sat up, set my BABOW down on the table with a thunk and leaned forward. "A creepy ass woman knocked me out of my body earlier, and I don't even know her name. So yeah, we're gonna talk about that. All night. And I'll *still* enjoy my goddamn wine."

Casper sighed. He looked like I was asking him to walk the plank. I leaned back and waited.

"This might be a little convoluted at first, so you'll have to bear with me. And if you want to take a break at any point, or you get tired—"

"I'm fine. What the hell was that vortex of awfulness you pulled me into? And how are you able to teleport things all of a sudden? Who was that woman, and how did you find her?"

"Her name is Lovonia Fontenot, and she . . . kind of found me."

I raised my eyebrows.

"I decided to check any kind of occult type place in the city. Hers was the fourth place I visited. It was starting to seem like a huge waste of time, so I was standing outside her store, deciding whether it was even worth it to go inside, and she walked out like she knew I was there and invited me in."

"Okay, that's . . . yeah, okay, go on."

"She had to help me shift my perception of my place in the world, so that I can affect things that are on a slightly different vibration than I am."

"Lost. What is your perception of your place in the world?"

"Well, every ghost has a perception of themselves. What you're seeing right now is my perception of myself as it fits into this world that I've chosen to inhabit. If you were to die right now and become a ghost, your perception would probably match what you look like right now."

"But the Jimani does not look human. At least, the clearer he gets to me."

"Ghosts' perceptions of themselves can change over time, as mine has. My world was centered around you, so my perception changed as you changed. The Jimani likes fear and intimidation. His perception of himself has changed to reflect what he wants to present. That's why you're so rare. What you're seeing is someone else's perception of their own essence."

"But why did this suddenly start happening? Had you never tried to touch me before the accident?"

"Well, according to Lovonia, we were already linked, and then I possibly saved your life, which creates a deeper link, but she also said that you probably already had seer tendencies that were . . . awakened. Trauma does that sometimes too, but it likely was a combination."

Although I was totally fine, my chest tightened as I thought about the accident. I took a deep breath. "Okay, so you altered your perception of yourself or the world or whatever. And now you can move things?"

"It's very difficult to explain, which is why we were hoping you would just be able to instinctively *do* it earlier, like I was able to, but I'll try."

"Wait, wait, waitwaitwaitwaitwait. You got sucked into the vortex of bad and you . . . what? Didn't get blown to pieces because you have a superior perception?"

"For starters, you were not getting blown to pieces, I wouldn't let that happen, as I hope you know by now. Your . . . essence—let's use that word—can assert itself against other essences and even absorb them if they're something you need. It just may be harder for you to grasp because you're used to having a corporeal form."

"Oh, you fucking think? Seriously, Casper, this was your plan? Yank me out of my body with no explanation and hope that I would somehow figure out how to . . . wield my essence?"

"You're already a seer! That happened on its own, so you have some latent talent for this somewhere. The problem is . . ."

He trailed off and stared at his shoes. *Or the perception of his shoes.* For several seconds.

"Raely, can we please stop here for tonight?"

"Um, no, I'm finally getting answers that are interesting, even if they are also infuriating. What is 'the problem?'" I tossed up finger quotes.

"The problem is that you have some significant trauma in your life that you want to avoid. You don't want to deal with it, so it just sits there, ready to attack you. It makes you even more vulnerable to certain spirits because you're like a hair-trigger emotional bomb. And if you're going to 'wield your essence,' as you put it, you need to incorporate all those parts of yourself that you don't want to deal with. Everything that's happened to you has informed your soul and can strengthen it, but you have to accept the things you think are unattractive, allow yourself to be vulnerable and . . . allow yourself to receive support. But you won't do those things—you just push it all away."

I set my glass down. I stared, unfocused, at nothing as I tried to untangle my jumbled emotions again. Grief really wanted to climb to the front, but I felt I'd given it enough time tonight already. Anger was once again my buddy as my mind sped through hairpin turns down a dark tunnel. Why did I have to do this? How come no one else had to sit in their ratty apartment, watching videos of a dead person who was worth more than they were, drinking cheap wine and listening to a ghost tell them about how to wield their essence? And enumerate their failings as a soul.

Not just personal failings. My soul wasn't strong enough. That was what he was telling me.

Anger slipped a little. Guilt and grief stepped up, and they were once again fighting for top position, but I no longer cared who won. My eyes burned as they focused on the flash drive. A ringing sound pulsed against my eardrums.

"Or maybe I'm just not supposed to be here," I whispered.

"What?" Casper's eyes went wide.

"Maybe," my voice trembled, "you should have let me die on that train. Maybe that's what was *supposed* to happen, and you fucked it up."

"Raely, no—" Casper reached for my arm, but I jerked away and stood up. My breath was now coming in gasps. My chest was so tight my lungs didn't have enough room to expand. My throat constricted.

Everything was closing in. The tears I refused to shed blocked my nose. I needed space. I needed air. I needed something to hang onto. I was drowning.

"*You* did this." I focused on Casper, now standing two feet from me, one hand slightly outstretched like he wanted to close the distance but was afraid of making the wrong move. My stupid lungs continued to try to breathe. My heart thundered, loud and insistent. Trying to keep me alive. "I'm supposed to be dead, but then you wouldn't have me to follow around and manipulate anymore, would you?"

"Raely—"

"And I *wouldn't* have become a ghost. I would have vanished into the ether or whatever the . . . like Joe did. And then I wouldn't have to be dealing with wielding my essence or fucking psychics yanking me out of my body." I was shouting now, in between gasps. "Or *you* following me around and making me act like a crazy person. I'd just be *dead*. And that would be *fine*." My voice cracked.

The pressure inside was unbearable. I hugged myself as if I were physically holding my insides together, stepping around aimlessly, before dropping to my knees, still fighting the sobs that worked hard to force their way out.

Casper knelt in front of me, his face twisted with emotion. Could ghosts cry?

"If I was dead, I wouldn't have to feel this," I wheezed.

"That's not necessarily true," he whispered back.

I took three long, shuddering breaths. Forced my hands to unclench from my ribs and planted them on the floor in front of me. Another breath. I looked at Casper.

"Get out."

He stared.

"Get out! I don't want you here. I've *never* wanted you here. Ever since that accident, my life has gotten worse and worse. You shouldn't have pulled me out. I shouldn't be here and *you* shouldn't be here.

Go . . . move on! Go wherever dead people go who aren't ghosts." I stood up and stumbled into the bathroom, slamming the door.

"Raely, please don't do this."

"Leave. Me. Alone!"

I curled up on the rug and finally gave in to the sobs. And I felt it when Casper left.

13

I WOKE UP ON THE BATHROOM FLOOR several hours later. Blitz was scratching at the door and meowing. I twisted the knob and pulled it open wide enough to let him in. Then I turned just in time to vomit into the toilet.

You're a mess, I told myself in between heaves. *You have to stop this. The booze isn't helping.*

I cleaned up, brushed my teeth, drank several glasses of water, and popped some Advil. Then I pulled the bathroom door fully open.

"Casper?"

My chest hollowed out. I knew he wasn't there.

I dragged myself into my bedroom. It was 5 a.m. I put my dead phone on its charger and climbed into bed.

I stayed in bed for most of the day.

Other than occasional trips to the bathroom—and into the kitchen to feed Blitz and retrieve the other box of Cheez-Its—I dozed throughout the day. Blitz, at least, enjoyed cuddling with me. It was snowing again and blustery outside. I watched the snow drift past my windows and wondered if the wind could buffet your essence around.

Casper didn't come back.

～っ⌒～～っ⌒～～っ⌒～～っ⌒～

ON THE MORNING of Joe's funeral, I woke numb and drained, a husk of a person. No essence inside whatsoever.

And still no Casper whatsoever.

So I was going to the funeral alone. I didn't blame him.

You could have had your mom. You could have gone with James. You've pushed everyone away. Telling myself didn't help.

I smudged the entire apartment again, then spent a long time sitting with my amethyst, thinking painful thoughts about everyone I loved. Guilt sat heavily in my stomach. I didn't have it in me to forgive myself. And to hope for happiness was ridiculous. After that, I cleaned up my detritus from two nights ago and took a very long, very hot shower.

I found some black wool leggings and a black skirt. I'd have to wear my black 'punk rock' boots, as Joe had called them. They had the best traction in the snow and no heel. They did have more buckles than necessary, but not falling was more important than dressy footwear. I didn't have a clean black sweater, at least not one that wasn't slightly sparkly, so I wore a black T-shirt with black hoodie on top. I felt like I was in a costume for some absurd minimalist play. When did black become the funeral color? I dug around for a necklace to dress up the ensemble and found one that had a bloodstone hanging from it. Why not? Maybe it had some weird-ass protective properties I didn't know about. And I'd always thought the deep green stone was pretty with its dark red splatters. In fact, I remembered that Joe had given it to me during our first year in college, specifically because it was called bloodstone and he thought there was something morbidly funny about it.

I checked the time. I knew I was cutting it close. I was dreading the pre-funeral mingling almost as much as the actual funeral. I hadn't seen most of our mutual friends since the accident, although several had come by the hospital. I tucked my amethyst into one inside pocket of my coat and the flash drive into the other and headed out.

I decided to take the bus as far as I could before summoning a Lyft. It didn't feel like good luck to take the train today. Once off the bus, I walked to a nearby Walgreens and bought a card. I filled it out in the office supply aisle using a pen that I then put back. As I stood in line to buy the card, I kept watch for errant ghosts. I spotted a few hovering around a bar across the street, and hoped I was in less danger because I felt absolutely nothing.

In the Lyft, I tucked the flash drive inside the card and did my best to seal the envelope. Then I sat back and stared out the window until we pulled up at the funeral home. Inside, I caught a glimpse of myself as I passed a hall mirror. I felt a momentary drop in my stomach before the feeling dissolved into numbness again. I was the one who looked dead. I looked like an Addams family reject, except paler and thinner, if possible, with deep purple circles under my eyes. I looked away.

I passed through a room with collages of photos glued to poster boards propped up on easels between bouquets of flowers evenly spaced around the perimeter. I didn't stop. People were slowly making their way around photos. Usually in pairs, sometimes in threes or fours, making quiet comments, some sniffling softly into tissues. I didn't look at any group too closely. I didn't want to see anyone I knew.

I paused at the guestbook. I almost kept walking, but . . . it seemed rude. I picked up the pen, scrawled 'Raely' on one line, then continued. No one else had my name. They'd know who it was.

At the door to the remembrance room, I held my breath. *Just rip the Band-Aid off.* I stepped inside and exhaled in a whoosh when I saw that the casket was closed. Good. I didn't want to remember Joe like that. My mind started to consider why it was closed, and I steered it sharply away. I continued into the room and finally saw the person I wanted. Joe's mom was sitting off to the side of the casket, surrounded by pockets of family and friends as they stopped to offer their condolences. She was holding together very well, I thought. I clenched my jaw as I passed the casket, refusing to look at it as I wound a path through other mourners. Joe wasn't in there anyway. Not really. This ceremony was for everyone he'd left behind.

She caught my eye before I had entered the circle of well-wishers surrounding her. She stood, began crying, and opened her arms. "Oh, Raely!"

I walked toward her embrace, water ringing my eyes and turning the world into a fishbowl. I blinked just before I reached her, and the fishbowl collapsed, cascading down my cheeks. One long tear for each eye. She swept me into a hug, and I allowed myself to sink into it. For one second, we let ourselves cling to each other, then we both pulled back as if we both knew that one moment longer and we'd be weeping uncontrollably. *I hate funerals.* She held me at arm's length, fingers clasping my shoulders, as if she were reluctant to let go. I kept my hands loosely on her arms. Both of us had new fishbowls growing.

"You look like you're walking so well, Raely. I asked some of Joe's cousins to step in for the pallbearing service. If I had known that you might be able to—"

"No. No, that's fine. I'm not as . . . stable as I look. I'm . . . I'm only just getting good at walking okay." *Oh Jesus, thank you for not asking me to put Joe into the ground.*

Her clear blue eyes, so like Joe's, scanned my face. I forced a smile. She pushed a lock of hair behind my ear. "Oh honey," she said, "you can't fool me." Then she hugged me again.

My heart swelled. My eyes watered like fountains. Where had all these tears come from? I had to pull it together. There were still hours to get through. I disengaged gently.

As she took the card I put into her hands, I pulled a paper towel out of my other coat pocket and wiped my nose. "When I was getting you the pictures for today, I found a lot more," I explained, wrangling myself back under control. "So there's a flash drive in there with some videos and some other pictures. I . . . didn't know if you would want to see those right away but . . . but I thought maybe someday you might want them. If not, you can just . . . give them to Mia or throw them away or . . . whatever."

Joe's mom held the card in one hand and ran the other one along the edge as I talked until her fingers found the bulge of the flash drive. She pulled up a watery smile and went in for another hug that I couldn't refuse.

"Thank you for being such a good friend to him, Raely," she whispered into my ear. She pulled back and smoothed another strand of hair back from my face. "I know you have other people to see. I'm sure I'll love whatever you say."

I pulled on a smile through my tears, forced a stiff nod, then turned away. She expected me to speak.

I was not going to speak. What could I possibly say that would bring any meaning to this or provide any comfort for anyone here? I wasn't good at this kind of speaking. I was an amateur comedian, for fuck's sake. *It's fine. It's fine. There are a billion people here. So many people are going to talk that it won't matter.* I kept my head down as I moved up the aisle away from the casket.

"Raely." Lawyer James and his wife Lindsey had found me. "Hey, how you holding up?"

"Oh, hi. Uh, I'm fine." I swiped beneath my eyes with my paper towel to catch any stray mascara. "I just talked to Joe's mom, so . . ."

"Aw, sweetie." Lindsey leaned forward. Too many hugs. They made it difficult to hold back the tears. James rubbed my back for a second and then went to fetch Kleenex, which was really much more practical than my wad of paper towels.

As I cleaned myself up with James's less abrasive tissues, I glanced around. I was amazed that there were no ghosts. It seemed like all this emoting would be a spirit buffet. Then I remembered: Something about gravesites and funerals was taboo.

I realized I had been looking for Casper to turn up. And that I should stop.

James and Lindsey asked if I wanted to sit with them and I agreed for several reasons. One, who says no to that kind of thing at a funeral? Two, if I was with James and Lindsey, it would prevent other people from asking me to sit with them, or maybe even talking to me altogether, especially if they made the connection that James was my and Joe's family's lawyer. Three, I knew them well enough to be comfortable sitting with them, not well enough that I feared them asking any questions that were too intimate. It was almost as good as sitting next to Casper on the train.

Con: They picked a place three rows from the front. I had been hoping to blend into the background.

Pro: James had the foresight to grab an entire box of Kleenex just for us.

Joe's parents were the first to address the room. They spoke together. Joe's dad had traveled a lot for work, and I didn't know him as well as I knew his mom. He looked like a wilted version of the man I remembered. I wondered if he regretted all the time away. They had a slideshow going behind them with a montage of images from different parts of Joe's life, timed with their speech. To their credit, some of it was funny. Joe would have liked that. Joe's sisters took over at a certain point. One of them was a very good speaker, funny and sad. We were laughing and crying at the same time. Joe had never mentioned Angela's comedic chops to me. She was older than him and a veterinarian. I hadn't spent as much time with her as the other two.

Mia spoke next. She cried throughout her speech, and so did I. How do you meet the love of your life, find out that he's going to propose to you, and then deal with his death? And the death of everything they had hoped for together. I hadn't spoken to Mia since our awkward hospital visit just before I was discharged. I had her email address. I had her phone number, but we had only hung out with Joe. We'd never been friends separately.

Watching her up there, watching her share her pain in front of everyone, I felt stupid for not calling her. I could have at least texted. Yes, she could have called or texted me too, but I was the best friend. I had been in Joe's life longer; I should have been the one to reach out. I had really shut myself away.

James passed me Kleenex at regular intervals.

During the next few speeches, I managed to keep my tears mostly under control. Joe had a few cousins who spoke, but I hadn't known them, and they mostly talked about times when Joe was little, which didn't hurt so much to hear about. Then a few of his comedy friends got up in groups of two or three. There was a point at which I realized that people were looking back at me.

Everyone who knew me was expecting me to speak.

My numbness warped into panic, and my mind flipped to Casper. I don't know what would have changed for me if he had been there, but I felt bereft and vulnerable by myself. I wanted Casper there. I wanted someone there. Someone who knew what Joe meant to me and knew why I couldn't get up there and talk right now. Someone who knew me and knew Raely-and-Joe.

It was probably only a handful of people, but I felt like *everyone* kept glancing at me.

Another comedy friend shuffled to the podium, but it was obvious that Joe's best friend was supposed to speak.

Fuck.

Why had I not expected this?

At the next break, I reached over, pulled three tissues out of the box James was holding, clenched them in one fist and inched my way into the aisle. It took forever to walk to the front. Everyone was way too quiet. The casket loomed as I approached. Where I had ignored it before, now I couldn't tear my eyes from it. I knew that Joe's *essence* wasn't in there. Everything that had made him Joe to me was gone, but I also knew that what was left of his body was lying in that shiny box.

Tears slid down my cheeks as I grabbed onto the podium and hauled myself around, facing away from the casket and toward the crowd. I looked down at the scuffed brown wood that I was denting with my thumbnails and took a breath. The tears dropped down from my cheeks to splat against the scarred surface. One. Two. Three. Then stopped. I dabbed my eyes with a tissue, used the same one to swipe the moisture from the podium, then looked up toward the back of the room.

"Hi, my name is Raely." My voice in the microphone startled me. I paused and placed my trembling hands flat on top of the podium. Smashing my tissues against the wood. "Joe was my best friend." I stopped. What the hell was I supposed to say? *Improvise, Raely. You used to know how.*

I cleared my throat. "I was going through some videos last night and found one we had taken on New Year's. Joe had big plans for this year. For both of us. Apparently, I was going to have regular sets at Second City." There was a small smattering of laughter. "Sorry, Joe, I don't think that one's going to work out." Another sprinkling of laughs. People wanted a break in the sadness. It was natural. "Joe was also going to get married, or at least propose." I looked at Mia, she was weeping into a fistful of limp tissues. Someone, probably her mother, had her arm around her shoulders, squeezing as if she were holding her together. I pulled my gaze away and looked back out over the heads of Joe's friends and family. "I was going to be Joe's best man. That was a speech I had thought about a couple of times in my head. I'd thought of a few good stories to tell, appropriate to the occasion, some funny, some heartwarming, stuff like that . . . I never thought about this speech."

Everyone was quiet again. There were a few sniffles. I was careful to avoid looking at anyone in particular. *Just keep going. Get through this.* "I did not want to do this speech. This speech means I'll never get to do the other one. It means I'll never talk to Joe again. Never do anything with Joe again. I'm having a hard time with that."

My throat constricted. I looked down, spread my tissues on the podium and smoothed them out until the ache eased. I raised my eyes again. "I was on the train with Joe, as I'm sure most of you know. I'm having a hard time with that, too. Why am I standing here, while he's lying behind me?" Moisture stabbed at the corners of my eyes again. I looked up at the ceiling and counted to three. "Joe was a good guy and always trying to be a better one. If I could swap places with him, I would. In a second."

My voice cracked on the last word, and I paused. I looked down at the brown particle board of the podium I was clinging to. I had said all I wanted to say, but I knew I couldn't leave it like that. It was so bleak. *Just one more thing, Raely, just one more, then you can be done,* I told myself. I thought of Joe. What would I say to Joe if he could hear me? I half turned, glancing at the casket behind me.

"I don't remember how to laugh anymore, Joe. I can't seem to smile. My jokes are all biting and sarcastic. I don't know where the rest of me went." I cleared my throat. Turned forward. Looked back out over the crowd. "But I'll keep trying to find it. Because I know you would hate for me to quit. You used to give me advice. On everything, all the time. And I used to get annoyed with that, occasionally. But I'm going on the record right now. If you want to give me some advice on how to keep going, how not to quit, I'd be really happy to hear from you. Anytime. I miss you. So much." My face crumpled then, I snatched up my tissues and clomped quickly back down the stairs and to my seat. I held my coat to my face and cried into it as quietly as I could while the officiant asked if anyone else wanted to talk. When no one did, he gave directions on how to proceed to the gravesite.

I ADMITTED TO James that I didn't have a ride, claiming that it fell through at the last minute, and rode with him and Lindsey in the funeral procession. We spoke very little. We also kept the box of tissues.

Chairs were arranged on either side of the grave. We ended up in seats facing Joe's family. I couldn't watch Joe being pulled from the hearse and carried over to the gravesite. I stared at the toes of my boots until that was done. I could hear his parents and sisters crying. The funeral director introduced the priest, who cleared his throat to speak. Then I looked up.

And saw Joe.

My heart stopped, my breathing stopped, everything stopped, and then restarted twice as fast as normal. I watched Joe's ghost walk over to his parents, put his arms around them, and whisper into their ears. They seemed to calm as he spoke. Then he moved on to each sister.

I suddenly knew why ghosts weren't supposed to haunt funerals. This was the last goodbye for spirits who were choosing to move on.

Joe knelt right in front of Mia, put his hands on hers and looked up into her unseeing face while he talked to her. I watched her face crumple and smooth several times as he spoke until finally, she looked up, still crying, with a quavery half-smile on her lips.

Joe turned and looked over his shoulder, right at me.

No.

I stood up, mumbling apologies, and stumbled away from the gravesite. My limping run carried me through the snow, halfway back to the parking lot before I slipped on a root and fell to my knees behind two trees.

I was not going to say goodbye.

But Joe was never one to give up.

When I looked up, he was there, kneeling in front of me. I started sobbing in earnest.

"No, no, no, no, no, I am not saying goodbye. I don't want to hear it—"

"It's not your funeral, kiddo, it's mine. I can say goodbye if I want to." He smiled, but his eyes were bright with silver tears.

"It's not fair," I said, my thick words barely intelligible. "You had plans. You didn't get enough time. You were just getting started."

"Everyone who dies had plans, Raely." Joe didn't question how I was able to see him. I didn't question the hand he put on my shoulder. "I'm okay. And you're going to be okay, too. We're both going to move on from this place and do the things we're supposed to do now. Plans have changed."

"No!" I banged my fist into the snow. "I don't *want* to move on. I want to go *back*. I want to wake up from this stupid reality and go back to the one where you are alive and trains stay on tracks and I don't see ghosts and everything makes sense."

"We don't have that option, and you know it." He squeezed my shoulder. Later I would wonder if all ghosts were able to do that just after they died, or if Joe was just as fast a learner after death as he had been in life. Or if I had merely longed to feel the pressure and affected his perception. "I don't have a lot of time left, Raely, please let me say goodbye to my best friend."

I cried harder and shook my head, but Joe kept talking.

"Thanks for making the last several years of my life so much fun, Raely. You've always had my back, and you've always called me out when I needed it. I did so much more than I would have without you in my life. You've always pushed me to be better. I'm never going to forget you."

"That was you," I said finally. "It was you who did all those things for *me*."

"We were a pretty good team." He smiled, glowing a bit brighter, a glittering confetti surrounding him. "But you have always, *always* sold yourself short. I want you to stop that now. You are braver than you believe, and stronger than you seem, and smarter than you think—"

"Okay, Christopher Robin," I hiccupped.

"I've been saving that one for you. You like *Winnie the Pooh*." Joe smiled again, but the glitter was now flying away, and bits of Joe with it. "I'll always be with you, Raely. Now put yourself back in the world. And own it."

And in a flash of golden sparkles, he was gone.

I crumpled from the inside out. Sobs wrenching themselves from my core. My frozen fingers clenched the dirt and snow as the world blurred. I lifted my burning eyes back up to where Joe had been, and my blood went cold.

The Jimani was striding across the graveyard in the distance. Straight for me.

14

I FROZE, CROUCHED ON THE GROUND, my mind screaming for Casper, suddenly aware that the snow had seeped through the knees of my leggings, that my fingers were white and numb, and that I was shaking. All physical sensation rushed back to me, but I still couldn't move. I stared, trembling, at the black, horrifying figure striding closer and closer.

Hands wrapped around my upper arms and hoisted me up. I yelped.

James.

"C'mon, girl. Let's get you out of here. Lindsey's pulling up the car."

I deflated in relief and nodded silently as he threw his arm across my shoulders and steered me toward his waiting SUV. I glanced behind us as James opened the door for me. The Jimani was still there, still pacing in my direction as if he had all the time in the world.

"Get in, you're shivering. We'll get you home," James said.

I scrambled into my seat and stared out at the Jimani, my heart hammering in my chest as James took forever switching places with

Lindsey and adjusting the seat. Finally, we pulled away, the Jimani receding in the distance, but my trembling only increased. Couldn't he just appear in the car next to me at any moment? Could he wreck us? Would he care if he killed James and Lindsey also? Of course not.

After thirty seconds, he still had not appeared. My brain began to thaw. Dylan. I was supposed to go to Dylan. He was the absolute last person I wanted to see right now, but he had promised to help me. He'd said they would be ready for me. Ready for any ghosts that I brought with me. They could help me take care of this. After all, I had no other options.

"Thanks for the ride," I said to James, unable to keep my voice from quivering. "I actually have some friends waiting for me, if you could take me to their place instead?"

"Absolutely. Great idea to be with people after a day like that. What's their address? I'll put it in the nav."

I gave him the ghost hunters' address, texted Dylan that I was on my way, to please be prepared to ward off a ghost attack, and fumbled for my amethyst. I clenched it in my still-thawing fingers while I stared out the window, certain that the Jimani was going to appear at any second. By the time we pulled onto Dylan's street, I was vibrating with fear, but my heart was still leaden with grief. The remains of tears still tracked down my cheeks. I had never been so crushed with sadness and alive with terror at the same time.

I squeaked out a thank you to James and Lindsey as I slid out of the car and shut the door behind me. I looked to the right and then to the left—

The Jimani was striding up the sidewalk, black trench coat floating behind him on a phantom wind. The air around him darkened, as if he pulled night along in his wake.

I hurled myself at Dylan's door, twisting the knob and then pounding on the door when it refused to yield. "Dylan, it's me!" I shouted. The Jimani was less than half a block away. I could see the dark hollows of his eye holes glinting. His lipless mouth pulled back into a sneer as he turned his head toward me.

The door opened, and I flung myself over the threshold.

"The Jimani! He's here. He followed me." I was near hysterics. My breath coming in gasps, my eyes still burning from crying. "He found me at the funeral he—"

I took in my surroundings. The detritus of my previous visit had been cleared away. The center of the room was completely empty. I was standing in the middle of a taped-off hexagon. Two cameras faced me on tripods. Greg sat at one table manning a softly beeping computer, and Chris busily adjusted some meters off to my left. Dylan shut the door. His eyes were flashing, and he was smiling. Excitement wafted from him as he pushed me to the center of the hexagon.

"That's good, Raely, just what we were hoping for. You texted just in time; we're set up perfectly to record. Just stay in the taped-off area." He adjusted me slightly, then practically danced over to one of the cameras, grabbing a handheld meter en route. The other furniture, tables, chairs, and boxes of equipment had all been pushed to the walls and haphazardly stacked out of the way.

I shook my head, trying to pull myself together. "Wasn't I supposed to sign . . . something . . ."

The room noticeably chilled.

"Whoa, did you feel that? Look at the thermometer—and check the EKG." Greg's blunt-featured face was alight as he tossed instructions to Chris.

"What happens if I step outside of the tape?" I asked Dylan. Was it some sort of protective circle? *Please let it be a protective circle.* My breath clouded the air in front of me as the temperature continued to plunge.

"Then you're outside the range of the cameras," he said distractedly. "We want to make sure we get everything on video. Hey, Chris, are you recording these readings?"

I turned toward the door just as a dark shadow flowed through solid wood, coalescing into the Jimani, grinning at me with too many teeth. The lights dimmed.

Casper! My mind screamed as Dylan, Chris, and Greg babbled excitedly about their readings. My heart thundered at an impossible speed, the rest of me paralyzed with fear as the Jimani glided closer. *I'm going to have a heart attack. I'm going to have a heart attack right here and die.*

He spread his arms wide, waving his skeletally thin fingers like underwater reeds. "*Juuuuuuuuullllleessssssss . . .*" he hissed through his teeth.

I shook my head and backed away. "I don't know what you want. Please leave." My voice quivered. The remnants of the funeral tears were half frozen on my face.

Hollow eye sockets fixed on my face, and his head slowly canted toward his shoulder. One hand remained extended from his side, palm upturned, but with the other he reached out in front of him, curling three fingers back toward himself and leaving one pointed at me.

"*Jewels . . . where?*" He drew out every syllable as though the vowels were reluctant to leave his throat. I couldn't understand what he wanted.

"I don't know what you want." I was backing in a circle now, running out of room.

Greg muttered something and shoved me back within the boundaries of the tape. I stumbled desperately toward Dylan, swiping salt roughly from my face with the sleeve of my coat. "*Do* something!"

He didn't take his eyes off the camera, just waved one hand in a circular motion, like he was telling me to keep going and gave me a thumbs up with the other.

"Are you fucking kidding me right now?" I said, just as the Jimani lifted one of the crates of equipment and hurled it across the room. I flung myself to the floor in time, but the crate spun as it flew, scattering everything it contained in a wide direction. Some of it hit me. Some of it hit the others. Chris ducked beneath his table, cursing, as Dylan continued to man his camera.

"Chris, keep recording! We cannot miss this shit!" he shouted.

I scrambled to my feet and bolted for the door, but the Jimani shoved a table full of equipment into me, ramming into my hip bones and knocking me on my ass as everything on top slid off and fell on and around me.

Something heavy cracked against my skull. My head ricocheted off the floor. I lay dazed, trying to refocus my eyes as the Jimani laughed—deep, rusty, and cold.

Wield your essence, Raely. Figure it out, it's now or never. I clenched the amethyst hard, but nothing happened. What good was it? I heard more crashing as the Jimani hurled another milk crate full of crap at a cowering Chris. Dylan was still filming and still shouting at Chris to get his act together. He was still filming after I'd had a table full of shit thrown on me.

Something snapped.

I may not be able to wield happiness, forgiveness, or love, but I sure as hell could wield my anger. I pushed myself up and grabbed the thing that had fallen on my head. It was a broken waffle iron. I shoved the amethyst into my boot and gripped the waffle iron with both hands as I got my feet beneath me. I gripped my anger too.

"Hey. Skelator," I snarled. The Jimani turned to me.

I heaved the waffle iron and my anger at him, full force.

The waffle iron didn't pass through him as I'd expected. It crashed into his left shoulder, knocking him back. Shocked, I grabbed a can opener and lobbed it at his head, but it flew right through him.

"That's it, Raely, keep going, this is *fantastic*! We're sure to go viral!" Dylan had the camera trained on me.

My anger flared again just as the Jimani lifted a wooden chair over his head. "Fuck you!" I screamed at Dylan as I grabbed the edge of the table and shoved it across the floor into the Jimani, making sure to *push* with my anger as well. The table crashed into him, but he still managed to throw the chair in my direction. I ducked and raced for the door as the chair crashed into the wall behind me.

My fingers grazed the doorknob, but I was hauled back, my damp boots squeaking as they slipped. The Jimani had the edge of my coat in one hand, a lamp base in the other, held high, ready to swing. He laughed. Shadows caressing his edges, writhing around him like so many snakes.

He yanked on my coat, pulling me closer. I tried to drag my anger up, but I was scraping up dregs from the bottom of a nearly empty jar. The last of my rage abandoned me as fear surged through my core, lodging in my throat. I was going to be beaten to death on film by a ghost.

NO. Do not quit.

I tore the front of my coat open, scattering buttons. My arms slid free of the sleeves as I fled, leaving it behind. I yanked open the door and sprinted up the walk, my bad leg screaming. I ignored it as I pelted toward the bus stop, arms pumping, knees lifting higher. I prayed that I wouldn't hit a patch of ice. Prayed that the Jimani would stay to play with the fears of Chris, Greg, and Dylan, and give me time to get on a bus. Any bus.

I was five feet from the corner when a number 74 bus flew by.

"Wait!" I shrieked, but it sped on. I turned onto the main street and gave chase. The next stop was three blocks away. My bad leg threatened to give out. My lungs were on fire. I pushed so hard a yelp of effort burst from my throat.

There was traffic on the street, none on the sidewalk. I was running alongside the bus, then pulling ahead. I made it to the stop, grabbing the sign to halt my momentum, two seconds before the bus pulled up. The doors swung open, and I stumbled on. As the driver shut the doors and the bus lumbered forward again, I clung to the railing at the front, eyes squeezed shut against the pain in my leg. I gasped to fill my burning lungs.

"You okay, miss?" the driver asked. "You was running like someone was chasing you."

I nodded and slapped at my pocket for my pass as I turned to face him, one hand still clutching the railing.

My pass was in my coat.

"Oh, shit," I gasped. "I left my bus pass in my coat—"

"Miss, you are bleeding everywhere! Was you attacked by someone?"

I reached up and touched the side of my head where the waffle iron had hit me. It was damp and sticky. My fingertips came away red. Wetness that I had unconsciously written off as sweat streamed down the side of my face.

"I was . . . I was kind of attacked, yeah." I giggled slightly hysterically as I searched my other pockets. Thankfully my phone and wallet were in my hoodie. *Please let me have cash.* I fumbled with the zipper of my pocket with shaking, freezing hands.

"Hey, I gotchu." The man sitting directly behind the bus driver leaned over, pulled his pass out of his back pocket, and tapped it on the reader. "You go on. Sit down."

I puffed a thank you to the man and limped to the back of the bus. Although it wasn't crowded, the other passengers were all unabashedly staring as I passed by.

I was still breathing heavily, I had nothing to wipe the blood off my face, and my leg was in so much pain that I was moving with a pronounced limp, making liberal use of the handrails as I made my way back.

I would have stared at me too.

I sat heavily in a seat near the back and leaned the uninjured side of my head against the upright railing. At least the blood wouldn't show on my black clothes. My eyes felt itchy and hot from exhaustion and excessive tear production. My heart was still hanging heavily in the middle of my chest like a lead balloon. I let my eyelids drift shut for just a second.

"What the hell happened to you?"

I opened my eyes, and my heart cracked in two. There was Casper. In his olive-green jacket, just like the one Robbie had owned that I had so envied. His blue converse, identical to the ones I had worn until they disintegrated. Shaggy hair flopping into his eyes. I realized his shaggy hair looked just like Hei's—a character from the *Darker than Black* anime series that I had loved.

I lifted my head from the railing, relief threatening to choke me.

"Casper," I breathed, my voice shaking as my entire body trembled with cold and shock. "I've had a shitty day." *I'm sorry about what I said. Don't leave.*

The apology was composed in my head, but I couldn't get it out. I swallowed against the sandpaper coating my throat.

To my intense relief, Casper sat down in the empty seat next to me. He touched his cold fingers gently to the side of my head where a lump was forming. "I'm sorry I was late," he said. "I've been working with Lovonia, and I was still recharging when I felt that something was wrong. It took me a minute. Who hurt you?"

I forced shaking fingers to pull my phone and headphones out of my pocket for show and quietly told him about the Jimani following me from the funeral to the ghost hunters' house. I mentioned seeing Joe, but it felt like knives in my chest when I thought about it, and I wasn't ready to process my last goodbye in depth. I made sure to mention *pushing* with my anger, that the amethyst was useless, and my bus pass was gone.

"I'm sorry about what I said," I told him finally, using the sleeve of my hoodie to wipe away an errant bloodstream that threatened to cut a path across my cheekbone. "I don't know who you are or why you're with me, but I don't want you to leave."

"Didn't take much for you to admit that, did it?" he said, but one side of his mouth had quirked up. "Just the saddest funeral ever followed immediately by a murderous ghost attack."

"I really want to say something snarky to you, but alas, I seem to have run out of fucks to give."

He chuckled. "You used up all your anger. That's the problem with pulling from emotions only. And just one emotion at that. Don't worry, it'll come back. Where would we be without Raely-snark? Let's get off here, we need to get you another pass and switch buses."

"Where are we going?" I pulled the cord, signaling the driver to stop.

"Lovonia. We need a plan. Can we agree now that the ghost hunters are bullshit and go with my idea?" We stood and made our way to the rear exit.

"Just say, 'I told you so,' and get it over with," I said without bite as I pushed the door open and held it unnecessarily.

"Say 'Casper is the smartest, and I will listen to his plans from now on.'" He hopped down onto the curb.

"I'm not saying that."

"It's okay. I know you're thinking it." He followed me into a train station to buy the new transit pass.

"I've noticed that you copied your hair after an anime character." I jammed my credit card into the machine. My heart was a million times lighter now that he was back with me. "Nerd."

"I'm not the one who watched it obsessively and drew the characters all over their notebooks in college. *College*. When you're supposed to be an adult." He leaned against the machine, watching me, a tiny smile pulling at his lips.

"I am very tired of adulting. You take over for the rest of the day." My new pass clattered into the slot. I retrieved it and turned toward the exit. "Can we wait in here until the bus is close? I'm freezing my ass off."

Casper gave me a once-over. "Where's your coat?"

"The Jimani was hanging on to it. I had to lose it." The bus had been warm, but now I was shivering violently. I could no longer stop my voice from shaking. "That's how come no pass."

"I don't like that he has something of yours. Anything with your essence on it is going to make you easier to track." Casper took another look at the side of my head. It had stopped actively bleeding, but I still looked like an extra from a zombie apocalypse movie. "We should be able to get you cleaned up at Lovonia's. It's not far. We could walk it if you had a coat. Or do you wanna spring for a Lyft?"

"Let's save that for the way home. God, I'm gonna eat that whole fucking pizza tonight."

<hr />

CASPER OCCASIONALLY POPPED out to check for buses while I stayed in the train station and trembled like a scared rabbit. We made it to Lovonia's without further incident. I still experienced gut-clenching dread upon approaching the place, but I forced myself up the stairs and inside anyway. Lovonia didn't seem surprised to see us, nor was she shocked at the blood coating one side of my head. In fact, the first thing she remarked on was my necklace.

"The bloodstone. Where did you get it?" She fingered the green and red rock.

"My friend Joe gave it to me a long time ago. His funeral was today."

"Hmmmm." She let it drop back to my chest. "It is drained. Needs charging."

"I haven't used it," I said, reaching down to dig the amethyst out of my boot and setting it on her counter. "I tried to use this, but it didn't—"

I stopped when one of her dark, raspy chuckles scratched from her throat. "You used both today. Both are drained. You do not tell the stones when they are to be used, they lend their energy when they are needed."

She handed me a wad of mismatched fast-food napkins from a stash below her counter and pointed me toward the bathroom. "For your head."

"Thanks." I started walking in the direction she had indicated, then paused. "Wait, what's the bloodstone do?"

"Many things, but mostly it lends courage. It is for warriors." She smiled, her face crinkling more deeply. "Also called heliotrope."

I found the tiny bathroom by limping through a beaded curtain and past several tables in a dark hallway with shadowy items on display. I didn't examine them too closely, though I was almost certain I saw a skull. The bathroom was entirely paneled in dark wood with a Pepto Bismol pink sink and counter. I left the door wide open, as this entire place gave me the creeps. It wasn't long before Casper came to check on me. I was swiping the side of my face and neck with damp napkins and tossing them into the wicker wastebasket once they were completely red.

"You should just stick your whole head under the sink. It would be faster."

"And I'd go hypothermic on the way home with wet hair and no coat." I soaked a fresh napkin and scrubbed dried blood out of the inside of my ear. "I'm just going to do enough so that I don't, like, start attracting flies or vampires. I'll shower later."

He peered at the gash on my head. "Maybe you should go get stitches."

"Although I'm sure that everyone in the emergency room would love to see how well I'm getting on"—I tossed my ear napkin and wetted a new one for the actual cut—"I feel like we have enough to deal with."

He made a dissatisfied noise as I gingerly pulled my matted hair away from the cut.

"If it's still bad tomorrow, I'll get it checked out, okay? But it stopped bleeding."

He grunted but didn't say anything else. I finished cleaning myself up enough that I could pull my hair back into a slightly-damp-on-one-side bun. The casual passerby, or vampire, would have no idea that I had sustained any head trauma.

When we re-entered the main store, I was surprised to find Lovonia attending to actual customers. A trio of thirty-something goths were asking questions about some items in one of the "for conjuring" baskets. They looked up when I came out, stopped talking, and stared at me. One took a step back. I waved awkwardly. I wondered if I had missed some blood somewhere? Surely, I fit the ambiance with my black ensemble and punk rock boots.

As if nothing unusual had happened, Lovonia excused herself, walked over to me, handed me the amethyst, and said, "Here. It is charged. The séance room is opposite the bathroom. You wait there with brother ghost."

The small séance room was thankfully not creepy. In fact, it was almost serene. The walls were a deep purple, completely unadorned. A round, dark, wooden table with four chairs sat at the center, taking up most of the space. There was a small, three-drawer nightstand wedged in one corner topped with one unlit Tiffany lamp. The only window faced the brick wall of the building next door but was covered with gauzy blue and lavender curtains. The only other light in the room came from a bulb screwed into the center of the ceiling, covered with a blue paper lantern. Casper and I squeezed our way around the table to two chairs opposite the lamp and nightstand.

"Why does she call you that?" I imitated Lovonia's accent. "Brother ghost."

"I don't know. She says she'll use my real name once I learn it." He shrugged.

"How the fuck are you supposed to learn your 'real name,'" I finger-quoted, "if you don't already know it?" I crossed my arms on the table and laid my cheek on top of them.

He shrugged. "I don't know, but I didn't know a lot of stuff that I've learned in the past few days. When you . . . well, had your tantrum—"

My heart dipped in remorse. I narrowed my eyes at him but didn't interrupt.

"—I figured I should give you some space for a few days. And I decided it would probably help both of us if I learned tools to defend us against other ghosts. Maybe I could help teach you to defend yourself better if I understood more. I've been working on throwing my own energy and moving things in this plane . . ."

I wasn't sure when my eyes closed, or when Casper's words started weaving into a dream. Images from the day mixed with what Casper was saying. Seeing Joe, Mia, James, the Jimani, Dylan . . . then the images melted into colors . . . then pure feeling. Lovonia joined the dream.

"Leave her," she said. "This will be easier. Less resistance. Ground her where she is."

I felt Casper sidle into the dreamscape, as if he were standing by my side. I wanted to look at him, but it was as if I had no eyes, or he had nothing to see. When I tried to see him, I felt him there with me as clearly as if I had watched him reach out and take hold of my hand.

It's going to get windy. I felt the thought, rather than hearing his words.

I like windy days, I thought back.

Lovonia's alto chuckle rumbled through me. It didn't unnerve me in the dream.

The wind picked up, and electricity spritzed through my being. I found I was weightless, with no contact to the earth. I "looked" again for Casper and used him to pull myself down. I sat deeper into myself and found that, although the wind was pushing even harder, I was more stable.

"Already better." Strangely, I heard Lovonia differently than Casper, as if she were speaking into ears that I had left behind.

The "wind" began to change. It had flavors. Some were warm and sweet, but many were bitter, cloying, ashy. I wanted nothing to do with any of them. I curled in on myself, trying to turn away from them. I struggled to find stability and pulled on Casper.

They won't hurt you. Invite them in.

I don't know how.

Don't know or don't want?

A distant heart I had left behind pounded faster. Telling myself that it was just a dream, it couldn't hurt me, I forced myself to uncurl. With effort, I turned to face the distasteful flavors, letting them wash over me and settling back into myself. It was as if I were standing next to Casper rather than hanging onto him and trying not to be blown away. A spicy flavor swept forward and plunged for my essence. I let the spice run through me. I welcomed it, embraced it even. I felt myself reaching for Casper's approval.

That was your anger. I could feel him smiling. *I told you it would come back. And we already know you like that one. Just do the same with the others.*

I hesitated and slipped. *The other ones scare me.*

I'm here. I'm not leaving no matter what happens.

I had to try. Nothing else was working. I needed to try to listen to Casper. I turned into the wind, and a cloying, ashy flavor buffeted me. Although it terrified me to do it, I flung myself open and let it run through me. I was twisted and pulled. My heart ached from somewhere in my essence, but I stood stable. Casper was still with me. I felt choked by the ash, nauseated by the sickliness, but I stood. The awfulness of this wind wrapped up with the spice, wrapped up with the rest of me, and became part of me.

I had no chance to rest. A bright, warm wind swept around me next. It was too bright, too warm after the last one. I shrank down against it and felt myself sliding away. Casper pulled me up.

You can do this.

It's too bright!

You're just not used to it. It won't be after a second. Just try.

I forced myself to stand, using the spice, the ash, the bitterness already in me. I tried to open to the bright, warm wind, but I was terrified that the rest would be blown away.

Nothing would be left. The heat and light would burn it all.

Just try.

Like stepping off a cliff, I flung myself open.

The warm wind swept in, stirring up the ash, mixing the spice with the sickly sweet. It all roiled within me, an uncomfortable mash of flavors and emotions. But I was stronger somehow, more stable. My wispy "self" had more weight. I looked over and I could "see" Casper's essence next to mine.

That was pretty good. I felt the smile. *Now try letting go and finding me again.*

No! Don't leave!

I won't leave. Just see if you can let go and grab back on.

I felt lungs that I had left behind panting in terror, a heart that I used to be connected to galloping faster and faster.

Everything else you've done has been great. Just try this one last thing.

I pulled everything in me together. Pulled in all the flavors. Gathered all the uncomfortable feelings.

And I let go.

I was still there. I hadn't blown away. I could still "see" Casper. I reached back out and grabbed onto him. I felt him grab me back.

"Goooooood." I heard Lovonia with my other ears. "Let's come back now, little seer."

I felt as though I were gently melting. Spreading. Less like a backwards whirlpool than a warm waterfall.

My head ached. My leg hurt. My arms were numb. I lifted my face from my forearms and the blood rushed back into them. I was back in my body. Lovonia was seated at the table across from me, a grin splitting her face. Casper was perched on a chair next to me, one of his hands on my shoulder. He let go and sat back, smiling when I shook my head.

"Was that a dream or . . .?"

"Very well done," Lovonia said. "Now you begin to see. It can be done in this world also. Reach out, touch brother ghost."

I turned to look at Casper, smiling in the chair next to mine. He was clearer than he had ever been. If I hadn't known he was a ghost, I might have mistaken him for a normal person. Except that he seemed to have a light emanating from him. Almost as if he were sitting in the sun while I remained in the shade. I reached out a finger, which went right through his arm and left me feeling as if I'd swiped it through ice water.

"Close your eyes," Lovonia instructed. "Remember letting go and holding on in your . . . dream. Do it that way."

I closed my eyes and tried to get the feeling back that I'd had in the dream. It was more difficult, but I remembered the way I had pulled everything together inside of me. I could *feel* Casper next to me. As soon as I lifted my hand, it went away. I stopped, focused again on the feelings, the uncomfortable mush swirling around inside of me, sat deeper into myself and "looked" for Casper. I reached out first with my essence and let my hand follow. My hand found something solid . . . and warm. I blinked open my eyes. My hand was on Casper's arm. *Don't freak out.* I settled deeper into myself, letting my essence go first, I wrapped my fingers around his bicep and tugged. His arm moved toward me.

"You pulled me!" Casper was delighted. "Do something else."

I let go of his arm, concentrating on spirit first, body second, I curled my fingers into a fist, then punched him in the shoulder.

"Ow, hey."

I grinned.

"You're mean."

"Sorry." I briskly rubbed the spot where I had punched. "Why is he warm now?"

Lovonia chuckled. I was getting used to the sound. "Now you connect spirit to spirit, not spirit to body. Spirits are on the same plane. Same vibrations."

I poked Casper a few times in the arm, the shoulder, testing until he got annoyed and started poking me back.

"Enough. Practice is good, but do not waste energy. You need to prepare your home."

We stopped. "Like, something other than the smudging?" I asked.

"The Jimani will come to your home. It knows your essence well now, which means you will need to defend yourselves there. It does not matter what you do; it will happen, sooner or later."

My stomach dropped. "How do we prepare?"

"Remove any distractions. Any objects you cannot stand to see broken or damaged. He will use these against you."

"Blitz." My stomach iced over. "I have to get Blitz out of there."

"You could take him to your mom's," Casper suggested.

"Yeah. Yeah, I'll tell her they're doing construction on the building or something. I wonder how soon we can get a train out there." I pulled out my phone. A million messages and missed calls from Dylan. I had silenced my phone for the funeral, which seemed like it had happened weeks ago. I ignored the messages and opened the app for the commuter trains to the suburbs.

"Go tonight if you can. He will find you in the city." Lovonia stood, gracefully navigating the sliver of space around the table and heading to the door. "Practice touching and moving, but do not exhaust yourself. Recharging is easier for ghosts."

I shimmied out of my chair and edged around the side of the table, meeting Lovonia in the doorway. She stopped me with one hand on my shoulder and pulled my chin around with the other. She peered into my face, her dark eyes unblinking. "Eat," she said, then released me.

"I will." I moved my jaw from side to side, still feeling the ghost of her grip. We continued up the hall. When we had passed through the beaded curtain, I glanced at her. "Thank you for all of this."

Her smile creased her face so that her glittering eyes were almost hidden in the folds. "You are welcome. I have been waiting for you for a long time. Go now. Move your Blitz."

15

HOURS LATER, CASPER, BLITZ, AND I were on a Metra train bound for the suburbs. I had done a double smudge of the apartment before we left. No matter what Lovonia said, I didn't fancy coming home to a Jimani-wrecked place if I could avoid it. We climbed the narrow stairs to the top level of the train for the single-seaters. Casper sat in the one facing me, and I put Blitz's carrier in the narrow floor space between us, propping one foot on the corner of Casper's seat and crossing the other on top. For a few minutes we just stared out the window, each silently willing the train to get moving before any ghosts, Jimani or otherwise, were attracted to our car.

My mom had been effusive in her welcome when I asked if I could drop off Blitz and spend the night. The funeral had been hard, I'd told her—not a lie—and it had completely slipped my mind that construction was starting in our building, and we were supposed to relocate our pets for a few days. She assured me that she could work half a day from home in the morning to have breakfast and lunch with me and then drop me off at the station on her way into the office. She loved her grand-cat, as she called Blitz, and would be happy for his company for a few days. I had been intentionally vague about how long he'd be staying.

Casper broke the silence. "I'm looking forward to seeing your mom."

I blinked. "Oh yeah?"

"Yeah, I mean, for all intents and purposes, I grew up with her too."

"Oh, I guess I never thought of it that way. So . . . you don't remember your parents at all?"

Casper stared out the window. "I don't remember anything before you and your family. There are some early parts of that I don't even remember. I still don't know where I came from, Raely."

"I . . . I'm sorry." For the umpteenth time, I fought down a swell of emotion. I searched for something comforting to say and came up empty. *I should be nicer to him,* I thought. *Maybe just slightly.*

I changed the subject. "Do you know where the Jimani came from?"

He cleared his throat and pulled his gaze from the window. "Jimani can come from anywhere," he told me. "From what I understand, they start out as regular ghosts but enjoy the fear and pain they can create, so they change in response . . . and there's the whole soul-hunting aspect." I shuddered but didn't interrupt him. "Like the way a Lixivier enjoys growing negativity that already exists. They all start out looking like . . . people."

"Is there a fancy name for the kind of ghost that you are?"

He smiled, peering at me through his anime hair. "I'm an Aural spirit. At least right now. Apparently that can change."

I focused my energy and tapped his leg with my foot, proud of myself when it connected. "What's an Aural spirit then, when it's at home?"

He smirked. "Basically, according to Lovonia, when we die, our energy, essence, whatever you want to call it, is released from our corporeal body. Some . . . move on, whatever that means, and the ones that don't . . . well, I attached myself to you. What was left of myself—my personality, intelligence, all of that—I bounced it off you. I'm still me. But . . . just like the people around us tend to influence our personalities and behaviors, you influenced mine. So I became what you needed."

I swallowed. "I feel like I should apologize for that? I know it's not my fault, but . . . it seems sad that you based your existence on me. Like, what did you get out of it?"

"You were the person I was drawn to, so I was happy. I'm just sorry it all started going down like this." He stared down at Blitz in his carrier. "I never wanted to bring bad things to you."

"It's . . . I mean, it's not fine, but it seems like it would have happened at some point anyway." I waved my hands in what I thought was a mystical and spooky way. "I had latent seer tendencies just waiting to pounce near my twenty-seventh birthday."

"Oh, man! Your birthday is coming up."

"Please. I'm ignoring it this year. It's the worst year ever."

"That's all the more reason to celebrate it. Say goodbye to this shitty year and start a new one." He grabbed my booted foot and shook it.

I half-smiled. "Let's just get me there first."

<hr />

MY MOM PICKED us up at the station on her way home from work. She gave me a long hug and teared up a bit over Joe. Then she grabbed Blitz's carrier and briskly led the way to her car. Her brown ponytail, with one long streak of gray through the right side, bounced behind her. When I glanced at Casper beside me, his eyes were shining. I realized that he might be affected by Joe's death more than I thought, as Joe had probably been his de facto best friend also.

For some reason, it felt weird for my mom not to acknowledge Casper. I made a mental note to be careful about addressing him in front of her. I was getting far too used to talking to him in public.

Casper settled into the backseat next to Blitz, and I found myself really bothered that he didn't buckle his seat belt. *Ugh. Get a grip.* I slid into shotgun and asked my mom about her day. She set up payroll for various companies, so she always had personalities to deal with, but a lot of her day-to-day wasn't thrilling, so it was pleasant to listen to her break down what and who she had interacted with. The problems and dramas seemed so small and manageable compared to what we had left behind in the city.

I watched her face as she talked, the streetlights flashing overhead at regular intervals as we drove. No foundation, just eye makeup and lip gloss. A few crow's feet bracketed her eyes, some faint lines visible on her forehead. She looked younger than she had before my dad died. Then, she had often applied full foundation to hide a bruise or dark circles beneath her eyes. I'd been eleven when his temper and penchant for drinking and driving had culminated in him wrapping himself around a telephone pole.

On the very night mom had packed our bags and—for real this time!—left him. He'd been driving around town trying to track us down after stopping at a few bars. I felt like our life had really started that year, after he was gone. Although, for the first several months, Mom was severely haunted by his memory, almost like he was still there. It took an army of friends, relatives, and therapy to pull her out. I was still proud of her almost sixteen years later. It had taken a lot for her to move past that.

"I like your hair," I said, pushing her ponytail so that it swung. "I hope mine does that when I'm your age."

"Thank you!" she said. "But I think you have your grandma's hair. It's so wavy. Her hair just got darker and darker until she was almost seventy."

We pulled into the carport and chatted as we brought Blitz and our baggage inside. Casper followed us with his hands in his pockets, a little bounce in his step, his expression blandly content. I gave him a little smile behind Mom's back to let him know I hadn't forgotten he was there.

We got Blitz settled and—after a brief debate where I talked her out of the mom-guilt—decided cheese, crackers, olives, and hummus would be just fine for dinner. She even dug out a bottle of white zinfandel she had nestled in the crisper with the bagged spinach so that we could toast to Joe.

"Seriously, Mom, this is fine. I totally sprang this on you, and this is so much nicer than what I've been eating anyway—"

"Raely Mynor Videc. You had better be taking care of yourself. You just had a serious accident!"

"Oh, really? I guess that slipped my mind." I popped some cheese into my mouth and took a polite sip of the terrible wine.

"You do look thinner, honey. I know it's been a hard time but . . ." she looked down, her lips pressed into a tight line. Blitz took the opportunity to walk his front paws up her pant leg. Her face relaxed, and she broke off a corner of cheese to toss to him. She lifted her glass of wine. "To Joe. A wonderful friend who was pulled away far, far too soon."

I blinked several times as I touched my glass to hers. Casper was watching Blitz chow down on his bit of cheese, his eyes bright. He still looked like someone I knew from somewhere. Not just an anime character.

"Mom." I set my glass down. "Did I ever know someone who died? Like . . . when I was really young? Like even younger than kindergarten. I feel like I remember that someone died." I made a cheese-and-cracker sandwich with some of the last on our plate as I asked. I had the entire double decker in my mouth, crunching away when I noticed that her face had paled. "Oh my God, what?" I said around my food. It came out "ofmugofwhuu?"

She drained her glass, set it down, and stared at the floor for several seconds. I glanced at Casper. He shook his head slightly and shrugged. Without saying a word, she got up and walked out of the room.

"Holy shit, what the fuck?" I whispered.

"I don't know," Casper said, brow furrowing. "I mean . . . she didn't seem pissed off or anything, just . . . shocked?"

She was gone for several minutes. I nervously fed Blitz an entire slice of cheese and then finished off the tray while she was gone. I poured her another glass of pink wine just in case. I even went to the bathroom and came back. I was on the verge of telling Casper to go find out where she had gone when she returned with a dusty wooden box.

She set it down on the table, then picked up the wine I had poured and took a long drink. Because of my father, my mom rarely drank, so I was surprised to see her top herself off. "I probably shouldn't have kept this from you for so long." She opened the box, pulling out photographs and setting them to one side until she found a yellowed piece of paper folded in thirds. She unfolded and smoothed it out, face down. She stared at the back of the paper without speaking.

Casper moved to stand next to me.

"What's going on?" I asked, taking a sip of my own wine, forcing myself to stay at just a sip.

Without a word, she flipped the paper over and pushed it toward me. Then she got up, taking her wine with her, and crossed to the refrigerator.

I watched her go, then pulled the paper over to where both Casper and I could read it. It was a birth certificate. It was *my* birth certificate. My name wasn't the only live birth listed.

I was a twin.

Gooseflesh sprung up over my entire body. "Mom . . ."

She plopped an ice cube into her glass, closed the freezer and walked back to the table. "Your brother died when he was two." Her voice cracked on the last word.

"Holy shit." I took a less polite sip of grape sugar.

"Your father . . . he said it was an accident . . . we lived on the second floor, and your grandpa had gotten me a job interview. Your father wasn't happy about staying home with the two of you—he never was—but . . . I was determined to . . ." She sat back down and pushed the photographs around as she talked. "He fell off the balcony. Your brother."

I set down my glass so that it wouldn't slip through my numb fingers. Electricity fizzed through my veins. *How could I not have known this?* I dragged my gaze up to Mom. She took another swallow of wine, her eyes brimming with tears. "Your father called 911 but . . . Anyway, it was ruled an accident." She swallowed. "They offered me the job, but . . . I . . . your father said it was my fault. He was never as attentive as I was when it came to the two of you—"

Ingrained protectiveness roused me enough to interrupt. "Oh my God, please tell me you don't think this was *your fault—*"

"Oh, not anymore, honey." She patted my hand. Another sip of wine. More photograph rearrangement. My gaze snagged on those photographs and my heart twisted. I wanted to see him. With me. With us. Even if only in a picture. But she stacked them up again. "I never wanted to leave you alone again. I turned down the job and stayed home."

Trapped. Like he wanted you to be, I thought. I shoved my wine back from the edge of the table, reached across, and fanned out the photographs. One of them was of her and my dad when they were very, very young. Before he had become . . . what he became. The long, straight nose. The dark slashes of eyebrows. My breath caught and I looked up at Casper.

He looked like he was about to faint.

My eyes snapped back to the birth certificate. My mouth had gone dry. "Julian Clay . . ."

"He was older than you by two minutes. Your Aunt Cathy wanted to call him J. C. but I was already calling him Jules." She slid one of the photographs toward me. It was her: younger, looking incredibly tired, in a hospital room surrounded by machinery, and she was holding two impossibly tiny babies wrapped in blankets. I picked it up, gazed at it for a moment, then put it on the table where all three of us could see. "Which one is he?"

She started to cry as she pointed to the baby on the left.

"I'm so sorry, Raely." She took another pull of wine. "I know this probably wasn't the best time to bring this up, with you already mourning Joe . . . I thought I might have lost you in that train accident, Raely. I just . . ." She dabbed her eyes with a corner of the tablecloth. We'd forgotten napkins with our casual dinner. "It's interesting that you asked me that question tonight. I've been thinking about your brother often since the accident. I talked about him at first, a little bit, but then . . . I don't know if you remember this, but you used to have this imaginary friend, and you started calling him Jules. 'Jules wants to go with us,' or 'Jules wants to be pushed on the swings, too,' and . . . I just couldn't take it. I told you that you needed to find a new name for your friend, that he couldn't be Jules—I snapped at you, I hope to God you don't remember, it wasn't my finest moment—and then I forbid anyone in the family from talking about him in front of you and . . . I guess I just never brought it up again."

I risked a peek at Casper.

"You did call me Jules for a while. I remember now . . ." He stared at the picture of the three of us together.

I finished my wine and topped both of us off with the rest of the bottle. I noticed my hand was trembling as I poured. I tried hard to think of something to say.

"I'm so sorry, honey." She could no longer absorb her tears with the tablecloth corner. "I know our life could have been better if I had gotten out sooner. When I look back, I can't believe—"

"Mom, it wasn't your fault," I said. My chest felt like a cage for electric butterflies.

"I know. I just wish I'd seen the signs and left him earlier." She sniffled once, futzed with one more piece of paper in the box, then pushed it back down. "If it's okay with you, I'll go ahead on to bed and let you look through the rest of this on your own tonight. I can answer any questions in the morning. I love you so much, honey." As she stood up, she grabbed my shoulder and planted a firm kiss on the top of my head. Then she took her wine with her and strode to the back of the house. "C'mon, Blitz."

The traitor trotted after her without even a backward glance at me. But I guess she needed him more just then.

"She taught me how to lock my door from the inside when I was so little that I can't remember," I said. I tugged out the sheet of paper she had been fiddling with. "I didn't even know it was weird until my first sleepover when I tried to lock the door to my friend's room, and she asked me what the hell I was doing." I unfolded the page. Death certificate for Julian Clay Videc.

Julian had arranged the pictures before him in a line. There was even one of the two of us together next to a cake with a number one candle on it. I had frosting all over my face, having taken a bite out of the side of the thing, and looked like I was having the time of my life. Jules was clapping his hands and laughing at me. Another picture showed the four of us together. Our dad held both of us and was gazing at Mom, but she had one arm half around me and was reaching for Julian with the other.

"You look like Dad did before . . . before he was the big, mean drunk that I knew," I said, fighting hard to push some lightness into the atmosphere. "You're a combination of Dad and Hei. Nerd."

"I'm your older brother," he said, pressing the folds of the birth certificate into the table. I shoved the death certificate back into the box.

"You're my *twin* brother. You are the same age as me."

"I'm older by two minutes."

"Oh my fucking God. So you have two whole minutes of wisdom on me. Please, tell me what the fuck will I learn in the next two minutes, oh wise sage?"

"Now I know why you're so obnoxious. Bratty little sis."

"So I guess we can stop calling you—" My stomach dropped to the floor. The hair on the back of my neck reached new heights and my mouth dried out. I set my wine down, gripping the edge of the table.

"What?"

"He knew your name," I whispered.

"Who?"

"The Jimani. When he attacked me at the ghost hunters', he was looking for Jules."

16

WE SPENT SOME TIME QUIETLY GOING OVER the pictures before heading to bed. Cas—Julian had no helpful answers or even decent theories as to how the Jimani knew him. I peppered him with questions: Had he pissed off any evil ghosts in recent months? Did bad ghosts maybe always fight with good ghosts? Was there a ghost, good or bad, that he'd hung around a lot as a child? I stopped after getting an increasingly terse *no* in response to every question. He was more caught up in the fact that we were his real family and that he wasn't just some creep ghost following me around for no discernible reason. He was thrilled that his protective instincts were validated and that there was a reason he had attached himself to me, even after days of me being various degrees of difficult toward him.

I couldn't blame him. Honestly, it made me feel better too. After my initial freak-out, I had accepted him so quickly that I'd been concerned I was projecting Joe onto him. That I felt so much more comfortable with him there had alarmed me. I'd thought I might be going insane. And honestly, I hadn't cared. But this made it better. There was a reason. He was my twin.

Still, I didn't sleep well, even with Julian sitting vigil at the window the entire night.

I was up well before the sun. Rather than risk waking Mom by banging around in her kitchen, I did my physical therapy for the first time in a while. My leg had ached on and off throughout the night. I also practiced *pushing* with my energy while Jules coached. I thought I could now discern when my gemstones were charged. When they were "full," they had the same look as Jules, as if they were sitting in the sun, and they felt warmer. Jules was better by leaps and bounds. He could pick things up and put them down as if he were alive.

When I heard Mom beginning to move around in the next room, I headed to the kitchen to make breakfast. I found a muffin mix that only required an egg, half a cup of milk, and some energetic stirring. Jules insisted on doing some of the stirring while I greased the muffin tin. I let him have at it, deciding to enjoy my brother's help. Although I did wonder what it would have looked like to someone just walking in. After I slid the muffins into the oven, he wanted to try to give me a piggyback ride. I told him to save the show-offy stuff for when we were fighting the fear demon.

Mom was subdued during breakfast. Our father had blamed her for losing Jules, and for years, she had been beaten down enough to believe it. It had taken a lot of therapy for her to let go of the guilt, to stop wondering "what if," but I doubted it would ever completely wash away. I ached to tell her that he was here, right next to me, and didn't blame her at all, but Jules and I had decided it wasn't a good idea. There was every chance she would assume I was cracking up over losing Joe and simply force me into therapy. In the unlikely event that she did believe me, we'd have to tell her about the Jimani and all the other ghosts, which would terrify her. Jules also didn't want to risk her unearthing seer abilities of her own—who knew which side mine had come from—and drawing the attention of malevolent ghosts. We had enough to worry about.

By lunchtime, she had brightened a little and was looking forward to having Blitz as company for a few days. I forced a sunny demeanor until we were back on the train, then dropped it like a heavy mask.

Jules was lost in his own thoughts, staring out the window. I took the opportunity to listen to the plethora of messages that Dylan had left me. He changed tactics in each voicemail. At first, he tried to tell me how amazing the footage was and asked when I might want to come and review it so we could talk strategy. Then he told me he needed my signature on the release forms or his partners said he couldn't continue giving their aid for free. Then he switched to telling me that I had left my coat there and could come get it any time. Next up, he was outside my apartment and had my coat with him if I would come down. Finally, he told me to check my email.

Mouth tightening, I swiped open the email app and saw one from Dylan. I opened it.

There was a TikTok link.

My stomach flipped. I clicked on it, and the air seemed to be sucked out of the train car.

Jules looked away from the window and raised his eyebrows.

"That jagoff Dylan," I wheezed, then turned my phone screen so he could see.

Despite everything I had said, Dylan had posted a cut of video from the Jimani attack on TikTok. He had even put it to trending audio with the flashing headline *Ghost troubles? We're here to help! *cute ghost emoji**—and it was on its way to going viral. He had left the original audio in the clip as well, and I watched Julian's jaw slowly drop away from the rest of his face as I heard my own voice screaming, "*Are you fucking kidding me right now?*" followed by the crashing of detritus.

He grabbed my arm to pull the phone closer. I glanced around quickly to make sure no one was around to witness my odd movements, then whispered to Jules, "He's called me like ten times asking me to sign release forms. I didn't agree to this, I told him I didn't want my picture anywhere . . ." I trailed off, my heart hammering. What if Mom saw this? What if my *boss* saw this?

Julian's face had gone from slack-jawed shock to Liam-Neeson-in-*Taken*. "They just watched while he beat the shit out of you? And filmed it?"

I yanked my arm back, the video playing on a loop. I watched the views increase in real time. Already over 50K. Some self-destructive impulse had me click to the comments.

That's some good acting there. How much she get paid?

@CleverBoi89 Look, I told you ghosts were real!

crying laughing emoji Someone rigged a buncha shit to fly at that poor girl! She gonna need so much therapy!

I swiped the app shut, my breath coming quick and fast. "Fuck, if Mom sees this—" I opened my text message app and started a text to Dylan, telling him I hadn't agreed to this. Then stopped, deleted the text, and composed a reply to the email. "Emails are legal documents," I narrated as my fingers flew over my screen, my voice still breathy and high. "I . . . did not . . . agree . . . to my likeness . . ."

Julian's eyes narrowed, eyebrows dropping lower. "Tell him he's about to see what it feels like to be a haunted person if he doesn't take that shit down."

I smiled despite myself. "Yeah, I'll just say my ghost brother will beat him—" I gasped and looked up from my phone. "She *knew*! Lovonia!"

"Oh." Jules blinked. "I guess so. I told you she was amazing."

I glared. Little flames wrapped around my breastbone. "Seems like she could be less cryptic sometimes and save us a shitload of trouble."

I finished the email, then read it over for spelling errors.

He furrowed his brow and examined his shoes for a moment. "I dunno." He glanced up. "I feel like she lets us find out things on our own intentionally."

"Does she hang out with any other ghosts?" I asked, an idea sparking. "Maybe she's been talking about you and that's how the Jimani—"

"Stop it." He predictably defended his darling Lovonia. "She's not a gossip. I hardly think she'd tell any other spirits my name if she wouldn't tell us."

I grunted, not convinced. We'd only known her a few days, so how did Julian know she wasn't a gossip?

I sent my terse email and glowered at the passing cornfields for a few minutes.

Jules pulled out the end of my shoelace. We were trying to practice in discreet ways as often as possible. "Do you have to work tonight?"

"Oh, shit, yeah. Will you come along?" I fully untied my shoe, then put my foot up on the chair for him to retie.

"Hell yeah. I'm not leaving you alone again if I don't have to. Until we get this Jimani shit resolved." He effortlessly retied my shoe. Now the other one felt loose.

"Good." I held up my other foot. He untied it.

"Just don't get trashed and throw me out again." He retied my shoe with a double knot.

I looked into his blue eyes, peeking out from beneath his messy, messy hair. The corner of my mouth twitched. "I make no promises."

One side of his mouth curved upward. "Jagoff."

───※───※───※───

BACK AT MY Blitz-less apartment, in the darkness of a February late-afternoon, Jules suggested moving a few things that he felt were important into an almost-hidden side closet. It looked like it had been an entrance to an attic when perhaps this apartment had been part of a single-family home.

"Okay, but seriously, if we move anything in there, it should probably be like . . . my financial statements or something . . ." I glanced at the pile of lawyer files from the accident stacked on a scuffed end table.

"There are copies of those in other places! Your lawyers have them. The insurance agencies and doctors have them. You need to be putting photo albums in there and your quilt and band posters and—"

"Jules?"

He was floating four feet above the ground. "Oh my God, I'm sorry." He dropped back to the floor.

"You're sorry because you suddenly got floaty or because you're flipping out about physical possessions when you're an incorporeal being?"

"I just . . . I've really been trying not to freak you out, and it burns a dumb amount of energy, but sometimes when I get stressed or I hate what you're doing, I float—"

I started chuckling.

"What's funny?" He crossed his arms across his chest.

I pointed, my laughter ratcheting up to a cackle. "You float when you're upset. That's so haunted house." I flopped sideways on the couch, giving way to glee. "We should drape you in tissue paper for Halloween . . ." I howled until I could barely draw breath. "Or maybe a bedsheet with eyeholes . . ."

"Raely . . ."

It wasn't pretty. Mascara-blackened tears cut tracks down my cheeks. I couldn't stop. My inhales were raspy wheezes in between chortles. It wasn't *that* funny, but the seal had been broken, and laughing felt so good. I rolled from the couch onto the floor.

Jules lifted his feet off the ground and hovered over me. "Woooooooooo!"

Tears pushed through the slits of my eyelids. "Stop!" I wheezed. "I can't breathe!"

He spun in a slow circle above me waving his hands. "Woooooooo!"

I tried to tell him to quit but I had no breath left. All I could do was mouth the word. Tears were streaming down my face. I thought I would die from suffocation. Then the lights cut out.

17

"JULIAN."

"I'm here."

Our laughter had extinguished as completely as the lights.

As one, we retreated toward the bathroom with our arsenal of stones. I'd rooted around in my childhood rock collection while we were at Mom's and found a quartz and an obsidian to add to our assemblage. They seemed small and ineffectual right now.

"Maybe there was just an electrical failure," I whispered. But the water vapor puffing from my mouth with each word belied that theory.

"It's not. Close your eyes for a second."

I knew what he was asking. I closed my eyes and tried to push past my fear and find my center. The spicy, bitter, confused self that was able to stand on her own in the place of wind. I was able to see more easily without using my physical eyes. I could *see* Julian next to me. I could *see* my own essence around me. And I could *see* something dark, smoky, horrific, and powerful, ascending the staircase.

My eyes flew open.

"Holy fucking shit, Jules." My legs were shaking.

"We're going to be fine."

"Do the thing you did with the groceries and pull me out of here."

"Moving you is not the same as moving groceries, Raely. Just get in the bathroom and you'll be more protected."

"But you can't come into the bathroom!" My breath was coming faster. I was nearly hyperventilating. The smoky *thing* was hovering just outside my door. How long would the smudging keep it out? My entire body trembled.

Jules shoved me toward the bathroom, and I stumbled over the threshold. "Stop freaking out. Take a breath—"

My ears popped as if experiencing a sudden drop of air pressure. A metallic fizz coated my tongue. A rush of static shot through the apartment as the smudge work was obliterated and the door smashed open.

The Jimani flowed through the doorway, somehow darker than the blackness of the stairwell behind him. He paused just over the threshold, grinning though he had no lips. He was wreathed in writhing shadow. He lifted his skeletal hands, cupped together in front of him, arms outstretched, then spread them wide. "*You again . . .*" he rasped, eye sockets glittering.

We have to get out, we have to get out, we have to get out.

"Get out of here," Jules told him, taking a step to his right, blocking the entrance to the bathroom. "You're not welcome."

I saw the heel of his shoe dip past the threshold and knew that my wards on this room had been decimated also. There was no safe place left in the apartment. *Focus, Raely, focus.* I tried to drop down into myself. To find that stable place I had discovered with Julian and Lovonia just yesterday. I could barely sense it, like reaching out with my fingertips for the edge of a blanket to pull up against the chill. I stretched myself toward it, straining to find purchase . . .

The Jimani hurled himself at Jules like a gunshot. I screamed as Jules crashed against the bathroom sink, his glow shuddering. The Jimani wrapped long fingers around Julian's throat. Jules was writhing, trying to throw him off. I pulled myself together, grasping at my essence with fumbling mental fingers. *Got it.* I gripped hard and punched the Jimani in the face.

He staggered sideways into the bathroom doorframe, releasing Jules, who fell to the floor, unbalanced.

The Jimani grinned at me, cackled, then yanked the towel bar out of the wall and swung it at my head. It connected with a dull thud. I staggered back, my calves hitting the bathtub. I fell backward with a crash, pulling the shower curtain down as I landed painfully in the tub, my left hip, shoulder, and previously injured side of my head all clanging against the porcelain. The Jimani brought the towel rod down again and again as I kicked out ineffectually with my legs, trying to shield my head with my arms.

A flash of light, and the Jimani was jerked away. I forced my battered body out of the tub. *Movemovemove.* I stumbled to my feet. Jules was wrapped around the dark ghost, struggling to pull him from the bathroom. The smoky shadows emanating from the Jimani snaked themselves around Julian's arms, torso, and neck as the two spirits thrashed into the living room.

"Get out, Raely, get out!" Jules shouted. "You have to run! I'll catch up—"

The Jimani threw Jules off. He seemed to swell as he glided toward him, extending his arms outward, as if gathering the surrounding darkness to himself. Shadows unfurled from his limbs, lengthening, curling, solidifying, and wrapped themselves around Jules like massive black pythons. For a moment, his sunny glow was enhanced by the contrast, then it shuddered spasmodically as the shadows contracted, squeezed, and stabbed into him. Jules screamed, writhing on the floor as the shadows engulfed him.

My mental fingers snapped around the shield of my essence, hauling it up. For one instant, everything crystallized. I sat down into myself and thrust my shield out like a battering ram. It connected solidly with the Jimani. I felt the force of the impact clang through me, but I stood strong, watching him fly through the wall. His shadows unraveled, spinning away from Julian and evaporating.

We didn't speak. We just fled.

⁓⁓⁓

I HAD NEVER run down three flights of stairs faster than I did in that moment. The lights in the building sputtered back to life as I smashed through the entryway doors. I must have knocked the Jimani good, but I had no idea how much time I had bought us. Julian materialized next to me as soon as I was in the courtyard, neither of us checking our speed as we tore toward the street, turning right out of the courtyard to sprint to the train station.

I smashed into something solid and crashed to the side, landing hard in snow-shrouded shrubbery, the branches snapping beneath me, snagging in my hair and clothes, scratching my face.

"Raely!" Jules must have seen my graceless derailment, and what had caused it. "Oh, shit."

I thrashed around, terrified, desperate to detangle myself from the bush and regain my footing. *Essence, essence, where is my essence?*

"Raely!" Not Jules, a different voice. Living human voice. *Laughing* human voice. "That was graceful." Someone grabbed my upper arm and hauled me out of the foliage. "I was just looking for you, so lucky to literally run into each other." I started to fight the grip holding me until I recognized that fake laugh.

Dylan. I allowed him to help me up but then shook him off, glancing up and down the street. The lights were blinking back to life in all directions.

No Jimani so far. I brushed evergreen needles and snow from my clothes and pushed past him. I didn't have time for this.

"Jesus, are you alright?" Dylan stepped in front of me, forced to walk backwards when I refused to stop. "Hey, I brought your coat, I thought maybe we could grab a drink and have a chat. You kinda look like you need one." Another unearned chuckle. He swept his right arm toward the main street, where presumably drinks, warmth, and comfort awaited. My coat was draped over it. He grabbed my arm hard with his other hand. "Slow down, doll—"

I yanked out of his grip and snatched my coat back, thrusting my arms into the sleeves. I stomped away from him. "Not a good time."

"Tell him to take down that goddamn video," Jules bit out, intentionally stopping in Dylan's path, forcing him to walk right through him. Dylan shivered. Jules smirked.

"Look, Raely, I know you were probably a little emotional after the funeral, which you have to admit was stellar timing on our part. I knew it would be perfect conditions to attract the Jimani, and I don't know if you saw, but we did get some great footage—"

"I didn't agree to be blasted across TikTok getting attacked by a ghost on one of the worst days of my life." I didn't look at him, just sped up. My bad leg was going to need more therapy after this week. I suppressed the limp, aided by an electric jolt of fury surging up from my core to join the adrenaline still thundering through my blood. "I said I didn't want to be on social. I specifically told you to take that down."

"Look, doll, let's have a chat about this. You're being a little squirrelly for no real reason. The exposure is good for you too!"

"Unfuckingbelievable," Julian said, and flicked Dylan's earlobe.

Dylan shook his head slightly, rubbing his ear, and increased his pace. He grabbed my arm again, forcing me to stop. "Honestly, doll, aren't you an actor? Comedian? Something? A bit of notoriety is not going to hurt your career. I did you a favor. Okay, let's talk strategy. I have the release papers here." He patted his pocket, then dipped his hand inside and pulled out a pen, fingers still digging into my bicep. "You can just sign them now, and we can go wider with the footage, which is helping to fund our expenses by the way, then we can go over the videos together—"

I jerked my arm from his grip, simultaneously slapping him off me with the other hand.

"Don't touch me again. I'm not sure where the disconnect is, but I will not be signing anything in the middle of the sidewalk, and I *never* agreed to be put on your social media. You never said this was how compensation would work, and I would never have gone to your place had I known you'd be posting this. Not to mention that you've actually done nothing at all to help me. If anything, you seem more interested in making my situation worse so you can get TikTok views. Now, if you'll excuse me, I just had the shit beat out of me in my own home by the same ghost that attacked me then, so—"

My mouth snapped shut as Dylan whipped out his cellphone and began filming me. He flicked his fingers across the screen, zooming in on my face, scanning my wounds. My anger flared white-hot. *Is he kidding me right now?* Bile rose, coating my throat, shoving any remaining fear to the side. My fingers curled into fists, nails biting into my palms, the bruised muscles of my forearms aching in protest.

"If you don't tell him to fuck off—" Jules threatened.

"You said that same ghost came to find you at home?" Dylan grabbed my arm *again* and pushed me six inches over so that I was standing within the orange glow of a streetlight. I smacked his hand away as he continued. "How badly are you injured? Tell me what that was like, what are you going to do now?"

"Stay. Away. From. Me," I growled, pushing as much threat into my words as I could. I shoved past him and stalked toward the train, positive that the ice on the street was melting in my wake. Behind me, I heard the satisfying sound of Dylan's phone clattering to the frozen sidewalk, his subsequent yelp, and Julian's triumphant cackle.

AFTER WE HAD traveled several stops on the train, Jules was fairly certain we had temporarily lost the Jimani. I tried to assess the damage to my body. While I was sure that the fluorescent lights did me no favors, peering at the disheveled girl reflected in the scratched windows had me doubting that even the most sophisticated filters and softest lighting would have eased the impact. A bruise was already forming along my jaw, blood crusted the side of my nose, and there was a cut across my temple near my right eye. Not to mention my hair was partially matted where yesterday's wound had reopened. It looked like I had tried to style it with a juniper bush.

My image disappeared and reformed as streetlights whisked by on the other side. Jules plopped down next to me, following my gaze. I blew out a breath. His reflection nodded at me.

"You do look like shit."

"Thanks, I wasn't sure."

"Here to confirm."

I sighed and tried to tug a few twigs from my hair, wincing as my shoulder protested. I hoped I hadn't seriously damaged it when I crashed into the tub.

"Stop. Let me do it; you're hurt." He stood and sorted through the detritus that was my hair.

"Someone will see shit being levitated from my head," I protested weakly. I really didn't care what anyone saw.

"No one is in this car. Let me try to get what I can before that changes."

I closed my eyes and let him wrest foliage from my tangles. I let go of any concerns about what anyone else might see. I let go of worrying about the energy it was costing him. I took all the pain my body was throwing at me, categorized it, then packed it up into a box to deal with later. I had to think.

Julian is my brother. This explains why he's been with me for so long. It explains why I've felt comfortable with him. It explains his tendency to be bossy and my tendency to rebel against it. But why does the Jimani know his name?

Treat the cause, not the symptom.

I'd been working on symptoms. Keeping the ghosts that I could suddenly see away. Running away from the Jimani, trying to level out my feelings so nothing would sense them. Going to the ghost hunters like I would down a cold medicine. Lovonia wasn't really treating the cause either. She was like physical therapy, concerned with helping me build the strength to survive these new circumstances.

Who is the Jimani? Why is he after us?

From what I understood, ghosts tended to fixate on people that they could manipulate to get what they wanted. Had the Jimani figured out that I could see him that day in the coffee shop and been looking for us ever since? But that didn't explain how he knew Julian's name. Then again, those Oracles Jules had mentioned knew things about the people they tormented long before they crossed paths with them. Perhaps he had gleaned that Julian was my brother and had known he could toy with both human and ghost emotions by targeting us simultaneously. Then if he destroyed me, he may as well have both our souls, as Julian's was somehow tethered to mine. I gritted my teeth. I would not let that happen.

"How do you destroy a Jimani?" I asked Julian, opening my eyes. "Oh, that looks better actually, thanks."

There was a small circle of pine needles and twigs ringing our area. My hair, although not at its best, at least wouldn't attract attention. I carefully gathered it into a bun, my movements slow and limited. I had definitely fucked up my shoulder.

"I don't know if it's possible to destroy a Jimani," Julian mused, watching my painful hair styling attempt. He held one hand behind my injured shoulder, ready to support my arm if it failed.

"It has to be," I said through clenched teeth, finally securing the bun. "If he made himself, it must be possible to unmake him."

Jules blinked at me.

I wet my finger and rubbed a bloodstain on my jeans. "Energy can neither be created nor destroyed. Only converted from one form to another. Basic physics." I raised an eyebrow at him. "Or did you skip that class?"

Julian muttered something about physics being boring. "Wait, so you want to convert the Jimani?"

"Didn't he convert himself? Isn't that what you said? All ghosts start out the same and then they become . . . whatever? Like, you attached yourself to me, and since you're an Aural spirit, you gradually became my protector, or whatever, because you decided that's what I needed or what you wanted to be to me. If he's become this, then, I dunno maybe we can . . . unbecome him . . ."

"We're heading to Lovonia's . . ." Jules realized.

"She knows more than she's letting on." I leaned back against the wall of the car and stretched my legs across two other seats, not giving a shit for once if I was taking up too much space. "And I'm tired of being left behind."

The train ride seemed to last ages. I agreed to change to the Green Line to save time. I didn't want to open us up to any chance of the Jimani homing in on us before I was ready. Julian kept up a constant stream of conversation, talking about nothing in increasingly higher frequencies as we neared the spot where Joe had died. I eventually told him to be quiet.

That I was fine.

Liar.

I watched him stand where Joe had stood, watching me. Concerned. Waiting to see if I would break down or get angry. The lights flashed by just as they had the night of the accident, illuminating Julian's dark hair just as they had highlighted Joe's blond, although the sun had set long ago. I tensed as we approached the corner, heart pounding in my ears, but this time the train slowed. We rounded the curve as we should have weeks ago. I tried to look down at the spot where we had crashed, but it flashed by too quickly.

Then it was over. And it was just another train ride.

❦ ❦ ❦ ❦

LOVONIA'S STORE WAS very clearly closed when we got there, but I knocked anyway. For an obnoxiously long time. Julian was ready to go inside himself and open the door for me just so I could dodge pneumonia when she finally responded to my pounding. She took one look at us, nodded, then stepped aside to let us in.

The scents hit me all at once. Patchouli, candle wax, fast-food gyros, vintage wooden floors. My shoulders sagged. The adrenaline I had been running on abandoned me, leaving me drained. I was no longer afraid of this place. Somehow, it had come to mean answers, safety, and understanding. I walked two feet into the room before my knees buckled with exhaustion and my kneecaps cracked against the floor.

I squeezed my eyes shut against the jolt to my skeleton, all my injuries protesting loudly. I didn't even try to stand up. I let my feet splay out, my butt hitting the ground. I pressed my palms into my knees, digging my nails into my damp jeans, willing all the aches to settle down again as Julian crouched down in front of me.

"Raely?"

I shook my head, keeping my eyes shut and taking deep breaths. "I just need to sit here for a minute."

In the background, Lovonia was moving from one area of the room to the other. She sounded like she was reciting psalms, a kind of toneless chanting. I recognized none of the words. Probably putting extra protection spells on the place now that we were inside. *Well, good,* I thought. *Hope they're stronger than mine were.*

Julian rubbed my uninjured shoulder for a moment, then I felt him move away. As Lovonia's chanting slowed, I heard Jules catching her up on his name and history, along with how the Jimani had found us and how we had tried—and utterly failed—to fight him. How terrified he was that I would be killed.

My heart squeezed as I listened to Jules beg this woman to help me.

"She tried, but she doesn't know how," he said as she muttered enchantments and scattered . . . *something* beneath the windows. "Sometimes she has a good hit, but I know she doesn't know where it came from and . . . that thing wants to kill her. I can tell. It wants to kill her and probably take her soul. And it wants to scare her while it does it. Please. Please, anything you can do. You've done a lot already, I know. We'll find a way to make it up to you. I promise. Please. I don't want my sister to die like—"

"Like you did?" Lovonia finally spoke. She dusted off her hands. Whatever she had been sprinkling around the perimeter of the room darkened her striped pajama pants.

Julian didn't say anything. He stared at his shoes. Next to her, he still looked like he was illuminated by the only sunbeam to exist at 9 p.m. indoors on a Thursday.

"You do not want her to die scared and defenseless like you did." Lovonia was pointing at Julian now. "Yes or no?"

My insides were coming to life again. My buddy Anger scratched against my sternum, lighting a little fire in my belly, stoked by Lovonia's insensitivity. *How dare she.* Muscles protesting every movement, I forced myself to my feet.

"No, I don't," Jules replied.

"Leave him alone," I snapped. I wanted to stride forward, but all I could muster was a grumpy hobble. "How would you know how he felt when he died? And Jules, stop agonizing over my hypothetical impending death."

Lovonia wasn't fazed. For someone who had been pulled out of her nighttime routine and surprised in her pajamas by a battered twenty-something and her ghostly brother, she was remarkably unflappable. "Let me ask you the same question, *cher*. What do you know about your brother's death?"

"It was an accident."

"Do you believe that?"

"I wasn't there, I don't think. At least, I don't remember it. My mom said it was an accident, and she has no reason to lie."

"But she never left you again." Her unblinking coal-black eyes locked on to mine. Something clicked.

"The Jimani?"

She nodded. Her gaze intensified.

A chill ripped through me. The Jimani was an old ghost. How long had he wrapped himself in negative energy? For all I knew, he'd already absorbed a few other hapless souls.

"I need to get stronger," I said to Lovonia. "Fast. I need to get rid of him for good."

LOVONIA PUT ME on the couch in her apartment above the shop. She added protection spells on that floor also. I offered to help, but she refused, saying that spells themselves left the mark of the caster and it was best if my signature was hidden. I was forbidden from touching windows, door knobs that led outside, and any air vents, faucets, or—highly annoying—toilet handles. Anything that caused an exit to the outside world might carry a signature.

Lovonia left one faucet dripping, which she said was better for the pipes anyway in this cold, and told me just to shut the toilet lid if I used it and she would flush it herself in the morning. She had to turn on and off the water for me to shower.

"This stinks," I complained to Jules in a whisper, nestled on the couch in a T-shirt of Lovonia's that was like a dress on me. I watched the snow float past a streetlight through a crack in the curtains above.

Julian had stretched out along the back of the couch and was also watching the snow. He turned his head. "It's only for the night."

"Is it?" I asked. "How long until I'm able to handle this thing? How long until I learn enough? Also, I missed work today. I hope I still have a job." The guilt of this realization had given me an extra dose of crabby.

"Can you tell them you were sick?"

"I can, but I should have called before. I'll have to think of something better."

"You could just send them a picture of your face and tell them you were mugged."

I chuckled, because sadly, he was right. "Okay, remind me in the morning. I'll take one and send it to Luck and see what he thinks I should say. They'll probably want a police report."

My heart hung in my chest like a lead balloon when I thought about Luck. I'd left him high and dry behind the bar. He was probably mad at me. And I didn't exactly want him to see a picture of me looking craptastic.

"Just tell him you were freaked out and ran to a friend's house. Tell him it happened right after the funeral. Which it did." He sighed. "I felt how upset you were. I'm sorry I didn't show up."

"You told me that you weren't supposed to," I said, patting his arm. That small contact was still satisfying.

"That's right . . ." he trailed off, staring out at the snow. "I remember now . . ."

I waited. I counted thirty seconds. "You remember why ghosts aren't supposed to go to gravesites?"

He just nodded.

I pushed myself a little higher up on the wadded-up blanket I was using as a pillow against the couch arm. "So tell me. Is it because the dead who are moving on are supposed to say goodbye to their families? Because that's . . . what Joe did . . ."

"Yeah." Jules swallowed and crossed his arms behind his head, staring fixedly at the orange of the streetlight and the snow swirling past it. "I'm sorry about Joe. Do you want to talk about it?"

I sat all the way up, curling my knees toward my chest. "No . . ." I put a hand on his elbow. "I want to talk about you. I want to know what you remember."

He didn't speak. We were both still. Just the snow flurrying by, my hand resting on Julian's elbow, the sound of the radiator fizzing to life, then . . .

"I remember my funeral."

I brought up my other hand and wrapped both around Julian's arm, but I said nothing. Julian's gaze remained fixed on the streetlight.

"I didn't remember it until today. Until Lovonia—" He pulled his arm out of my grasp and sat up. For a moment, he obscured the shaft of light the gap in the curtains had provided. His edges were gilded in the apricot glow, and I was once again reminded of an anime character.

Then he slid off the couch and plopped down to the cushion near my feet. He still wouldn't look at me. I held very still.

"I think it's instinctive, or something, to say goodbye. At least, that's what I started to do. And I was only two." He looked down at his hands, pressed his fingertips together. His eyes flicked to mine for an instant before settling back on his hands. "I remember saying goodbye to a lot of people, and I wasn't upset. I said goodbye to aunts, uncles, grandpa . . . I went to say goodbye to Mom, and that was hard . . . but I was still okay. And she looked . . . better. But she hugged you tighter. Pulled you onto her lap. I was about to say goodbye to you . . . and you looked at me, you smiled and waved . . . and . . . I just decided to stay."

"Do you . . ." My voice rasped, I swallowed. "Do you remember the Jimani . . . the day you . . . fell?"

He shook his head. "I don't remember that day. But I think you're right. I'm sure he was there. There's a . . . feeling. Maybe I'll remember more. All I know is I wanted to be with you. I felt like you needed me."

"I do seem to have become incredibly high-maintenance as of late."

He cracked a smile. "You've just got a lot to learn in a short amount of time. You'll get it. We both will."

"Or we'll die trying."

18

THE NEXT MORNING, I HAD JULIAN HELP ME take a picture of my face, which did look worse. He was so thrilled with his new ability to both hold and operate the phone that he insisted on taking pictures of my scalp wounds so that I could fully appreciate them. I relented and asked for shots of my back too. There were enormous bruises blooming where I had landed in the tub.

I did have a few missed calls from Luck and one voicemail saying that I'd missed my shift and he hoped everything was okay. I sent him the best (worst) picture of my face and told him that I had been assaulted and to call me when he had a chance.

He called immediately.

I answered on the first ring, pleased that my voice sounded tired and a little scratchy. My heart picked up speed when I heard him speak.

"Oh my God, what is this picture? Did you really get mugged? Are you okay? Did you call the police? Did they catch the guy? Did anyone help you?"

Shit. I really should have gotten my story straight in my head before texting him. I decided to stick as close to the truth as possible. "No one saw it, and I don't know who it was. A guy who followed me home. I . . . I don't think he took anything, but I guess I don't know . . . as soon as I could get away from him, I just ran to a friend's house."

"Holy shit, what did the police say?"

"I . . . haven't called the police."

"Why? Raely, seriously!" Genuine concern colored his voice, and a fragment of tension left my shoulders. He didn't think I was lying. He didn't think I was making it up. *Which you're not,* I reminded myself.

"I know, it sounds stupid. I just . . . I don't have any witnesses or evidence. I don't even have a good physical description. What are they going to do? They probably wouldn't even believe me."

"Raely." His tone changed. Gentled. "You know you could tell me if something was happening. I won't judge you, and I can try to help you figure things out. No one has the right to beat you up like that."

I'd forgotten that he knew about my dad. I closed my eyes and stifled a sigh. "I—thank you. For saying that. And I do know. But I promise I don't know who this guy was, and I—"

"So this has nothing to do with that guy who's been coming to the bar asking for you?" Luck's voice hardened. Whoever this person was, he didn't like him.

"What guy?" As soon as the words were out of my mouth, I groaned inwardly. Of course.

"Some guy named Dylan. Claims you went on a date with him. Left your coat at his house. I told him if you weren't returning his calls then it was probably an indication that the date didn't go as well as he thought, and he should back off. Not that it's any of my business, but I think you deserve better."

Julian looked over his shoulder from where he had been practicing floating books across the room at unbelievably fast speeds and gave me a thumbs-up. *I like Luck,* he mouthed.

He can't hear ghosts, you can talk out loud, I mouthed back.

He flipped me off.

"Dylan's a jerk, and I didn't go on a date with him," I told Luck, switching my phone to the ear farthest from Julian. "I had what I thought was a . . . meeting with him about some work—potential work—and he did pay for the meal and kissed me afterward, but it wasn't something I . . . invited." *God, Raely, just stop talking.*

"That doesn't sound great, Raely."

Julian gave me a meaningful look and tapped his nose.

I rolled my eyes. "Yeah, I know, my choice of company has been suspect lately."

Jules glared, then resumed Harry Pottering his books around.

"Well, if I see the guy again, I'm having him shown out."

"That's absolutely fine with me," I said. "Luck, I hate to do this, but I don't think I'm going to make it in tonight either. My shoulder is killing me, and you've seen my face. I think I'm just going to lay low at my friend's house for a day or so until I know if this guy is really following me or . . . or what. I know I should probably call George, but I don't have his number."

"That's fine, Raely, I'll let George know what's going on. Just please, please file a police report, okay? This is serious. I don't like seeing you get hurt."

My stomach swooped a bit. "Okay, I'll . . ." I stopped. I didn't like outright lying to Luck, and I had no intention of going to the police. "I'll talk to my friend about it and see what she says."

"Good. Can I call you in a couple of days to see how you're doing? Or will you call me and let me know?"

"Yeah, of course. Either. Both. Whichever happens first." My cheeks warmed. I had a ridiculous urge to smile.

"Okay. Please take care, Raely."

"I will. Thanks, Luck."

I ended the call and stared at the phone.

A book whizzed by my head. "Why are you smiling at your phone?" Another book flew toward me.

I caught it. "I'm *not* smiling!" I threw the book back at Jules. It hit him in the arm with a satisfying *thunk*. "*Now* I'm smiling."

⁓⁓⁓⁓

WE STAYED INSIDE that day, mostly in Lovonia's apartment, so she could handle whatever business came her way. She didn't want either of us making contact with any customers, lest some of our *essence* float out with them and alert the Jimani to our presence. Eventually, our essence would become mixed with hers, she said, and it would leak out, but she would buy us what time she could.

I worked on finding myself as I had in my fugue state, but it was harder while conscious. Julian was better by leaps and bounds, which was a relief to both of us, but my improvement had plateaued. I was able to touch him, and most of the time I was able to block his attempts to touch me, but tossing things at him was hit-or-miss, and I couldn't move things like he did.

"Is that even a thing I'm supposed to know how to do?" I asked as I tried so hard to lift a pen without touching it that I was sure I'd bust a blood vessel. "Like, you're a ghost, you can levitate shit, fine, but humans don't. We don't . . . levitate . . . shit. I give up." I slumped, panting slightly.

"Everything is connected, Raely," he said patiently, while an outdated globe spun lazily in the air in front of us. "You're already affecting things on both planes. It's not a huge leap to access this third plane also."

Every now and then, I would get a glimpse. Everything would glow slightly, like Jules did, and moving *anything* felt easy. But it was just a flash, and then it would be gone. My first flash came after Luck's phone call, when I threw the book at Jules. Right after that, he swore that I levitated the phone in my hand and shot it at him. I thought I'd just tossed it at him. We eventually agreed to disagree.

We were still hard at work when Lovonia came up around lunchtime with some sandwiches.

"Lovonia, Jules thinks I can levitate shit like he does, can you please tell him that humans—"

I shut up when she levitated the sandwiches over to us. Julian picked one up, held it toward me and winked. I took it automatically, then turned to gape at her.

She chuckled. "Listen to your brother. He's been doing it all for longer. Use *all* of yourself. I'll come back later." She chuckled again as she went back to the shop.

⁒⁒⁒⁒

ONCE I KNEW it was a real possibility, I was determined to make it happen. After finishing the sandwiches, I tried to levitate the plate but eventually had to admit I was just tossing it into the air. After not catching it a couple of times, Jules suggested that I switch to something less breakable to avoid destroying Lovonia's flatware and getting glass all over her apartment.

"Explain it *better*," I said through clenched teeth. I was coated with sweat and had levitated nothing. We'd been working on the couch cushions, which Julian was able to pull on and off the couch without touching.

"I'm trying to explain it—"

"No, you're saying the same thing over and over again. I'm not getting it that way. You have to try saying it differently. Or showing me differently. Haven't you ever taught anyone anything before?"

He folded his arms and stared at me.

I deflated. "Sorry, of course you haven't. I'm just really frustrated—"

"No, I have. I taught you how to climb a tree." He was still staring at me, his head cocked to the side. "You were trying to do it like these older boys were doing it, but your arms weren't as strong, and you were much shorter. I showed you how to get up."

"Oh. I don't remember that . . ."

He was still staring, but no longer seeing me, gazing into the middle distance like a statue. I was about to say something sassy about him posing for a mostly-dead fashion magazine, when he unfroze all at once, crossed to me, pulled off his right shoe, and held it out. "Touch it."

I raised my eyebrow at him, but I did as he said and poked the luminous shoe. It shifted in his hand.

"Good, now here, take it."

"You want me to hold your stinky shoe?"

"It's not stinky—I don't have body odor—and yes, hold it please." He thrust it toward me impatiently.

I grabbed the tongue of the shoe between my thumb and forefinger.

He removed his hand. "Now, what are you holding?"

". . . your shoe?"

"What are you holding it with?"

"My . . . essence?"

"You're holding *what* with your essence?"

I blinked at him. "We've been over this."

"Answer the question."

I sighed. "I'm holding your shoe with my essence."

"What's my shoe actually made of?"

My insides froze. I stared at him. I stared at the shoe dangling from between my fingers. Back at Jules.

"Answer the question."

"I . . . I don't know what your shoe is made—"

"Yes, you do. Think. What could *my shoe* that looks just like *your* old shoes possibly be made of?"

My insides thawed as electricity crawled through my veins. "Your shoe is made of . . . your essence?"

He nodded. "And what else?"

What else? What else could there possibly be? I looked back at the shoe, pulled it closer to my face, studying it. Then clutched it with both hands. The shoelace . . . the aglet was missing on one lace and had been replaced with blue electrical tape. Just like my old shoes. ". . . and *my* essence?"

Jules's face split into a grin. He nodded slowly. "You loved those shoes so much."

I set the shoe across the palm of my hand, gazing at it like a piece of leprechaun gold.

"Use your essence. Find the bit of *you* in the shoe and then, without moving your hand, *push* it back to me." He stepped back and held out a hand, palm up, waiting to receive.

I nodded. And somehow it was easier to drop into myself. The room warmed and glowed as I dropped my hand from beneath Julian's shoe and *pushed* it away. It rolled over and over, but it slowly traveled the two feet over to Jules.

He caught it, smiling. "Sometimes you do better when you learn backwards. You had to climb down the tree first, before you were able to climb up without help." He pushed the shoe back toward me. I stopped it without touching it.

It floated six inches from me. I pushed it back.

"Everything has some kind of essence," Jules said. "The shoe was easy because there's a bit of both of us in it. But you can move anything." I was concentrating so much on the shoe, I didn't overthink it when Jules floated a couch cushion toward me, I just pushed it back.

Then I squeaked.

"Don't stop!"

I clung to my focus, grinning like a fool, as we pushed the shoe and the cushion back and forth.

"Now, without dropping these, try to pick up something else. Anything," Jules suggested.

I nodded, my breath quickening as I fought to maintain my tenuous grasp on this new skill while daring to glance around for something else to lift. A trickle of sweat skated down my left temple, but I ignored it. The first thing my eyes landed on was the empty sandwich plate. I hesitated, trying to find the right moment to reach out for it without dropping the cushion or the shoe.

"You can use your hands if you need to, just to start with," Jules said.

I nodded again. Sometimes it was easier for me to reach with my hands—like a conductor or a Dr. Strange wannabe—when I was trying to direct my essence. Julian wanted me to be able to do it without "waving around" eventually. It was a crutch and a tell, he said. Since he apparently knew everything with his "I'm two minutes older."

I extended one hand toward the shoe and cushion, continuing to *push* them gently back toward Jules when they came at me, then I reached the other toward the plate and flicked my fingers upward. It lifted.

"Eeee!"

"Focus."

My cheeks ached from smiling as I slowly guided the plate into rotation with the shoe and the cushion.

"That's it," Jules encouraged, "almost there—"

My phone rang.

I flinched and lost everything. All three items flew in opposite directions. Julian managed to catch the plate one inch from smashing into the radiator. His shoe flew through my head, disorienting me, and the cushion smacked into the door with a surprisingly loud thunk that I was certain was audible downstairs. I scrambled to track down and silence my still-ringing phone.

I located it against the far wall, hooked up to a spare charger of Lovonia's.

All lingering warm fuzzies from my successful levitation exercise vanished when I laid eyes on the screen.

Dylan.

I jabbed the button to silence the call then sent it straight to voice-mail, with Julian peeking over my shoulder.

He made a sound like a pissed-off tomcat.

I plunked down on the floor next to the outlet, feeling the effects of my levitation efforts, and wiped the sweat from my hairline. The voicemail notification pinged. Jules joined me, scooting closer as I put the phone on speaker and played the message.

"Raely, Dylan here. Look, I've been trying to do this nicely, but I don't appreciate being shut out so rudely. We had a verbal agreement. You've agreed to let us take some footage in exchange for my team looking into your issue. We're not making any money on your case, so obviously we used a snippet to grow our platform. We did not use your name or identify you in any way. Now, we've looked into your problem, and I've offered to meet with you and show you our findings. That offer has been rebuffed. Okay. You've changed your mind or have decided to seek another service. That's your prerogative. However, you still have an obligation to uphold your end of our agreement. I need those re-lease waivers signed so that we can use the footage for our platform as we agreed."

"I never agreed to let him social media me," I muttered, my shoulders creeping toward my ears. "I specifically told him I *didn't* want that."

"I've tried to reach you at work, as I assumed that would be a neutral place to get this business finalized, but your coworker told me that I'm banned from the premises. He's threatened harassment charges, which is just laughable, Raely. It really didn't have to come to this, but I've contacted an attorney, and you'll be hearing from their office unless I hear from you and get these forms signed by the end of the week. Cheers."

I stared at the screen, my jaw dangling unattractively from my face.

"Vomit," Julian said. "Did he actually say 'cheers' instead of good-bye? What is he, faux British?"

"That means he hasn't taken it down." I immediately went and checked Dylan's ghost hunter TikTok page. Not only did the original video have over a million views, he had put up three new ones. Clips from different sections of the footage he had taken after the funeral, set to different music and some run through slo-mo or different effects. They all had over 80K views and climbing. All of me being attacked by the Jimani. Although I could see him on the screen, I knew the average person wouldn't be able to. The sandwiches tried to crawl out of my throat.

"Stop it, put that away." Julian took my phone from me and swiped the app shut. I was impressed that he did that so easily.

"He can't—Is he trying to sue me? He never actually *helped* me even! He can't do that! I'm pretty sure he can't do that. I hope he can't do that."

"Who can't do what? And what was all that noise? I had to tell my customers I had ghosts up here." Lovonia entered, chuckling at herself. "Good for business actually." She was carrying a Brita pitcher and an enormous plastic beer stein from a German street festival. She offered me the stein. "Thirsty?"

"Play her the voicemail from Dylan. That jag."

I gave the smallest eye roll then played the voicemail for Lovonia, drinking deeply from my plastic chalice as she listened. Just hearing Dylan's condescending tone emanating from my phone again raised my ire. I wondered if Lovonia would chastise me for even going to the ghost hunters, but I found that I didn't care if she did. It was nice to have another "adult in the room," for once.

She listened carefully, her normally continuous chuckle complete-ly absent.

She turned to me. "This man has video of you?"

"Yeah, they manipulated me into bringing the Jimani to their house after Joe's funeral and filmed me while it was attacking me. I barely got out. They posted it online—actually, they put up *several videos*—and won't take them down." My stomach flipped. "God, if anyone at work sees that . . ." I prayed Luck wasn't on TikTok.

She nodded, her eyes never leaving mine. "You have a lawyer, yes?"

"Oh. Yeah. James Cantor."

"*Ça c'est bon*, call this lawyer, tell him that these"—she waved her hand around like she was shooing flies—"ghost hunters film you, attack you, then post it to pretend for their . . . platform? He says 'platform?'" She shook her head muttering, "*Moi, j'connais pas* . . . platform."

"I'm supposed to tell a *lawyer* that I was chased by ghosts?" I had drained the stein. Lovonia refilled it.

"You tell him *these people* say they ghosts. They be crazy. Not you. Who gonna believe them? You bring ghosts in. Ha!" She put the empty pitcher down, shaking her head. "Trying to impress this 'platform.' Ha!" She did air quotes around the word "platform."

Julian chuckled. I even smiled a bit.

"Yeah, I could call James. Or email him." I picked up my phone, then sighed. "He's going to want me to go down there."

"You have to go out eventually, cher . . ."

19

WE WERE READY.

Julian and I had worked relentlessly for three days. Lovonia had taught me protection and cloaking spells to conceal my essence as I traveled. They required some concentration, but when I was focused, I could feel it. We'd also learned how to throw shields up across the second dimension. I was thrilled. My levitation wasn't nearly as good as Julian's, but it was getting there, and my pushing and pulling in his dimension was coming along.

Lovonia reminded us that we hadn't been tested under pressure, but admitted that we were greatly improved. I felt ready to at least get to the law office. If the Jimani tried to hit me with a towel rod, I could lift up a shield, pull something out of his dimension, and blast it into him. And Jules was getting so good I literally *felt* my chest inflate with pride.

It was fool proof: Don't give in to fear, fight back, and he'd leave us alone and find someone else to get his fear fix from.

"It makes complete sense," I told Jules, hurling a couch cushion through his dimension and watching it bounce off his shield. "That's what they always tell you in self-defense classes. You know, don't make it easy, make yourself more trouble than you're worth. Same thing with bullies. They don't like it when you fight back."

"Right, and emotions. Just try not to get emotional, and he probably won't even be attracted to you."

I nodded. "We got this. We can fight now. And there's two of us."

Jules and I were priming to leave Lovonia's as if we were heading into a caveman battle. I had so many stones in my pockets and hanging around my neck—not to mention sage stuffed in my boots. I even had rings with stones on them.

"I look like a fucking hippie goth," I said, watching my reflection as we passed the mirror in the hallway. "A hippie goth that very recently got beat over the head with a towel rod."

"Suits you. You should try to maintain the look." Jules smirked.

I elbowed him.

Lovonia was up front to give me the final inspection and see us out. "All charged. Good. Charge them again before you leave the lawyer's offices, if you can. If they need." She glanced outside. It was a bright, clear day. In fact, temperatures in the upper thirties were being rumored. "Lots of sun left. Least popular time for ghost. Although it doesn't really matter."

Helpful.

As I had predicted, James was enthusiastic about my email, but did insist that I come down to the office to fill out paperwork and go over what happened. "You always bring me the best stuff, Raely. This is bonkers. I've checked out this guy's website. GeoCities. Were you even born when GeoCities was big? Doesn't matter. When can you come in?"

Lovonia planned to use our absence to purge her place of our essences and do a "reset," which would make us harder to track to the area if we came back. She did say *if*, which was slightly disconcerting. But I supposed she felt that if we were successful in fighting off a Jimani attack, I might be able to return to my apartment. She did suggest that if we had enough daylight and felt it was safe, we should stop back by my place to pack a bag. I'm sure she was getting tired of lending me her shirts and the one pair of drawstring shorts she had that could be made to fit me. There was also that day where I wore one of those big shawls she sold as a sarong while we washed my underwear. It took me a minute to get over being underwearless in front of Jules, but I managed.

My bank account was dwindling quickly with a few days off work, but I sprung for a Lyft down to James's office. Although we were ready to throw down, Jules and I both felt that we shouldn't *invite* a Jimani attack. Jules opted to meet me at the office. Lovonia confirmed that the Jimani likely would be more drawn to us when we were together, and it was easy for Jules to slip from one location to another if they weren't too far apart.

My easy bravado dimmed the moment he'd left my side. I spent the ride anxiously looking out of windows and over my shoulder. I didn't pause, tipping the driver and giving him the star rating before he had even fully stopped. I sprang out of the car and up to the door. Jules was inside and opened it for me, sparing me the need to call reception for entry. That was actually one of his most handy qualities. If I ever decided to support myself with burglary, all I would have to do is convince my brother to cooperate. *I must discuss visiting the casino with him at some point,* I mused. *We could rack up some rent money at the blackjack table with him telling me what cards are coming up.*

Helen was a little surprised that she hadn't had to buzz me in. I told her I'd grabbed the door off someone going for a smoke. Since they shared the building with some "advertising goofballs"—James's words—she took that at face value and showed us—me—into the conference room to wait for James. We didn't have to wait long. Helen had only just given me coffee—my first coffee in *days*—when James came bustling in with the usual clipboard of printer paper and the forms I had filled out online. James didn't like lined paper. He scribbled away on his printer paper like he was Picasso. It used to drive me crazy when I was working for him and had to transcribe those notes later into something coherent, but as a client, I kind of enjoyed it. Julian even walked around to James's side of the table so he could watch his scribbles right side up.

"So let's figure out the big thing: Why were you at his place? How did they get you there? And be honest with me."

"Well, you dropped me off there," I said. He froze. Blue pen poised above blank typing paper. Eyebrows slowly encroaching upon hairline.

He pressed a hand to his chest. "*I* dropped you off there?"

"After the funeral," I clarified. "He said I could come by after the funeral. We had . . . well, we had gone out to dinner, which was not a date, but he kissed me at the end of it, kind of aggressively, and . . . anyway, he said I should come over after the funeral." I hated the slow burn that crept over my skin. I dropped my eyes, studying the table's surface. I felt so stupid.

"Okay." James scribbled away. His brusque manner soothed me. "How did he get you to go out to dinner? How did you meet him?"

"I thought I might be seeing a ghost after . . . after the accident. I wasn't . . . sure." I squeezed my eyes shut and sucked in a shaky breath. *He's going to think I'm unhinged.* My embarrassment tossed beneath my skin as if trying to break free. My mouth had gone completely dry. I massaged my temples and cleared my throat several times. I couldn't come unglued right in front of everyone.

James excused himself to grab a bottle of water for me.

"Are you okay?" Jules said.

"No!" I hissed, dropping my hands. "I'm upset, and I feel stupid." I grabbed the edge of my sleeve and swiped at my temples. I was so warm, a little sweat was forming. "I'm really ashamed, and I'm not sure where this is coming from."

"Well, you're probably upset that this dude actually *did* play you and is growing his business by using video of you getting beat to hell. And that a lot of people commenting obviously think you were faking or that you're stupid or crazy. And you're worried that someone you know might see it and think that too."

Wow.

WOW.

He was right, though. Dylan had played me. And he'd tried to keep doing it. Even now, he was trying to coerce me into agreeing to put it all out there publicly. What did he care if everyone thought I was crazy? I was just an actor or a comedian or something, right? We're all easy to buy with some wine and happy to be on film no matter what's happening to us. My stomach turned over, but I straightened in my chair. This was going to be embarrassing, but I would get through it. Kissing me in my courtyard was one thing. He didn't get to use my image and my pain to grow his business. When James came back with the water, I was steadier. I thanked him and took a sip. I explained that Dylan had said he would be able to investigate the ghost issue for me, that I had specifically stated I did not want my likeness to be public, had signed nothing, and that he had encouraged me to come by the house right after the funeral. He had known based on our conversation what funeral I would be going to and had insisted that that's when I would come. It was clear to me now that he was trying to get me at my most emotional.

"Okay, so tell me again what happened when you got in the door." James had called in Sara, his associate, to take notes also. Apparently, this was kind of a big deal.

"I was upset. Visibly upset. I told him I thought someone might be following me. I had seen someone walking up the sidewalk after you dropped me."

"I remember seeing you look to the side and practically sprint to the door. I thought you were just emotional from the funeral." He cleared his throat. "I'm sorry."

"It was not your fault. I thought I was safe there." That wasn't a lie. "Anyway, once I got there, they had cleared the room and had this big taped-off area in the middle. They told me to stay inside of it, or I wouldn't be in the frame. Then they started talking about the meters jumping around and stuff."

James nodded, scribbling. I felt like I was at a press conference. Jules was standing behind James, watching his pen dance across the page, tossing me the occasional nod. Sara was standing near the door, also writing, although she apparently preferred a legal pad. Even Helen lingered in the doorway, initially arriving to bring more coffee but never quite making it back to her desk. I shook myself and pulled my focus back to James.

"I mean, the original video is still up. I emailed him to take it down, but he hasn't. And he's put up more." I swiped open my phone and reluctantly pulled up the first video, sliding my phone across the table to James once I had it going. I hated watching it. I hated hearing it. My shoulders crept up toward my ears as James, Sara, and Helen muttered variations of "my goodness," "good Lord," "holy shit," and even one "oy gevalt!" Julian's face grew stony as he watched the videos through again over James's shoulder.

"My God, Raely, were you hurt?" James asked, passing my phone to me after watching all four videos twice. "What was that thing that fell on your head?"

"A waffle iron," I muttered.

"Do you have a picture of that wound?"

"I still have the actual wound." I pulled my hair to the side. James jumped up and motioned to Sara. "Do you have a picture of this, Raely?"

"I probably took a picture of that when I took a picture of your other head stuff," Jules reminded me. I swiped open my phone.

"I think so." I pulled up the photo app and scrolled through the recent pictures.

"Whoa, whoa, whoa, whoa, what is *this*?" James plucked the phone from my hand. The image of my banged-up face stared up from the screen. James's eyes raked my face. The yellowing remains of those bruises were still evident.

"I don't actually know who did that."

They all stared at me. Even Julian. Like he was just watching to see what the fuck I would come up with.

"I went to visit my mom after the funeral . . . after everything, and when I came back to my apartment . . ." My cheeks flamed, and I couldn't keep my fingers from fidgeting with the edge of my sweater, but I plowed on, knowing there was no way to just brush this under the rug. "The lights cut out in the whole place, and I got scared and ran into the bathroom. Something—someone, dressed all in black, ripped the towel rod off the wall and hit me with it. I fell into the tub, but I got away. I was outside trying to get the hell away from there when I ran into Dylan."

They were all staring at me. My voice audibly shook despite my attempts to steady it, but I finished with a description of my confrontation with Dylan.

"Raely, did you file a police report?" James asked.

"No. I—I know this is bad, but I just didn't think anyone would believe me." I dropped my gaze to my antsy fingers and took slow, deep breaths. "I don't think Dylan was behind that attack, but I really want him to leave me alone, and I want those videos taken down."

I felt Julian next to me. "I know you hate talking about this, but you have to protect yourself. You can't let people fuck you over just because you can see things that other people can't. You're not lying about anything, really. You have nothing to be ashamed of. You've been traumatized, and it's okay to be upset about it. And fuck Dylan. He's the one who brought this shit down."

I opened my eyes, dropped my shoulders, and gave Jules the barest wink.

"We can get this guy off your back," James promised. "At the very least, he owes you damages for what was done to you on this video. Forward me the email that tells him to take the video down, and the link to the video. All the videos. Everything will be time-stamped. We'll have you get a statement from your coworker stating that Mr. Barrett came by several times looking for you. At the very least, we can get an order of protection and let this guy know he's to keep his distance. There's nothing they can do to you. If any legal representation contacts you, tell them they're to speak to me. You have my card. In the meantime, send us those injury pictures—"

The lights flickered.

"That's hysterical, given what we've just been talking about," James said.

Then they cut out completely.

"Oh God," I breathed. *Not now.*

"Nobody panic." James pulled out his phone and hit the flashlight app. "Crazy coincidence, but let's all keep calm and head to the exit. Go get some pastries or something while the city takes its sweet time fixing things."

"Oooo, it sure got cold quickly, didn't it?" Helen was rubbing her arms. She snatched her coat off the back of her chair as we trooped toward the door.

"Jules . . ." I exhaled in the barest whisper. I could see my breath.

"Start finding your essence, just like we practiced."

What about the three clueless people here with us? I wanted to ask. My mind was going a million miles a minute. I had *just* told them about two ghost attacks. In both of them, the lights had gone out, and it had gotten cold. Maybe I could get into the stairwell first, fight him off before he did anything.

Ludicrous, Raely, terrible plan. I tried over and over to bring the second dimension into focus, but I was failing, failing, failing. I'd never practiced while upset. My legs were shaking.

Stop stop stop! I told myself. *Stop being afraid!* It was about as effective as you'd imagine.

The advertising goofballs were spilling out of their office into the hallway. They were in high spirits, tossing around some kind of glow-in-the-dark ball with a logo on it and even whooping occasionally. I heard James mutter something that sounded like "idiots" under his breath as we all clumped up near the entrance to the stairwell.

"There you are . . ."

Goosebumps erupted from my neck to my arms. The voice had come from . . . everywhere. My eyes found Julian's, and I wondered if mine were just as wide. In his, I could see a glint of determination. I tried to dredge up some of my own.

I glanced over my shoulder: Nothing but blackness. I knew there were some untenanted offices in that direction, but currently there was nothing but darkness and a small, faraway exit sign at the other end of the hallway.

No sign of the owner of the disembodied voice. The trembling spread from my legs until my entire being was vibrating. One piece of hair had come untucked from my ponytail and hung near my eye. I could see it shivering, a physical display of my lack of control. I pushed it back.

"Don't worry, Raely, I know it's a little eerie considering what you've been through, and these assholes have pushed us to the back of the line, but we'll get you out," James said in a slightly-louder-than-conversational tone of voice, earning a couple of goofball glares.

"I'm fine," I panted out between rapid, shallow breaths. I wiped my sweaty palms on my coat, fishing clumsily for stones in my pockets, desperately trying to reel my emotions back in.

"Clearly," Jules said flatly. "Clearly we're all fucking fine."

Something crashed in an office behind us. I jumped, one of the advertising girls shrieked, and a few of them giggled as they pressed into the stairwell in a little knot of bodies.

"OhGodohgodohgodohgod," I whispered. Once again, I tried to slow my breathing.

James patted my shoulder. "Don't let these hysterical children and their dramatics get to you, Raely, we're almost there."

"Pull it together!" Julian's advice.

Helen and Sara were already descending, James stood just inside the stairwell, pulling the open door toward him and gesturing for me to precede him. I took two steps forward, that much closer to safety, and then the floor beneath my feet trembled. At first I thought it was my own shaking, but the vibrations cascaded up my legs, intensifying as if an earthquake had struck. My eyes locked with James's and I watched as his knees bent and his other arm swung forward to grip the door as the shuddering off-balanced him.

"Go!" Jules yelled. The emergency lights winked out, then back on, then out . . . then on. The shrieking from the goofballs was no longer accompanied by giggling.

I lunged for the stairwell just as the door was ripped from James's hand and slammed shut in my face. The emergency lights went out for good.

20

I'D BEEN A NANOSECOND TOO LATE. I banged on the now-closed door and pushed at the handle bar, which didn't give a centimeter. "C'mon, c'mon, c'*mon*!" I panted. I yanked out my phone and flicked the flashlight app on.

"Raely!" James's yell was muffled by the steel of the door.

"I can't open it!" I hollered back, unable to prevent fear from ratcheting my voice up an octave. I struck the handle again in frustration. It held as if frozen. My stomach twisted. Everywhere not illuminated by my phone—or Jules—was pitch-black. I backed up and kicked the handle three times with all my might. Nothing. I was panting, a bead of sweat trickled into my eye. *Don't lose control, you've been* training *for this.*

"The door must've gotten jammed somehow. Go to the other end!" James yelled. "There's another stairwell there! Don't panic. I'll tell the responders that you're in here. If you want, just go back, sit in my office, and take a nap. This will be over before you know it."

I giggled hysterically at the thought of attempting a nap right now. "Okay. Okay, I'll try the other door!"

I spun away from the door to face Jules. My eyes burned. My lungs seemed to hold less air.

"You have. To pull. Yourself. Together." He planted his hands on my shoulders and shook me slightly with each word. "Close your eyes and try to find it."

I nodded. Closed my eyes. Took a steady breath.

"*Together . . .*"

My eyes flew open.

Jules stared back at me, deep blue boring into dark brown. He swallowed. "C'mon. Just try."

I released the amethyst I had been clutching in my pocket and grabbed onto the bloodstone at my throat. Courage. I narrowed my focus to nothing but Jules. Seeing nothing beyond his dark shaggy hair and dilated blue eyes. I could almost hear him thinking, *We can do this.*

There it was. The hallway became luminous. I felt it. I had a grip on it. I sat down into myself. I nodded, and Julian released my shoulders. As one, we turned toward the dark hallway. Ready.

The Jimani flowed toward us. His fleshless lips were pulled back in a skeletal grin. He seemed to glide on air, his coat billowing around him, his arms outstretched, as if in greeting. He was even less solid than the last time I had encountered him. His trench coat was nothing but swirling shadows. Nothing but darkness where his feet should have been. Aside from his thin, white fingers, the brightest spots were the hard, glinting sparks where eyes would normally rest.

I was ready. I pulled up a shield in front of us, floor to ceiling. It was a beautiful thing. Golden, glittering, transparent yet solid. I *pushed* and it expanded to either wall. He was completely cut off from us.

"Nice," Jules said.

The Jimani laughed, a deep, harsh sound that bounced off the concrete walls and ceilings of the building. A spritz of static danced up my spine. I tested my shield, it was strong. Why was he laughing so hard?

Jules shifted closer and slightly to the front.

The Jimani lifted his face skyward and thrust his arms up, the burst of movement incongruous with his usual, flowing motions. His brittle fingers curled in toward his palms as if he were gripping an invisible handle. Slowly, he pulled both elbows in toward his sides, his gaze returning to us, his grin widening.

The walls and ceiling bowed inward.

My secondary vision shuttered. I bolted, ripping open the door to the advertising office and hurtling inside. Jules followed. I glanced over my shoulder and saw my shield guttering. The Jimani continued to cackle, his gaze never leaving us.

"Where are you going? There's no way out!" Julian threw up a glittery, silver shield of his own behind us, but it wasn't as substantial as mine. For whatever reason, when I could do it, my shields were the bomb.

"I dunno, I dunno . . ." I gasped, looking around in desperation. We should have been attacking. The plan was to *attack*. But him being able to warp the fucking walls and shake the floor wasn't part of the plan.

I had never been in this office before. It was an open concept, with cool ad office accoutrements, like a pool table and a snack area. Their windows faced an alley toward the river. Slightly nicer view, as you could catch a glimpse of the river between buildings, but still an alley. Their office was longer than the law office. It spanned the length of the building.

Then I saw it. The tiny flickering exit sign. They had a fire escape.

I fumbled for my center, grasping the amethyst and pulling from its energy. The second dimension settled into focus as the Jimani shattered Julian's shield. I pelted toward the escape. Julian tossed small shields behind us as we fled—nothing large enough to block our pursuer completely, but they would slow him down. I *pulled*, and a large box flew from a high filing cabinet, flying over our heads, bursting open as it sailed.

I spun around and saw several balls flying out of it, glowing as soon as they made contact with anything. I *grabbed* as many as I could, solidified them in the Jimani's dimension, then flung them hard.

His cackling silenced as they pounded into him. I'd bought us time.

We burst through the door to the fire escape. My eyelids slammed shut, momentarily blinded by the brightness.

I didn't hesitate. I grabbed onto the escape ladder just like in the movies, swung my feet onto the bottom rung, hit the release, and rode it to the alley floor. The ladder slammed into the pavement. I fell off, butt smacking to the ground. James was there immediately, scraping me off the concrete and telling the fireman near him I was the one who'd been trapped in the inexplicably shuddering building.

"We gotta go. We gotta go!" Julian was motioning with his hands as if that would speed things up.

"No, thank you, I'm fine. I'm just spooked. I don't need medical attention," I told the firemen. Two of them were trying to get me to sit down so they could check me out. I tried to catch my breath. I couldn't stop glancing up. Any second he'd appear.

"Are you sure, Raely?" I could tell James was going to insist.

Julian was practically jogging in place. I cut James off as politely as I could. "I just really want to get home after all that. Really. I'm fine. Very tired. Need a nap and to be somewhere . . . safe."

"Let me call you a Lyft at least." James was already punching my address into his phone. How was he so organized? "Look there's one . . . not even a minute away."

Jules nodded. "Take it. I'll see you there." He vanished. No doubt to check out the apartment before I arrived.

"Okay, yeah, that'd be great, thanks." I pasted on a smile. While I waited for the Lyft, I forced myself to answer a few of the fireman's questions and proved that I could keep my gaze on his fingertip while he waved it back and forth.

I stumbled into the Lyft, taking out my remaining charged stones and placing them into the door handles. I took a few sage leaves and placed them on the floorboards near the door. This time I wasn't shy about muttering the protection spells that Lovonia had taught me. On the way over, I hadn't wanted to freak the driver out. Now, I didn't give a shit. He tried to make some hesitant small talk to which I replied, "I'm really sorry, I've just been attacked, so I feel a strong need to pray right now. I don't want to freak you out, but I hope you understand."

He nodded. "Uhhh, yeah, sure thing! You do you!"

I continued chanting protection and cloaking spells all the way home. I hoped James's star rating didn't get docked because of my performance. I made sure to take the sage and the stones with me when I got out of the car.

My apartment building looked more foreboding than ever.

And Julian was nowhere to be seen.

I SPRINTED TO the entrance, the stones and sage clutched in my hands. I managed to unlock the main door without losing anything and pelted up the stairs, hoping that Julian was waiting for me and not anything else. Just to be safe, I slowed and stopped at my apartment door, listening hard. Quiet. No sound other than an occasional car moving through the slush outside, the muted sounds of a television playing in an apartment somewhere below, and my panting.

I grabbed the knob and turned. Unlocked. Not a surprise, I reminded myself; we'd left in a hurry.

Still gripping my sage and stones, I took a deep breath and tried to pull the second dimension into my focus. I opened the door and stepped inside.

"What took you so long?"

I jumped and dropped everything I was holding. "Jesus Christ, Jules, you scared the crap out of me."

"Sorry . . ."

I bent down and picked up the stones, leaving the crumpled sage leaves where they had fallen. My heart was getting a workout today.

"Start grabbing what you need. I'm gonna move some of your photo albums and stuff into this closet." Jules walked into my room.

"Julian, do you think this is really necessary?"

"Yes. That stuff isn't replaceable, and if the Jimani does come back here at some point, he might wreck shit you care about, like Lovonia said." He pulled a stack of photo albums off my bookshelf.

I shook my head and yanked a duffel bag from under my bed. I didn't want to waste time arguing. And if it made him happy, fine. Once I had a random assortment of clothing shoved into the bag, I dragged it into the bathroom and threw my toiletries inside. I was debating tampons—would I be at Lovonia's for that long? If so, I'd have to start paying rent—when I heard a crash and some ghostly cursing from the living room.

Julian had been trying to pull open the small closet while holding the photo albums, lost focus, and dropped the albums. A few photos had exploded out of one and were strewn across the room. I sighed, zipped the duffel, and marched into the room. "Just leave it—"

"No! These are my memories, too, you know."

My heart squeezed. That hadn't occurred to me.

He stuck the albums onto a closet shelf and snatched up the photos one at a time.

I knelt down, grabbing the ones nearest as quickly as possible. "Save your energy," I said. I tugged a photo out from where it had wedged itself underneath a coffee table leg and froze when I saw the image.

It was a picture of my dad next to a car he'd just bought. The car he'd ended up dying in. He was wearing a black trench coat and fedora, holding a cigar in one hand, a drink in the other, and posing for the camera with both arms out and a self-satisfied smirk on his face. A buzzing filled my ears, growing swiftly to a dull roar. The edges of my vision darkened and my focus narrowed tightly on the photograph. The air left the room.

No.

It couldn't be.

One disconnected part of my brain registered that Julian was calling my name from the other end of a very long tunnel, while the rest of it grappled with the image I held in my hands. *He uses fear. He can alter his appearance the way he wants. He would have known that our dad used to scare us. He would appear like him . . .*

But I hadn't even remembered that my dad wore a trench coat and fedora. Was he wearing it the day he died? Was it just something he felt powerful in? *No. Nonononono, the Jimani is not my father.* But then, how did he know Julian's name?

"RAELY!"

My catatonia shattered. Julian was crouched next to me, yelling into my face and looking freaked. I unzipped my duffel a trifle, stuffed the photographs inside, jerked the zipper shut, and stood. "Let's go."

21

SOMETHING SETTLED IN ME AS WE MARCHED TO THE TRAIN. As we walked, I charged the crystals, ate a granola bar, and ignored a few text notifications on my phone. I shifted in and out of the second dimension a couple of times while waiting for the train. A newspaper blew toward me, caught up in the wind. I waited until it was about to smack into me, then punched it with my essence. It turned into confetti.

"That was really good," Jules whispered.

I didn't answer.

I wasn't thinking. I wasn't feeling. I was disconnected. For some reason, it made shifting from one dimension to the other easier. It made using my essence easier. It was as if pushing all other thoughts and emotions aside had allowed space for a clearer understanding. Two more trains whizzed by in opposite directions. I boarded neither of them. I exploded a few more pieces of trash that were buffeted in my vicinity.

"Raely? Are we going to go somewhere?"

I couldn't stay like this. I needed to make a decision. I turned to look at Jules, willing my numb brain to chug back to life as I stared at him. Go home to mom's house. Get answers. That was an option. What if she had no answers? What would I even ask her? *Hey, so after dad died, were you ever like, haunted by anything slightly murderous?* And what if we brought the Jimani straight to her? I bet that would be a fucking field day for him.

Back to Lovonia's? It seemed the logical place to go. She could probably confirm whether the Jimani was our dad or not . . .

But if I was honest with myself, I knew. I knew it was him. And I knew she knew, too. I didn't need to ask her.

Fuck Lovonia for never clueing us in to this shit. How did she know anyway? Flickers of my anger began to curl around the edges of my numbness. But, like flames on damp kindling, they didn't catch and quickly extinguished.

My phone pinged again. I pulled it out robotically and checked the messages I had missed. They were all from Luck. Crap, I had forgotten to update him. He wanted to know if I was coming in or if I needed more time.

I made a decision.

"Let's go to the club," I said to Julian. "I'm going to go to work tonight. We can go to Lovonia's after."

As if validating my choice, a train to the Loop pulled up. As I boarded, I texted Luck that I was on my way and apologized for not checking in sooner. When I looked up, Jules was sitting next to me, watching me as if waiting to see whether I was going to break apart or explode.

I gave him a forced smile, then stared out the window, shifting in and out of the second dimension, occasionally lobbing my essence at passing trees, knocking the snow off the branches.

"Raely, are you going to tell me what's going on with you right now? Are you pissed because I dropped your photo albums?"

"What? No." I pulled my attention back to Jules. He was looking down at his fingers, which I now recognized as his emotional discomfort tell. I patted his arm, then belatedly looked around to see who was watching us. Fortunately, the car was largely empty. I popped my headphones in just in case. "I'm not upset with you at all."

"So, what happened? What's going on?"

I blasted snow off another tree branch. I should have felt a thrill of elation or at least a smidge of satisfaction. I was controlling my essence so effectively. It was as if the shock had nudged me into my groove. "I just need to think for a bit." I wasn't sure why I didn't tell Julian. I could have just shown the photograph to him and let him draw his own conclusions. Maybe the Jimani even looked different to Jules. How would I know? But I continued stewing inside of myself, inventing alternate explanations then disproving them, over and over.

Why was he fixated on us? And, not that I wished it upon her, but why wasn't he going after my mom? *Our mom*, I corrected myself. Alive, he had been obsessed with her. He'd wanted her all to himself. He probably would have been happier if we'd never been born.

A tree branch from which I was aiming to *push* the snow exploded into tiny fragments.

My face tingled. I pulled my gaze from the window to focus on my hands, clenched deep into the folds of my duffel bag. I shook my head to clear it and forced my fingers to relax their death grip on my bag. It was still possible that I had this all wrong.

"Jules," I whispered, but when I looked around, he was already standing by the doors. I scrambled to hoist the duffel bag up and scoot out of the seat in time to exit the train. When I caught up with him on the platform, he was glancing up and down its length.

"Hey, I'm just gonna meet you there, okay?" He vanished before I could answer. I supposed he figured it was safer this way. Still, I felt a hollow gnawing at the base of my throat once he disappeared. I slung the shoulder strap of the duffel crossways over my chest and marched to the exit staircase. Without Julian to talk to, my thoughts began to trundle back down the rut I had been creating.

If the Jimani *was* our father, did that mean he killed Julian? When he was just two years old? I shuddered. Mom said she had been at a job interview. She even got the position but didn't take the job. She never left my side again, until our father died. The Jimani was a ghost, which meant he either wasn't our father, or he wasn't there when Julian died. My insides hollowed out. Was I trying to rationalize the existence of a ghost? Hoping to prove that a ghost was responsible to avoid laying blame on our father? Whether it was an accident or not, Julian had died on our father's watch. And yet, he had blamed our mother. Never taken any responsibility.

I had been scared of my father, but I didn't remember him actively trying to scare me . . . did I? I remembered doing my best to stay out of his way or to defuse a situation that had become too tense. I was an excellent peacemaker by age eight. Although, the older I got, the less I cared to make peace and the more I chose to go toe-to-toe, which was probably why there were more instances of me staying with my aunts or my mom "running away" with me, as my dad had called it, after I hit ten.

Memory flashes flipped through my brain like a montage. My first sleepover, where I learned that not every kid locked their bedroom door from the inside when they heard shouting. My dad coming home in a screaming temper, and my mom shoving me behind her into the laundry room so hard that I fell in the dirty clothes basket, covered myself in the clothes, and curled up in the basket with my fingers in my ears. Turning on the football game at seven when I could feel an argument heating up. Pouring chips into a bowl, getting a beer—that he most certainly didn't need—distracting him enough to let it go. Watching him smash a glass into the sink where my mom was doing dishes while my first white-hot rage surged through my chest, pushing the fear and self-preservation instincts aside. I'd hurled a jar of giardiniera at him as hard as I could. I never got to see if it landed, because my mom grabbed me and fled the house.

I knew it was wrong, but it was all I had known. My first romantic relationships were short and rocky. I gravitated toward guys who were controlling and physical. Fortunately, I never got too entrenched. I always saw the signs—the shoving, painful arm-grabbing, belittling during arguments—and ended it. Even when I didn't want to. Even when the pattern felt comfortable and familiar. I now wondered if any of that had been Julian's influence. For a while I'd sworn off dating until I had examined my own paradigm and found a group of friends I felt safe with. Joe and I had platonically roomed together for a while during that time. Watching my mom go through her own therapy was helpful. She'd put me in counseling after my dad died—once she had a job where she could afford it—but by then I thought I was coping on my own and wasn't interested in digging up old wounds. I also saw it as an expense she could cut, so I told her I didn't think talk therapy was working for me.

I found comedy, which helped. Comedians can throw things out in bits that would be uncomfortable in normal conversation. I wove variations of stories and pieces of what I had been through into my acts. It helped. I really felt like I was on my way to becoming a fairly normal adult.

Until recently, until the accident when my best friend died. When I started to see my brother again. The incident in the coffee shop had started a domino effect, and I'd slid into all my worst habits, like pushing away anyone and anything that offered a light in my life. This man had come back into my life, after death, and was somehow managing to destroy me from the inside out. And I had been helping.

I will obliterate him. I kicked open the door to the comedy club.

22

"NICE, LADY-LIKE ENTRANCE," Jules quipped from the booth nearest the door.

"Hands were full," I said. They weren't. "And the door gets stuck in the cold." It does.

"Hello? We're not open yet!" Luck's familiar voice echoed from somewhere backstage. My heart did a little skip.

"Okay, look." Jules put his hands on my shoulders. I pulled my focus away from the stage, still keeping an ear out for Luck. "I think you're okay here for now, so I'm going to head back to Lovonia's to tell her what happened and see where we went wrong. I might also recharge a bit."

I turned my head toward the shuffling and muttered oaths from backstage.

Jules gave my shoulders a little shake to reclaim my attention. "Whatever's going on, we'll figure it out. If for some reason he comes back while you're here, don't lose your head. I'll be back before long."

His eyes raked my face. "Are you sure there's nothing you want to tell me?"

The words caught in my throat. What was I supposed to say? *Yeah, so I'm pretty sure the thing that killed you and has been trying to kill us is our father.* Surefire way to make Jules feel like shit. I hesitated, then tossed out a professional smile and shook my head. "Let me know what she says."

He pushed a smile back, which didn't reach his eyes, and vanished.

Dammit, I thought belatedly as I scanned the club. *I should have asked him to take the duffel bag.*

Without planning it, I had arrived at that magical time between the lunch and evening shifts, the mid-afternoon cleaning hour. Most of the chairs were upended on their tables to allow for easier mopping, and the bar was glistening from a recent wipe down. Luck pushed through the backstage curtains, broom in hand, ready to explain to some walk-in that we were, in fact, closed, and no, they couldn't wait at the bar for the next show. He caught sight of me, and his no-nonsense expression dropped.

"Raely!" He sounded . . . glad to see me? My stomach backflipped in response to the concern in his voice and the naked relief on his face.

He jumped off the stage, leaning the broom against the nearest table and strode over. He was wearing dark jeans and a gray button-down that looked like it had actually been ironed.

It was then that I realized the only thing containing my windblown, tangled, wavy hair was my knit hat. My makeup consisted of Lovonia's "lightest" dark brown eyeshadow, eyeliner, and the stain of a dark red lipstick that she sold at the store. Apparently, people occasionally bought lipstick for themselves when prepping for rituals. I was wearing the dubiously laundered, wrinkled, post-recent-ghost-attack clothes that I had worn the day I ran out of my house—*why* couldn't I have taken two minutes to change into something fresh? My buttonless coat, some fading bruises, and an enormous duffel bag completed my look. I awkwardly tugged a few hanks of hair out from beneath the duffel's shoulder strap. I found myself blushing as Luck's attractively put-together self reached my frazzled mess.

"I hope you didn't feel obligated to come in, I just hadn't heard from you—"

"No, no, I wanted to come in, I'm fine—" I unslung the duffel bag, ripping out a few strands of hair as I untangled myself, and plopped it onto a nearby booth. For some reason, I felt embarrassed to meet his eyes. *Ridiculous*, I told myself, and looked up.

Luck was right in front of me. A natural, innocent inhale pulled in his fresh, clean scent. My body froze, but my core warmed. Whatever I had been about to say vanished from tongue and brain. He gently pulled off my hat and pushed my hair back from the temple where a half-healed cut and the most colorful of my bruises remained. His brows contracted, a crease forming between them as he examined the area. "Damn," he muttered. He lifted his other hand as if to touch my face, then dropped it to my shoulder instead. My heart pounded loudly in my ears. *Can he hear my loud-ass heart right now?* I looked him in the eyes. Wow. Gray, ringed with black. Never noticed that before.

"Are you sure you're okay to be here right now?" He handed my hat back to me without breaking eye contact.

I took it and swallowed. My mouth was oddly dry. He smelled awesome. Like a freshly showered human who also might have access to bodywash of some kind. I probably reeked of sage, patchouli, and Lovonia's couch. "Yeah. Yeah, I . . . totally wanna be here right now."

My cheeks warmed.

I cleared my throat, stuffing my hat into a pocket as I stammered. "I can, uh, fix my hair and stuff before people get here, and and and and shove this"—I gestured vaguely at the duffel—"wherever it's out of the way."

"Don't be overly concerned about your hair. It's a comedy club, not the Ritz. And I think it looks fine, by the way." He flashed a quick smile that squeezed my lungs, then picked up my bag and walked it to the back. "You going somewhere?"

"I'm still staying with my friend. I stopped home to pick up some stuff." *Move. Legs.* I stumbled along in Luck's wake, tripping once over my own feet but catching myself before he noticed. *Smooth.*

"Did you file a police report?" Luck's tone softened. He glanced at me once then focused on the ladder as he climbed halfway to the light booth and shoved my bag underneath the board.

"I saw my lawyer today," I said, then lost my train of thought, oddly hypnotized by how his shoulders flexed beneath his shirt as he pushed my bag into place. I quickly looked down at my toes. "He's going to get me a restraining order and—oh right!—he said if I could get a statement from you saying that Dylan had come by here a few times, that would help."

Luck dropped down from the ladder. "Of course. Do you want it emailed, or do I need to sign something?" He closed the gap between us and held out his hand for my coat.

"Um, I think . . . I think email is fine." My mouth went dry as I handed him my coat. He hung it for me where we always hung our coats, but suddenly I found these simple everyday interactions completely distracting. Forming words was difficult. Was I the only one feeling warm?

Finished with my coat, Luck turned back to me. I was suddenly aware that we were alone in the building. A little thrill clambered up my spine to fizz out as goosebumps across my skin.

"I'll email something then." He put his hands on my arms and gave a gentle squeeze. "I've really been worried about you, but I didn't want to bother you too much. Are you sure you're okay?"

I nodded, all verbal capacity reduced to cinders. We were so close. He smelled so good.

He nodded back. "Good. If you're sure . . ." Was he leaning in? Was I leaning in? *Are we leaning in?*

Then the fucking lights cut out.

23

I SUCKED IN A BREATH AND INSTINCTIVELY GRABBED onto Luck's arms. He was still holding mine and huffed a laugh. "I promise I didn't plan that," he said.

Two thoughts collided in my brain: One, did that mean he *had been leaning in*? And two, I needed to get him out of here!

"Maybe we can just go out the back," I said, my voice husky. There was a part of me that was still ready to *lean*, but as the temperature dropped, that feeling dissolved, like water poured onto a campfire.

I fumbled around for my essence while Luck said, "If we wait a second, they'll probably come right back on." Oh fuck, making out had seemed like a cool idea a second ago, but right now it was bad bad bad. How did I put a stop to it without quashing all future possibilities? *Is this literally where your priorities are right now?* I asked myself.

Yes! If we make it out alive, I want to kiss him! I answered me. *Touché, let's make it out alive.*

I gave myself a mental fist bump.

"Luck, I'm kind of scared," I said. Not a lie. "Both times I was attacked, the lights were out. I really want to get out of here."

A rasping inhalation sounded from all around us. No coherent words, just a long, rattling intake of breath. Little hairs shot to attention over my entire body. *JulesJulesJules!* my mind screamed. He had said he was able to tell when something was wrong. I prayed he was able to sense this.

"That was kind of a creepy noise," Luck said. "I think heading out back is a good idea. Maybe we can see if it's the whole block or just us." He took my left hand in his right and reached over to grab our coats before walking carefully toward the alley door. The hairs on my neck were still standing on end, but my stomach was wriggling like a puppy at the feeling of his hand wrapped around mine. *Essence, Raely, find your essence.* I wrenched myself into survival mode. The second dimension formed . . .

Another wheezy inhalation, followed by a gravely exhalation that reverberated through the club. I clung hard to my essence. The second dimension made the route to the door a little clearer. I took the lead, pulling Luck behind me. I grabbed the handle.

It was so cold it burned.

I yelped and snatched my hand back, shaking it. "Fuck, that's cold!"

Luck tried and reacted similarly. "That's . . . incredible. I'm not sure how . . ." He rubbed his hand on the leg of his jeans.

I grabbed my coat off Luck's arm and tried to use it to turn the handle. Not only did the cold singe through the wool of my coat, but the handle refused to budge. It was as if it were made of stone and had never been intended to move. Luck tried himself, to no avail.

JulesJulesJules, pleeeeeeeease!

"We'll just have to go out the front," Luck said, taking my hand again. We had both put our coats on. Nonetheless, I started to shiver. I needed to rally, and I needed to find a way to get Luck out. We left the bar area, and I saw the exit sign flickering ahead of us. As we wove between the tables, Jules materialized next to me. I pressed a hand to my chest to keep my heart from cracking with relief.

"Where is he?" Jules whispered.

I shook my head.

The wheezing inhalation stretched over our heads again, this time tumbling into a rusty cackle. My stomach churned, and I braced myself, trying not to vomit.

"What *is* that?" Luck said.

Jules looked at me. "He can hear it?"

I nodded.

"This isn't good."

We were ten feet from the door when an upright piano that had been tucked against the stage slid across the floor, blocking the exit.

"What the—" Luck stopped in his tracks.

"Oh shit," I said.

He didn't flow in from a dark space or glide out from around a corner. No, this time the Jimani materialized right in front of us as if poured into shape from the surrounding air.

I flung a glittering shield between us. He laughed. The building began to tremble.

"Backstage door!" I screamed. I didn't care if Luck thought I was crazy, I hauled him with me and took off.

We didn't get far. I heard my shield shatter like glass, then one of the tables tipped over, shedding its two chairs. It shot toward us like a battering ram.

I dodged, pulling Luck with me, but we would have been hit had Jules not sent a table of his own right into the Jimani's, knocking it off course. Luck cursed, but thankfully kept pace with me. I looked over my shoulder and sent two chairs right into the Jimani. He knocked one aside, but the other caught him on the right side of his chest. His cackling ceased.

His dark glinting eyes slowly grew red.

My legs turned to water. I tore my gaze from him after throwing another hasty shield up behind us. Jules grunted from the impact of the table the Jimani had shoved at him, knocking him sideways. He staggered but stayed upright and flung up a weak shield of his own.

Jules, Luck, and I hurtled over the lip of the stage as one. I heard our shields smashing behind us as we sprinted toward the curtains. We seemed to be running in slow motion. My spine barked with pain as the back of a chair slammed into it, knocking me to the ground and ripping my hand from Luck's. "I'm fine, keep going!" I yelped when I saw him stagger-step to a halt. Jules sent the chair that had hit me back into the Jimani and threw a shield over me as I struggled to regain my feet. Luck had turned around and was reaching for me.

Metallic groaning and snapping sounded from directly above us. The Jimani was laughing again, arms flexing in that hideous pulling motion. My head snapped up just as the light grid came crashing down.

"Luck!" I screamed, tossing a shield over him. Too late.

Julian's shield deflected the grid from colliding with me. I was able to roll before it shattered, trapping my right leg. My shield had prevented full impact, but I hadn't been able to cover Luck completely and the grid slid off the edge, grazing his head and connecting with his shoulder. There was nothing I could do as he crumpled to the ground, nearly hidden beneath it.

Julian was fighting the Jimani on his own, and tiring. I tried to yank my leg free, crying out when jagged metal ripped into my calf. Pushing myself to a sitting position, I tugged my phone out of my pocket and held down the emergency button, letting it go through to 911, hoping they would trace our location. Still trapped, I sat down into my essence, pushing all thoughts and feelings to the side.

I focused on the Jimani. He had just thrown another table at Jules, who barely dodged. I gathered up every spicy, ashy, bitter, warm, bright thing inside of me. And *punched*. The Jimani staggered back. I didn't give him time to recover. I *punched* again, again, again.

Flashing lights illuminated the windows at the front of the club. I scarcely heard the sirens growing louder as I continued to pummel the Jimani with my essence. I only missed once, exploding a stack of programs near his head. Jules *pulled* the piano out of the way as the police hammered on the doors.

I was fading. I fell back to my elbows. I felt the bloodstone necklace settle against my breastbone and *pulled* from it. A small, shimmering shield bloomed in front of me. The police shoved through the entrance just as I slammed my shield into the Jimani and passed out.

24

"THAT'S IT, RAELY, OPEN YOUR EYES." I heard Julian first, then other sounds filtered through. Strangers were saying things about concussions, trauma to certain limbs, swelling . . . I felt my body being moved. Someone was wrapping my right leg. My mind thrashed desperately at the weighted blanket pressing me into paralysis. A small sound pushed from my throat.

"Hey, hey, I think our girl is coming around," said a voice I didn't recognize, almost as if he were talking to himself.

"She's conscious?" called a no-nonsense woman from what felt like a short distance away. Then the voice came closer. "Can she answer some questions?"

"Mel, she's just starting to move around. She hasn't even opened her eyes. I think you might have to wait for the hospital to—"

"Raely, forget what I said before. Don't open your eyes until this pushy cop has gone away," Julian said.

I couldn't help it. It was funny. I laughed, but it came out a cough.

Unfortunately, once I started, I couldn't stop. I eventually hacked my way back into my body, opening my bleary eyes into a bright, tear-stained world filled with strangers' faces and a ridiculous amount of activity.

"Okay, just take it one breath at a time, you're safe, you're okay." An EMT was sitting next to me, patting my hip with one hand, stabilizing my right leg with the other. I was near the edge of the stage, a gurney situated nearby, as if they had been about to transfer me onto it. A trim, crisp—there was no other word for her—police officer stood next to the gurney, arms folded, staring at me emotionlessly.

The lights were back on. The furniture was still in disarray. There were several police inside, as well as a few firemen and the odd EMT.

"Luck," I wheezed. "Is Luck okay? Where is he?"

"Your friend is going to be fine," the EMT said, still holding my leg still. "He's probably got a concussion, maybe a broken bone or two, but he's stable and we've got him in the ambulance to the hospital. He's probably there by now. We'll just pop you on this bed here and you can join him."

I glanced at Jules, who was crouched by my shoulder.

"Your leg's not broken, the club owner is here, and he just doesn't want to get sued. You probably should get stitches, but they patched you up pretty good. We should go."

"I'm okay," I told the EMT. Fully aware that I sounded anything but. "I don't need to go in the ambulance. Thank you so much for getting us out . . ."

"If you're okay, then maybe you can answer some questions?" Crisp Lady Cop was ready for me. Shit.

"Mel, she's obviously not okay, please back off," said the EMT. "Sweetie, what's your name?"

"Raely. And I know I'm banged up but—"

"Raely, I'm Ryan, and I really think you should come get checked out. Okay?"

"Nice to meet you, Ryan. And thank you. But I honestly have shit insurance and I can't afford the ride. I probably can't afford what you've already done." I gestured to my gauze-swathed leg. I pushed myself more upright. He was still holding my leg.

"What happened here?" Lady cop seized her chance.

"Obviously the grid fell on us," I deadpanned. I could have sworn I saw EMT Ryan smirk, but it vanished so quickly I couldn't be sure.

"*How* did it fall? What *happened* in here? Tables and chairs are all over the place. It looks like a bomb hit."

"Mel—" Ryan sighed.

She cut him off. "You do your job, I'll do mine."

"Just say whatever you think Luck is going to say and let's try to get out of here," Jules said, glaring at Mel. "She's not going to let you go, and you can't get stuck in a hospital right now."

"Well . . ." I leaned into my fatigue, letting myself feel every ache on my body. "It's kind of fuzzy, but . . . we were hanging our coats up in the back and then the lights went out. We . . . yeah, we put our coats back on and tried to go out the back door but neither of us could open it, so we came out here . . ." I paused. What was Luck going to say? He had to have seen furniture flying around. I didn't have to explain it. "This is going to sound nuts—"

She had been writing in a little pad, nodding along. I didn't think they still did that. I would have thought they had tablets or something.

"Doesn't matter how weird it sounds, just tell me anything you remember."

"Well, it was as if there was a tornado in here. Chairs and tables were flying at us. We'd just run to the backstage door thinking that would be faster when the grid came down and I . . . I must have hit my head, but I got my phone and pushed the emergency button. That's all I remember."

In the end, no one was going to allow me to leave without a trip to the hospital, no matter how many forms I signed. I was allowed to retrieve my duffel from the light booth, but George—who really was there, as Jules had said—insisted on driving me to the hospital himself since I refused to incur the expense of an ambulance ride. He really must have been worried about an injury suit. The drive wasn't long, and I stuck to the story I had given Mel the cop, assuming that Luck's would match. George dropped me off at the emergency entrance, watched me limp inside and then sped off back to the club after making me promise to update him on my condition in a few days.

"He's gone." Jules reappeared at my side as I approached the intake desk slowly and painfully. "Let's head out to the train."

"Not yet," I said. "I want to check in on Luck."

"He was banged up, but you heard the guy, he's going to be fine. He's probably still unconscious anyway and won't even know you're—" Julian stopped speaking once he beheld my death glare.

"Fucking nice, Julian."

A slightly sheepish eye-roll. "Fine, I get it. Make it quick. Draw some hearts on a napkin or something—"

"Oh, fuck right off," I muttered. I was now in front of a rather harassed-looking intake nurse and inquired about Luck as nicely as I could. I was explaining who I was and what had happened when—

"No! Out!" A tall, bronze-skinned, middle-aged woman was striding toward me, her salt-and-pepper hair escaping what had probably been a tidy bun this morning. A wizened, elderly lady stood a few feet behind her, blocking the hallway they had come from, wringing her hands and muttering words I didn't understand as she focused her lamp-like gray eyes on me.

"I'm sorry?" I glanced at Jules, who looked taken aback himself.

"You will leave my son alone!" The woman was now jabbing at my face with her index finger. "You've brought him nothing but trouble, and he wants nothing more to do with you."

My insides froze. I stumbled back a step from her lethal-looking phalange. Luck's mother? "I never—"

She wouldn't let me get a word in edgewise, now instructing the nurses, passing doctors, other patients in the waiting room, anyone who would look at her, that I was not to see her son under any circumstances. Every time he mentioned me, it was in conjunction with some kind of drama and he was tired of it, she told me, in various ways, as she backed me all the way out of the hospital.

I was so stunned that I just stood in the parking lot for a moment, staring after her as she stalked back into the emergency room until Julian tapped my shoulder and jerked his chin toward the train. I swallowed against the hard lump in my throat and meekly followed my brother to the station.

Once I was fairly certain I wouldn't burst into the embarrassing tears of hurt feelings, I checked in with Julian. "Are you okay?"

"I fared better than you did. I'm a little tired, but I'll be alright." He looked me over. "You did a pretty good job at the end there. I'd imagine the Jimani's going to have to recharge for a bit before he comes at us again."

I nodded, releasing a sigh. I was bone-tired, and my heart felt like a shriveled balloon. When we arrived at the station, I started automatically toward the stairs that would lead us to Lovonia's train, but Jules yanked me in the other direction without looking at me. "We aren't going to Lovonia's." His jaw feathered with tension.

I blew out a breath and dug out my headphones as I followed him. "Why? Where are we going?"

A train pulled up just as we ascended the staircase and we hopped on. I found the least populated space in the car and chose a seat next to the window, settling my duffel between my feet. Jules sat next to me. "We're going home to Mom's."

I sucked in a breath, eyes widening. "No!" I tried to shove my way out of the seat, but he pushed me back. Heat flared beneath my ribs. I clenched my jaw and pushed him again. He pushed back more forcefully, his eyes cold. My butt hit the seat hard, and my leg gave out.

"Sit down. We're going to Mom's."

"Let's get two things straight," I hissed at him, barely reining in the urge to punch him in the face. "Number one, you are *not* the boss of me. Do *not* push me around. Number two, I am *not* bringing the Jimani to Mom's house under *any* circumstances. Now let me out; we're changing trains."

Julian wrapped one hand around the railing on the back of our seats and one on the pair in front of us, effectively blocking my exit unless I punched through him. Which I was *seriously* tempted to do.

"You're going to listen to *me* now," he said, pointing his finger in my face, infuriatingly reminiscent of Luck's harpy mother.

I slapped his hand away, grinding my teeth at his sheer nerve.

"Lovonia said we can find out how to get rid of the Jimani from Mom because she's done it before, even though she may not be aware of it. She said the Jimani will not follow us there. That we'll be safe at Mom's for a while."

A cool splash of surprise banked the fire inside my chest. "Did she deign to tell you *why* the Jimani won't follow us there?"

"She did not."

I snorted and rolled my eyes. "Typical."

"She also said"—he narrowed his eyes, the blue piercing through me—"that you have been keeping something from me, and it's time for you to stop."

My jaw dropped open. I shut it and sat back down in my seat, staring straight ahead for a moment before throwing up my hands. "How does she *know* all of this? Where the fuck is she getting her information? Don't tell me she's a real goddamn psychic. Jesus H. Christ." I glanced at Jules, who was still corralling me. "You can sit down; you've made your fucking point."

He didn't move. "I'm waiting. For my sister. To stop *lying* to me."

I pressed my lips into a thin line. There was no reason not to tell him. He was going to find out eventually. I was just pissed that he was physically blocking me. But I'd have been angrier if I'd found out he was keeping things from me too. I yanked open the zipper on the duffel and dug around for the photograph. "Fine. Sit down. Bully."

He sat. I found the photograph and thrust it at him. "Remind you of anyone?"

He froze, his eyes widening. "Holy burning hell."

25

ONCE WE HAD SETTLED OURSELVES ON A TRAIN to the suburbs, I made some calls. Mom was thrilled that we—that I—was coming even if she was freaked out about the "accident" at the comedy club, which was the reason I had given for my sudden desire to vacate the city. With my apartment "under construction" and my place of partial employment closed for repairs and probably investigation, there was every reason to get out of Dodge.

I also called the hospital where Luck had been taken—altering my voice slightly, just in case—and claimed to be a cousin, in addition to leaving a stuttering, highly inadequate voice message on his cell phone. So far, I hadn't been able to reach him directly, although the hospital told me that he was stable, expected to recover fully, and his family was with him. I considered calling Lovonia and grilling her about fending off the Jimani directly rather than hearing everything from Julian secondhand—I was convinced she was still holding some information back—and then realized that I didn't have her goddamn phone number. I thought about looking up the number to the shop, but that one small obstacle sapped the last of my energy. I tucked my phone into a pocket, leaned my head against the window, and stared out at the flat, snow-covered countryside flashing by in the gathering dark.

"Are you gonna show Mom your leg?"

I dragged my gaze to where Jules was sprawled across the two seats facing me, picking at his fingernails. We hadn't spoken much after our argument on the El. I was still a little irritated with him for pushing me around, and he was undoubtedly processing the possibility that the ghost who had been trying to kill us was our father. And he may have been mad at me for not informing him as soon as I'd figured it out.

"You're limping. She's going to ask about it," he said to his fingertips.

I sighed. "Then I guess I'll tell her."

"She's gonna make you get stitches if she sees it." He was still absorbed in whatever ghostly dirt was embedded under his nails, not so much as glancing in my direction. He sounded sullen.

"Either tell me what's on your mind or leave me alone. I'm tired." I watched him for a few beats. He didn't look up, just continued his poor man's manicure. I turned back to the window.

"It wasn't an accident."

Something in his tone made me push away from the window and face him. He was still staring at his hands, but now his fingers were worrying a thread he had pulled out of the cuff of his jacket. I waited. When he didn't speak, I said softly, "What wasn't an accident?"

I heard him swallow. Twice. Still twisting the thread between his fingers. "He killed me. It wasn't an accident."

My blood chilled. My shoulders rose toward my ears. I fumbled for something to say, the right thing to say.

"That picture . . ." His throat bobbed again. He cleared it. "Flashes started to come back when I looked at it. Nothing coherent. Feelings. Things I just . . . knew. From when I was alive."

His voice got quieter as he talked. The last sentence came out barely above a whisper. I realized I was holding my breath and made myself inhale. I cast my mind back, trying to see if I could dredge up any memories of my own, but there was nothing.

I thought of the little boy in the photographs my mom had shown me and tried to find him somewhere in the recesses of my brain. I came up empty.

"He didn't want us there." Julian's eyes flicked up to meet mine. "I remember always feeling like we were in the way."

I managed to dip my chin. I had felt similarly at times.

"He hated me more than you, though." He swiped a hand across his eyes. My own eyes started burning.

"How . . ." My voice trembled. "Why would you think that?"

He shook his head, once again focusing on the shredded thread. "I just *knew*. He pushed us a lot. Knocked us out of the way. Mostly when Mom wasn't looking. But he always pushed me harder and more often."

I was shaking but otherwise frozen to my seat, barely drawing in breath.

"He hated when we were both getting Mom's attention, or both of us doing something. It was as if he thought we were ganging up on him. We used to go into the closet to play together." He squeezed his eyes shut and pinched the bridge of his nose. "I know it doesn't make sense, but I remember the *feeling*."

"Do you remember when . . ." My voice sounded rusty. I couldn't finish the question.

He nodded, eyelids brimming with silver. "I remember," he whispered. "I don't wanna talk about it just yet."

He tossed the thread onto the floor, pressed the heels of his hands into his eyes briefly, then stared out the window.

I didn't spare a thought for who might be watching. I got up and sat next to him.

I found his dimension and wrapped my arms around his middle, leaning my head on his shoulder. He was still for several seconds, then he dropped his cheek down to rest on the crown of my head.

We stayed like that for the rest of the ride.

26

MOM STOPPED AT THE STORE AFTER WORK en route to picking us—me—up from the station and had obtained grocery store sushi for dinner. She made me tell her about the accident and I gave the barest details, sticking to my official story in case worlds ever collided, but I avoided talk of furniture flying around. There was no way around admitting that the grid had fallen on Luck and me, which of course upset her. Dissecting that incident monopolized our conversation for the entire ride home.

Blitz was thriving and didn't care about my arrival until I'd stopped trying to get his attention and sat down with Mom to eat. Then he wouldn't rest until he occupied my lap and at least one of my hands was giving him scratches. They'd been getting along well. Mom was even musing about getting a cat of her own once I took Blitz back. We'd never been able to have pets when Dad was around. It was a rule we'd unconsciously kept until I found Blitz in the dumpster behind the comedy club.

Jules watched us silently, not altogether unhappily, but definitely in a mood. I glanced at him frequently. Even tried to sit next to him on the couch, but he just scooted slightly away, half reclining against the arm on the opposite side. Mom was taking a half-day from work the following afternoon so that we could hang out after lunch and then have the weekend. I decided to leave any Jimani-related probing until the next day. I needed sleep, and I was concerned about Julian processing any more memories that night.

It wasn't a fabrication when I told Mom I was tired and wanted to head to bed early and that I'd see her in the morning. She was happy to oblige, telling me an early night would be best as she wanted to go to the gym before work anyway and wouldn't wake me.

Julian didn't follow us as we started to head back to the bedrooms. I glanced at my mom's retreating back and tip-toe-limped back over to the couch and poked him. "C'mon!" I whispered.

"I'm fine here."

"Please don't do this," I said. "You can sulk by the window in the guest room just as well as you can out here." When he didn't move, I added, "I'm going to worry all night if I can't see where you are."

He sighed and pushed off the couch.

While I brushed my teeth and puttered around, he did indeed take up a position sitting next to the window, looking out like a little glow statue. He hadn't moved by the time I turned out the light and climbed into bed. Blitz had already taken up residence at the foot.

"Love you, Jules," I whispered, burrowing into the covers.

He didn't respond. But he was there at the window every time I woke during the night. I fell quickly back to sleep each time.

WHEN I WOKE up, it was already edging toward eleven, and Jules was no longer by the window. I pushed myself up and felt every muscle in my body protest. I groaned and fought the desire to lie back down. I forced myself to toss the covers back. I swung my pajama-clad legs to the floor. Before I even took a step, I knew there would be pain. I sighed.

"Jules?" I called out, hoping maybe he'd just come back and I could stay here for eternity. No answer. My stomach grumbled loudly. I resigned myself to movement and took slow, painful steps toward the kitchen.

Well before I entered the room, I could see Julian sitting at the table. He had found the box my mom had shown us during our last visit and had spread its contents out across the table's surface. He didn't look up as I approached, even though I was moving and groaning like a B-movie zombie.

"Sleeping Beauty finally woke up, then?" he said without taking his eyes off the relics in front of him. "I thought you were going to sleep through the entire morning."

"What are you doing?" I said from ten feet away. I didn't have it in me to walk faster. Even to my ears, my words were varnished with pain.

Jules finally looked up. His brow furrowed. "Jesus, what's wrong with you? Does your leg hurt that bad?"

"My leg hurts. My back hurts. My fucking hair hurts," I moaned, staggering closer. Almost to a chair. So close. "And I'm sooooo hungry."

"Mom left stuff out for you." Jules pulled some of the photos and papers he'd strewn about into a more concentrated area of the table, clearing a spot for me to drop my head onto my arms once I had collapsed into the chair next to him.

"Don't you wanna eat?" he asked the back of my skull.

I didn't lift my forehead from the pillow of my arms as I grunted an affirmative.

For a beat, neither of us moved, then I heard Julian shift from his chair and walk to the kitchen counter. I continued to breathe in and out, cataloging the sore spots. *If I feel this bad, Luck must be ten times worse,* I thought. *At least he's in a hospital with access to lots of sweet drugs.* I heard rustling from whatever Julian was doing at the counter. He returned and pushed something against my arm.

"Here, it's a muffin."

I lifted my head and gazed upon an enormous blueberry muffin. After weeks of granola bars and oatmeal, it looked like salvation. With one forearm pressed into the table as my foundation, I swept the muffin into range with the other and took a large bite right out of the top. I closed my eyes against the delicious, light texture and the absolutely faint-worthy blueberry sweetness cascading over my tastebuds. "Mmmmmmmmmmmmmmmm." I put my head back down while I chewed, the muffin nestled safely in the crook of my elbow.

"You're pathetic," Julian said.

I tossed him a rude gesture and then chomped off another chunk of life-affirming muffin. After swallowing my second bite, I pushed myself up to sit like a human and a different kind of groan escaped me.

"If you feel this shitty, Mom is going to . . . 'mom' on you." Jules was putting his papers and photos in some kind of order.

"Can you please find me some drugs?" My back was still throbbing from my attempt at sitting upright.

"Raely, it's way too early for booze and cocaine," Jules said lightly, not lifting his eyes from what he was doing.

"Fuck. Off. Please go get me some Advil or something!" I wanted more muffin. I also wanted the waves of soreness to dissipate and to be able to function like a healthy person when Mom got back.

"You should take better care of yourself," Jules said sweetly.

"You're the one who said not to let them take me to the hospital," I wailed, easing myself against the chair back. "I bet Luck's getting all kinds of floaty drugs, and I bet people are being nice to him."

Julian tossed his photos down and stalked off toward the bedrooms, muttering something about using his powers for a life of servitude. Once he was gone, I reached for my muffin and took a glance at what he had been occupied with. I saw our birth certificates and his death certificate off to one side. My stomach twisted. The rest were mainly photographs of the two of us, although there was a slew of cards that I hadn't gone through before. Some of them looked like sympathy cards. Julian came stomping back into the room. I cupped my muffin and leaned back from the table.

"Here." He held his hand out to me. I opened my palm, and he dropped several pills into it. "I got you four, since you're obviously an inch from joining me on this side of the veil. Enjoy them with your last meal."

"God, you are in a delightful mood this morning." I took a bite of muffin and then crammed the painkillers in, swallowing both together. "What are you doing with that stuff?"

"Just . . . looking at it. Remembering."

I watched him while I finished my muffin, waiting for the meds to kick in. He didn't say anything else. Didn't even snap at me to stop staring.

"Do you wanna talk about any of it?" I asked.

"No."

I waited. Then, "Well, you should put it away before Mom gets back."

"Why?" His eyes were hard as he read through some of the cards. "We need to ask her questions about all this. That's why we're here, right?"

"Well, yeah," I said, trying to keep my tone reasonable, "but I wasn't planning on ambushing her with it right when she walked in the door. I thought I'd work up to it—"

"You thought you'd just have a little vacation and some fun time with Mom taking care of you and then maybe get around to it when it was convenient for you." He started throwing things back into the box. His face was set. I had never seen his eyes so cold.

"Julian . . ." I felt like he had punched me in the chest. "No. I just . . . this is hard stuff for her too—"

"That's great. So you guys can have a nice cry about how bad everything was and how you got through it together and have a nice fucking bonding moment." He slammed the box shut, stood, and stalked back toward the bedrooms. "You'll probably even hug. She'll cry and tell you how much she loves you . . ." He trailed off. I stumbled after him, ignoring the pain in my leg.

"Jules, what happened?" My chest was tight, my shoulders creeping up to my ears. "Please talk to me."

"God, you are so self-centered," he bit out.

I flinched as if he had slapped me, stopping dead in the middle of Mom's room while he strode to her closet, wrenched open the door, and shoved the box back on the top shelf. "What do you *think* happened, Raely? I fucking died. I was fucking murdered and all that's left of me is this goddamn box of bullshit."

I stood rooted to the spot. My lungs turned to concrete. I didn't dare move.

Julian slammed the closet door and turned to face me. "And now *you* get *my* mom. You get everything. You get to be hugged and given muffins and worried about and looked after. You get Christmas and birthdays and—" He blinked hard. His voice broke. "And you had someone with you. You got to go through it with Mom. I was alone."

"Julian . . ." I could barely breathe, and my legs were shaking.

"By the time Mom got there, I was dead. I didn't even get a hug—" He blinked, and a tear escaped. He wiped it away impatiently. "He pushed me off the balcony. I was dead right away. And I just lay there until the EMTs got there. He just stood next to me on the phone until they got there. Didn't even touch me."

"Oh God, Jules . . ."

"You saw it. You were there. He told you he was calling the hospital and that I would be fine and locked you in the bathroom and told you to be quiet." He sniffed. "I didn't really understand what was happening." He finally looked up at me, his eyes glistening. "You didn't either. Dad told you I would be fine, and I showed up as a ghost and you thought I was fine. Until you eventually stopped seeing me. Then I really didn't have anyone anymore. And I still don't."

"You have me." My voice trembled. "I know I'm not Mom and . . . I'm so sorry, Jules. I'm so sorry." Julian was right. It wasn't fair. And I wished I could give him some of the love I had had.

He stared at me from across the room, then dropped his gaze to his feet. I watched one tear fall from each eye. It didn't occur to me to wonder whether ghosts could cry until I saw them disappear without making a mark on the floor. Jules looked back up at me, and his face broke. He crossed over and pulled me into a hug. I fumbled a bit for his dimension, then clung to him.

"I'm sorry." I pressed my face into his shoulder, tears finally breaking free. "I wish I could share some of the life I've had." I wasn't at my most articulate, but he seemed to understand. We held on to each other until our sniffling abated and turned into hiccups. When he finally released me, he held onto my arms and looked at my tear-stained face.

"I'm sorry. I was a dick just now."

"You're allowed." I dabbed my nose on my sleeve. I was trembling all over. One of these days I was going to vibrate until my molecules just flew apart. "I would be mad, too."

"Oh, shit, your leg is bleeding."

27

I LOOKED DOWN AT THE LEG OF MY PAJAMA PANTS. A red spot was blooming over my right calf, gluing my pant leg to my skin. "Crap, I have to get this rebandaged before Mom gets here." I hobbled toward her bathroom.

"Don't you think you should tell her?" Julian trailed after me.

I ignored him and commenced with digging through the disorganized plethora of medical supplies in Mom's sink cabinet. I found a gauze pad and some medical tape that must have hailed from the '90s. "Woman never throws anything away," I muttered.

"I really think you should get it looked at." Julian sat down next to me, watching me roll back my pant leg and peel off the old bandage.

"Hand me that trash can," I said, gesturing to a small one in the corner. He obliged, and I stuffed my old bandage down to the bottom of it. I cleaned the wound as best I could with a washcloth, but it was still leaking. I smacked the gauze pad on top of it and taped it down. The tape was less than sturdy, having been created in the prior millennium, so I wrapped an Ace bandage around it for good measure. "Compression will help," I muttered.

"Why are you being stupid about this?" Jules was frowning at me. I was busily hiding the wrapping from the gauze pad at the bottom of the trash can next to my bloody bandage.

"It's going to be fine, and I don't want her to worry. She still freaks out if I get, like, a scratch . . ." I trailed off. We both knew why that was. Considering the feelings Jules had just expressed, I didn't want to steer us back down that road.

He was quiet while I put the cabinet back in order. The painkillers were starting to kick in, but I still dreaded standing back up. "I need to wash the blood out of my pants," I sighed. "Can you give me a minute?"

Jules got up and left, rolling his eyes. Shortly after that, while I was scrubbing furiously and pink foam was blossoming between the folds of fabric in the sink, there was a *whoosh*, a *thunk*, and then a pair of my jeans landed on the floor beside me. "Thank you," I called into the hallway. A sweater followed.

Fully dressed, my wet pj's hanging in the guest shower, I sat with Jules at the kitchen table waiting for Mom to come home. He was obviously unhappy with my decision to hide my injury from her but had apparently decided to shut up about it.

We debated ways we might work out how she managed to banish the Jimani without knowing it, and how we'd tease it out of her, all the while delicately skirting around the emotional implosion of the morning by unspoken mutual agreement. I spent a little time griping about Lovonia giving us information piecemeal. Julian, of course, defended her. We were in the middle of that dispute when Mom breezed through.

It still made me so happy to see her bright-eyed and full of energy. She immediately trotted out lunch options, as she was *starving*. There was a place near the mall we could try, get a glass of wine with lunch if we wanted to be "a little crazy," and then go shopping. I was turning over the options in my head, trying to figure out how I could do as little walking as possible, when I felt a tug at the hem of my jeans.

I glanced down. Julian was crouched there, snaking his hand up my pant leg. I pressed my lips into a thin line and yanked my foot away, but he had grabbed onto my ankle and wouldn't let go. I glared at him and gripped the table, preparing to kick, but he had already grabbed the edge of the Ace bandage and pulled it out until a good twelve inches was hanging out of my jeans. He retreated before I could kick him.

"Raely, what's that?" Mom had spotted Julian's handiwork. As. He. Had. Planned.

"Nothing, don't worry about it." I tried to stuff the bandage back up my pant leg, but it was no good. Ten minutes later we were on our way to the minute clinic.

"I can't believe you told on me. Tattletale," I spat at Julian under my breath as we climbed out of the car. He just smirked and walked bouncily into the clinic ahead of us.

Plans for the mall were shelved. I got five stitches and a lecture instead of a cobb salad and Pinot Grigio. We made do with protein bars in the car for lunch and headed back home. I tried to think of the best way to bring up the Jimani without bringing up the Jimani.

Since Mom had determined that we would be sedentary for the rest of the day, she swung by the grocery store to get supplies. Jules and I were sitting silently in the car. I was trying to call Luck—and deleting voicemail after voicemail after two dumb texts that I couldn't take back—when my phone pinged with a text from Mom. She was in the checkout line. She was excited about her purchases. She declared it movie night. The beginnings of an idea sparked to life in my frontal cortex. I mulled it over from a few different angles. Unable to foresee anything disastrous, I was about to turn around and run it by Julian when Mom bounced back into the car, slinging sacks of groceries into my lap.

"Ow, Mother, I am injured." I grasped the handles and balanced the bags on my legs, nonetheless.

"Oh, hush, look what I got us!" She somehow managed to flow into her seat, buckle her seatbelt, and start the car before her door had fully closed.

"Your ease of motion is enviable," I commented dryly. "Is there Advil in here?"

She rolled her eyes, put the car in gear, and answered without taking her eyes off the road. "Just look and see, goofball."

I dug around, narrating as I went. "A frozen cauliflower crust pizza, yum, oh, make that TWO cauliflower crust pizzas—"

"Well, I didn't know how hungry you were . . ."

"Incredibly. Perpetually."

"And I couldn't decide which flavor."

"Flavor. Okay, and stovetop popcorn. That's always fun. Ooooo, chocolate, nicely done, aaaaand . . . Is this . . . what is this. Is this a *box* of wine, Momma?"

"Read the front of it!"

"Battlefield Victory Big Red Blend. Wow."

"It won some kind of consumer award. And I thought the title was fun."

Julian was snickering in the backseat.

"It is. In a macabre Halloween-type of way." I rifled through the bags once more. "Detergent. Oatmilk. Ah! Gauze pads from *this* century—"

"Stop it."

"We really should go through your cabinets and check some expiration dates. Might be able to sell some shit to museums."

"Raely Mynor—"

"Okay, okay," I chuckled. "I still say *shit* is not a curse word. It's a noun. But whatever. So you *didn't* get painkillers then."

"There are plenty at the house. We can put these things away and decide when we want to have dinner and pick out some movies to watch. You can rest on the couch, take a nap . . ."

"I slept until almost 11 a.m.; I don't need a nap." I arranged the groceries on the floor between my feet. Jules snorted his agreement from the backseat. "I actually had kind of a fun idea."

"Oh really? Do tell." She took the turn into our neighborhood.

"I was thinking maybe we could—since it's movie night . . . day . . . time—go through some of the home movies. Ones where you, me, Julian, and Dad were all together. We still have some, right?"

The most awkward five seconds of silence in the history of the Videc family filled the car.

"Crickets," narrated Jules.

Mom recovered. "Sure. We can look around and see what I still have." She pulled into the carport, threw the car in park, turned it off and swung out before I could even pull in a breath to answer. I had started to awkwardly wrest the groceries back to my lap and nudge the car door open, but she was there before I could make much progress. She hauled the groceries from my grip and strode briskly to the door. Her mobility made me downright jealous.

"I can carry one of them. I'm not completely useless." I pushed painfully out of the car, shutting the door behind me, and limped after her. I needed more Advil. Stat.

"I think you surprised her," Jules said. "It's a good idea, though. At least a way to segue into the topic."

"I hate this," I muttered. I hated that Julian had been right. There was a big part of me that would love to just enjoy the downtime with my mom. I would have loved to relax into the chill evening she had planned for her accident-prone daughter even after having been blindsided by a trip to the clinic. If I were being honest, I didn't want to talk about my father. I didn't want to dig further into my memories and see if I had, in fact, witnessed Julian's death. I was terrified of what I might find. I hated that I really had no choice. I hated that Mom couldn't see Julian. I hated that Julian couldn't eat pizza with us and make snarky comments about Mom's groceries and drink unfortunately named wine. Maybe he wouldn't have even had wine. Maybe he would have been a beer person, and Mom would have bought him some crazy local six-pack with a weird animal on the front. Maybe he would have gone into the grocery store with her to help her carry everything. Maybe he would have said he hated chocolate so Mom would buy him something dumb like licorice. I would never know. Because the Jimani had taken that from all of us. Dad had taken it.

I was so wrapped up in my fictional depiction of a real, live Julian's family grocery trip that I straight up tripped over the threshold to the kitchen.

"Raely!" Mom shrieked from the other side of the counter where she had just stowed the oatmilk in the fridge.

I probably would have been seriously hurt—again—if Julian hadn't grabbed the back of my coat before my face smacked into the floor and gently lowered me the final three inches before Mom made it around the corner.

"Thanks," I breathed. Then louder, "I'm okay. Just scuffed my hand a little."

Despite my protestations of health, she wouldn't rest until I was bundled onto the couch in front of the television with a glass of water and some—finally, Jesus—anti-inflammatories. She wouldn't let me help her with the groceries and, in fact, declared that she was making cookies. She even wiped the tiny scrape on the heel of my palm with hydrogen peroxide.

"Mother, this is completely unnecessary."

"At the rate you're going, you'd get a staph infection, and then where would we be?" She slathered Neosporin over the decontaminated wound.

"She has a point. Your luck has been abysmal lately," Jules commented from where he was draped, upside down, on the couch. Mom bustled out of the room to toss her medical supplies into the Hotel California of bathroom cabinets, and I tilted my head to look at Julian.

"Obviously the blood doesn't rush to your head when you do that, so is the perspective just fun or what?"

"I don't need a reason for everything that I do."

I shrugged, then flipped my feet onto the back of the couch and lowered myself until I was also upside down. "I have to say, it's not as uncomfortable as I thought it would be."

He looked me up and down. "Yeah, but your face is getting all red and you've got a big vein sticking out in your forehead."

"This is what I get for trying to bond with a jagoff."

His mouth quirked to the side as he tried not to smile. "It's fun. That you tried."

"Well, I had to jump on it before the opportunity passed. Later I'll be drunk on Battlefield Victory and flipping upside down will be a bad idea."

"What on Earth are you doing?" Mom was back, carrying a battered cardboard box which she set down next to me before smacking my thigh. "Are you trying to make yourself sick? Sit up!"

"Oh my God." I flopped around, righting myself. "I just scraped my hand. I didn't give blood."

She shoved the box at me then marched off to the kitchen. "While I make the cookies, you can go through those and see which ones you want to watch."

The box was full of home movie DVDs.

"Oh, of *course*," Jules said, as if he had just intuited the equation for the theory of relativity. "You almost died walking through a doorway, so she's going to give you whatever you want. Brilliant move, sis."

"Oh, shove it," I said, secretly giddy that he'd called me "sis." I pawed through the discs while Julian chuckled. "Turn right side up and glide your transparent ass over here to help me pick."

By the time Mom had come back with the cookies, we had picked out some DVDs.

Jules had made the first choice, an early one.

"I'm kind of surprised we have any home movies," I admitted, dipping my cookie into my black licorice tea. A secret nod to what I thought Julian's favorite candy might have been. Mom had opted for chai.

"Well, your grandparents gave your father a camcorder when I was pregnant." She fiddled with the remote until the DVD screensaver illuminated the television. "He was excited about it. He's the one who put everything on DVD thinking that would be the best way to watch them. At the time, it was."

"Huh," was all I said. I tossed a glance at Jules, but his eyes were fixed on the screen. A moment later, I knew why.

There was Mom with an armful of babies. Laughing. And I could hear my father narrating in a voice I don't ever remember him using.

"Here's my beautiful wife, Jillian, holding our beautiful babies! Tell everyone what day it is, hon."

"Well, Julian and Raely are one month old today! We've just had a great checkup, and we're excited to see grandma and grandpa later."

"That was a good day . . ."

I looked over and Mom was white-knuckling the remote, her eyes glassy. "It was so different at first, Raely," she breathed. "I wish . . . You didn't get to see many of the good times, but you can bring some of these home with you if you want."

"I just wanted to see him. Julian." I looked away from Jules, my cheeks warming, but made myself ask, "Did we like each other?" I wanted to know if living Julian had been attached to me at all or if it was just some stupid spiritual tether that he hadn't had much choice about.

On the screen, our father continued to narrate in that bright, proud voice, zooming in on each of our faces individually, pulling back the edges of our swaddles with a careful fingertip to give the viewing audience the full chubby baby experience.

"Oh, sweetie. You were inseparable. I'm sorry I hid it away for so long. I didn't mean to." She exhaled slowly, moisture lining her lower lids as she watched her younger self tucking a baby Julian carefully into a car seat. "He used to give you his toys, or bottle, whatever he was holding, if you were crying. If that didn't pacify you, he would cry louder until I came into the room, then he would stop and point at you until I fixed whatever you needed."

My eyes flicked to Jules. He chuckled.

"Did I ever do nice things for him?"

She nodded, and her gaze slid off into the middle distance. "One of my favorite memories: Whenever you two got sick, you never got it as bad as Julian. I guess your immune system was just a bit more robust. He always had trouble sleeping through a cold, and you used to sing to him. Very quietly, so your father wouldn't hear, but I used to peek in to watch you. You would stroke his hair like I did for the two of you, and make up your own songs. I wish I had written them down. Some of them were hilarious."

"See, you weren't always mean to me," Jules said, smiling.

I gave him the side-eye. "We shared the same bed?"

Her face dropped again. "We were discussing when it might be time to separate you . . ." She trailed off and took a shaky breath, then she turned and pushed a smile at me. "I would *love* nothing more than to sit here and show you all of the videos of your brother." Her eyes shone a bit more brightly. It was an effort not to look at Jules. "He was such a delight. And he *loved* you. It's just . . . hard to see your father in the ones from before. It really shines a light on how bad things got."

After finishing the early DVD of very tiny Jules and Raely—with a father I didn't recognize at all—I grabbed another one at random and handed it to Mom. It was a Christmas morning a few years later. I was three or four, toddling around a small tree, hauling a large, plush dragon in a headlock, his tail and hindquarters dragging on the ground next to me. "That was mine," Julian said. "You always liked it, though."

What I saw next froze my heart. I stopped breathing for several beats. My sensory awareness only returned when the mug of tea I was clutching slowly scalded the fingers I had wrapped around it. "Oh my God," I whispered.

On the television screen, a little ghostly Julian trundled after me. Loudly proclaiming that I was holding his dragon incorrectly and that he didn't like to be held that way. Little Raely's mouth twisted sideways into a tiny frown. She adjusted her grip on the dragon, glancing once over her shoulder. We looked more like twins than ever. Both with curly mops of hair in obvious bowl cuts and dark lines of eyebrows accenting thick-lashed, almond-shaped eyes.

I dragged my gaze from the screen to check Julian's reaction. My jaw was still hanging open.

"Wow, your face is as white as . . . wait, can you see me? On the TV?"

I nodded. Even if I had wanted to risk speaking to him in front of Mom, I wouldn't have been able to form words.

"You loved that little dragon," Mom was saying. "You carried him with you everywhere. Talked to him all the time."

I gave an inarticulate squeak in response. There weren't a ton of gifts under the tree, but little Raely had one and little Jules had none. He tried to grab one or two of the packages, but his chubby hand swept right through them. His face crumpled in on itself. Little Raely noticed and placed the dragon in front of him, with a bit of ribbon on top of its head for good measure.

"Here you go," she said.

Little Jules was placated and concentrated on moving the ribbon, mostly unsuccessfully but contentedly, until the recording ended.

After that, we skipped around a little more. Julian was in all the videos of me. All of them. Some also featured our father. I noted a growing coldness and detachment in him as the videos moved up in years.

It was interesting, hearing my father's voice change. I never heard that cheerful, proud man that had narrated the very first videos when

Jules and I were newborns, but the earlier videos all had occasional slices of a lighthearted dad. Maybe not a happy person, maybe not even a kind person, but someone who still thought to film his wife and kid at Christmas and on a birthday. The later videos either had myself or Mom behind the camera. He always had a drink in hand. In a few of them, I felt I was witnessing him hollowing out into a husk of the person he'd been before.

"Wait, what's that?" I pointed at the screen. In one of the videos, taken around Thanksgiving, Dad was sulking by the grill, watching our Thanksgiving hamburgers sizzle and nursing a tall glass with a large helping of straight whiskey. But around his head and shoulders was a dark haze that I hadn't seen before. Or if I had, it wasn't this pronounced. It followed him around the screen.

"What's what?" Mom asked.

"That . . . fuzzy stuff around his shoulders . . ." When I looked at her, she was squinting at the screen. "You don't see it?"

"She can't," Jules jumped in. "I've only seen a few of those. I stay away from them. They're some kind of spirit. They attach to living people, but they can follow them into death. They're like parasites. I don't know exactly what they do, but they feel awful to be around. I don't know how anyone could stand to be near them long enough to let them attach themselves . . . I—wow, I totally forgot he had that. I guess because it was always there, but it got worse."

I made a show of blinking furiously during Julian's explanation. "Oh, oh no, it was just an eyelash in my eye. Sorry about that." I pretended to carefully extract the eyelash from the corner of my eye. The hazy thing attached to my father floated behind him. I didn't want to see anymore.

"Why don't we skip to some after . . . after it was just me and you," I suggested, and Mom willingly complied. I needed a break from that soulless face. Julian didn't voice any disagreement, and I wondered what he was feeling. I wished he would tell me.

Mom pulled a fresh DVD from the box. "Oh, this is your twelfth birthday. We had so many family members come in for that one, that would be fun to see." She slid it into the player and closed the drawer.

When the video played, I physically started. I couldn't stop myself from grabbing Julian's arm.

Jules scooted over next to me and rubbed my back. He didn't speak, and his eyes were glued to the screen, the corners of his mouth pulling down.

Mom didn't notice my shock. She was transfixed by her own image. She looked exhausted. Thin. Ten years older than she looked now, as if the life had been drained out of her. Yet she forced herself to carry a cake to the table, light candles, and interact with her family, who had indeed all come. Probably because they were worried about this shell of a woman who drifted around . . . with my father's ghost trailing after her. And by the looks of it, he was well on his way to becoming a Jimani.

"Wow, I really didn't remember how bad it got," she said.

I reached out to rub her back like Jules was rubbing mine. I kept my other hand on his leg, clutching his jeans like a life raft. Everyone gathered around a table to sing "Happy Birthday" to a tween Raely who looked a little feral, like she'd been allowed to run a bit wild and had been doing just that. She was chewing on her lower lip, trying not to smile at the gathering of relatives who were trying to pull her mother out of a hole. The ghost of her father stood in front of her mother. If he had been human, he would have been blocking her view of Raely and her birthday cake. He reached his thin, bone-white fingers up to cup the sides of Mom's face, the hazy black shadow darker and longer now, wrapping his shoulders like a cloak. His eyes were hard and black. I dug my fingers into Julian's leg. I had to stop touching Mom for fear I would do something similar.

"Where were you?" I breathed at Jules. He had been in every video until now. Why wasn't he here now when that *thing* was sucking the life out of our mother?

"I used to get . . . feelings," he said, his voice unsteady. "I figured it was just because things were so bad there for a few years. But sometimes I felt I needed to go take a break. Go somewhere else for a while. I was always with you at school though. Or when you were running around the neighborhood by yourself like a heathen."

I looked at him, brimming with questions, but one in particular.

He must have read it on my face, because he said, "I never saw him. Not once." He glanced past me toward our mother. "I don't think you or I were that interesting to him at the time. But I did stay away more right after he died. I mostly looked after you when you were off on your own. Which you were. A lot."

I glanced at Mom. Her eyes were glassy, staring at the screen. I didn't want to see anymore.

"We can take a break if you want. Just talk for a bit," I said. "Do you want more tea?" I reached for her cup and she unfroze, aiming the remote at the TV and thumbing it off before standing swiftly.

"I'll get it. You rest." She snatched up our cups and pushed the plate of cookies toward me before retreating into the kitchen. "We can chat for a bit and then pick out some movies. You can take all of these DVDs with you . . ."

I pried my claws from Julian's leg with an apologetic pat and scrubbed at my face with both hands. "What does this *mean*," I mumbled into my palms. I pushed the heels of my palms into my eyes until little stars danced across my eyelids. A tug on a strand of hair had me lifting my face from my hands.

"Mom's back," Jules said.

Mom had indeed returned, much faster than water could possibly have boiled.

She had two wine glasses in one hand and the box of Battlefield Victory in the other.

"Well, here we go," I said. "You are aware that it's barely four in the afternoon?"

"Hush. Help me open it," she said. "I've never had one of these boxes before."

I took it from her. Her hands trembled as she set our glasses on top of drink coasters. Any further teasing about the hour died in my throat. I opened the box, explaining the functionality of the plastic stopper as I poured two glasses. I wasn't sure if she truly had never worked a box before or just didn't trust her shaking hands, but if it was the latter, I decided to pretend with her. I lifted my glass to clink against hers, which she had cupped in both palms.

As much as I hated to pick at an open wound, it was a perfect segue to our ultimate mission. We took our first sips (gulps), and I waited to see if she would speak first. She didn't. Even Julian was quiet.

I opened and closed my mouth a couple of times. Took another sip of wine. Mentally reformulated my opening. Looked at Julian, who was of no help and didn't even meet my eyes. Finally, I gave myself a count of three and just blurted the first thing that came to mind, as if I'd been thrown into an improv. "You didn't remember it being that hard? Moving forward? After he was gone?"

She sighed and leaned back into the couch cushions, swirling her wine in her glass. "No." She watched her wine create a tiny whirlpool. "But honestly, so much of those first months after your father died were kind of a blur."

"Yeah," I said. Interrogator of the year.

"Ask her how she stopped it," Julian prompted.

I nodded. But said nothing. I couldn't even look at Mom. I reached for a cookie. Stopped myself. Started to reach again. Stopped. Julian exhaled in disgust and threw one at me. Mom snapped into the present at the sudden movement.

I recovered and broke the cookie in half, passing one half to her. She took it.

"I'm so sorry, sweetie," she said after chewing her tiny mouthful of cookie. She washed down her apology with a sip of wine.

"You have *nothing* to be sorry for. I'm serious. I was fine." I couldn't help a furtive glance in Julian's direction. After his outburst this morning, my survivor's guilt had revved up, coating any other feelings in an oily residue.

"You managed very well," she said.

"When did you get . . . better?"

She popped the remainder of her cookie into her mouth, followed by another gulp of wine. "The Battlefield Victory pairs really well with chocolate chip," she said, offering a tiny smile that somehow made me want to cry. "So, I press here?" She topped off her still half full glass.

"Yep," I confirmed. I was at a loss as to what to say to keep us on topic when neither of us really wanted to be discussing this. "I know I wasn't easy to deal with. I'm sorry I was such a—"

"Oh, Raely." Mom grabbed another cookie and tossed me one as well, practically commanding me to eat it. I wondered if we would even make it to pizza. "You were a *child*. And I was in a fog. You never did badly in school. You didn't act out in the traditional way, you just . . . decided to become responsible for your own whereabouts and safety much earlier than you should have." She sighed. "I guess I'm lucky either that you were very smart or that the neighborhood was very watchful."

"I'm pretty sure someone was always watching," I said. Not looking at Julian.

"I was," he said.

Mom bit into her new cookie and deliberately sipped her wine afterward. I decided to try the pairing myself. It wasn't bad. Mom swallowed and gave an appreciative nod. "Everything you did was to get my attention or to keep yourself afloat, I think. There was a time when I was in such a haze, I almost didn't see you." Another swallow. "I feel wretched about it now, Raely, I truly do."

At that moment, I wondered how many families had been splintered this way. How many Jimanis were out there in the world, pulling mothers away from their children, causing accidents and deaths, just to finish the bullshit they had started during their lives. There were some daughters who probably would have raged at their mothers, who might have said, "Yeah, actually, it sucked and it's your fault because you were all I had." And it did suck. And she was all that I had. All that I *thought* I had. But I knew so much more now, and despite all I had been through, all I felt at that moment was sorrow for her, awe at her strength, and gratitude that I was able to comprehend how much had actually been happening.

"I'm fine. We made it," I said. That oily guilt swirled through my stomach. Jules hadn't made it, even though he'd been essential in making sure that I had. "Dad was the one who caused all of this. If I'm mad at anyone, it's always him."

"Oh, sweetie," she sighed and patted my leg. "You can't let that eat away at you forever." She ate the rest of her cookie between swigs of wine, while I tried to think of a parent-appropriate response, munching my own cookie to stall. I even turned a pleading gaze toward Julian, but he was looking intently at our mother, as if he had never seen her before.

"When did the fog lift?" I asked finally. "And how?"

"Well." She set down her empty glass. "It took a lot of therapy, and a lot of help from my family, as you know, but in the end . . ." She stared off into the distance for so long that I thought maybe she was done, or that she just wasn't going to finish her answer. "It came down to me."

"What came down to you?" I had pulled my knees up under my chin and had my wine cupped in front of my face like a shield, as if it would perhaps ward off whatever awful knowledge she was about to impart.

She went to refill her glass, and her thumb slipped off the stopper, startling her. She laughed at herself. Her laugh had always been contagious, so both Julian and I laughed with her. His laugh had the exact same cadence as hers. I met his eyes. wishing that she could hear it. I offered him a cookie. He grinned but shook his head, then flicked it. I stuck out my tongue quickly before Mom could see and ask what I was doing. I longed for a way to pull him into our family.

"It came down to how *I* felt about everything that happened." She took a sip of wine, set it down, and took one of the last two cookies. "Your father's life was obviously over. When we were very young, we were very much in love. We really did want to take care of each other for the rest of our lives. I know you may not understand this, but I was hanging on to that person for as long as I could. Long after he disappeared. Long after he grew into something else. And in a way," another sip, "I was hanging onto the person that I had been before too."

Just to be doing something, I took a drink of my own wine. I didn't quite fathom what she was trying to say, and I couldn't discern any hidden ghost-killing wisdom in it, either. By the scrunched expression on Jules's face, he wasn't getting any more out of it than I was. "So you . . . changed who you were and got . . . better?"

She barked out a laugh, then smiled at me. "No, sweetie. Everyone changes. We constantly change. Finding those people who change *with* you is the challenge. And your father—" She stopped. Her face smoothed out in a way that I recognized. She was about to tell me a lie.

"Just tell me the awful truth, Mom," I said, and bit into my cookie. "Protecting me from things that have already happened won't help. Just tell me what I need to know. In case it ever happens to me and I need to find a way out of the same situation."

I saw the thought hit her almost before I had finished speaking. Her head whipped toward me, and I saw her cataloging all the injuries, the secretiveness, moving Blitz to her house.

"Oh fuck," Jules said.

I couldn't have said it better myself. Technically, the conclusion that Mom was careening toward wasn't wrong. I was being abused. But it wasn't by a boyfriend, it was by my dead father. I wasn't going to be able to explain that.

"This Luck person," she started.

"No," I said firmly. "Luck and I are not—I'm not dating anyone right now. I can just see that you're holding something back."

She sat up on the edge of the couch. I could see the wheels turning. I could see the guilt forming. I had to quash this now.

"Mom, I've done the whole repeat-the-cycle thing," I confessed quickly. "I had a couple of boyfriends that behaved like Dad, and I left them. I stopped dating for a while. I'm past it. That's . . . I don't need—" I swallowed. I glanced at Jules, his eyes were ping-ponging between me and Mom. "I just want to be able to move past Dad."

"Raely." Her eyes bored into mine. I had gotten her dark brown eyes, and Julian had gotten our dad's deep blue. "You keep showing up here hurt."

"Well, I did have an entire train wreck, which would have been a hell of an abusive relationship if a dude had managed to punch me with a train." She wasn't laughing.

Julian moved to sit next to Mom. "Raely isn't lying to you. You can tell when she's lying, she was never great at it."

I watched, spellbound, as he talked her down.

This is what he used to do with me before I could see him. As he continued talking to her, I could *see* her physically relaxing. I felt slightly manipulated, but also a little pissed that he hadn't jumped in earlier with this little trick. It was working! Jules made a circular motion with his hand as he raised his eyebrows at me, and I realized it was odd for me to be sitting here not saying anything. Although Julian was influencing her ideas, she couldn't "hear" him like I could. Her mood had shifted. I jumped back in.

"The past few weeks without Joe have just been really hard. And I've been thinking about the past a lot." Not really a lie. "I just wanted to know how you finally got out of that place."

Julian had stopped whispering in Mom's ear but stayed near her. Both of us were on the edge of our proverbial seats. What magic had our mother inadvertently discovered that had banished the Jimani? How had she shielded herself from him? Taken away his ability to hurt her?

She sighed. "I almost feel guilty saying it. I know you'll have a hard time understanding." She looked down at her interlaced fingers. "It wasn't easy, and it took a long time."

Both Jules and I leaned forward. *Here it comes . . .* However hard it was, I knew we were both determined to do it or die trying.

"I forgave him."

I blinked. "I'm sorry, what?"

"I forgave your father." She looked up from her hands and met my eyes. "I know it's difficult to—"

"How? How!" I sputtered. Julian stood slowly, his brows furrowed, looking at our mother like she had sprouted wings.

"It was just eating me up. The anger, the sadness, the blame, all of it. Once I forgave him, *really* forgave him, I was able to let it all go. The fog lifted, and it was as if life had color again. I don't know how to explain it better than that."

"This is utter horseshit," Jules said. "I can't fucking forgive him, that's an impossible ask."

I was inclined to agree.

28

WE TOOK A BREAK AFTER THE HOME MOVIES. Mom got started on the pizza. Julian lay spread out on the living room floor like a sacrifice, staring at the ceiling. I limped into the bedroom to change into my pj's at 5 p.m. Because why not?

I dug through my duffel bag for a fresh set, making a mental note to do laundry tomorrow so I'd have clean clothes when we left, and unearthed a few more old photographs that had tumbled out of the album Julian stowed away.

It seemed like weeks ago. I set them to the side as they surfaced. By the time I'd located the pajama top and bottoms I was after, I had a pile of seven pictures.

After I changed, I sat on the edge of the bed, holding the photos in my hands. The one with my dad in his fedora was on top. My eyes roved over his frozen face, finding bits of me in his almond eye shape, sharp cheekbones, and wide smile. There were bits of Julian in the dark slashes of his eyebrows, his long, straight nose, and his dark blue eyes.

I stared into those eyes. Somewhere in there was a person my mother had loved once. Someone she had found a way to forgive.

I got up from the bed and walked back into the living room, taking the photos with me. As much as it made me want to vomit, Julian and I had to find that person, the person our father had been before he was the horror that we knew.

Jules was still splayed out on the living room rug. I stepped over him carefully and set the photos down by the box of Battlefield Victory. Then I went to help my mom in the kitchen, the bones of a plan forming. We had tea while the pizzas were in the oven and easy conversation as we cleaned up the rest of the kitchen and pulled out plates. I shoved back the third one I had accidentally retrieved. Julian had joined us by the time we were slicing up pizza and debating the merits of which movies to include in our binge. Jules wanted *The Princess Bride*—"I need something with a happy ending right now"—so I lobbied for that one first.

We'd finished our teas, so I balanced tall glasses of water with our plates and napkins as I made my way to the coffee table. Mom followed with the pizzas. As I had planned, she saw the photographs once she sat down. "Where did these come from?"

"They were in my bag," I said, serving us a slice of pizza from each pie as I answered. "I was moving one of the photo albums before I left and dropped one. These fell out and I was in a hurry, so I just shoved them into my bag. I thought it was funny that they stowed away, considering everything we've been talking about, so I brought them out."

I monitored her reactions carefully as she slowly flipped through each photo in the stack. Julian watched as well, looking over her shoulder at the pictures. She had finished her rotation, still silent, and started again by the time I had swallowed my first bite of pizza.

"You said you had to forgive him to move on," I said quietly, glancing at a stone-faced Julian. "I don't know how to do that. I never knew the person he was before . . . before he was just awful."

Mom was still staring at the pictures. Julian's eyes met mine briefly from beneath lowered brows, then he frowned back at Mom. I sighed. I wasn't convinced either, but I couldn't just quit. We couldn't hide here at Mom's forever, living under the protective umbrella of her forgiveness. We had to find a way to move on for ourselves.

I leaned over and looked at the photo she was holding on top of the pile. It was of both our parents, young, flanked by two guys I didn't know. All four of them were in their winter coats, obviously in the middle of a thick snowfall, heads thrown back with laughter, arms tossed over shoulders to hold each other up. "Who are those guys?"

She blinked twice, as if she had forgotten I was there. "Oh. That's . . . well, this is Jasper . . . Jasper . . . wow . . . I forget his last name. Something with a D. And the one next to your father is Bill Cole. They were in your father's band."

"Hold up. Dad was in a *band*?"

"Oh, yes, before you were born. He gave it up shortly after." She smiled slightly down on the picture, as if the memory was a happy one. She flipped the photo over to the scrawl on the back that I hadn't been able to translate, and a laugh burst from her. She flipped it back over and smiled. "He was so funny, Raely."

"Who was funny?" I felt my brows drawing together.

"Your father," she said, flipping through the pictures again, a faint smile on her face. "I have never laughed so hard in my life. The things he would come up with. He could make anyone laugh."

"I don't remember that," I said sullenly, my shoulders stiff. I didn't look at Julian.

"Well, things changed." Her smile faded. "I'm sure you've heard stories, but the delivery wasn't easy on me or you. Or Julian." Jules whipped his head around at the sound of Mom speaking his name. My heart squeezed as emotion flashed across his face. She went on. "I was a waitress, and I couldn't go back to work for weeks. Your father's gigs were hit-or-miss with how much they paid, so your father needed to find a more regular job. But it was hard, because his band was *every-thing* to him. Bill was the best man at our wedding. He was . . . a good friend."

"Do you still . . . do you—"

"Oh, honey." Mom shook her head. "Your father drove everyone away. Bill tried for a while, though." She trailed off as she flipped to another picture. Our father and Bill Cole—who was imitating some kind of arabesque—with Ray cupping one of the larger man's feet in his hand at waist height. Both of them with goofy looks on their faces, arms held high, mid-flourish. As Mom stared at the picture, her face softened.

She laughed and looked right into my eyes. "You remind me of him sometimes."

My shock must have been visible.

"He wasn't always so angry, Raely." Her voice softened. "I have never laughed more often. I was just so happy during those first years with Ray." Her eyes dropped back to the photograph. She chuckled.

I glanced at Jules, who looked as gobsmacked as I felt.

The lines around her mouth tightened. "I don't know what shifted, Raely, but you remind me so much of his best parts. His humor, his . . . You even walk like him. You both have this careless confidence. I don't even know how to describe it. This effortless way to pull humor from even the darkest—"

"I don't remember him being funny," I whispered, staring at the faux ballerina photo.

She wiped her eyes. "Something changed when you two were small. We were under a lot of stress, and he just didn't handle it well, but there was so much light in him before. He would brighten up a room." She looked right into my eyes. "He was so much like you are. It made it easier to forgive him, to be honest. Just seeing you. All of what was good about him was right there."

I didn't know what to say. I couldn't look at Julian.

We went through the rest of the photos slowly, and she gave me a little more information with each one. Bill Cole was in three more of the seven photos. Apparently, he had been our father's best friend. Until Jules died.

"Why haven't we ever seen pictures of the band?" Julian asked.

I thought this was a good question, so I repeated it for him.

"Oh, I don't have many." She cleared her throat, put the photos face down on the coffee table, aligned her empty wine glass beneath Battlefield Victory's plastic spout and skillfully depressed the plunger. "He had a bad night about a year after you were born. Said some horrible things and burned a lot of them."

I pulled out one of the photos at random. It was Bill Cole in a striped shirt, playing piano on his knees, no piano bench to be found, with my mother perched on top in a blue dress, her hair curled, leaning on an elbow gazing at Bill while he made a comically grumpy face.

"Oh my God, are y'all pretending to be Lucy and Schroeder?" I waved the picture at her.

She didn't look, and her smile was tight as she answered. "Yep. We all went as the Peanuts characters for Halloween that year. Your dad was Charlie Brown."

LATER THAT NIGHT, after too much of *everything*, Mom and I both stumbled to bed, vowing to sleep in tomorrow. I hoped she would, but she never slept past 7 a.m. no matter what she'd done the night before.

We hugged goodnight with toothbrushes hanging out of our mouths and retreated to our rooms. My brain was still floating gently in Battlefield Victory, and my body was achingly suggesting that mayhap blissful unconsciousness would be the healing salve I desperately needed as I shuffled toward bed.

Julian was sitting on it.

I sagged like a marionette with cut strings.

Jules folded his arms.

I crawled onto the bed, hoping he would move. He didn't. I sighed, collapsing into a fetal position at the foot. "Jules, I'm so tired, my eyes hurt. Can we please deconstruct everything in the morning?"

"No." His sober ass was unrelenting. "We're talking about this now."

"Julian." I pitched onto all fours and shuffled forward until I was kneeling in front of him. "I did so much heavy lifting today." I put my hands on his shoulders. My eyes were half-shut with exhaustion. "I hated it, and it was hard." I wrapped my arms around his neck, deliberately hanging on to him. "Pleeeeeeeaaaaasseee let me into the bed. If you ever loved me at all—"

"Jesus H. Christ," he said, half hugging me back because he had no choice.

"Please, Jules, let me get into bed and I promise we can talk. Just let me lie down." I threw all of my weight into his dimension. "*Please.*"

"What are you *doing*?" He tried to shove me off, but my arms were still wrapped around his neck. I was getting stronger at interdimensional contact. He could either relinquish control of the bed or push me off it.

"I'm beseeching you," I mumbled into his shirt. "Let me into my bed. My physical body is in pain. You don't understand."

"Fine, just . . . stop slobbering on me." He moved aside, shifting me off him.

Victory was mine. I slid between the sheets with a sigh that was almost a groan. I let my head fall back toward the pillow that wasn't there. My skull bounced off the mattress, harder than I had expected. With all the wine, it was disorienting.

"No pillows until we talk." Julian held both pillows hostage.

"Fine," I said, eyes still closed, head swimming. I adjusted to the new latitude. I could live without pillows now that I had the bed. "What do you need to say?"

"What's your goal here? We need a plan. We can't stay here forever."

God. Had he even been paying attention?

"We're going to go see Bill Cole," I said slowly, as if I were *The Evening You've Just Experienced For Dummies*. "We're going to find out about our dad from him. We're going to try to see what he was before that . . . shadow thing. Before he was our horrible father. We're going to try to find it in ourselves to forgive him."

"Raely," Julian said slowly, as if he were *I'm Your Dead and Murdered Brother For Dummies*. "I cannot forgive him. He killed me when I was two years old."

"Julian," I said, keeping the tone going. "If you have any other suggestions that will prevent the Jimani from destroying both of us, then I would be oh-so-happy to hear them. And don't forget, your precious Lovonia sent us here to learn how Mom did it."

Julian was quiet for so long that I began drifting off to sleep. It occurred to me as I did so that this was probably the first time in a very long time that we had done a whisper-fight in the darkness to avoid waking our mom.

Julian had been matching my volume, probably without thinking about it, even though he didn't need to. Just as the thoughts in my head had started spinning themselves into dreams, he spoke again and hauled me back into the present.

"You don't even know where Bill Cole is."

"Yes, I do," I breathed, hoping to slide back into that dreamy spot quickly.

I felt him flop down next to me, intentionally bumping into me to shake me awake. "Where?" This time his voice was jarringly loud.

I sighed, the sleepy spot slipping through my fingers. "I found his social media while we were watching *The Shawshank Redemption*. He's still playing music. He's got a gig in Rosemont Sunday night. We just get off the train one stop before the city."

He was quiet.

"Now is when you should say, 'Thank you for doing all the work, Raely, you're an amazingly resourceful person and the best sister anyone could ever hope for.'"

A beat, then: "You were on your phone during *Shawshank*?"

"It was during the part where Brooks kills himself. That part makes me sad."

Silence again. Nonsense dreams wound tendrils through my brain. I let go of my breathing completely until it became slow, shallow, and automatic and my lungs might not even have been a part of me anymore. I floated, my body lighter and lighter until it finally grew so diaphanous that it floated away.

My ears were the last to go. I heard, "I love you, Raely," before they blew away with the rest of me.

29

MOM AND I DID SLEEP IN THE NEXT DAY. I slept later, but she slept late.
For her.

Julian finally prodded me into consciousness at 10 a.m., telling me
that Mom had been up for an hour and a half and that it looked like she
was waiting for me to eat. With that motivation, and my own growling
stomach and fuzzy head to urge me onward, I dressed quickly. I found
her in the kitchen looking at tea and cereal. I quickly nixed those ideas,
and we went to Starbucks for carbs and enormous coffees that someone else poured. We had a nice day.

We went shopping. We had our lunchtime wine. Julian was there
the whole time. Part of me wondered if Mom could sense him. She was
chattering away on the phone to one of her friends who had called to
discuss a Sunday night card game as we lugged our shopping to the
car. While digging for Kleenex in the backseat, she tossed the grocery
bags behind her to be held—presumably thinking I was the one back
there—and she handed them to Julian instead, without even noticing.

He just took them with a bemused smile. My hands were already full with the bags we were trying to load *into* the backseat. Although there were people going in and out of the store, no one noticed the briefly levitating shopping bags, and Mom took them back from Jules, tossing them back into the car and then reaching for what I had without breaking her phone conversation. For ten seconds, we were as close to a normal family as the three of us had ever been.

It was my favorite moment of the day.

I'd never seen Jules smile so much.

When we got home, we did my laundry and ordered Chinese for dinner. We watched one movie that night (*The Last Unicorn*). Mom and I folded laundry, Blitz played with Julian, and Mom laughed at how Blitz "just had the zoomies" while they ran around the room. We all went to bed early. Julian and I talked a little bit about our plans for the next day, but there wasn't much to say. We were both still glowing from our nice family day and didn't want to wreck it with too much talk of the future. We didn't even mention the shopping bag moment. It was one of those magical bonding times that was best left undissected.

THE NEXT DAY at the train station, I promised Mom that we'd figure things out with Blitz soon. She assured me that it was no bother and that maybe she should come up for my birthday anyway and bring Blitz with her then. I pulled in both Mom and Jules when we said goodbye, making it a group hug. She didn't notice anything strange.

WE GOT OFF the train at Rosemont an hour before Bill Cole's gig, but with nowhere else to go, I pulled the duffel bag's handles over my shoulders and headed toward the club.

"You know where you're going?" Jules asked.

"Devon got to do a short set here a few times and got Joe a gig as the host once. I came to see them. They do bands and other stuff too." There was no sidewalk leading away from the Metra station. We marched along the gravel shoulder for a few moments in silence.

"How come you never did any comedy here?"

I snorted. "I'm not that good."

"Yes, you are," Jules said. "You were, anyway. You were better than Joe."

My insides slowly twisted into a hurricane of emotion. Julian thought I was good. My *brother* said I was funny without any prompting. Better than Joe, he said. My own brain huffed that this was obviously a lie. Sadness that Joe was gone coated it all. *I'm probably done with comedy for good anyway, so what does it matter?*

Church Laugh Comedy Bar & Lounge was about a mile and a half from the Metra. By the time we arrived, my fingers, toes, and most of my face were numb. I had wrapped my extra-long scarf around the lower half of my face, leaving only my eyes exposed. My eyelashes were still frozen when I stepped into the club.

A piano plunked jangly cords into the blissfully heated air. In the main room, neat round tables were scattered about the floor, ringed by squashy booths. A long bar stretched from the door along the back of the room facing the stage opposite, which held a drum kit, a few music stands, and the piano, presently being commanded by a barrel of a man with flyaway blond hair shot with silver at the temples, totally engrossed in his dance with the black and white keys.

The bar was empty and the sound spectacular. Even the lone bartender didn't clock me as I walked in, engrossed as he was with watching the pianist sway back and forth with the energy of his music. He was arched over the keys, the spindly piano bench dwarfed beneath him. I marveled that the flimsy vessel of wood and ivory was even able to contain this behemoth and his explosion of sound.

Neither Julian nor I spoke as I drifted toward the stage, gradually loosening my winter gear. My coat was unbuttoned—new buttons sewn on by Mom—and I had just pulled my hat from my head when the pianist looked up from beneath his caterpillar eyebrows and caught my eye.

The rhythmic plinking skipped half a beat. He didn't break eye contact as he recovered and hammered out a finale. He gently shut the lid to the piano with spatula-sized palms and rested his elbows on it.

"Is this a Mynor I see before me?" a surprisingly soft voice inquired. The giant gave me a half smile.

"I—My last name is Videc," I stammered. "But my middle name . . ."

"Jillian's maiden name. And you look—goddamn you look just like her. You have to be Ray's daughter. Aren't you?" He stood up without waiting for an answer, dusted his palms unnecessarily on the sides of his slacks, and hopped off the stage with an agility at odds with his size.

He ambled toward me, his soft brown eyes unblinking, and extended his hand. I wanted to turn in on myself. I blushed, like he could already see too much of my past, secrets I wasn't even aware of. My shoulders tensed.

"He's not going to hurt you," Julian said in my ear. I instantly relaxed. I had almost forgotten I wasn't alone. Yes, I had to do the talking, but Jules was there to help me with the emotional part. I reached out and shook Bill Cole's hand.

The bartender arrived with two beers.

"Thanks, Joe," Bill said. My heart flipped at the name. Bill looked back at me. "You want a water too . . . ?" He left the space open.

"Raely," I filled it. "Yes, please. Water would be great."

His gaze cleared, and he smiled as if reminded of something pleasant. "Two waters for me and Ms. Raely Videc. Bring a menu when you come back. Just for fun, Joe."

"You got it," Joe said as he disappeared behind the bar.

I shoved my duffel against the stage as we sat down at a two-top below the piano. Julian perched on the edge of the stage near me.

"Wow," Bill said, lifting his beer to his lips, shaking his head slightly, his gaze still raking every inch of my face. It was as if someone had shown him the fossil of a prehistoric beast that he was certain he'd seen but had been unable to confirm with photographic evidence, and now the hearsay was officially validated.

I pulled my heavy coat off my shoulders and let it drape over the back of my chair, then unzipped my hoodie pocket and pulled out the seven photographs. I allowed their edges to shuffle against my thumb as I pressed them onto the table between us. His gaze dropped from me to the photos as I leaned back against the flimsy wooden frame of my chair and tilted the chilled glass of the beer bottle to my mouth with trembling hands. Much easier to appear calm if you have something to do with your hands.

"Don't get trashed," Jules whispered in my ear. I wanted to smack him for saying that after one sip of beer. I cut him a glare, but that was all I dared before turning back to see Bill Cole pulling the photographs toward him.

My hands were no longer shaking. My head was clear. The fire had banked. My jerk of a brother had done it to center me. I was equal parts grateful and pissed at how easily he manipulated me. If only I knew myself that well.

"Wow." Bill Cole was going through the photographs a second time, examining details, checking the inscriptions scrawled on the back, sometimes smiling, sometimes shaking his head. "I have not thought about some of these people in decades."

I cleared my throat and took a sip of water. "I don't want to take up too much of your time, Mr. Cole—"

The giant tipped back his head and laughed, his bear-paw hands falling to the table with a thud, still holding the fan of photographs between his fingers like playing cards.

"So sorry, darlin.'" He thumbed a tear from the corner of one eye, his apple cheeks reddened. "No one calls me Mister anything outside of when I'm makin' a deposit at the bank, and sometimes not even then." He winked. It was somehow much more charming than when Dylan did it. "Please call me Cole. Like your daddy did."

My spine stiffened. "Daddy" seemed like a term for a nice man, who had bounced his daughter on his knee, taken her out for ice cream, and called her "princess."

That man was so foreign to the one I had known that he seemed like fiction. I pushed past it.

"Thanks, Cole." It felt weird, but I went with it. "I just . . . according to my mom, you knew my father better than anyone else—"

"I thought so too, I thought so too," he said, almost absently, as he began to lay the photos out in front of him like tiles. "He got strange there at the end, but there was a time when I thought Ray and I would be in each other's lives forever." He shook his head. "I still can't believe he's gone sometimes."

Well, not entirely, I wanted to say. Instead, I answered, "I never knew he was in a band."

"No? You're kiddin' me." Cole slapped the photos on the table between us and took a swig of his beer. It seemed like a good idea, so I imitated him. He set his bottle down with a soft *thunk.* "You were what, nine or ten when he died?"

"Eleven."

"Eleven," he said. "And you never saw pictures? He never taught you any music? Never told you about it? You never saw his bass?"

I shook my head. "I don't remember him ever teaching either of us anything."

"That's right, that's right, there were two of you." He sighed and took an even deeper pull from his beer bottle. "Raely and Julian. Always thought that was cute." He finished his beer, waved at Joe and tapped the table, which vibrated a little with each prod of his thick finger. I stole a glance at Jules. He was staring intently at Cole, his arms folded across his chest, legs stretched out and crossed at the ankles. He'd dipped his chin, but his shaggy hair still didn't quite conceal the brightness in his eyes.

"Were you around when we were born?"

Cole chuckled. "You kidding? I was in the waiting room, handing out cigars! Weren't allowed to smoke 'em there, of course." He chuckled wheezily. "In fact, I have a photo at home somewhere of me holding each of ya in one hand. Holding you both out toward the camera like you was two little pies. You were both so tiny. Never knew they made people so tiny."

Joe arrived then with another beer, and Cole asked for a double order of fries after making sure that I wasn't "some kind of health nut" and would have some. I asked for some mustard to dip mine in, but otherwise agreed.

"You're so weird," Jules commented.

"You like licorice, so shut up," I tossed over my shoulder while Cole was busy tapping a few other things on the menu in consultation with Joe.

"Wait, what?"

"Hush." My face warmed. I'd forgotten that licorice was my invention.

"Never got the bass back, huh?" Cole said, turning back toward me with his fresh beer. "Well, I want to say I'm surprised, but I'm not. Not really. He would have done anything for Jillian. He sure loved that bass, though. Couldn't believe when he sold her. Almost feel bad for the girl," he chuckled. "She was his first love, after all."

For some reason that raised my ire. I'd never thought of my father as capable of really caring for anything. "Well, he was shit at loving things. He burned all the band pictures when I was young; that's why I never saw any. And the thought of him teaching me anything, aside from how to drink and hit by example, is laughable."

Our fries arrived then and Cole nodded at me through another swig of beer. He looked back at the photos on the table, then back at me. He gestured to the crinkle fries, moved the little cup of mustard over to my side of the table, then took a fry himself. "I guess I never asked you, Ms. Raely, why did you come visit me?"

I glanced at Julian before swiping a fry through mustard. I popped it into my mouth and chewed, stalling.

"Just tell him the truth," Julian said. "I mean . . . obviously not *all* of it. He seems like a decent guy, but I don't know that he's up for the whole shebang."

I nodded as I swallowed. "I've been walking around with this . . . bitterness. I'm full of anger at him, and I don't want to be." I shrugged and grabbed another fry. "It seemed like you knew him well, at least according to my mom. Maybe you can tell me about another side of him?"

Cole selected a few fries and arranged them onto the napkin in front of him before he spoke. "You know, I never knew my mother," he said. "She died when I was . . . oh, five. Six. Didn't have the complicated relationship you had with Ray, but my dad remarried a couple years later, and we never talked about her much. I never thought to go find out more about her on my own. By the time I thought I could have . . ." He stuffed two fries into his mouth and chewed, looking up at the ceiling. "I'll tell you what I can, Ms. Raely, and I hope it helps you. Ask me anything."

"Ask him how he met Mom," Jules said immediately.

"Thanks," I said at the same time. "I appreciate you taking the time. Do you remember how they met? My mom and dad?"

Cole chuckled. "Like it just happened." His face crinkled, and his brown eyes glittered as if lit from within. It was impossible not to smile back at him. "We were warming up for a gig, and she walked in during a snowstorm. Stopped just inside the door and stared up at the stage. Just like you did when you walked in here. I thought I was seeing a ghost." He tossed back another fry and used his beer to wash it down. "Couldn't help but clock her when she came in, but she was staring straight at Ray. I looked over at him, and I swear his fingers were on autopilot, because he hit a few sour notes just gaping at her before one of the other boys snapped at him to keep up." He chuckled again. "That was it for him. She was there for her first day waitressing. He played his best and worst that night while she was working those tables. Couldn't take his eyes off her for the first few songs and really threw us. We took a break and were in the middle of telling him to get his head in the game when she walked over with a little smile and handed him her number on a napkin. Played the best set of our lives after that."

"They started dating right away?" I was tossing fries into my maw like popcorn. Julian even uncrossed one set of limbs and leaned forward slightly.

"That very night," Cole said. "Ray waited for her to get off her shift to buy her a drink after we had packed up. Eventually, the closing crew had to kick them out. That was it. From then on, there was nothing he wouldn't do for Jillian. He practically moved into her place until they got their own. Proposed to her after six months. Sold his car for the ring."

"What?" I choked on my beer. "That's ridiculous and irresponsible!"

Julian muttered, "Seriously."

Cole threw back his head and howled.

"Not a big dramatic romance fan, eh, Ms. Raely?" Cole was still chuckling. "Well, we happened to agree with you. Not that we didn't love Jillian—she was the sweetest thing—but we worried about him getting to gigs with that bass on nothing but public transit. He said he'd be able to borrow Jill's car once she was his fiancée, and they'd work it out. He somehow always got his way in things like that. They lived near the train, which helped."

Joe brought over some fried calamari rings and a veggie tray. "Thought you might want some roughage," Cole said, pushing the veggies in my direction. "Help yourself."

I did. "I can't believe my mom got engaged after six months."

"Oh, Ray was quite the charmer." Cole anointed the calamari with a lemon wedge. "He was determined that Jillian was the one for him. He couldn't believe he had snagged the girl of his dreams. Didn't want to wait and risk her getting bored or falling for someone else. I think he may have actually said that. He promised her the moon. Said he'd make sure they had everything they needed. Everything she wanted."

"So she asked him to quit the band?" Julian said to me with raised eyebrows. "Doesn't seem like her."

"She wanted him to quit music?" I asked Cole, then burned my mouth on a calamari ring, slamming back the rest of my beer on top of it because the only other option was spitting it out.

"Hell no!" Cole said. "She never asked him to give up anything. Her one stipulation when he proposed was that she wanted a family. She wanted a baby."

My stomach twisted. I couldn't look at Jules. I concentrated on fishing an ice cube out of my water glass and pushing it into my mouth to mitigate my calamari damage.

Cole looked down at the table and once again pulled fries one by one onto his napkin before eating them, as if he were soliciting their advice. "Ray was never cut out to be a family guy. That's my opinion. He'd never hung on to anything stable in his life before Jillian. He liked traveling gigs, he liked odd jobs, didn't like to be tied down to a schedule. But he did. Not. Want to let go of her. They were cute together. I don't want to give you the wrong impression. Jill loved Ray. Came to all his gigs if she wasn't working. Even helped us put a website together. Helped carry equipment if she came on the road with us. Her friends liked him. Hell, even her family didn't throw too much of a fit when they decided to make the engagement short. They were all about each other."

"What happened?" Jules and I said together. Internally, I was imagining going back in time and shaking my mother for marrying someone she'd known less than a year. Love was so dumb. Maybe this was why I'd never heard these stories. I'd also probably shown very little interest.

Oily guilt swirled through me once again.

"Well . . . as these things go, Jill got pregnant right away. She was older, in her mind, and didn't want to wait. Oh, but she was over the moon. As soon as they hit that three-month mark, she was telling everyone. Couldn't have been happier."

"Was my dad happy?" I made myself ask the question even though I knew the answer. My dad had never been happy to be a father. Never.

"Overjoyed," Cole said softly.

I looked up at him, my eyebrows forcing creases into existence between them. I heard Julian snort beside me. He had recrossed his arms and was jiggling his leg. The look he was giving Cole . . . I wondered if that was how my face looked. It was as if someone had told a ten-year-old that no, Santa *was* real. All of that mounting evidence to the contrary had been a mistake. Jules looked like he wanted so badly to believe, but that he'd be an idiot to be taken in by the nonsense.

"You'll forgive me if I find that difficult to swallow," I said finally.

The corners of Cole's mouth lifted, but his eyes were shadowed. "Overjoyed," he repeated softly. "One of the guys in the band got him a part-time job with some steady pay, and Jillian had already started working part-time at a Starbucks opposite her waitressing gig for the insurance. We threw 'em a shower and everything. Hell, I helped build a goddamn crib with Ray over a few beers. He truly was happy. And Jillian just . . . glowed. They had it all worked out. She had some family not far away that would come in and help for a few weeks after you were born and . . ." He stopped, shook his head, and killed his second beer.

I looked at Jules. He was frowning down at his shoes. "Maybe he just didn't want both of us," he whispered.

It felt like a hot knife in my gut, but I had to ask. Julian wanted to know, and I needed to give him what peace I could. "Was it . . . was it because there were two of us? Is that what changed?"

"No," Cole said. "Don't get me wrong, that was a surprise, and of course it made things a little more challenging, but no. If I'm being honest, I think . . ." he stopped. He pulled more fries onto his napkin but made no move to eat them. Instead, he dragged his finger through a ring of condensation on the table. He was silent for so long, I thought he had forgotten I was there.

"What do you think?" I asked. He flinched and I asked again. "You said, 'if I'm being honest, I think . . .' then you stopped. What do you think?"

He sighed, scrubbed his hands through his hair and leaned back in his chair. "I don't know that you came here for my opinions. Opinions aren't facts."

"Um. I came here *explicitly* for your opinions." Heat began to scour the back of my sternum. "I'm not . . . collecting evidence for a jury. I'm trying to piece together a sense of who my father was and why he became such a hateful shit. And maybe . . . entertain the idea that he wasn't always like that."

"God, I wish he could hear the things I'd like to say right now," Julian said. He was scowling at Cole beneath his mop of anime fringe.

Cole slowly shook his head from side to side. "If I'm being honest," he spoke so quietly that I had to lean forward to hear him. "I think he thought he had your mother then. I think he thought that creating this life was an even more permanent tie between the two of them. That now she was even more indelibly *his*." He shook his head again, as if he didn't want to hear the words he spoke. "But then he saw how much she loved the two of you, and he saw that the love between a mother and her child—children—was different and even more permanent than how she loved him."

I blinked and sat up, spine locked against the back of my chair.

"He tried. He *did* try. She had a hard labor—you both came early, of course, not uncommon with twins. Her mother and aunt couldn't get off in time to come down when it happened. She couldn't go back to work. He went full-time. At first it was just going to be for a while, until Jillian got her feet under her, but then one of you got sick. I honestly don't remember which, and the bills were just . . . He had to sell the bass. We had to get someone else to play with us, because we were losing gigs. Everyone acted like it was temporary at first, but he got stranger and stranger. It was like he started going down some dark hole. Didn't want Jill to go back to work anymore. Said he was taking care of it. Almost didn't let her out of the house. Like he owned her. It was . . . strange."

My throat dried up. I took a sip of my water and almost choked.

"Ask him about when I died. Ask him if he saw him. If he hung out with him." Julian was standing next to me now, one hand on the back of my chair, leaning over me, glaring intently at Cole. I felt suffocated. I hated this. I hated everything about this conversation. I didn't want to know what our father had done. I didn't want to hear any more about Julian dying.

But there was no other way forward. Julian deserved answers. I stared at the mustard cup in front of me and consciously took three deep breaths. "Were you around much then?" I asked.

"I tried to stop by," Cole said, scratching under his chin. He didn't meet my gaze. "It was . . . uncomfortable over there after a while. Bringing up the band or playing or music at all would eat away at Ray, and that's . . . I mean, that's what I do. That's what *we* used to do. He didn't like his job, so that was a sore topic, and poor Jill . . . It was like she was being rung dry. So, after a while, I called less. And if he made excuses or didn't pick up, I let it go. Probably should've done more. Tried harder." He shook his head.

"Were you . . . I mean, did you see him after . . . after my brother died?" I couldn't stop the trembling in my hands and folded them into the sleeves of my hoodie.

"I went to the funeral." Cole's voice was low and husky. "That was . . . I never want to do that again."

I forced myself to ask. "Was he upset?"

Cole lifted his eyes to mine and held my gaze. His eyebrows contracted. "He was devastated. Blamed himself. Managed to get through the service somehow, then got blind drunk. It was one of the last times the original band was together, trying to wrangle Ray into the back of our van to get him home. Once we got him in there, he broke down, sobbing his heart out. Asking, 'What have I become?' Cursing himself because he felt his life was worthless now that one of his babies was dead. Wondering, how he could let this happen. I've never seen *anyone* so torn up. In fact, we all sat out there in the van, in front of your house, for hours with him. Couldn't let him in there like that. Jillian had family over. Hell, you were in there, all of two years old, still awake, probably wondering what the heck was going on. Terrible night." He took a gulp of water.

I glanced at Julian. His face was unreadable. He was no longer clenched up with arms tightly crossed, nor was he leaning over like he was in an interrogation room. He was standing beside me, staring at Cole.

"We lost touch after that," Cole continued. "I tried to go and check on your folks that week a couple of times. It was like a switch flipped in Ray. Wouldn't talk about the things he said. Wouldn't go get help. The Ray that I knew got eaten away. He was a little strange before, yeah, but when Julian died . . . as far as I'm concerned, that's when Ray died too. At least all that was good in him."

The corners of my eyes were burning. I blinked hard and swallowed.

Cole cleared his throat. "I'm sorry for what you and Jillian must have gone through over the next, what, nine years? Jesus. He did love your mother, of that I'm sure. Maybe too much. Lost himself somewhere along the way. And he did love you and your brother. He may have been shitty at it, like you said, but at least when I knew him, there wasn't a thing he didn't give up so that you would have a life. I know that doesn't make up for how things turned out, but I hope it helps you a little, Ms. Raely."

I was grateful for the numbness coating my body. At least I could be polite and not burst into tears or fly into a rage. "I know that you've probably gotta get ready for your show, but I really do appreciate this. Really."

After refusing my offer to pay for some of the food, Cole scooped up the photographs and thumbed through them one last time. "You sure you don't want to stay for the show tonight? A couple of the guys coming down used to play with Ray, too. They'd remember your mom also."

I pushed the corners of my mouth up into a smile. "I can't tonight, but if you play around the city regularly, maybe I could come another time?" My heart stumbled a bit as I asked. I didn't really know if this was a can of worms I wanted to open. Would my mom even want me associating with these people? But Cole had been kind, and he'd handed me a chunk of my past that I didn't even know was missing.

His grin split his face and was once again contagious. He dug out his wallet and teased a business card out from behind his ID. "I keep a couple of these on me in case we run into any talent scouts. Or cute girls." Another grin. "The guys would love to meet you. This has our website on it, and my email and cell number. If there's a gig you wanna go to, just give me a shout and I'll put you on the list. Or if you just want to reach out." He passed me the business card, and I tucked it safely into my wallet. "Oh, don't forget these." He picked up the photos. "Bring 'em back when you come to a gig, eh? The other guys would get a kick out of seeing them."

"Why don't you hang on to them for now," I said, a corner of my mouth drifting upward. "I can get them back from you. Next time."

30

CHUNKS OF SNOW TOPPLED OFF MY BOOTS onto the floor of the train. A small, brackish pond glistened around my rubber soles. I watched the water fill in the little trenches on the corrugated flooring, sliding back and forth with the motion of the train. My entire focus was narrowed to the part of myself that existed below the knees. The only part that didn't feel like cracking apart.

Julian and I hadn't spoken since leaving the club. We'd silently waited for a train that would take us to Lovonia's and now sat in suspended animation in a nearly deserted car. There were five drunk frat boys at the other end, but they couldn't have given a shit about anyone else on the train. Raely-of-two-months-ago would have resented their presence, but current-Raely appreciated their distracting energy. Any ghosts sniffing about would undoubtedly detect their vibe before mine.

Jules's sneaker edged into view. He had stopped his stationary vigil by the handrail and taken a seat next to me. Locating his dimension had become so second nature that I felt warmth from his presence as he scooted closer. He kicked my shoe with his.

I took my time pulling out my headphones and plugging them into my phone, although I honestly didn't think the frat party would notice even if I'd started conducting full séances. "Hey," I said to our shoes once I was finally situated.

"What's wrong?"

I almost laughed at him, because *everything* was wrong. Because I was being a coward, I said, "What do you mean?"

He sighed heavily and grabbed my face in both hands to yank my head around.

"What's. Wrong?" he said loudly.

"What the hell, Jules?" I yelped.

He released my face. "You won't look at me. And your—you feel off."

"Were you about to actually comment on my energetic *vibe*?" I rolled my eyes.

"Stop being a brat."

We glared at each other. I felt my mouth tightening as Jules's eyebrows dropped. I looked away first. I didn't know how to articulate what I was feeling. My mother believed that Julian's death was an accident. She had forgiven my father for that accident, and a number of other things. Julian believed that he'd been pushed, whether it was because a ghost was attached to my father, or . . .

I didn't know what to believe. Julian had said I was there, and I had tried hard to remember. As scared as I had been, I did try. But I couldn't even remember living in a place with a balcony. I couldn't even remember Julian-my-imaginary-friend. I was trying to wrap my mind around the probability that I would never really know what had happened or why, and I somehow needed to forgive my father either way.

"Sorry," I whispered.

He put an arm across my shoulder. "What are you feeling guilty for this time?"

I let my head drop forward, my crown smacking against his breastbone. For a full minute, I let myself close my eyes and breathe. Once I'd pulled myself together, I pushed upright and glanced at the frat party at the other end of the car. One of them had apparently tried to do a handstand against the far wall and—obviously—was unsuccessful. The others were enjoying his failure loudly. They hadn't noticed me at all.

"Jules." He was mirroring me. Both of us had our hands in our laps, palms up, and both of us were staring at our fingers. A faint smile flashed across my face at our twinning. "I feel like I'm betraying you by trying to forgive him."

And there it was.

For a moment, neither of us said anything. There was nothing but the motion of the train and the fluorescent lights and the backdrop of drunken laughter from the opposite end of the car.

"Raely," Julian said softly, still looking at his cupped hands. "These past few weeks have been the best and worst of my . . . life, for lack of a better term. You didn't want me at first; I freaked you out. But you let me in. I feel like we've been able to be brother and sister, and a lot of that is because of what you've done. I've always been here. I didn't know what we were, sure, but I knew that we belonged together."

I stared glumly at him. I tried to smile, but my mouth wouldn't work.

"You've had a terrible few months," Jules continued. "I know, because I've been around for your whole life. This has sucked."

That made me chuckle.

Jules smiled back. "Despite having the worst year of your life, you've somehow still learned how to find another dimension and move things telepathically, get to know the brother that you never knew you had, and basically let him move in with you." His eyes glistened. "I think you've been a pretty great sister. All things considered."

"Well, when you put it that way, I do sound kind of awesome."

Jules snorted. The train pulled up to our stop. It was lightly snowing as we stepped onto the platform. I made the first footprints in fresh powder. Jules didn't disturb it, which was still weird for me when we walked side by side.

"You never got birthday presents, or Christmas presents . . . but you were there the whole time," I said. It was an obvious statement, but it bothered me.

"I've made peace with all of this by now, Raely."

"I haven't," I said. "What do you want this year? I'll do something. We can do something for our birthday. And we can do something for Christmas too. Do you want to go somewhere? Do you want me to . . . like, get a dog or something? Go skiing? We can . . . do things."

My face burned, and I stopped talking. Maybe I'd been insensitive even to bring it up.

But Jules laughed, a light, easy sound. "I think Blitz would be upset if you brought home a dog, but it might be fun to go somewhere." He grinned at me. The joy in his face lifted me. "If you can afford it."

I chuckled, a knot in my chest relaxing. "I'll find a way. Or you can just enjoy cheaper places. Or let me bring friends."

"Yeah," he said. "Maybe you could bring Luck. He seemed like he could potentially weather the storm that is you."

My stomach dropped. I still hadn't heard from Luck. The hospital had said he was released the last time I called to check, but my calls and texts to him had gone unanswered. "You heard what his mom said. He doesn't want to see me. I should stop causing trouble in his life."

There weren't a lot of people out, and the glow of the streetlights catching on the flurries was beautiful. A fresh coat of snow always seemed to quiet the world. As much as I disliked the cold, I had always appreciated snowfall. And walking through fresh powder while your heart was cracking felt emotionally appropriate.

"But did you talk to Luck?" Jules asked.

I kicked at the sparkling snowdrifts with the toes of my boots.

"You should talk to Luck."

"I tried. I've texted, and I've left voicemails."

"If he was in the hospital, they could have deleted those."

I forced a laugh that I didn't feel. "I don't want to be a crazy stalker. If he doesn't want me . . ." I had to stop and focus on the soft powder being pushed aside by my scruffy boots in the orange glow of the streetlight. I hadn't realized until that moment how much I'd *wanted* Luck to want me. "If he doesn't want me, I don't want to push myself on him. Maybe we can still be friends."

We passed under a few more streetlights without speaking. The snow was falling swiftly and finely enough that it was gilding me in frost. Julian, of course, was untouched. I took a selfie of the two of us being snow pretty in different ways.

Lovonia's storefront was just ahead. Something tight in my center eased at the sight of it. This place that I had been so afraid of was now a haven.

"You need to talk to Luck face-to-face. Or at least get him on the phone." Jules stopped and admired a particularly attractive, swirly snowdrift being blown apart by a passing gust. "He likes you. And he's not an asshole. I think you should give it a shot."

I pulled my attention from the snow at my feet and looked Julian in the eye. He gazed back, unflinching. The streetlight illuminated his irises, displaying the unfair brilliance of his dark blue. *Why did I have to get brown?* I thought. "I'll call him," I promised. "Again."

The left side of his mouth curved up in the customary half smile, and he strode ahead to Lovonia's stoop. Five feet away, his steps faltered. I instinctively panned the area for danger and registered that the lights were off in the psychic shop.

All lights.

And the door stood ajar, moving slightly on a phantom breeze.

31

"MAYBE IT'S JUST A NORMAL BREAK-IN," I said, then giggled hysterically at the realization that mortal criminals were the best-case scenario here. For a moment, both of us stood frozen, the snow swirling around us, and stared at the swaying door.

"What do we do?" Julian asked me, as if I were a paragon of rational thought.

"We have to go in," I said, my heart hammering harder and faster against my ribs at the thought, but there was no other option. "I mean, we have to see if she's okay."

We peered at the door. Neither of us took a step forward.

"I'll go first," Jules said. "Get your shields up and ready."

"I should go first. My shields are stronger."

"I'm less breakable than you are."

"You're less *substantial* than I am in every way."

"I'm the oldest."

"Oh my God, like two *minutes*, Julian."

"Shhh!" He stalked forward, his silhouette backlit by a streetlight and accented by the falling snow. Ugh. He looked cool.

I was right on Julian's heels when we crossed the threshold. It was cold. The radiator wheezed in the corner of the room, fighting against the winter wind that was pushing at the doorway. Although I hated cutting off the exit, I shut the door behind me as softly as I could.

The room was dark, but the streetlights outside the floor-to-ceiling windows cast enough light that I could see the disarray. It was as if a small tornado had hopped through the front room, leaving some tables completely untouched and destroying others. The purple curtains had been yanked down, allowing the light to spill through the tall windows, illuminating heaps of detritus.

I stepped carefully around a scattered tumble of crystals, making my way to the back hallway.

"Lovonia?" I whispered, my voice trembling.

Julian was steps ahead of me. He paused in the black frame of the hallway and reached his hand back behind him. I took it, throwing a shining shield in front of us.

"Can you see?" I breathed as we shuffled forward.

A raspy voice emerged from the shadows. "He's been looking for you."

My entire body flinched away from the sound, crashing into the wall beside me. I accidentally yanked my shield back, smashing it into Julian and knocking him flat on his ass.

The voice chuckled rustily.

"Jesus Christ, Lovonia," I gasped, leaning weak-kneed against the wall, pressing a hand to my chest to keep my heart from bursting through. "I know it's on brand for you, but you are really fucking creepy sometimes."

Scraping himself off the floor, Jules muttered something about heart attacks in the afterlife while Lovonia, still chuckling, handed us each an unlit candle and then waved us into the front room.

"He likes to shut off the lights, your father," she said as she plunked a fat candle onto her counter and lit its three wicks. "Flair for the dramatic."

My veins turned to ice, and I spun around, scanning for that shadowy skeletal face, although I knew that I would have felt his presence by now if he were still in the building.

"At least *you* come by it honestly," Jules snarked at me.

I squeaked indignantly. "I am *not* dramatic!" I said, part of me realizing that once again he had pulled me back from blind panic by being annoying. "Drama happens to me."

Julian snorted and placed his candle on an undisturbed table, lighting it with a snap of his fingers.

"Hey, that was cool. Can I do that?" I placed my candle on the nearest surface and snapped at the wick several times with no result.

"You have to pull heat from your core," Jules said, then snapped my candle, lighting the wick for me.

"You don't even have a core," I muttered.

He opened his mouth to retort but Lovonia barked at us to help her right a table.

While the three of us carefully hauled the long, heavy piece of oak upright, I decided to hell with preamble. "Why didn't you tell us any of this before? Like Julian's name. That the Jimani was our father," I asked, tugging my end of the table toward me and centering it in the room. "If you knew what we had to do this whole time, why send us all over the place trying to figure it out?"

Lovonia pulled the beaded table runner out from underneath her scattered merchandise as she answered. "When you come here two weeks ago, with your broken heart and your chip on your shoulder, what do you think you would do if I say"—she gestured at Julian—"that he is your brother"—she pointed toward the door—"and the Jimani is your father." She flung the table runner along the table. "Learn to shield, forgive your father, you be okay?"

I leaned down and picked up an overturned basket with the label "For Protection" still pinned to it. I placed it on the table, smoothing out a wrinkle in the runner. "I probably would have said a lot of bad words, stormed out, and gone for a swim in a bottle of wine."

"Accurate," said Julian, plopping two purple stones into the basket.

"I would have cursed you out, too," I spat.

He smirked. "What a change that would have been."

"You had to find the answers on your own," Lovonia interrupted our bickering. "You cannot rush this kind of healing." She bent down, collecting items from the floor and placing them on the table, presumably to sort through afterward. "You cannot rush finding and using your gift, *ma dompteuse de fantômes*. Everything must happen in its time."

"What's that mean?" Julian dumped two handfuls of crystals and jewelry onto the table. "What you just called her?"

"*Dompteuse de fantômes*?" The candle she had placed nearby on the table illuminated her various creases. Her eyes glittered like stars. "*Ghost tamer*. That is the closest. She quiets the ghosts. Settles them. So they can move on."

"Yeah, I'm real good at that," I muttered under my breath, thinking it was Julian who usually settled me and not the other way around.

"You are new." Lovonia continued to scrape her livelihood from the floor and pile it onto the table, unconcerned. "Just learning. One step at a time."

"So how do I 'tame' my father? Just run after him and tell him I forgive him?" I found two other baskets and tried to sort items into them correctly.

"You must separate your father from the Lespri attached to him." She pulled out a piece that I had incorrectly sorted and carried it to another table. "Destroy the Lespri, send it back to its own dimension, and your father can receive your forgiveness and move on."

"Oh, well, if that's all," I said.

"What's a Lespri?" Julian asked. "I thought he was a Jimani."

"Lespri is the demon that attached to your father in life. Lespri can only exist in this world by attaching to and controlling a soul born here. A Jimani is its most powerful form."

"I'm sorry, did you say *demon*?" I asked just as the lights flickered back to life.

"And the Jimani is its final form?" Julian raised his eyebrows at me. "You should have played more Pokémon."

Lovonia smacked Julian on the arm, muttering in Cajun French as she ambled past him to blow out the candle on the counter. "Demon," she said again, righting the Tiffany lamp near her cash register and checking it for damage before turning it on. "It likes a sensitive soul in pain. Easier to drown a sensitive soul." She emerged from behind the counter, blowing out and collecting the candles we had lit. She placed them next to each other. "It uses the pain and darkness already present in a soul and . . ." She extended her arms out and away from herself. "Magnifies . . . overwhelms."

She scooped up some gauzy shawls and scarves from the various areas they had been blown as she trundled past Julian and me. We were no longer helping but staring after her with our jaws on the floor. She went about the business of folding and arranging them on the table against the far wall. "Sometimes a soul will give up. Then the Lespri can take control. Drive out any good and light. Root in deep with its own darkness. If it follows the soul into death, it is harder for the soul to fight it off. Eventually the two can intertwine, and the Jimani is born. The soul is trapped in its darkness. Only a vehicle for the demon."

For a moment, there was only the soft swishing of the scarves as Lovonia continued to fold and drape them back onto their display. Julian's face was slack, as if someone had just dumped ice water over his head. He shook himself and blinked at me.

"Well, shit," I said.

Lovonia chuckled. "He come here looking for you." She gestured around. "Make a mess, turn off lights."

"I'm so sorry."

"Ach." She waved away my apology. "I knew he would come eventually. It took him a long time to track you here." She grinned wickedly. "And I am not an easy target for any demons. I send him packing."

"How?" asked Jules.

She winked at him. "I am older than I look. I have many tricks."

Julian and I looked at each other, eyebrows raised.

"He will find you again. He must rest, but not for long."

"I'm guessing you'd rather we were somewhere else when he does find us?" I asked, scanning the mess.

"I would appreciate it." She nodded at the séance room. "I have set some things aside for you. Go, Raely. Pick those which call to you. They are all charged. Julian will help me here."

"Thank you." I wrapped my fingers around the bloodstone necklace as I walked toward the hallway. It charged easily now, before I had even reached the little séance room. Lovonia had indeed laid out a few pieces of jewelry made of various stones. A bracelet of rose quartz spoke to me most, which surprised me, as pink wasn't normally a color I gravitated toward. However, when I held it in my hand, I felt a lightness flow through me, as if a clog had cleared after a long while. I glanced around at the other pieces, but none of them tugged at my essence. I put the bracelet on my left wrist and walked back into the main room.

Lovonia and Julian were finishing up what looked like a heart-to-heart. Both their eyes were shining, and they were smiling at each other. She patted him on the arm when I walked in and turned to me. "Let me see . . . ahhhhh, wise choice. Very good." She held my left hand in both of hers as she smiled down at the rose quartz. She didn't release it as her gaze slid to mine. "Are you ready, *ma dompteuse de fantômes?*"

"As ready as I'll ever be, I guess." My pulse quickened. "I'm ready for it to be over."

She continued holding my hand and my gaze. Her smile turned wistful. "It will be harder than you think, cher. It is difficult to lose something you never knew you had when you are only just finding it. Be brave. Use this." She stabbed a pointer finger into my chest, right over my heart.

"Ow," I said.

She cackled. "*Au revoir, ma dompteuse de fantômes.* I will see you soon." She released my hand. "And you, brother ghost. *Adieu.* Safe journey."

"Thanks for everything," Jules said.

"Yes, thank you," I said. "We'll let you know how it goes." I held open the door for Julian, and we stepped out into the snowy night.

32

MY SKIN FELT LIKE IT WAS VIBRATING along with the track as the Green Line came barreling toward us. Julian and I had decided that my apartment would be the likeliest place for the Jimani to show up again. Although I wasn't thrilled at the probability that I wouldn't be getting my deposit back once we had a full-blown magic fight inside, I couldn't think of a more logical place to go.

It was dark, cold, and getting late. Julian and I were the only ones in the car we boarded.

"Do you think you can do it, Jules?" I asked, looking up at him where he stood near my seat. "Forgive him?"

Julian exhaled slowly through his nose, hand clenched around the handrail. He opened his mouth to answer but snapped it shut when a sudden frost crept up every bit of metal in the car. The temperature plunged.

The fluorescent lights guttered but didn't entirely cut out. The continual, patternless strobe effect was almost more disconcerting. The hairs on my arms were standing on end beneath my layers as I slowly rose from my seat to stand next to Julian in the center of the aisle.

"*There you are . . .*" The rasping whisper skittered along my bones like spiders, but the Jimani did not yet appear.

Julian flung up a glittering, silvery shield. "Remember. Use your heart and all that bullshit." He stared straight ahead, jaw clenched.

"Remind me to nominate you for pep talk of the year when we're done," I answered, pulling up a golden shield to brace his silver one.

"You really can't turn off the snark, can you?"

A rattling, threatening exhalation filled the air, seeming to come from all around us.

"I'm serious, I'm gonna embroider that shit on a fucking pillow for inspiration." My voice was steady, but my legs trembled as shadows at the other end of the car began to flow together, folding and draping over each other like vaporous eels.

"As if you can sew," Jules said, *pushing* into his shield to lengthen it across the car. "You'd stab yourself with the needle more often than you'd get a stitch. The only thing that pillow'd inspire would be vampires."

"Fuck you, I am excellent at crafts," I said, my heart kicking against my ribs. I *pushed* into my shield, and it filled out alongside Julian's. The shadows at the other end of the car were assembling into a humanoid shape. "I'm gonna start up an Etsy site as soon as we get home. Pithy Pillows. I'll embroider all your pearls of wisdom." My throat dried up as the Jimani took shape. "Make a million dollars . . ."

Julian took my hand in his. "You're funny. You should try comedy sometime."

The Jimani lifted his hands, flicked out his fingers, and shattered our shields into nothing.

We held on, teeth gritted against the frigid wind blasting around us. The car shuddered. Even as it bounced and swayed along the track, the windows visibly flexed. The roof bowed inward. Julian released my hand, flung out his arms and *pushed*. The car stopped collapsing in on itself but continued to tremble. Julian was breathing hard between clenched teeth, his lips pulled back in a snarl as he held firm against the Jimani.

Here goes nothing. I leaned into the gale and took a step forward.

"Dad!" I shouted. "I know you're in there!"

The Jimani's hard, black eyes glittered threateningly as it angled its head, a predator sizing up prey. My brain stalled. "Uhhhh. We could use a little help, Dad. Anytime."

"Embroider that on your fucking pillows while you're at it," Julian barked, then yelped as the Jimani flexed its wrists inward and the car groaned again. Julian's eyes widened in panic. "Raely," he gasped. My stomach twisted. I stepped in front of him.

"Let go of our father!" I shouted and *pulled* from my core. I thought of Blitz, of my mom, of Julian, of Lovonia, of James, and I *pulled* that love and affection forward, cupping my hands in front of my chest. A spark shimmered to life between them. I looked up at the Jimani and flicked my palms flat. The spark shot toward him, a beam of swirling color boring into his chest.

The Jimani laughed. "*Pathetic.*"

"C'mon, Raely," Jules panted behind me, still pushing against the vibrating walls of the car as the train hurtled forward. The Jimani glided toward us.

I reached deeper, finding the pricklier parts of my heart, adding Luck, thinking about him leaning in. About his mom telling me to stay away. My unanswered voicemails. The sound of his voice in the outgoing message. The way he'd smiled when he saw me last. My heart ached, but my beam of light grew wider.

Still, the Jimani came forward. He curled his fingers into his palms and Julian groaned behind me, pushing with everything he had. I felt the impact as his knees buckled and hit the floor. The windows on the left side of the car cracked. The lights guttered wildly.

The rose quartz on my wrist burned as I desperately grabbed for the most broken shards of my soul. I pulled up Joe. The way he'd looked on this very train, the last time I saw him alive. The beam widened. I thought of him as a ghost, saying goodbye to me. Moving on. My chest cracked, but my energy intensified. I thrust out my hands and light exploded from them—from me—and slammed into the Jimani. He paused but didn't stop.

I pulled up memories of my father, most of them painful, but I shuffled through them, pulling forward the tiny glimmers of affection that I had locked away and refused to look at: A Band-Aid for my knee when I slipped on ice and sliced open my jeans. A surprise hug when my favorite blanket had been torn apart in the wash. A music box playing *Für Elise* on my eighth birthday. There was a time when I had stored away every scrap of affection so that I could pull them out when he was especially horrible, to convince myself that he cared. As I got older, I stored them away for a different reason, locked them up and threw them into the depths of my memory. I hauled them all out now and added to them what I knew from Bill Cole. What I knew from my mother. What I had learned from Lovonia.

"I forgive you, Dad," I said, my voice cracking with tears, then I PUSHED.

The Jimani was thrown back. My light shot into him and around him, piercing the shadows. He released his hold on the car, which crackled back to its original shape. Shadows writhed as he fought the light stabbing into him. I pushed harder. Beneath my sweater, my spine was slick with sweat. My hair damp with it. My lungs heaved. Still, I *pushed*.

I felt Julian stand up behind me. He put his hands on my shoulders and added his energy to mine. His memories cascaded through me. Mostly thoughts of me. Of Mom. Some were even from the last few days: Mom, handing him groceries in the parking lot. Me, hugging him on the train. Then came fuzzy, faded memories from a much smaller person. A living person. Tiny, tiny Raely sitting across from him on a seesaw screaming with laughter. A wading pool where Mom splashed with a tiny baby Raely while chubby baby Julian's fists wrapped around two calloused male fingers, using them for balance as he took his first steps. The angle changed as baby Jules looked up into his father's smiling face. My heart burst with Julian's as he whispered, "I forgive you."

Our light grew vicious. It tore at the shadows and ripped them to shreds. The Jimani screamed, a hideous, shrieking sound like metal rent asunder. We *pushed* harder. A flash of a human face before shadow swirled around it again. A piercing blue eye. Then—

I got a glimpse of the ghost of our father when the demon released him. He looked like a thinner, waner version of the man in the earliest pictures. I saw him, briefly.

Then the Lespri hurtled for my soul.

33

I WAS KNOCKED BACK INTO MYSELF. My heart stumbled, exhausted. I heard Julian screaming my name as if he were on the other side of a wide canyon. I tried to push back against the darkness, but it was heavy. It wrapped around me tightly, squeezing. My soul squirmed against the black, but the Lespri found the cracks. There were so many fissures that I had only just begun to heal, and even more that I'd tried to ignore. It oozed into them and widened them, wrenching me apart. It showed me all the reasons to give up. It pulled up all the pain and despair I had been content to nest in and showed me how easy it would be to just let go. Like falling asleep. I teetered on the edge, my will relaxing.

Then I heard his voice. Not the bitter, dull voice I had come to know as I grew up. The one from the first video, right after Julian and I had been born. "You took my son from me, but you *will not have my daughter!*"

My soul stiffened. A crack sealed closed. I fought to struggle back from the edge. Room, I needed room. I thrashed against the darkness digging into me and tried to make space to push it out. It was heavy, suffocating.

"Julian!" The voice again. "You have to help me, son!"

"Raely!" Jules screamed. I stretched toward their voices, desperate to free myself, but the darkness was desperate too. It held on hard, shrieking back at them.

"*Push*, Raely! Don't let it take root! Find those pieces of your heart again and push it out!" I twisted toward my father's voice, trying to pull up the light I had just wielded. There was no room. The dark squeezed me too hard.

"Where's that fucking smart-ass now?" Julian yelled. "C'mon, Raely, you're meaner than this thing! Where's my brawler of a sister? Let's go!"

A light gleamed. Just a spark, but I set my sights on it. That's where they were. I grabbed onto my favorite weapon—my thorny anger and snark—and *shoved* it outward like porcupine quills. The darkness didn't let go, but it did flinch. I grabbed for the space, wedged into it, and pulled up the light from my heart, as tired as it was. I wrapped it around the thorns of my anger and *pressed* outward in all directions. The unearthly shrieking filled the air again, and I knew that I was winning. I heard Julian, heard my father, saw the glimmer of light in the distance expanding. I dug for every last scrap of myself. Everything I was and ever had been. Every last bit of life, love, and energy. And I leapt for that light.

THE TRAIN WAS rocking rhythmically. The lights gleamed, harshly fluorescent. My entire body ached as I pushed myself off the grimy floor. Hands wrapped around my biceps and helped haul me to my feet.

I looked up to find Julian on one side, my father on the other.

No Lespri to be seen.

I was trembling all over, but when Julian grinned at me, I couldn't help but smile back. "I think we won," he said.

We both looked back at our father. Ray had tears in his eyes, but none of the shadow and bleakness that I had come to accept as a part of him during his life. "Thank you," he said, his voice cracking. "I don't know that I deserved it, but you've freed my soul. You're both . . ." His face crumpled with grief . . . and love. "You're the best things to have ever come from me."

And then our father began to glow as if the sun were shining out from him, bathing all of us in it. Sparks separated from him and moved away. I had seen this before, I realized, with Joe. Like he was shedding golden confetti.

He was moving on.

"Raely, I'm so proud of you," he said as more and more of himself drifted away. "You've become so resilient and strong. But you've somehow kept your heart."

A sob pushed against my burning throat. Lovonia was right; this was harder than I had thought. "Thanks, Dad, I wish . . . I wish . . ."

"I know, baby. I do too." He brushed a hand across my cheek, wiping away a tear before the hand itself became cascading bits of bright soul. "Keep that resilient heart, my girl."

He turned to Julian, his face breaking. "I'm so sorry, Jules. I wish I had been stronger. I should have been stronger. Fought harder. If I could go back . . ." He swallowed, his hair flaking away, bits of his face beginning to follow. "You fought for me, and for your sister, harder than I ever could. You truly are the better version of who I should have been. I'm so proud of you. I love you both, so much." His brilliant blue eyes were the last to dissolve into golden dust. "I'll see you soon, son."

It took me a second to realize that I was still surrounded by gold confetti flecks, but they were coming from . . .

No.

I looked at Julian, who was glowing brighter than the sun. Shedding bits of himself into the ether. He smiled at me through his tears.

"No," I sobbed. "I can't lose you! I've only just found you!"

It hit me like a kick to the gut. This is what Lovonia had meant. She had known, like she had known every other fucking thing, that once Julian had forgiven our father and seen me safe, he would move on. And she knew I wouldn't want to let go.

"Julian!" I cried, grabbing onto his arms, as if I could hold him together, hold him in this life. My life.

"This is the goodbye that I didn't finish twenty-five years ago," he said. "You're going to be okay, Raely."

"I'm sick of goodbyes! I can't handle another one. This isn't fair, Jules." His shaggy hair was floating around his head, parts of it flaking away. I squeezed his arms harder. "I don't mind sharing my life. I just want . . . I want my brother in it."

"I know." He pulled me into a hug. "A part of me will always be with you."

I knew that this was right. I knew he had to move on. But I clung to him, sobbing.

He pushed me back, one hand on either side of my face. So little of him was still corporeal. He glowed brighter and brighter, and disappeared still more swiftly. "Listen to me. I need you to promise me three things."

"Okay," I said, my voice high and watery.

"One, you're going to do comedy again. In some form. Don't give up on yourself. Two, you're going to go see Luck. Not call. I'm moving on, so I get to demand bigger gestures. Three, you're going to embroider my wisest saying, 'Don't get trashed,' on a pillow so I know you have some accountability."

I sobbed a laugh. Julian was almost gone. "I love you, Jules. Say hi to Joe for me." The pressure of his hands dissolved into a warm whisper of wind. My heart cracked open.

"You've got a great life to look forward to, ghost tamer. Don't be afraid to go after it."

I reached out to him one last time, but my fingers slid through the dancing golden flecks of his soul as they slipped off to the next place, leaving me behind.

EPILOGUE

ONE MONTH LATER

"VIDEC, YOU'RE ON DECK!"

"Ready, thanks." I stood up and accepted some "break-a-legs" from the other comics in the green room at Church Laugh, glancing toward the door that led backstage. A crackle of adrenaline warmed my chest. I took a deep breath. *It's just ten minutes.*

Warm hands wrapped around mine. I pulled my gaze from the doorway and locked eyes with Luck. "You've got this. You're more than ready." He pulled me into a quick kiss, and my nerves fled.

About a week after the accident, I'd forced myself to follow Julian's advice—demands, whichever—and stopped by Luck's place to find out why he wasn't returning my calls. He was so frosty at first, I was afraid he wouldn't let me in, but apparently, I'd looked pretty pathetic standing on his doorstep, impaling myself on the thorns of the dozen roses I'd been clutching. After some initial verbal sparring, we quickly figured out that he'd never received any texts or voicemails that I'd sent while he was in the hospital.

His grandmother, who Luck explained had immigrated from Haiti, had been going on about a girl surrounded by dark spirits who needed to be kept away. Luck, who was admittedly on a lot of drugs after surgery to put pins in his severely broken leg, never took it seriously. He claimed his grandmother was always muttering about some spirit or demon, and so never even considered that the girl they mentioned was me. And although he remembered them answering his phone for him while he was out of it, he never thought they'd go as far as screening his calls and deleting messages.

Apparently, the problems I'd caused that his mother had alluded to when she ran me off were work-related. Unbeknownst to me, Luck had gone to bat for me with George when they discussed bringing me back on after the train crash, promising to take shifts alongside me and pick up any slack if I was slow off the mark. When I hadn't shown up the day after my attack, he'd gotten into some hot water. By the time I learned this, I'd already made up for it by picking up as many of Luck's shifts as I could while he recuperated.

"I'm gonna go and sit with everyone else now," Luck said, flashing me a grin and giving my hands a final squeeze. "Break a leg. You don't have to work in the morning, so we can celebrate a little, right? I mean, it is your birthday."

I nodded, my heart squeezing at the reminder that I no longer shared it. "Lovonia said I could have the whole day off."

I had started working at Lovonia's shop part-time. She said eventually I could go full if I wanted, but we'd work up to it. She was a pretty shrewd businesswoman, and I was making a decent hourly wage. More, when I did readings or séances, both of which I was learning more about under her guidance.

Interestingly, I came to find out that, about twenty-seven years ago, a slightly-less-ancient Lovonia had been doing palm readings in the French Quarter, minding her own business, when she was interrupted by a vision of a broken pair of twins, one a latent psychic with a chip on her shoulder and the other a sensitive ghost held to this world by grief and worry. They appeared to her in a frosty city backdrop that she had not yet come to know.

Over the next two decades, she would occasionally receive flashes about these twins, some of them images happening concurrently, many of them insights from the future. But when Julian found her, she was already waiting for him, knowing his sister would end up being her protégé if she could guide them carefully to where they needed to be. I'd asked her a few times if she knew anything else about my future that I should be made aware of, but she only chuckled and waved a finger at me.

No one was more surprised than me at my embrace of the occult arts, especially after my dealings with Dylan. After one communication with James, the videos of me were yanked down. After a few more, Dylan ended up settling with me for damages. His lawyer had apparently been a fabrication. Between that and the settlement checks from the train crash finally rolling in, I was able to pay off my medical debts and actually had some savings for the first time ever.

Devon was hosting Church Laugh's Comedy Nite tonight. From the sounds of it, the crowd was nice and warm. I took a peek between the curtains and scanned the faces. I couldn't rein in my ear-to-ear grin when I spotted Luck sliding into a seat next to my mom and Bill Cole at a table near the center. *Good job,* I thought. I'd forbidden them from going up front, too distracting. My heart stumbled a little when I saw Mia hurry to join them, drinks in hand. She passed one to my mom as she sat down next to Cole. She had said she would try when I texted her. I never let myself hope that she would show.

As it so often did, even now, my subconscious reached for that second dimension, brushing up against an empty space where, once, another soul had been tethered to mine. For the first few days, that emptiness had caused a gnawing pang, especially at night, when I tried to connect and Julian wasn't there. As if I was missing my right thumb.

Something small and vital I'd taken for granted because it had always just been there, whether I'd been aware of it or not.

I'd often woken in the middle of the night, in a cold sweat, sometimes from a train- or ghost-induced nightmare, but always grasping for something that wasn't there to catch me. The nightmares weren't as bad when Luck was with me, as he was more often than not, but they still woke me.

And I still missed Julian like a fierce ache.

So here I was. Keeping my promise to Jules and Joe. Devon had suggested me for the warm-up act when he'd agreed to host. He looked over at me now, grinning broadly as he introduced me to the crowd, stepping back from the mic and sweeping his arm toward me. My cue.

I smiled back as I crossed the stage, turning the smile toward the politely applauding audience and tossing them a wave halfway across. I pulled my attention back to Devon as we shook hands and switched places. I adjusted the mic stand, my hands steady, energy fizzing through me.

"Welcome, everybody. Thanks so much for coming out. There's so much you can do with your weekend, and we're all happy you chose to share it with us." I put my hands in my pockets, smiling at the front row. "And you all made it here, too! That's great. So awesome when you arrive at your destination. I used to take that for granted. Then a train I took went flying. Literally into the air! I know what you're thinking, did she say 'train' or 'plane'? Cause trains aren't supposed to fly, are they?" Sprinkles of laughter. They were warming up. "No, no they're not. I'll save you the suspense; that's still true. My train maybe flew for half a second before it remembered who it was. Like, 'Oh, sorry, passengers, I tried the *I-think-I-can* chant that worked for that other Little Engine, but I guess I still need rails?'" Louder laughs. I had them with me now. "The rest of us were like, 'No, cool, this is a new experience for everyone.' Spectacular? Yes. Did I get where I was going? Absolutely not. Not that day. Or for a couple days after, if I'm being honest." I grinned, looking out over the crowd. It felt good to let this go. "I take much less for granted nowadays, I can tell you that. So, congrats on getting here."

I reached for that empty space, that part of my heart that felt so bereft. Tonight I brushed against a flutter of warmth. A little spark. A little glow. My smile grew.

Wherever he had gone, Jules was okay too.

ACKNOWLEDGMENTS

⁓✺⁓✺⁓

I WILL ADMIT TO NOT LOOKING FORWARD to this part. So many people have been a part of my writing career thus far, and I'm petrified that I'll forget to thank someone essential. I'll start by thanking you. If this book is in your hands, whether you bought it new in hardcover, checked it out at the library, borrowed it from a friend, or found it in a donation bin, thank you for spending your time in my little world. I hope it was fun.

Next, I have to thank the original Nashville Novelists writing group: Melissa Collings, Cheryl Rieger, and Emily C. Whitson. You were the midwives to this project when I was at one of my lowest points creatively, lacking in self-confidence and motivation. This quite literally would not have been written had you not been there, with enthusiasm and encouragement, Sunday after Sunday. Thank you always.

To the Richland Park Library Long Form group, for that first full read and the most intimidating group feedback Zoom I have ever experienced: Thank you, April Bailey, Kyle Gordon, Samantha

McEnhimer, Mark Rice, Pamela Murray, Dean Rieger, Cheryl Rieger, Melissa Collings, Russ Rupe, Tariq Lacen, Michael Sobie, Thomas Clouse, Pam Jones, and to Drew Dunlop for creating this enormous, amazing support group of writers. Your feedback was essential to getting the book where it is today.

To my editor, Helga Schier, whose text message—at 8:42 p.m. CST on October 2, after she finished her first read—I may or may not have saved and printed out. There were hitches in this story that I knew needed tweaking but couldn't quite see the path forward on my own, and your comments cleared the way with seeming ease. I don't know why anyone ever complains about edits. This was easily the most fun part of creating this book. Thank you.

To Maryann Appel, for the fantastic cover and layouts. I kept the cover on my phone and showed it to anyone who would indulge me, far before it was released. To Laura Wooffitt and Abigail Miles, for putting far more work into marketing this book than I'm sure I'll ever be aware of. To Bill Lehto, for patiently answering all my questions about book sales and contracts, usually immediately. To Gabe Schier and Jessica Homani, for all the podcast and media support. To Kayla Webb, Nicole DeLise, and Camryn Flowers, for all the essential behind-the-scenes things you do every day that I'm sure most people never see but heavily rely upon. To Cassandra Farrin and Susan McGrath, for co-pyediting and proofreading, respectively. I was so thrilled when I saw these two expert names attached to my little book. To Piper Goodeve and Mosaic Studio for bringing Raely's voice to life.

To my mom, who reads more books than anyone I know, and does not think I'm crazy when I talk about characters like my real-life friends. She did the first full read of *Ghost Tamer* and was so relieved to find out that her daughter was actually a decent writer. "Because what was I going to say if it was terrible?" We've all been there.

To my dad, who is not a reader, or an actor, or a pianist, or even a painter, but always supported every wild bohemian passion that I threw myself into without hesitation. (Well, he wasn't crazy about the boxing.)

To my husband, Dean, also not a reader, who cleaned up the kitchen and did the laundry when I was deep down a writing hole. Thank you for your uncomplaining patience in keeping the house livable while I subsisted on peanut butter and crackers, snarling in a cave of blankets, clutching my laptop. And to Aang and Cloud, for sitting on my keyboard, my head, my mouse, my arms, everywhere but my lap while I tried to write around you. Your buttholes in my face and headbutts to my fingers added some additional interesting characters and were truly an inspiration. All three of you are essential to my daily well-being.

To Chicago, for your stupid weather, awesome trains, fantastic theatre scene, amazing people, and terrible drivers. Seventeen years was both too short and way too long. You'll always have a place in my heart, ya jagoff.

And last, but certainly not least, to Sue Arroyo, for making it rain chances. I know that I'm not the only creative whose life you've enriched with CamCat, so I will thank you, not just for myself, but for all of us. Your dream continues to hatch dreams. Thank you.

ABOUT THE AUTHOR

MEREDITH R. LYONS STARTED WRITING BEFORE she properly learned to spell. Technically, her first novel was finished when she was thirteen. It currently resides in a three-ring binder in her hall closet, and consists of mismatched, college-ruled pages, scrawled upon with both lead and ink in an assortment of colors. Her stories have steadily improved since then. Born and raised in the New Orleans area, she collected two degrees from Louisiana State University before running away to Chicago to be an actor. In between plays, she got her black belt and made martial arts and yoga her full-time day job. She fought in the Chicago Golden Gloves, ran the Chicago Marathon, and competed for team U.S.A. in the Savate World Championships in Paris. In spite of doing each of these things twice, she couldn't stay warm and relocated to Nashville. She owns several swords but lives a nonviolent life, saving all swashbuckling for the page, knitting scarves, gardening, visiting coffee shops, and cuddling with her husband and two panther-sized cats. *Ghost Tamer* is her first (legible) novel.

Feel free to hang out with Meredith on social media.

She's on almost all the platforms as:
@meredithrlyons

or on her website at
www.meredithraelyons.com

If you've enjoyed
Meredith R. Lyons's *Ghost Tamer*,
we hope you will consider leaving us a review
to help our authors.

And check out another great read
from CamCat,
A Dagger of Lightning by Meredith R. Lyons.

CHAPTER ONE

If you don't know where you're going, fine, just make sure you know what you're looking for. —Solange Delaney

"IM. IMOGEN! YOU'RE OKAY. You're all right, you're okay."

I awoke gasping, my ears throbbing as if my heart had established satellite locations. My eyes immediately locked onto a familiar shape, the feather swaying back and forth, dangling from the chain on our ceiling fan. *I'm safe. I'm in bed. With Keane. I'm okay.* The orange glow of a streetlamp filtered in through the open curtains. I reached up and lightly clasped Keane's forearm, his warm palm still gripping my shoulder, although he had stopped shaking me. I turned my head toward him, trying to take slower breaths. He'd angled himself just far enough away so that I wouldn't accidentally strike him. I must have been flailing.

"I'm awake. Sorry. Was I loud?" I never remembered these dreams when I woke. Only a sensation of falling and some vague knowledge that my grandfather had been there, either falling with me, or trying to keep me from falling, or . . . something . . .

"You didn't shout or anything this time, just thrashed around." Keane flopped back onto the pillows, sliding an arm beneath me and hauling me to his side. I let him, even though I was very warm and wanted air. The sheets beneath me were damp with sweat. I shoved the comforter down to my waist.

"Sorry I woke you. I've been trying to rest my ankle and didn't run yesterday." I always slept better if I was exhausted. I didn't process emotions the way most people did, and if I was unable to channel them physically, they liked to ambush me when I was unconscious.

"That's all right," Keane sighed, trailing his fingertips up and down my arm. Keane had been a good friend since college. Neither of us had ever married, in spite of cycling through many long-term relationships. At some point, after spending a mutual friend's wedding together as bridesmaid and groomsman for the umpteenth time, Keane had suggested that if we hadn't found anyone by forty, we should just wed each other. I'd drunkenly agreed. Now I was forty-five, Keane was nearly fifty, and six months ago he'd finally gotten my yes. I accepted a ring after insisting upon dating first, living together first, then living together for at least a year . . . until I'd run out of excuses. There were none. Keane was great. We got along great. Sex wasn't bad. Cohabitating was cheaper and made maintaining a home easier. And it was nice being on his insurance plan.

Settling, Imogen. You're settling is what you're doing. She'd been gone sixteen years and I could still *hear* my grandmother's exhale, could practically see her tossing a gauzy scarf over a small-boned shoulder as she gave me a look from beneath her lashes. But what was wrong with that at my age? I'd come to the conclusion that true love was a fantasy—although my grandparents had sure seemed to have it. Perhaps it wasn't in the cards for everyone. I'd looked around long enough. Fortunately, I'd never wanted kids, so I'd never felt that pressure.

"So, what are your plans for today?" Keane yawned, still lightly stroking my arm.

My stomach tightened. He had some kind of agenda. "Some more job applications, maybe—"

"You know, you don't have to get a job right away—"

"I want a job. I need to contribute—"

"I know, Im, and you will, but you don't need one in the next twenty-four hours. Your dad's coming in next week, and"—he rolled toward me, pulling me even closer—"the guest room is still a mess."

My eyes dropped away from his. I turned my face skyward again and focused on the feather. "I know." The guest room would have been nice if it weren't for the large pile of cardboard boxes. All mine.

I *had* tried to whittle them down. But I didn't know what I'd need. I didn't know where I'd fit in this new place. Keane had received a dream job offer in New Orleans. He'd convinced me that this would be a great life for both of us. Wasn't I tired of the cold in Chicago? Wasn't I able to find friends wherever I went? Weren't we going to get married now? I had no good arguments, so I went with him. It made sense. We were engaged.

Why not? I rolled my shoulders against the tightness threatening, trying to make a little more space between us. I didn't want to go through the boxes downstairs. Going through them meant getting rid of them, and I hated to let go of those little parts of myself.

I'd never found my calling. I liked to hop around. I was good at a lot of things, never great at any one thing. I never had a "crowd," but I was good at getting along. I'd find a job here too. Find things to like about it. I was good at adapting. I could wedge myself in.

Grandma would have told me to keep searching. *You're different, Imogen, and that's okay. But you have a place. We all do. You'll know it when you find it. Just keep looking.* Well, she wasn't here. Besides, maybe this would be it.

"Okay," I said, taking a deep breath. "I'll go through the boxes today. Try to put some away."

"You could make a donation pile too," Keane said, pulling the covers back up around us. "What about all that martial arts stuff? You haven't fought in over a decade."

Something twisted at my center. "I liked fighting though," I said, quietly. I had loved sparring. It was another effective outlet for emotions packed down too tightly. And I'd been good at it. Although I was technically too old to fight competitively anymore, I could still train. "Maybe we could find a place here, we could do it together—"

Keane chuckled. "I'm still sore from soccer two days ago." He yawned again and pulled me even closer, eliminating any space I'd created by wrapping his arms around me. He pressed a kiss to my forehead, one hand rubbing my back. "You know, I was thinking when your dad's here next week, we could set a date for the wedding. Like, an actual date. Maybe something in the fall."

I felt myself go rigid in his arms. "Not the fall," I said. Keane's hand stilled on my back, but he didn't let me go. This was the only thing I had ever pushed back on consistently.

"Imogen—"

"My grandma disappeared in the fall. I don't like the fall."

"Imogen." Impatience simmered under his voice. "Everyone on Earth has lost a grandparent—"

"Lost, yes, had one disappear, no."

His chest inflated against my arms where I was still smashed against him.

He exhaled slowly. "She was one-hundred-and-two, Im. You know she died. She probably left because your grandpa had just passed on and—"

"Her car was still there. All her stuff was still there. And she left me that message." The muscles between my shoulder blades tightened painfully.

Keane sighed. "She was quoting Stephen King—"

I knew exactly where this conversation was going and how I would feel afterward, but I couldn't help it, I took the bait. "No, she said, There might be other worlds to see,' not There are other worlds than these,' there's a diff—"

"So she misquoted—" Keane cut himself off when I started pushing out of his embrace. "Okay, baby." His voice lifted on the second word like he was asking a question. He held me slightly away, pushed my short hair back from my face, then tilted my chin up so I was forced to look at him. "I know you don't like to talk about this, so I'm not going to push it but . . . it's always something. First, you wanted to wait until I was sure about the job, then you wanted to wait until after the move, and now I just feel like you're making excuses."

"Just not the fall," I said. "Any other season—"

"How about this summer then?"

It was already June. Summer was technically days away.

"You want to get married in summer in New Orleans?" Honestly, this far south it felt like summer had been sitting on us for months already.

He didn't answer, just stared into my eyes, his fingers still at my chin, his arm at my waist, still holding me to him. Keane knew how to wear me down. If it was this important to him . . . what difference did it really make when it happened?

"Fine. Summer," I said, although a surge of distress simmered beneath my skin. "We can talk about it when Dad's here."

"Really?" Keane grinned, the corners of his eyes crinkling. My heart softened. He really was a handsome guy. And he was good to me.

"Really," I said, smiling back.

He kissed me softly. "I love you, Imogen."

"I love you, too." The words came easy. We'd been saying them to each other as friends for decades. I forced another smile, the distress coalescing into eels tossing against my stomach. "I'm gonna head out for my run. The sun's gonna come up soon."

"Okay." He gave me a squeeze and released me. Keane knew what I was doing. And he was letting me. "Text me when you're close, and I'll go out and get coffee for us." He snuggled back into the downy comforter.

"'Kay." I rolled out of bed and padded to the dresser in the soft brown light of near dawn. I snatched up some running shorts, a sports bra, and socks and slipped into the bathroom to get dressed. My sore Achilles still ached in spite of my rest day, but I ignored it. I couldn't get out of the house fast enough.

I stopped long enough to do a few heel drops on the front step to warm up my ankle before setting out, but that was it. The sky had lightened to pink by the time I hit the pavement. I loved the warm June mornings. Although I was leery of hurricane season, I couldn't complain about being warm all the time. No more treadmill-exclusive winters. I took off toward the levee. Running along the top at dawn was my new favorite way to greet the day. I tried to shake off the tension from this morning's conversation as I ran. No one understood how hard I had taken my grandma's disappearance. We'd had a different bond. Even my father had said that he felt like an interloper sometimes when it was just the three of us together. I had a nagging feeling that Keane had used that attachment when he suggested the fall to push me into a summer wedding. I shoved that thought away. If he had, it was done now.

My mother had died when I was eight, which was about when I'd stopped emoting in the "normal way." I had to let it out physically. Running, fighting, acting. I wasn't a crier and I wasn't a talker. I think it was one of the things Keane liked about me. If something upset me, I waited until I felt safe to let it out, or I channeled it through my body.

Not for the first time, I wished my grandma was around so I could run this wedding thing by her. Ask her why I had these conflicting feelings about what was so obviously the right decision. I mean, I'd already followed the guy across the country.

Keep looking, Imogen, she would level her green eyes at me. *Keep exploring. No need to pin yourself down to this one. You've got time. I don't care what anyone says.*

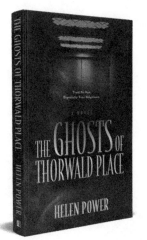

CamCat
Books

VISIT US ONLINE FOR MORE BOOKS TO LIVE IN:
CAMCATBOOKS.COM

SIGN UP FOR CAMCAT'S FICTION NEWSLETTER FOR
COVER REVEALS, EBOOK DEALS, AND MORE EXCLUSIVE CONTENT.

CamCatBooks   @CamCatBooks   @CamCat_Books   @CamCatBooks